P9-CDT-368

IN A DISTANT GALAXY,
THE PEACEFUL PLANET LORIEN
WAS DECIMATED BY
THE BRUTAL MOGADORIANS.

The last survivors of Lorien—the Garde—were
sent to Earth as children. Scattered across the con-
tinents, they developed their extraordinary powers
known as Legacies and readied themselves to defend
their adopted home world.

The Garde thwarted the Mogadorian invasion of
Earth. In the process, they changed the very nature
of the planet. Legacies began to manifest in human
beings.

These new Garde frighten some people, while others look for ways to manipulate them to their benefit.

And although the Legacies are meant to protect
Earth, not every Garde will use their powers for
good.

I AM PITTACUS LORE.
RECORDER OF THE FATES,
CHRONICLER OF THE LEGACIES.

I TELL THE TALES OF THOSE
WHO WOULD SHAPE WORLDS.

NORTH PORT PUBLIC LIBRARY

13800 S. TAMIAMI TRAIL
NORTH PORT, FL 34287

31969025945626

THE LEGACY CHRONICLES

TRIAL BY FIRE

NORTH PORT PUBLIC LIBRARY

13800 S. TAMIAMI TRAIL
NORTH PORT, FL 34287

PITTACUS LORE

HARPER

An Imprint of HarperCollinsPublishers

The Legacy Chronicles: Trial by Fire

The Legacy Chronicles: Out of the Ashes, copyright © 2017 by Pittacus Lore

The Legacy Chronicles: Into the Fire, copyright © 2018 by Pittacus Lore

The Legacy Chronicles: Up in Smoke, copyright © 2018 by Pittacus Lore

All rights reserved. Printed in the United States of America. No part of this book may be used or reproduced in any manner whatsoever without written permission except in the case of brief quotations embodied in critical articles and reviews. For information address HarperCollins Children's Books, a division of HarperCollins Publishers, 195 Broadway, New York, NY 10007.

www.epicreads.com

ISBN 978-0-06-249407-8

18 19 20 21 22   PC/LSCH   10 9 8 7 6 5 4 3 2 1

❖

First Edition

CONTENTS

THE LEGACY CHRONICLES

CHRONICLES

OUT OF THE ASHES

CHAPTER ONE

SIX

NEW YORK CITY, NEW YORK

THE CITY WAS COMING BACK TO LIFE.

As Six and Sam walked up Fifth Avenue in Manhattan's middle latitudes, they were surrounded by crews repairing the damage from the Mogadorian invasion that had taken place more than a year earlier. While huge swaths of the city had been reduced to rubble, new buildings were rising from the ashes of the old. All around them, New Yorkers went about their lives: cabs honked, shoppers peered into storefront windows at mannequins wearing the latest fashions, a dog walker stopped to let her six charges anoint a tree that still bore the scars of a piken's claws.

It was the first time either Six or Sam had been to the city since the battle that almost destroyed it. During the time they'd been traveling the world, they had seen other cities that were recovering from the invasion, but mostly they'd stuck to places where they were not reminded of those terrible events. The point of their trip had been to enjoy the beauty in the world, and to give them time to be alone with one another. Being in New York put them right back where so much of it had happened.

Passing a bus stop, Six noticed a poster about an exhibit at the American Museum of Natural History commemorating what was being called the Battle for the Boroughs. It featured an image of a huge dinosaur-like creature. *The Mogosaur,* Six thought, remembering Daniela's name for the monster that would have killed her friends and thousands of others had it not been turned to stone by Daniela and John. She hadn't faced it herself, as she'd been dealing with her own problems in Mexico at the time, but she'd heard all about it. She glanced at Sam to see if he'd noticed.

"I guess they fished the pieces out of the river," he said. He looked at the poster for a long moment before adding, "We should visit him."

"John?" said Six, knowing he didn't mean the petrified beast. "We will. Soon."

She thought about the Loralite pendants their friend had left for her and Sam on that beach in Montenegro. They could have used them at any time to travel to John's compound in the Himalayas. But they hadn't. They hadn't even talked about the possibility much other than to agree that they weren't quite ready to go. They weren't angry with John or anything like that, even if he and Six had disagreed about how to handle both the Loric's relationship with the human world and the issue of the emerging Human Garde. She and Sam just wanted some time to be normal—or as normal as they could ever be, given who and what they were.

Then, a week ago, just after they'd returned to the United States and were hiking the first part of the Appalachian Trail in Maine, an email had arrived in their in-boxes. It was from someone asking to speak to them about possibly working on some kind of task force involving the Human Garde. Six had deleted it without finishing it. Sam, however, had read it, and a few days later brought it up while they were eating dinner by a particularly beautiful lake. Six immediately objected. But Sam worked on her over the next few days as they continued on the trail, and eventually she'd agreed to meet with the sender, if only to shut Sam up.

Now, after hitchhiking to Bangor, taking a bus to Boston and then a train to New York, she wasn't so sure about it. Seeing the poster for the exhibit only reinforced her belief that it was too soon to get involved in Garde activities again. She stopped and readjusted her backpack. "Sam, what are we even doing here?"

Sam, a few steps ahead of her, turned around. Dressed in hiking boots and clothes better suited for the woods than for the concrete jungle, he looked out of place in the sea of smartly dressed people who walked around him. He also needed a haircut and a shave. "We're just going to have a talk," he said. "That's all."

"I don't see the point," Six told him. Her head was rapidly

filling up with memories—ones she had worked hard to put behind her—and she suddenly wanted to be anywhere else. "Whatever it is, I'm saying no. I said no to John about the Declaration. I said no to heading up the Human Garde Academy. How is this any different?"

Sam looked at her for a long time before replying, and for a moment she thought he might agree to turn around and leave. "Maybe it won't be any different," he said, shrugging. "But what else are we going to do? We've been wandering around the world for over a year, Six. We've been to more countries than I can count. It's been great having you all to myself, but I'm tired of living out of a backpack. And I want to *do* something. Something to make a difference. It's time to figure out what's next."

"Can't you just volunteer with a rebuilding team or something?" Six asked.

Sam walked back to her. He took her hands in his. "Let's just hear what this guy has to say," he said. "Please?"

Six looked into his eyes. "Does this mean you don't want me all to yourself anymore?" she teased.

"Ten minutes. That's all I'm asking you for. Give him ten minutes."

She sighed. "All right, but I'm only doing this for you. And when the time's up, I'm out that door and headed for Penn Station. That trail isn't going to hike itself. Got it?"

"What was the nickname that guy had for you at the sleeping shelter the other night after you lectured him?" Sam asked, putting his index finger on his chin and pretending to think. "Screech Owl?"

"Very funny," Six said. "Especially since *he* was the one snoring and keeping everyone awake all night."

They walked until they reached the southern edge of Central Park, then followed it over to its western side and continued north. Like the rest of the city, the park was recovering, and here nature had worked more quickly than humans. Already it looked almost as it had before, with the exception of a few ruined buildings scattered across the green landscape and some deep gashes where Mog ships had crashed and burned.

The towering stone buildings of the Upper West Side rose like castles into the sky. Six and Sam passed through the doorway of one of them, entering a lobby tiled in marble and ornamented with gold accents. It looked more like a hotel from a bygone era than the office building Six had been expecting. Despite her reservations, she found herself intrigued.

In the elevator, she leaned against the wall as they rode to the twenty-third floor. When they stopped and the doors opened, she stepped out into a small room that felt like it belonged in an old mansion. The gleaming wood floor was covered by an elaborately patterned carpet straight out of a Persian marketplace, and two leather couches sat on it, facing each other. A chandelier hung from the ceiling, filling the room with soft, warm light. Opposite the elevator were two closed pocket doors made of the same dark wood that paneled the lower half of the walls, the upper halves being covered with a red paper featuring an Art Deco design of black-and-gold flowers.

Standing in front of Six and Sam, his hands held behind his back, was a man. Six estimated him to be in his late twenties. He was wearing a tailored blue suit over an obviously well-muscled body. His skin was colored by a fading tan, his light-brown hair was cut short, and he looked at them with pale-blue eyes.

"McKenna?" Six asked, retrieving from her memory bank the name of the man who had written to her and Sam.

Before he could answer, the doors on the other side of the room slid open and another man appeared. He walked towards them. He wore a brown suit, and Six quickly appraised him: late thirties or early forties, shorter than average, medium build, reddish-brown hair and beard, green eyes. He met her gaze head-on and, she could tell, was performing his own assessment of her even as he held out his hand and said, "Peter McKenna."

Six took his hand. His grip was firm, but not overly aggressive. "Thank you for coming," McKenna said, releasing her hand and turning to greet Sam. "It's a pleasure to meet both of you."

His accent was Irish, but from which part of the country, she couldn't identify. It didn't matter, as this would be the one and only time they met. She would listen to what he had to say, then leave. She was only here because Sam wanted this meeting, and she wanted to make him happy.

McKenna gestured to the open doors behind him. "After

you," he said, indicating that they should walk through. He followed, shut the doors, then led them down a hallway lined with more closed doors. He opened one, and they stepped into an office or library. Large and airy, it featured built-in bookshelves that took up three of the walls. A fourth was lined with floor-to-ceiling windows that faced the street and let in lots of light. A desk was positioned facing the windows, with two armchairs in front of it. McKenna sat down behind the desk. Six and Sam shrugged off their packs and took the chairs.

"Nice place," Six remarked. "Yours?"

"Not mine personally, no," McKenna answered. "But it does belong to us."

"And who exactly are 'us'?" Six asked.

McKenna leaned back in his chair. "I'm hoping it will be myself and the two of you."

"What about the guy who answered the door?" Six asked. "Or is he just for decoration?"

A smile teased at the corners of McKenna's mouth. "James would be part of the team as well."

"Well, as wonderful as that news is, I'm not interested in government work," Six informed him.

"What makes you think I'm with any government?" McKenna asked.

"Aren't you?" she asked.

"I represent the intelligence services for a coalition of countries interested in maintaining an ongoing surveillance of Human Garde activities."

"Translation—government," Six persisted.

"Only as much as intelligence is a part of government," McKenna said. "Which I realize is an oxymoron." He smiled at his joke.

Six didn't return the look, but she did ask, "Which countries?"

"The US," McKenna answered. "France. The UK. Germany. Japan. Sweden. Others."

"China?" said Six. "Russia?"

"No," McKenna said. "They are not involved."

Six made a dismissive sound and shook her head. "Sounds *exactly* like a government program to me. Maybe nobody told you, but I didn't sign the Declaration. And the Human Garde Academy is bullshit."

"Yes," McKenna said. "I understand you made your feelings about those things quite clear."

Six was already getting angry. McKenna was jerking them around. As she'd expected, this was a waste of time.

"We'll be going now," she said as she stood and started to shoulder her pack. "Don't get up. We can see ourselves out."

Sam looked at his watch. "I thought *we* agreed on ten minutes," he said. "It's been less than three. That might be a new personal record for you."

"My son has developed a Legacy," McKenna said calmly. "He's not going to the Human Garde Academy."

Six stopped, but did not turn around. "That's in direct defiance of the Declaration."

"It is," McKenna agreed.

Six turned. "What's his Legacy?"

"Insect telepathy," he answered. "He's particularly adept at getting the spiders in the house to infest his sister's bedroom and cover it with webs."

A face flashed across Six's memory: A boy, dark haired and round faced. Bertrand. He too had been able to communicate with insects. She had liked him. And now he was dead, killed by the Mogs like so many others.

"What's his name?" she asked. "Your son."

"Seamus. He's fifteen." He took a framed photo that stood on his desk and turned it around. It showed a family of four: McKenna, a pretty woman with long dark hair, and two teen-agers whose faces contained a bit of each of their parents.

"Why isn't he at the HGA?" Six asked. "Don't you and your wife think he should go?"

McKenna looked her in the eyes. "My wife is dead," he said, setting the photo back in place. "She was killed during the invasion."

Six walked back to the chair and sat. "Tell me more about this operation of yours."

"As I was saying, it's been put together by the intelligence arms of various countries," McKenna said. "Should anyone inquire, our work is part of a special NATO program."

Six groaned. McKenna held up a hand. "But no one is going to ask. The only people who will know exactly what we're doing are sitting right here in this room."

Six shook her head. "That's impossible," she said. "You've got more than half a dozen countries funding this. They're all going to want to pull the strings."

"You let me worry about that," McKenna said. "All you and Sam have to worry about is, well, everything else."

Six looked at Sam, who shrugged. "Everything else," he said. "Sounds easy enough."

She turned back to McKenna. "And what, exactly, would everything else be?"

"Our primary role is to investigate any Garde-related incidents or activities that fall outside of acceptable parameters."

"That sounds like a press release." Six tilted her head and raised an eyebrow.

McKenna smiled. "I suppose it does," he said. "I've been working in government too long. All right, how about this: it's important for the ongoing success and safety of the Human Garde that the public believe them to be under control and of no danger to the general population." He paused. "And for those with Legacies to believe that they are in no danger either. But we know that that isn't entirely true, in either case. What we have is a population of young people who have suddenly developed extraordinary abilities. In some cases—perhaps many—they do not have the emotional maturity to wield these newfound powers in an appropriate manner. The HGA has been established to address this. But a school setting is not one that all will respond to. In fact, some will actively reject it."

He hesitated again, and looked toward the window.

"From what I understand, they won't have a choice," Six

said. Forcing Human Garde to attend the HGA was one of the things she resisted.

"That's the plan, yes," said McKenna, returning his attention to her and Sam. "But teenagers have been rebelling against authority since the first child reached their thirteenth birthday. Part of our job will be monitoring for Human Garde who have, for whatever reason, failed to report their Legacies."

"And do what with them?" Six interrupted.

"Encourage them to attend the HGA if that's appropriate," McKenna said.

"But that's exactly what—" Six began.

"Or," McKenna interrupted, silencing her.

"Or?" said Six.

"Or provide them with an alternative."

"Which is what?" asked Six.

"That's something we'll discuss in greater detail if we decide to work together," said McKenna. "Secondly, we will be monitoring for activity that threatens or seeks to exploit them. These young people are an exceptionally valuable resource, and, as with all resources, there will be those who want to use them for personal gain. We have already seen some evidence of this."

Six cringed at the word "resource" being used to describe the kids. "They're not *resources*," she said. "They're people."

"Precisely," McKenna agreed. "But there are those out there who see them as tools or weapons. Our job is to prevent that from happening."

"So, basically, Earth Garde is the public face and will make it look as if everything is going smoothly," Sam said. "Meanwhile, we'll be making sure it *actually* does."

"More or less," said McKenna.

"Still sounds like politics as usual," Six said.

"We have extensive resources at our disposal," McKenna continued, ignoring her jab. "We'll be able to draw information from the intelligence communities of numerous countries. And you'll be headquartered here."

"In New York?" Sam asked.

"Specifically, here in this building," said McKenna. "We occupy this floor and the one above. I doubt you'll be around much, but this would be home."

"There's that 'we' again," Six said. "You live here too?"

McKenna shook his head. "I live downtown, where my wife's art gallery is. Or was." Again, he looked distracted. Then he brightened. "When James and I aren't here, you'll have the place to yourselves."

Sam looked at Six. "Sounds good to me."

"Too good," Six countered. "Nobody does something like this without wanting something in return. Especially governments. Sure, it might help the new Human Garde, but who stands to benefit from it?"

McKenna took a moment to answer. "I've been involved with governmental agencies my entire career," he said. "And you're correct. They are, for the most part, only interested in maintaining power. However, within every organization there are people who honestly want to do good. I like to believe that I'm one of those people."

"That's great," said Six. "But you still have to answer to someone."

"The people involved are ones I trust," McKenna replied.

She laughed. "Isn't that always how it starts? Until someone turns out not to be trustworthy?"

"Do you have a better idea?"

Six turned to Sam, who had asked her the question. He shrugged. "Well, do you? I know you want to help these new Garde understand their Legacies. How are you going to do that on your own? You have to trust *someone*, Six."

"I mentioned my son earlier," McKenna said, drawing Six's focus back to him before she could start arguing with Sam. "You asked why he isn't attending the HGA."

"I noticed you avoided answering that question," Six said.

"The truth is," said McKenna, "it doesn't matter whether I think the HGA is a good place for him or not, as I don't know where Seamus is."

"He's missing?"

"For two months now," McKenna said. "He was afraid he would be forced to report. Like you, he mistrusts the government. So he ran away."

"And you can't find him?" Six asked. "With all the resources available to you?"

McKenna smiled ruefully. "My son is a brilliant young man," he said. "Also, the anti-HGA movement is larger than most people know. I believe he's tapped into that and has gone underground."

Six studied McKenna's face. He wasn't lying. He was deeply concerned for his son, and this concern extended to the young people struggling with their newly developed Legacies. Sam was right, too. She did want to help. But she still wasn't convinced that becoming involved with this operation was the best way to do it.

"I'm hungry," Sam said suddenly, interrupting her thoughts.

"I can have something brought in," McKenna suggested.

"No," said Sam, standing. "I think we'll go out."

McKenna, looking bemused, said nothing.

"Six?" Sam said. "You coming?"

Six had no idea what he was up to, but she said, "Okay."

"We'll be back in, like, half an hour," Sam said to McKenna as Six stood.

They left the office and returned to the front room, where they waited for the elevator in silence. When the elevator doors opened, they stepped in and Sam hit the button for the ground floor. Six waited for him to say something, but he just stood there. When they were out on the street, he finally spoke.

"I thought we should talk somewhere where no one else might be listening," he said.

"Didn't you magic the cameras off when we walked in, Mr. Technowizard?" Six asked.

"Obviously," said Sam. "There's no record we were ever here. But you can never be *too* careful."

"Now who's paranoid?" Six snarked.

Sam ignored her, walking to the corner. Lining the side-walk along the edge of the park were food carts. Sam walked up to a hot dog vendor and ordered two hot dogs, complete with onions, relish, and mustard. He handed one to Six as they entered the park and found a bench to sit down.

"I know you *want* to do this," Sam said as they ate. "It's everything you think needs to be done to make sure the Human Garde become what they should be."

"I'm not John or Nine," Six said. "I don't play well with others."

"Which is exactly why you're perfect for this job." Sam chewed thoughtfully. "I think you're afraid that if you say yes after saying no to the UN thing and the HGA thing, you'll look like you're agreeing with John."

Six didn't respond. He was right. Sort of. She'd made a big deal about not signing the Declaration. And she'd turned down a job at the HGA. But it wasn't John or Nine or anyone else's opinion of her that she was worried about. It was her own. She didn't think the government should have anything to do with Garde activity. Saying yes to something like they were being offered felt like betraying her own ideals.

"You're a good teacher, Six," Sam continued. "I wouldn't be here right now if it wasn't for you."

"Don't start," Six warned. "You know that greeting card stuff doesn't work on me."

"I know you were thinking about Bertrand when McKenna talked about his son. So was I."

Six didn't deny it. There was no point. Sam knew her too

well for her to pretend he was wrong. Instead, she finished her hot dog and crumpled up the paper wrapper it had come in. "Damn it, Sam. What do you want me to say?"

He looked into her eyes. "I want you to say yes. You'd be good at this. *We* would be good at this."

Six said nothing, watching traffic coming and going on the transverse road that cut through the park and linked it to the Upper East Side. As a cab passed by, she saw that it sported an ad for the HGA. A smiling girl pointed her hands at a levitating boulder as Nine, looking every inch a model, watched her. *Claim Your Legacy* the sign said.

Six bristled. "All right," she said. "I'll try it. But if *one* thing seems off, I'm done."

Sam popped the final bite of hot dog into his mouth and chewed. "Deal," he said. Five minutes later, they were back in McKenna's office.

"We're in," Sam told him.

"Good," the man answered. "Then let's get started. I already have your first assignment."

"Shouldn't we have a new-employee orientation first?" Six said. "Talk about the health plan? Retirement accounts? Get IDs?"

"This is more of a learn-as-you-go type of job," McKenna said.

He picked up two folders that were sitting on his desk, as if he'd been expecting them to come back all along. This irritated Six, but she said nothing.

"There have been several incidents of Human Garde who

exhibit healing Legacies disappearing," McKenna said. "We have to find out where they've gone, and why. I need you to go to the location of the most recent incident and see what you can find out."

Six opened her folder and scanned the first page of information. "Australia?" she said.

McKenna nodded. "Your plane leaves in two hours."

CHAPTER TWO

"WHEN HE SAID 'PLANE,' I HAD AN ENTIRELY different picture in my head," Sam said. "I was just hoping I'd have a window seat."

"All there is are window seats," Six remarked as she sat down in one of the Gulfstream G650's white leather chairs and spun around. She ran her hands over the gleaming woodwork. The jet was gorgeous.

"Have you seen the big-screen TV?" asked James, walking into the cabin. "There's a digital library. You can watch virtually any movie you like."

"*Mothra vs. Godzilla*?" Sam asked, going immediately to the control screen and ordering it to tell him what it had stored in its collection.

"You like *kaiju* films?" James asked.

"Absolutely," Sam said. "They're awesome. Gamera. Rodan. Hedorah."

"Hedorah!" James said. "The smog monster! He doesn't usually get any love, but he's one of my favorites."

"Not you too," Six said, groaning.

"I'd think that maybe after being attacked by what was basically a *kaiju* last year, that kind of film might be, you know, triggering," James said to Sam.

"Oh," said Sam, looking thoughtful. "Right. The Mogosaur. You know, I never really thought about it that way. But I guess you're right." He turned to Six. "Hey, I bet I could write an awesome script for *Godzilla vs. the Mogosaur.* Syfy would love that."

"We have a fully stocked pantry," James announced as Six shook her head. "Mostly ready-to-eat stuff. Behind this cabin is a smaller one with a couch that can be made into a bed. These chairs also fold out so you can sleep in them. There are lavatories both fore and aft. The rest you can pretty much figure out for yourselves."

"Now all we need is someone who can fly it," said Six.

"I could," Sam suggested, looking excited. "I just have to tap into the flight control system." He turned his head, focusing on getting into the plane's internal systems.

"I'm sure you could," James said. "But I suspect the FAA would have some problems with that. Fortunately, I'm a pilot."

"You?" Six said.

"Captain Kirk, at your service," James said, saluting.

Six fixed him with a look. "How convenient," she said.

"Nobody doubts that you can look after yourselves," James said, picking up on her insinuation. "My primary role on this mission is to fly the plane. However, I may be of further use. Despite your unique abilities, the two of you are still teenagers, albeit world-famous ones. There will be occasions when my presence will make it easier for others to accept your involvement and for you to do your jobs."

"Wait a minute," Sam said. "You're Captain Kirk. James Kirk."

James grinned.

"Please tell me your middle initial is *T*," Sam said.

"For Thomas," James said. "Not Tiberius. Although it's entirely accidental. My parents didn't do it on purpose. They have no sense of humor."

"I don't understand any of this conversation," said Six.

"For an alien, your knowledge of human sci-fi is seriously lacking," Sam teased. "How long have you lived here, and you don't know who Captain James T. Kirk is?"

"Apparently, it's him," Six said, pointing at James.

"If that thing has *Star Trek* on it, you're getting a history lesson," Sam said, indicating the TV.

"I need to prepare for takeoff," James said. "Air travel time to Darwin is slightly over twenty-four hours. We'll have to make stops in Copenhagen and Singapore, but you won't need to deplane. We should be in Darwin tomorrow afternoon, Australian time."

James disappeared into the cockpit. Sam sat down. Not

long after, James's voice came through the speakers, telling them to prepare for takeoff. Six and Sam secured their seatbelts, and Sam watched out the window as the plane taxied into position, then roared to life, rumbled down the runway, and lifted up in the air.

A few minutes later, James spoke through the speakers again: "Attention, passengers, you are now free to move about the cabin."

Sam laughed. "I like him," he said.

"Hmm," said Six. She took out one of the folders McKenna had provided for them with information about their mission, and started looking at the papers inside. Sam opened his own copy of the file. He started to read, but he kept glancing over at Six. She had that expression on her face that meant she was processing information, trying to fit pieces together so that they made sense. It was a look he'd seen a million times before. And it made her more beautiful than she already was. He felt his heart stutter a little. Six looked up as if sensing this.

"What?" she asked.

Sam shook his head. "Nothing," he told her. "I'm just admiring your mind."

"It *is* pretty amazing," Six said. "But listen. This incident doesn't make sense. Fifty people were massacred. An entire village. All so that whoever did it could take one kid. Why?"

"So that no one could give a description of who took him?"

"If you're concerned about that, wear masks," Six said. "There are other options besides killing fifty people. You only do that because you *want* to."

"You think it was Mogs?" Sam asked. "That's something they would do."

"Could be," said Six. "But unlikely. Most of them have been contained. Definitely somebody with a sadistic streak, though."

Sam returned to the file. There was one survivor of the attack on the village, a five-year-old girl named Miah. They'd found her hiding under one of the houses. She was the one who had told the rescuers that a boy had been taken. She was also the one he and Six were on their way to see.

"How much will this girl be able to tell us?" Sam wondered.

"We'll find out," said Six. "But we might be surprised. Kids notice a lot of things adults don't, or at least different things. She might be a good source of information."

Or she might be so terrified she remembers nothing, Sam thought.

✧ ✧ ✧

Several hours later, somewhere over the Atlantic, they sat on the couch, eating pizza they'd heated up in the galley oven and watching old episodes of *Star Trek.*

"Is every episode about Kirk trying to hook up with a sexy alien?" Six asked.

"Not *every* episode," Sam said defensively. "Besides, what's wrong with wanting to hook up with a sexy alien?" He leaned over and kissed her on the cheek. "Want to watch another episode?"

Six shook her head. "Five is more than enough, thanks," she said, pushing her plate away. "We should get back to the file."

Sam held up the can of soda he was drinking from. "How about a toast first," he said. "To our new jobs."

Six clinked her can against his, then drank. "Don't get too excited. These might be temporary positions," she said. "I still haven't decided. We'll see how this first mission—" She was interrupted by Sam kissing her.

He tasted the cola on her lips, the softness of her mouth. Even after more than a year of kisses, it still always felt like the first one to him. He pulled away. "Sorry," he said. "Were you saying something?"

"It's not important," said Six, and leaned towards him.

Just then, James emerged from the cockpit. He looked at their faces. "How's everything going out here?" he asked as he opened the refrigerator and looked around inside.

"Fine," Six and Sam said in unison.

"We should probably get back to those files," said Six.

For the next two hours, they reviewed every scrap of information they had. When the words all started to blur together and Sam was sure his brain couldn't hold any more information, he closed the file and said, "I think it's time for another break. How about we watch that Godzilla movie?"

"Do we have to?" Six asked. "I thought I did my duty watching *Star Trek* with you."

Sam reached over and took the folder from her. "Come on," he said. He stood up and grabbed her hand, leading her through into the other, smaller cabin. The couch in there was positioned across from another television screen. With a little maneuvering, the couch opened up into a full-size bed.

"Haven't I suffered enough?" Six asked as she sank onto it.

Sam sat beside her. "Trust me, you're going to love it," he said as he concentrated on interfacing with the entertainment system and told it to play the movie.

"Show-off," Six said, leaning against him.

Sam put his arm around her. "Admit it," he said. "You've always wanted to date a human remote control."

Six made it less than halfway through the film before falling asleep. Because he was enjoying being with her snuggled on the bed, Sam didn't wake her. Then he too fell asleep. Maybe because of the movie, and maybe because of the poster he'd seen in New York of the Mogosaur, he dreamed about fighting a giant monster. He couldn't see it, but he knew it was coming. He heard it, and he felt its footsteps shaking the ground. Then he realized the shaking was the plane landing. He forced his eyes open.

"We must be in Copenhagen," said Six, who was also awake. She yawned. "It's still the middle of the night."

"Come back to bed," Sam teased, reaching for her hand. He pulled her against him, his arm sliding around her. He closed his eyes, expecting to have trouble getting back to sleep. But a moment later, he was dreaming again, and this time not about monsters.

The rest of the trip was uneventful. They landed in Singapore just after lunchtime, then flew the last, shorter leg to

Australia. When they finally landed in Darwin, it was the afternoon. There, they traded the luxurious Gulfstream for a decidedly less-comfortable Jeep. Still, it was nice to be out of the plane after more than a day in the air.

"The girl has no living relatives," James reminded them before they set off for the city. "She's been living with one of the social workers assigned to her case, so that's where you're going. Her guardian thinks that you're members of a government task force investigating the massacre."

"Government," Six said meaningfully as she slid into the driver's seat and put on a pair of sunglasses.

"Drive safely," James said, ignoring the little jab. "I'll be standing by in case you need any backup."

"Don't wait up, Dad," Six said, and pulled away.

The house in question was in a quiet suburb, unassuming and slightly boring. Six parked the Jeep, and she and Sam walked up the neat concrete path to the front porch. When they knocked, the door was opened by a young man.

"Hi, I'm Six, and this is Sam."

"Oliver," the man said. Behind him, a small brown-and-white terrier barked excitedly. The man turned. "Quiet, Graham. These are friends."

The dog ignored him, and kept barking. Then a small girl appeared. She had the dark skin and black hair of the Yolngu people indigenous to Australia's Northern Territory, and she regarded them with large brown eyes. "It's all right, Graham," she said softly. Immediately, the dog quieted down, wagging its tail happily as the girl petted him.

"You must be Miah," Sam said to the girl.

The girl nodded. Oliver opened the door. "Please, come in."

They walked inside the house, and Oliver showed them into a cozy living room. Miah followed, with Graham padding along at her side. She sat down on a rug and started playing with a pile of Legos. Sam sat down cross-legged next to her, while Oliver and Six remained standing, watching them.

"I recognize the two of you," Oliver said. "You were involved in fighting the invasion." He hesitated a moment, glancing at Miah, before asking, "Is what happened in Arnhem Land connected to that?"

"No," Six assured him. "Not to the invasion. But possibly to what's going on now with humans developing Legacies. I assume you know about that."

Oliver nodded. "Yeah, of course," he said.

As Six and Oliver continued to talk, Sam focused on Miah. "What are you building?" he asked her.

"A castle," Miah told him. "For the princess to hide in when the dragon comes. The last time he came, he burned everybody up with his fire breath."

Sam felt a wave of compassion wash over him. The child was obviously channeling what had happened to her into her game, trying to make it something she could control. He hated having to ask her about it. But that was why he was there.

"Miah, can you tell me about what happened the day Bunji was taken?"

The girl didn't answer. Instead, she picked up a Lego figure of a boy and placed it on the rug. Then she picked up some more figures and arranged them around that one. Finally, she took the figure of a girl—the one she had indicated was the princess—and held it up. "When the dragon came, the princess hid," she said. "She was afraid of dragons. So she hid under the castle and watched. Then the dragon breathed fire on everyone and burned them up."

With her free hand, she knocked all the figures down, leaving just the boy standing. "Then the dragon took the boy and flew away," she said. "The princess didn't come out for a long time. Not until people from the next village came to see what had happened and told her it was all right."

"I see," Sam said. "You told that story really well. Can I ask you one thing?"

He waited for Miah to answer. Finally, she nodded.

"Can you tell me what the dragon looked like?"

Miah nodded. "He looked like you," she said.

"Like me?"

The girl nodded again. "A boy with white skin. But he wasn't a boy. He was a dragon pretending to be a boy."

"A dragon in a boy costume, huh?" Sam said, trying to joke.

"You don't believe me," Miah said. "Nobody does."

"Oh, no," Sam said quickly. "I believe you. So, this dragon boy had white skin. Can you tell me anything else about how he looked?"

Miah shrugged. "I don't remember," she said curtly.

Sam suspected she *did* remember more. But now she thought he didn't believe her. He tried a different tack. "What can you tell me about Bunji?"

Miah picked up the boy Lego figure and held it in her hand, looking at it for a long time. "He was nice," she said. "He could make people feel better."

"Feel better?" Sam said. "You mean like he made them feel happy?"

Miah nodded. "And he fixed us," she said. "When we got broken." She held her hand open, showing him the palm. "I cut myself once," she said. "On a piece of glass. Bunji made it not hurt anymore."

Sam ran his fingertips over the skin of the girl's palm. "Good as new," he said.

Miah laughed. "Good as new."

"Thank you for talking to me, Miah," Sam said. "I'm going to go talk to Oliver for a minute, okay? Then maybe I can come back and help you with your castle."

Miah looked at him, her big eyes pleading. "Are you going to find Bunji?" she asked.

"I hope so," Sam told her.

"And kill the dragon?"

"I don't know about that," he said. "Dragons are pretty hard to kill. But we'll try to make sure he doesn't hurt anybody else. How does that sound?"

"Okay," Miah said. "I'll tell the princess."

Sam stood, and he and Six walked into the kitchen with Oliver.

"She's been telling that story about the princess and the dragon ever since we brought her here," Oliver said. "Do you really think you can find Bunji? And why would anyone slaughter an entire village to cover up taking one boy?"

"We don't know yet," Six answered.

Oliver again looked at Six and Sam. "Does it have something to do with what you all can do? With what Miah says Bunji can do?"

"Very likely, yes," Sam admitted. He didn't want to scare the man, but he saw no point in lying to him either. "What's going to happen to Miah?" he asked.

"She'll stay here until we can figure out a long-term plan," Oliver said. "Everyone she was related to was killed, so finding an appropriate place for her isn't easy. You don't think she's in any danger from the monster who did this, do you?"

"No," Sam said. "Most likely, he doesn't even know there was a survivor, or doesn't care. But if anyone contacts you asking about her, you be sure to let us know, all right?"

While Six and Oliver continued to talk, Sam returned to the living room. Miah had given up playing with the Legos and was now playing with Graham. He was sitting on the rug in front of her, his head cocked as if listening intently.

"What are you doing?" Sam asked her.

"Telling him to go pick up the ball over there," Miah answered. She pointed to a red rubber ball that sat on the floor some distance away. "But I don't think he hears me."

"Try telling him again," Sam suggested.

Miah looked at Graham. She didn't speak, but Sam saw

her brow furrow in concentration. A moment later, the dog scampered off, picked up the ball, and returned it to the girl. "Good boy, Graham," she said, ruffling his ears.

"Have you taught him a lot of tricks like that?" Sam asked her.

Miah shrugged. "A few," she said. "Watch." She again focused her attention on the dog, but said nothing. After a few seconds, Graham flung himself on the ground and rolled over, his paws in the air.

"That's great," Sam told the little girl. "Is it just Graham you've taught to do that, or can you talk to other animals too?"

Miah shrugged again. "I don't know," she said, suddenly seeming shy.

Sam picked up the Lego princess. Focusing on it, he used his telekinesis to levitate it so that it floated over his palm. Miah looked at it, then smiled. "Bunji and I played like that sometimes," she said.

"Can you make her float?" Sam asked.

Miah stared hard at the princess, her face scrunched up. Sam stopped levitating it. For a split second, it seemed like the figure remained suspended in the air before falling onto his palm. Miah looked sad.

"It's okay," Sam assured her. "Do you want to try again?"

Miah shook her head. Sam, who suddenly had more questions about the girl than he'd arrived with, considered pressing her. But he didn't. Instead, he watched her play with Graham for another few minutes, until Six and Oliver emerged from the kitchen. Then Sam said good-bye to the girl, promising to come see her again if he found Bunji.

Back outside, as they walked to the Jeep, Sam said, "I think Bunji might not be the only one in that village with a Legacy." He told Six about the way Miah had interacted with Graham, and about the Lego princess. "It was just for a second," he said. "But I swear it felt like she was the one holding it in the air."

"She's too young to be exhibiting signs," Six said. "She's probably just good with animals."

Sam nodded. "I know," he said. "But I felt *something* from her."

Six stopped. "Should we go back in and test her some more?"

Sam glanced back at the door. "I don't think so," he said. "Not yet, anyway. She's been through a lot. And she seemed uncomfortable when I pushed her even a little. But we should keep an eye on her."

"I still say she's too young," Six said as they resumed walking to the Jeep and got in. When Sam didn't answer, she said, "What?"

"I'm just thinking," Sam said. "Humans aren't Loric. Maybe the energy won't always work the same way in them—in us—the way it does in you."

"It has so far," Six said.

"That we know of," Sam rebutted. He looked again at the house. "But you know what they say about rules—they're meant to be broken. Maybe that little girl is breaking one of them."

"Maybe," Six said as she started the jeep. "Like you said, we'll keep an eye on her."

As they were pulling away, Sam's phone rang. "It's James," he said as he answered it.

"Where are you guys?" James asked.

"On our way back," Sam told him.

"Did you find out anything new?"

"Maybe," Sam said. "We'll see."

"Okay," said James. "Well, get back here. Something's happened."

"Oh?"

"There's been another kidnapping," James said.

CHAPTER THREE

SIX
MANILA, PHILIPPINES

"TO MEET WITH THE PRESIDENT'S DAUGHTER?" Six said. "In Manila?"

She and Sam had just returned to the plane. Now, James was telling them that they were about to take off again.

"My dad met her and her father last year," Sam said. "He tried to help Melanie with her Legacy. Is that why we're going?"

"We're going because the president asked us to," James explained. "Or, rather, he asked McKenna to. The two of them are friends from way back."

"Really?" said Six. "The president of the United States asked us to talk to his daughter when probably every Secret Service, CIA, FBI, and whatever other kind of agent that exists is already on it?"

"Not to mention the Earth Garde," Sam added.

"As I said, McKenna and President Jackson have known each other for a long time," James explained. "He simply wants every avenue explored, and McKenna said he would do what he could to help with the investigation."

"Does this mean the president knows about our secret club?" Six pressed.

"It means he knows McKenna is someone who is good at getting answers," said James.

"And what, exactly, happened?" said Six.

"Melanie has been in the Philippines as part of the Earth Garde, assisting with disaster recovery following the earthquake that occurred there three weeks ago," James explained. "It's a goodwill tour of sorts. Last week, while returning to their hotel, they were ambushed. Melanie was knocked out. Vincent Iabruzzi, another Earth Garde member, was taken. He's a healer."

"So, probably the same people who took Bunji," Six surmised.

"That would be the logical conclusion, yes," said James.

"This happened a week ago?" Sam said. "How come we didn't hear anything about it?"

"Earth Garde put their public relations department into high gear," James explained. "They don't want people to be scared, so they downplayed the whole thing and kept Iabruzzi's disappearance out of the news. Melanie stayed in Manila and is making appearances so that everybody thinks things are fine. But believe me, she's got eyes on her at all times. Now buckle up. We need to get going. It's about a five-hour flight to Manila."

He went into the cockpit, leaving Six and Sam to discuss this new development.

"Melanie's Legacy is superstrength, right?" Six asked Sam.

He nodded. "Yeah. It's not the most interesting, but she's really enthusiastic about being part of the Earth Garde. She has millions of followers on Twitter, and her Instagram is a parade of selfies designed to make every teenager in the world want to attend the HGA."

Sam called up her profile on his phone and showed Six some of the photos. They all depicted a cute girl with curly blond hair. Most of them showed her doing typical teenage things: eating ice cream, playing with a black Labrador, making stupid faces with friends at a sleepover. But others were clearly staged to show off her using her Legacy for good. In one, she helped lift a pile of rubble in New York. In the most recent, she was seen assisting with cleanup in the Philippines, then being hugged by a woman whose home she helped unearth.

"I can see why they picked her to be the face of Earth Garde," said Six. "She seems very . . . perky."

✧ ✧ ✧

Hours later, when they met Melanie Jackson face-to-face in a room at the US embassy in Manila, she was far less perky than she appeared in photos. She looked exhausted. Her face was covered in fading bruises, and there was a bandage on her forehead.

"You're Six," she said wearily, sitting down on a couch. She pulled her legs up and hugged them, staring at her visitors over the tops of her knees. She darted her eyes at Sam. "And you're Sam. Your dad was kind to me when mine asked him for advice about my Legacy. How is he?" Her tone was. unreadable.

"He's good," Sam said. "How is yours?" He blushed and laughed nervously, realizing what a funny question it was, given that hers was the president of the United States.

Melanie didn't laugh. "Did he send you?"

"Kind of," Sam admitted.

Melanie snorted. "I guess the eight million marines stationed around this place aren't enough," she said. "Like that would stop them anyway, if they really want to get in."

"So," Six said. "Can you tell us what happened?"

"I've already told this story about a hundred times," Melanie replied. "Do I really have to tell it again?"

"We'd like to hear it directly from you," said Six. "If you don't mind."

Melanie pushed a piece of stray hair behind her ear. "We were coming back from spending the day helping out with earthquake stuff," she began. Her voice was slightly flat, as if she just wanted to get it over with. "I did a lot of heavy lifting. Vincent healed people. Using his Legacy always wears him out more than using mine does me. I guess healing is harder. Anyway, he was pretty wiped out. We both were. We just wanted to take a shower and get something to eat. But we had to wave and have our photos taken and all that. You know, for Earth Garde publicity." Her voice took on a bitter edge. "And that's when it all went wrong. I don't actually remember a whole lot. I saw Vincent go down, and tried to get to him. Then something pricked my neck. They told me later it was a tranquilizer dart. I don't remember anything else until I woke up a couple of hours later."

Six looked at Sam. This was pretty much what they already knew from what James had told them. They'd been hoping to get some additional information from Melanie.

"They say there must have been people with Legacies involved," Melanie said. "The way Vincent disappeared so quickly and all. Someone who could teleport."

"It's certainly possible," Six said.

Melanie shook her head. "That's pathetic," she said. "Legacies are supposed to be used to help people, not hurt them. Then again, it's not like any of us asked to get them." She glanced at Six, then looked away.

"Legacies are inherently good," said Six, reminding herself that the girl was under a lot of stress. "If people use them in a negative way, that's because they've chosen to." She thought about Five, and how his mind had been twisted to make him use his gifts to hurt his own people.

Melanie sighed. "I used to think the hardest decisions people my age faced were about drinking and sex. Now we've got this whole other thing to worry about."

"It's not easy," Sam agreed.

"You haven't had yours much longer than the rest of us, though, right?" Melanie asked. "And you seem to be handling it just fine."

"Yeah," Sam said. "But I didn't have much choice. Mine manifested right in the middle of the war, and I had to figure out pretty quickly what was going on." He looked at Six. "Besides, I've had a lot of help getting used to it. Trust me, it takes a while before it doesn't feel weird. Before *you* don't feel weird."

Melanie put her feet down but crossed her arms over her chest, still guarded. "I'm getting there," she said. "Sort of. Every time I use my Legacy, I'm surprised it actually works. It still feels a little like a magic trick. For the longest time, I had this weird fear that maybe somebody was playing an elaborate practical joke on me. Like somehow there was machinery or something I couldn't see that was doing the real work, and that I was being filmed for one of those hidden-camera shows. That's dumb, I know."

"It's not dumb," Sam said.

"Plus, there's always somebody watching," Melanie continued. "I mean, I'm used to everyone watching everything I do because I'm the president's kid. Everyone waiting for me to slip up and do something stupid. But that's nothing compared to this." She sighed. "Sometimes I just want to go to the mall and look at earrings without it having to *mean* something." She looked at Six for a moment. "Somehow, I don't think you ever go to the mall to shop for jewelry."

"I don't get a lot of time for that, no," said Six.

"That's one of the things I thought I would like about Earth Garde," Melanie said. "It's supposed to give you a positive outlet for all this."

"But now?" said Six.

"Now, I don't know," Melanie admitted. "Nobody told us that people would want to hurt us or . . ." Her voice trailed off. She shook her head. "I don't know."

"Did Vincent ever mention anyone contacting him?" Six asked, trying to get the interview back on track. "Threatening him?"

"No more than the usual," Melanie answered.

"The usual?" Six repeated.

"You know," Melanie said. "The emails from crazy people telling you you're possessed by demons. The comments from people who think you can give them a Legacy by sleeping with them. I had one guy who wrote to me a bunch of times asking if I would donate my blood to him so he could experiment with injecting it to see what would happen. You guys get that kind of stuff too, right?"

"Actually, no," said Six.

"But we've been pretty much off the grid," Sam added. "You guys are more public than we are right now."

"Maybe," Melanie said. "Anyway, it's not all creepy like that. Sometimes it's people who want to hire you to do stuff for them, or who want to buy your story. There's a company that wants to make action figures of us. That would actually be sort of cool. But it's against Earth Garde regulations or something to profit off our Legacies. Anyway, any emails or letters we get like that, we turn over to Lexa at the HGA to look into."

"Lexa?" said Six.

"Yeah," Melanie said. "She's the tech expert at the academy, and she offered her help to the Earth Garde. If anyone was really threatening Vincent, she would know about it. I can give you her contact info if you want."

"Oh, we know how to get in touch with her," Sam assured her. "Is there anything else—anything at all—that you think might be helpful?"

Melanie shook her head and yawned. "No," she said. "And I'm really beat. Are we done here?"

"For now," Six said.

"Thanks for talking to us," Sam added.

Melanie stood up. "Are you going to find Vincent?"

"We're going to try," Sam said.

"Try hard," Melanie said, and headed for the door.

When she was gone, Sam said, "Looks like we'll be talking to Lexa."

"So much for keeping a low profile," Six remarked.

"Melanie will probably mention to the Earth Garde that we came to see her anyway," Sam reminded her.

"Let's get back to the plane," Six said. "I'm ready to go home."

Sam chuckled.

"What?" Six said. "Did I say something funny?"

"You said 'home,'" Sam replied.

"Don't get excited," Six said. "I meant it metaphorically."

They returned to the Gulfstream. James wasn't there. Before they could even start wondering where he was, though, Sam's cell phone rang.

"Lexa!" Sam said, answering it.

"The one and only," Lexa said. "How are you two doing?"

"We're great," Sam told her. "Funny enough, we were just going to call you."

"Figured you might be," Lexa said. "How'd everything go with Melanie Jackson?"

Sam laughed. "Can't do anything without you knowing about it, can we?"

"Well, you know I like to keep an eye on things."

"Hang on. Let me put you on the big screen so Six can talk to you too."

He rerouted the call to the plane's television set. Lexa's face filled the screen. Sam interfaced with the electronics and made it so that she could see them as well.

"What kind of fancy flying hotel room are you two in?" Lexa asked.

"You know," Six said. "Just jet-setting around the world. How's everything going there?"

"There" was the Human Garde Academy in Point Reyes, California, where Lexa was helping Nine get things going. In answer to the question, Lexa shrugged. "I got myself an office with every toy a hacker could ever want," she said, indicating the room behind her. She tapped on a keyboard. "It's Nine's way of trying to make sure I stay for a while."

"Looks like it's working," Six said.

"There are worse places to be."

"How is Nine?" Six asked.

"King of the castle," Lexa said. "We'd love to see you two. You know, when you're not busy with whatever it is you're doing."

Sam laughed. He suspected Lexa somehow knew more about their activities than she was letting on, but he didn't ask. "Have you talked to any of the others lately?"

"Yeah, everyone is doing fine. John, Marina—"

"Even Five?" Six said.

"Well, you know," Lexa said. "*Almost* everybody."

"I'm guessing you didn't call just to catch up," Sam said. "What's up?"

"Two things," Lexa said. "One, you know about the healers that have been disappearing."

It was a statement, not a question. Sam nodded. "We do."

"Well, we found a potential healer. Girl named Edwige Pothier. She's developed a reputation. There are claims that she can help with everything from getting pregnant to curing terminal illnesses. Only thing is, she's been doing it long before the Legacies started showing up in humans."

"How?" Sam asked.

"Supposedly, with hoodoo."

"You mean like sticking pins in dolls?" said Sam.

"That's voodoo," Lexa said. "Hoodoo is a kind of folk magic. Whatever she calls it, it could be a Legacy. Or it could be nothing at all. The point is, someone who is collecting healers would be very interested in a girl like Edwige. You should get to her before someone else does."

"Why not go yourself?" Six asked her. "Why ask us?"

"I got enough to do here," Lexa said.

"You mean you thought it might get us to change our minds about working with the HGA," Six countered. "Nice try."

"All I'm asking is for you to make a little trip, check her out," Lexa said. "I'd consider it a favor."

"We'll do it," Sam said.

Lexa nodded. "Much appreciated. And while you're there, I got someone else you might be interested in talking to."

"Oh?" Six said. "Who's that?"

"You ever look at the YouTube videos of people who supposedly have Legacies?" Lexa asked. "It's a whole thing now. Some of them are so good, even I can't tell right away what's real and what's not. Well, take a look at this one."

She typed something on her keyboard, and in one corner of the screen, a video popped up. An image of a pair of hands appeared. One was cupped, and on the palm rested an origami horse made from folded paper, blue with tiny silver stars on it.

"Pretty," Six said.

"Just watch," Lexa told her.

The second hand moved so that it hovered over the horse. Two fingers pressed against the thumb as if whoever the hands belonged to was pinching something between them. Then the fingers moved in tiny circles as the hand traveled back and forth over the horse.

"It's like she's pretending to sprinkle salt on it," Sam remarked. "Or fairy dust."

The second hand disappeared, and only the one holding the horse remained in the frame. For a moment, nothing happened. Then the horse lifted its head and shook. It stretched out a leg and tapped its paper hoof against the palm of the hand, pawing at it. Its paper tail twitched jerkily. It moved its head from side to side as if testing muscles it was using for the very first time. Finally, it reared up on its hind legs awkwardly before toppling over onto its side, where it lay still.

"What was that?" Sam asked. "Some kind of animation?"

"That's a good word for it," said Lexa. "That's the first video she posted, about six weeks ago. There have been a lot more since. I'll play a couple."

She showed them two more videos. In the first, the girl animated another paper figure, this one a frog. After doing the sprinkling thing, the frog hopped across her palm before leaping off. In the second, the origami animals had been replaced by an action figure, which Sam informed Six was a person named Luke Skywalker from some movie called *Star Wars*. When it came to life, it immediately powered up its tiny light-up sword, swinging the glowing green weapon from side to side as it looked for a nonexistent enemy.

"Those were uploaded four and three weeks ago," Lexa said. "This one was posted two days ago."

The final video was slightly different. There was no hand holding an origami animal or an action figure. In this one, a marionette of a ballet dancer sat in the grass in a garden.

The figure looked to be made of papier-mâché, its l...
together with twine. It wore a pink paper tutu, and i...
tures were painted on. Strings connected the hands, fe...
and head to a pair of crossed sticks.

As in the previous videos, a hand appeared, picking up
the sticks. The ballerina stood, trembling at the ends of the
strings. Then music began to play, and she danced.

After about twenty seconds, a second hand appeared,
holding a pair of scissors. With quick motions, the scissors
severed each of the strings holding the marionette up. But
the ballerina didn't fall down. She kept dancing, lifting her
arms, kicking her legs, spinning around.

"Looks like stop-motion to me," Sam remarked. "Really
well done."

"It's not animation," Six said. "It's real."

Sam laughed. "Right. Lexa, those are great, but I don't
really know what they—"

"Six is right," Lexa said. "At least, I think she is."

"You think that puppet really came to life?" Sam asked.

"Not life," said Six. "They aren't alive. But they might as
well be in terms of what they can do."

"It's not all that different from your technopathy, Sam,"
Lexa said.

"I just get machines to do what they're built to do," Sam
objected.

"Isn't that what she's doing?" said Six. "She made a paper
horse act like a real horse, and a paper frog jump like a real
frog. She made the ballerina marionette dance."

"I guess," Sam admitted. "But we've never seen a Legacy like that."

"There are all kinds of new Legacies popping up," Lexa said.

"Who's the girl?" Six asked.

"I don't know yet. Not exactly, anyway. Her user name is Geppettogirl. I've traced her to New Orleans, where she does her act for tourists in Jackson Square, but that's as far as I've gotten. It gets more interesting, though. I found a story in the *Times-Picayune* this morning. Little thing, buried way in the back. Gentleman by the name of Tarvis Mendelson had a break-in at his antiques shop in the Quarter. Somebody made off with a couple of rare coins."

"That's interesting?" Sam said.

"No," said Lexa. "But this part is. Mendelson told police he was pretty sure he saw a couple of dolls walk out with those coins. Dolls dressed up like pirates."

"Sounds like Tarvis has been drinking a little bit," Sam suggested.

"I'm sure that's what the police think too," Lexa said. "And maybe that's what happened. Or maybe somebody like Geppettogirl used her Legacy to get those pirates to do her dirty work."

"You think somebody should look into her," said Six.

"It couldn't hurt. And since you're going to be there anyway, doing me that favor . . ." She let her words trail off.

Six groaned. "Fine," she said. "We'll try to find her."

Lexa grinned. "Thank you," she said. "I'll text you the

info on Edwige Pothier. Give me a call when you have some news."

The connection was terminated. Six leaned back in her chair. "She's up to something."

Sam laughed. "Congratulations. You are officially the most paranoid person I have ever met."

"She didn't even ask us who we're working for," Six continued. "Like she already knows."

"You're worrying about nothing," Sam assured her. "This is *Lexa*. She's our friend, remember?"

Six nodded. "I know. I know. You're right." She sighed.

James, walking through the doorway, said, "Sorry. I had to go file our flight plan back to New York. Anything happen while I was gone?"

Six looked at Sam, who nodded, then back at James. "About that flight plan," she said.

CHAPTER FOUR

SAM
NEW ORLEANS, LOUISIANA

THE SHOP THAT EDWIGE POTHIER WORKED OUT OF was unmarked, tucked into an alley on the edge of the Faubourg Marigny district, away from the crowds that filled the more popular French Quarter. Six and Sam walked right by the nondescript door, with its faded light-blue paint, and at first mistook it for the back door to somewhere else. Which, in fact, is what it was, or had been, as the shop was located in what used to be the servants' kitchen of a house that faced the next street over.

Once they realized that they had found the place they were looking for, Six opened the door, and she and Sam went inside. They found themselves in a small, windowless room lit by a single bare lightbulb screwed into a fixture in the ceiling. The floorboards, painted white, were worn smooth.

Shelves lined the walls, crowded with glass jars that were filled with dried herbs, flowers, grasses, and other botanicals. Scattered among those were other jars containing more unusual items: teeth, graveyard dirt, coffin nails, silver dimes.

In the middle of the room was a rectangular wooden table. Its top was covered with small piles of some of the things found in the jars on the shelves. Seated there was an old woman whose skin was creased and browned by years in the sun. She wore a faded-blue work shirt with the sleeves rolled up to the elbows. Her gray hair fell in a long, thick braid down her back. She was picking up pinches of this and that and tucking them into a small red flannel bag. When she looked up, she regarded Sam and Six with one blue eye and one the color of milk glass.

"Hi," Six said. "We're wondering if you can help us find Edwige Pothier."

"What you want with Edwige?" the woman asked. She spoke with a heavy Cajun accent.

"We just want to talk to her," said Six.

"'Bout what?"

"We understand she's a very skilled healer," Six said.

"You sick?" the woman asked. She cocked her head. "Don't look sick." She turned her gaze to Sam. "He don't look sick neither."

Six shook her head. "No."

"Somebody else sick?"

"Nobody's sick," Six said.

"Then what you need Edwige for?"

Six wasn't sure how to continue the conversation. The woman was obviously suspicious of them. She decided that the simplest thing would be to tell the truth. "She may be in danger."

"That so?" the woman replied. She seemed unconcerned.

"May I ask your name?" Sam asked.

"Evella."

"Evella, I'm Sam. This is Six. Do you know who the Garde are? What a Legacy is?"

The woman nodded. "Heard somethin' 'bout that. Spacemen and whatnot." She gave Six a meaningful look, but said nothing else.

"Yeah," Sam said. "Well, if Edwige really can heal people like we hear she can, she might have a Legacy. A gift."

"Oh, she got a gift, all right," Evella said. "But it don't come from outer space. She been healin' since she was seven years old. Long before any of what's happening now started up."

"And how exactly does she do her healing?" Six asked.

"She don't do the healing," said Evella. "God do. Edwige, she just know how to ask the right way for his help."

Six looked at Sam.

"What's wrong?" Evella said. "You don't believe in God?"

Six shook her head. "It's not that."

"Let me ask you something," Evella said. "Where these Legacies come from?"

"From a source called the Entity," Six told her.

"That a person?"

"Not really," said Six. "It's more of a power. A force. It awakens Legacies in certain people."

"What people? How it choose who to work through?"

"I don't actually know," Six admitted.

"Sounds like God to me," Evella said. "Just goin' by a different name." She looked from Six to Sam. "You two got powers." It wasn't a question.

Sam nodded. "Several."

"Like what?"

Sam focused on a small pile of what looked like dried roots that lay on the table in front of Evella. They slowly rose up in the air. Sam turned the roots in a circle, then lowered them back to the table. He waited for Evella's response.

"Suppose that makes clearin' the supper table a whole lot more fun," she said. She turned her good eye to Six. "Whatta you do?"

Six went invisible. Then she reappeared on the other side of the room. "That," she said. "Among other things."

"How'd you do that?" said a voice.

Behind where Evella sat in her chair was a doorway to another room. Now, a teenager stood in it. She was short, slight, with long, brown hair that fell almost to her waist. Her wide eyes were the same blue as Evella's one good one. She was wearing a sleeveless dress, yellow with a pattern of pink roses on it, and she was barefoot.

"Edwige?" Sam guessed.

The girl nodded. "How'd she do that?" she asked again.

"It's her Legacy," Sam explained.

"Is it magic?" Edwige asked.

"Something like that, I guess," Sam answered. "Is what you do magic?"

"Some people call it that," Edwige said. She glanced at Evella, who snorted derisively.

"You don't?" said Six.

The girl shook her head. "I call it hoodoo. Conjure. Rootwork. It's got different names. But it's all God."

"How did you learn how to do it?" Sam asked.

Edwige pointed to Evella. "She taught me."

Evella clicked her tongue. "I taught you," she said. "But you're brighter than I ever was. Brighter than anyone I ever saw."

"Brighter?" said Sam.

"She means stronger," Edwige explained.

"When she gets working, she glows with the spirit," said Evella.

"What do you think makes her so good at it?" Six asked.

"Some folks just is," said Evella.

The talk about glowing sounded to Six a lot like what those with a healing Legacy described. She turned her attention to Edwige. "How do you do it? The healing."

Edwige shrugged. "Different ways," she said. "Depends on what's wrong."

"Can you show me?"

"There's nothing to show," Edwige told her. "Unless you want to watch me grind up some roots and hear me say some prayers."

Six looked down at the table. A knife rested there, which Evella was using to scrape herbs into piles. Six picked it up and quickly drew it across her palm. The cut wasn't deep, but blood welled up. She held her hand out to Edwige. "Can you heal this?"

If she's a healer, she'll take my hand, she thought. For a moment, it looked like the girl might do it. Then Evella picked up a handkerchief and held it out to Six. "She ain't no sideshow attraction," she said. She waved the handkerchief in the air.

Six waited a moment, then took the cloth, wiping her hand with it. "She's not a healer," she said to Sam. "At least not the kind we're interested in."

"Maybe not," he said. "But if someone else *thinks* she is, she could still be in danger."

"I'm not afraid," Edwige announced.

"You should be," Six told her. "Someone is hunting teenagers with healing Legacies."

"But I'm not one," said Edwige. "Not like that. You said so yourself."

"Unfortunately for you, you have the appearance of one," Sam said. "You're the right age. And if whatever it is you *do* do really works, there might be people who want to take advantage of that."

"She got a gift, all right," Evella asked. "What she supposed to do, pretend she don't?"

"Stop healing," Six said. "Spread the word that you're a fake."

"But I'm not," said Edwige.

"Then start a rumor that your powers have left you," Six said. "I don't care what you say. But for you to stay safe—if that's even possible at this point—you need people to believe that you can't do what you supposedly can do. Because somebody's talking. We heard about you, and if we did, other people will too, and they might not be people you want to meet."

"I'm sorry we don't have a better suggestion," Sam said.

Edwige smiled softly. "I'll be fine," she said. "God will protect me."

"I hope that's true," said Sam. He went to the counter, picked up a piece of paper and a pencil and wrote something down. "But just in case you need some help, call this number."

Edwige took the paper, glanced at it, then slipped it into a pocket in her dress. "Thank you." She then turned to Six. "It was nice meeting you," she said, and held out her hand.

Six took it. A moment later, she felt a warmth penetrate her skin. Surprised, she looked into Edwige's face. The girl looked back at her, expressionless, and almost imperceptibly shook her head. She held Six's hand for another moment, then let go. Six ran her fingertips over her palm. There was no cut. "It was nice meeting you too," she said. "Maybe we'll see you again."

Six and Sam left the shop and stepped into the sunny afternoon.

"She *is* a healer," Six said to Sam, holding up her hand.

"What?" Sam said. "You just said she wasn't."

"I don't think she always was," Six said "But she is now."

"You think she was faking it, then just happened to be gifted with a healing Legacy?" Sam said. "That seems weirdly convenient."

"Maybe she's always been a healer," Six said. "Maybe she was given a Legacy because she was predisposed to it."

"Have we seen that before?" Sam asked.

"You're the one who said maybe the Loric energy works differently in humans," Six reminded him. "Who knows? Maybe some of the kids it's chosen already have certain abilities, and it supercharges them."

Sam turned back to the door. "We have to go back inside and convince her to—"

"To what?" Six interrupted. "Come with us? Go to the HGA? You can tell she's not ready yet. She needs time."

"She might not have time," Sam reminded her.

"She has enough time for us to get something to eat," Six told him. "Seriously, what can happen to her in the next hour? Let's get lunch. Then we can come back and see if Edwige will talk to us again. Okay?"

"I guess it's kind of a plan," Sam said. "Hey, you ever had an oyster po'boy?"

"Do I want to?" asked Six.

"You absolutely do," Sam said. "Hang on." He took out his phone and tapped into it, telling it to call up local restaurants. "There's a place not far from here," he said. "Come on."

They started walking. Their route took them into the

French Quarter and through Jackson Square, where there were numerous stalls with vendors selling art. There were also tables set up where people sat giving palm and tarot card readings. The café they were looking for was not far past that, with tables outside. They sat and ordered, then waited for the food to arrive.

"Do you think she really healed people with roots and prayers and whatever else she uses?" Six asked Sam. "I mean, before her Legacy kicked in?"

"I don't know," Sam said. "Half the stuff I take for granted now we used to think was science fiction. People from other planets? Superpowers? They were only in comic books and movies. Now, the president's daughter is lifting trees on the nightly news. The whole world has changed. So, who's to say what's impossible or not?"

When Six didn't respond, Sam looked at her. She was staring at something in the square.

"What are you looking at?" Sam asked her.

Six pointed. "Look," she said. "That girl."

Sam turned his head. Twenty yards away, an African American girl was standing. She was dressed in jeans and a white T-shirt. Her hair, a mass of dreadlocks, was tied back and hung down past her shoulders. There was a cardboard box on the ground beside her, as well as a bowl in front of which was a handwritten sign that said *Donations Thank You!* The girl was holding a piece of paper in her hands, folding it.

"What's she doing?" Sam asked Six.

"Origami. I don't know of what, though."

The girl finished folding the paper and held it in her palm. By this point, a handful of people had stopped to watch her. The girl waved her fingers over the paper, and it lifted up from her hand, a pair of wings moving jerkily. She had made a butterfly. The girl repeated the sprinkling motion, and the fluttering became more graceful. The paper butterfly flew around her head several times, then winged off across the square, rising up until it disappeared. The people assembled around the girl clapped.

"That's the girl from the videos," Six said. "Lexa said she performs here, remember? Come on." She stood up.

"But our po'boys!" Sam objected.

Six ignored him, walking over to where the girl was performing. Sam called out to their waitress, "We'll be right back," then followed.

The girl was now working with an origami frog. It was hopping from one hand to the other, then back again. The crowd laughed and applauded, drawing the attention of even more passersby. Coins and a few bills were deposited in the donation bowl.

Sam and Six stood at the back of the ever-increasing audience, watching as the girl animated a series of things: little plastic animals, a rag doll, a New Orleans souvenir figurine of a saxophone player that swayed back and forth as he performed a silent musical number.

"How is she doing that?" a young woman asked her friend.

"Invisible string," the young man said. "Like fishing line.

It's probably tied to her fingertips or something."

The girl, overhearing the conversation, said, "Give me something of yours, and I'll make it come alive."

The man searched his pockets. "I don't have anything."

"I do," his friend said, rummaging around in her purse and pulling out a key chain that had a Hello Kitty toy attached to it. "How's this?"

"Perfect," the girl said, taking the little figure.

She performed the maneuver with her fingers, and Hello Kitty began to do an awkward little dance. The keys made it difficult to move gracefully, but she did her best, dragging them behind her as she spun on her feet, her paws raised like a ballerina's.

"That's awesome," the young woman said. She nudged her friend. "Now what do you think?"

"I still think it's a trick," he said. He looked at Sam. "Right?"

"Sure," Sam said. He was distracted by the phone in his back pocket vibrating with an incoming message. Taking it out, he looked at it. "We have to go," he told Six.

"Tell James he'll have to wait," Six said. "We're talking to this girl."

"It's not James," Sam said. "It's Edwige."

He turned the phone around so that Six could see the message.

HELP ME

CHAPTER FIVE

SIX
NEW ORLEANS, LOUISIANA

WHEN SIX AND SAM ROUNDED THE CORNER ONTO the street where the shop was, they saw Evella hobbling towards them, using a wooden stick to help propel herself along. A moment later, she was *flying* towards them. A dozen feet behind her stood a boy with his hands raised in front of him, a look of concentration on his face. Six had only a moment to react and use her telekinesis to slow Evella's speed. The old woman hung suspended in the air for a moment, a look of indignant surprise on her face as she waved her cane around and kicked her feet. Six lowered her gently to the ground.

The boy ran inside the shop. The door slammed shut.

"What's going on in there?" Six asked Evella.

"They have her," she said angrily. She started walking

back towards the shop. Six stopped her.

"How many?" Sam asked.

"Three," said Evella. "The boy and two girls."

Sam looked at Six. "Could be the ones kidnapping healers."

"Only one way to find out," Six said, starting for the door. Evella and Sam followed.

Opening the door was no problem. It was locked from the inside, but Six simply used telekinesis to tear it off its hinges, sending it clattering into the street. "Stay here," she told Evella as she and Sam stepped inside.

The front room was empty. A moment later, however, the jars on the shelves began to rattle. Then they rose up in the air. They hovered there, shaking, making a racket as whoever was controlling them shook them. Six gave a slow clap. "Very good," she said. Then she cleared her mind and pictured the jars returning to their places. They obeyed. "But I'm better."

The jars exploded, sending shards of glass and the contents of the containers in all directions. Instinctively, Six and Sam pushed back with their telekinesis, and before any of the pieces could reach them, they stopped and hovered in the air. Then, slowly, the detritus began to turn in a counterclockwise direction, creating an ominous, swirling cloud that sparkled with bits of glass.

"Okay," Six said. "That's more impressive."

"You're not doing this?" Sam asked.

"No," Six said. She nodded at the doorway on the other

side of the room. "Someone in there is."

The cloud spiraled in on itself, turning over and over as if waiting for them to make the first move. Coins, roots, and teeth mingled with pieces of glass.

"It's a neat trick," Sam said. He reached out with his mind, testing the strength of the person controlling the cloud. Sam was stronger. He forced the bits and pieces to the floor, clearing the way to the door.

"You're ruining their fun," Six said, grinning at him as she walked down through the cleared space. Then she was through the doorway. A brick oven was built into one wall, the chimney rising up through the ceiling. A wooden chair stood unoccupied in a corner, a book on the floor beside it.

Standing on the other side of the room was the boy they had seen running into the shop. Now they got a better look at him: on the short side, a little heavy, white skin with a spray of freckles across the cheeks and nose, a mop of red curls. He was wearing jeans and a black T-shirt, both of which looked like they could use a wash.

With him were two girls. One of them, thin, with light-brown skin and straight black hair, was standing with her eyes closed as if she was concentrating. The second girl stood behind Edwige, holding her arms behind her back and glaring at Six and Sam. She reminded Six of the girl who gave her and Sam a tour of some temples in Vietnam a few months earlier. Her hair was colored a bright turquoise hue and cut in a short, spiky style that matched the angry expression on her face.

"Did you do that out there?" Six asked her.

"What if I did?" the girl snapped.

"Who are you?" Six asked her.

The girl ignored her, glancing at the other girl. "Come on, Ghost. Do it!"

"I'm trying, Nemo," Ghost said.

"Try harder."

The four teens flickered. That was the only word for it. Their bodies faded out, then immediately came back into focus. Then it happened again, a kind of rippling effect. This time, they winked out altogether. A moment later, two of them—the boy and Nemo—reappeared. Ghost and Edwige were gone.

"Damn it!" Nemo said. "She wasn't strong enough to take us all!"

If they're kidnappers, they're not very good at it, Six thought. "Where'd she teleport to?" she asked.

The boy shook his head. "It could be anywhere," he said. "Ghost isn't really great with specific directions."

"Shut up, Max," the girl snarled. She lifted her hands, and Six felt her trying to use her telekinesis to throw Six and Sam. Six easily canceled out the girl's attempt at telekinesis with her own. The girl's scowl deepened.

"Come on, Nemo," the boy said. "You know who they are. We can't beat them."

"He's right," Six said. "So, we might as well talk."

A shout from outside distracted her. There was more yelling.

"That sounds like Ghost," the boy said.

Gunshots rang out. "Does she have a gun?" Six asked.

Both teens shook their heads.

"Stay here," Six ordered them. "And I mean it." She turned to Sam. "Come on."

They ran through the outer room and out onto the street. Ignoring her orders, Max and Nemo followed. But Six was too busy taking in what was happening outside to yell at them. Halfway down the block, Ghost lay on the ground. A puddle of blood was quickly forming around her. Not far from her stood a huge man. In one hand, he held a gun. In the other, he gripped Edwige's wrist. The girl was struggling and screaming. Evella was stumbling toward the pair, calling out Edwige's name.

The man raised his gun and pointed it at Evella. Six, focusing on his hand, sent the weapon lurching to the side. The man's arm went with it. The gun went off, the bullet embedding itself harmlessly in the brick wall of a building. The man yelped, and the gun fell from his hand. Six lifted it up in the air and sent it flying way, out of his reach. But he still had a grip on Edwige, and Evella was still coming at him, her fists raised.

The man placed his forearm across Edwige's neck and pressed. She gasped. "I'll break her neck!" he shouted.

Evella stopped dead, only a few feet away. She reached out her hand.

The man began to walk backwards down the street. Beside Six, Nemo stood bristling with fear and anger. "*Do something," she hissed.

"I told you to stay inside," Six said.

"Do I look like someone who follows orders?"

Nemo closed her eyes and clenched her fists. Behind the man, the cobblestones that made up the street pulled themselves free of the ground and rose up in the air. The man who was holding Edwige didn't see them forming into the shape of a spinning sphere behind him. And he didn't see them rushing at him until it was too late. The ball struck him in the head. He went flying, and Edwige fell to the ground as the stones swept over her.

Nemo ran toward Ghost, followed by Sam. Six went and lifted Edwige up. She started to walk with her back to where the others stood when suddenly two more figures appeared from an alleyway. One was a man, the other a teenage boy.

"I knew that was too easy," Six muttered. "Run," she told Edwige.

Edwige ran. Six turned to face the two newcomers.

The older man—tall, muscular, and covered in tattoos—smiled. "That was an impressive display," he said, glancing at Nemo. "Maybe we should take her too."

Nemo was still on the ground, cradling Ghost's head in her lap. She looked up. "She's dead," she said, her voice shaking with rage. "He killed her."

"No, she's not dead," said Sam. He was holding his fingers against the girl's neck, checking for a pulse. "But she's badly hurt. She needs to get help. Now."

Six, anger rising insider her, raised her hands and sent a

blast of power at the two figures in front of her.

"Mirror!" the man shouted, and the teenage boy raised his hands.

A second later, Six felt her own blow hit her in the chest. It wasn't as strong as she'd sent it out, but it was enough to knock her backwards. She stumbled, righted herself, recovered. The boy was looking at her, a triumphant grin on his face. She'd never encountered a Legacy like this, one that reflected her own back at her. She wondered what, exactly, the boy could do, how powerful he really was. But there was no time to think about it right now.

"All right," Six said. "We'll do this the old-fashioned way."

She leaped at them. The boy went down with her first punch, knocked out cold. The man fought back. He wasn't a Garde, but he was strong, surprisingly strong. A leering smile remained plastered to his face as he and Six traded punches. His fists were like hammers. She matched him. Time and again, when he should have gone down, he didn't.

Six had no time to wonder what the others were doing. The fight had become her focus. Part of her was irritated that the man wouldn't give up; another was excited to have an opponent who truly tested her. She switched tactics, using various martial arts moves to catch the man off guard. None of them did. He was like a chameleon, moving from one style to another with ease, always ready for whatever she threw at him.

"Why don't you use one of your superpowers?" the man taunted.

"I save those for real opponents," Six shot back.

The man caught her arm, swung her hard. She hit a wall. The pain was momentary, invigorating. She responded with a kick to his midsection that sent him stumbling backwards, but he quickly righted himself. Then they flew at each other, limbs flashing, bone against flesh. Six saw an opening, landed a blow to his chin. The impact lifted him off his feet and sent him flying through the air. He landed hard. This time when he got to his feet, his eyes were looking at something behind Six.

Sam, Nemo, and Max stood in a row. Their hands were raised. All around them, items of various sorts hovered in the air: rocks, broken pieces of metal and glass, screwdrivers and keys and nails. They were all pointed in the direction of the man who was fighting with Six. Behind them, Edwige knelt beside Ghost. Her hands were on the girl's chest as she attempted to heal her.

"Four against one doesn't seem fair," the man said, and smirked as he wiped blood from a cut on his face.

"Who are you?" Six asked the man.

"His name's Jagger Dennings," Max said.

The man's face lit up. "The kid's heard of me."

"He's an MMA fighter," Max continued.

"World *champion* MMA fighter," Dennings added.

"Good for you," said Six. "Who are you working for?"

Dennings shook his head. "I'm afraid I can't discuss my employer's identity," he said. "Confidentiality clause in the contract."

Evella gave a shout. Six looked, and saw that Edwige had vanished.

Dennings laughed. "I'd love to stay and chat," he said. "But I'm afraid my ride is here."

A boy appeared next to him. Before Six could get more than a quick look at him (tall, skinny, light-brown hair tied in a ponytail), he put his hand on Dennings's shoulder. They both disappeared, popping out of existence. A moment later, the newcomer appeared again, this time touching the boy Six had knocked out, who was lying on the ground. Then they were gone. Shouts of outrage went up from Nemo and Max. All around them, the items they'd been helping to levitate fell to the ground.

"Where is she?" Evella shouted, turning around and around. "Edwige!"

Sirens sounded, not too far off.

"The police," Sam said. "We need to leave. If they find Garde here, we're going to have some explaining to do."

"What about Ghost?" Nemo objected. "We have to take her with us."

"She needs to get to a hospital," Six told the girl. "And you need to go. If you're here when they arrive and they discover you have Legacies—not to mention that you're runaways— who knows what'll happen. And Edwige was healing Ghost; she's going to be okay."

Nemo looked at Ghost. She nodded. "All right."

Evella was still looking around as if she could find Edwige if she just searched hard enough. Six went to her to try and calm her down.

"Where is she?" Evella asked again.

"I don't know. But we'll find her. I promise. Right now, though, we need to get these kids out of here, and that girl needs to get to a hospital. Can you handle the police? Tell them that man attacked the girl. That's it. You don't know anything else."

Evella nodded.

The sirens were getting closer.

"Six, if we're going, we need to go now," Sam said.

"I know," Six said. To Evella she said, "We'll find her. And we'll contact you soon to see how Ghost is doing."

Six looked at Nemo and Max. "Come on," she said. "We have some things to talk about."

CHAPTER SIX

SAM
NEW ORLEANS, LOUISIANA

"WHAT EXACTLY WERE YOU DOING WITH EDWIGE?"

They were back in Jackson Square. As Six waited for Nemo or Max to answer her question, she scanned the area, looking for the girl she and Sam had been watching earlier. Finding her again had now fallen a few places on her to do list, but she hadn't forgotten about her. The tarot card readers were still there. The man selling paintings was still there. But the girl was gone.

"Who are you looking for?" Nemo asked, watching Six's face.

"Nobody," Six said. "Now, answer the question."

"Who cares?" Max said. He was visibly shaking. "Ghost might die." He turned on Nemo. "That wasn't supposed to happen. You said this would be easy—come in, get that girl, and get out."

"It's not my fault," Nemo shot back. "And if these two hadn't shown up, we *would* have been out of there."

Sam put his hand on Max's shoulder. The boy shrugged it off. Sam tried again, and this time Max let himself be comforted. "I know what it's like to be worried about a friend," Sam said gently. "And I know you're upset about Ghost. Right now, though, we need to make a plan."

"We *had* a plan," Max said.

Nemo started to say something in response, but Sam held up his hand. "Enough," he said. To Six he said, "Maybe now isn't the time to look for the girl."

"Girl?" Max said. "What girl?"

"She calls herself Geppettogirl," Sam answered. "We don't know her real name."

"Geppettogirl from YouTube?" Max asked.

Sam nodded. "You know her?"

"She's on our list," Max said.

"Shut up, Max," Nemo barked, nudging him in the ribs.

"Knock it off," Max said, rubbing his side.

"What list?" Six asked.

Max looked at Nemo, who frowned. "We have a list of kids we think might have Legacies," he said as Nemo shook her head. "We're here checking them out. That's why we were trying to talk to Edwige."

"Talk to her?" said Sam. "You mean kidnap her."

Max shook his head. "It wasn't like that," he said. "We

72

saw you go to her shop before. We thought *you* were trying to make her go to that Human Garde Academy thing."

"We know who you are," Nemo added. "And I think we're done talking. Come on, Max. We're out of here."

The girl turned and started to walk away. When she'd gotten a few feet away and Max hadn't followed, she stopped and looked at him. "Come *on*, Max."

Max looked away from her.

"They almost got Ghost *killed*," Nemo said.

"They didn't almost get her killed," Max argued. "We did."

Nemo's face darkened. "Stop blaming that on me," she said, her voice trembling with rage. "She's my friend too."

Max shook his head. "I think we should talk to them."

"You can talk," Nemo said, pointing a finger at him accusingly. "I'm done."

She stormed off. Sam started to go after her, but Six put a hand on his arm, stopping him. "But—" Sam began.

"I'll trail her," Six said. "She needs to blow off steam. Trying to force her to stay will only make things worse."

"What about Edwige?"

"We can't do anything about her right now. We don't know where they took her. Maybe these kids know something that can help. You and Max talk. I'll deal with Nemo. You could also contact James and see what he can find out about this Dennings guy. And maybe look for Geppetogirl; she might still be around."

"Anything else?" Sam joked.

"I'm going to be *invisible*," said Six. "And on the move." She sighed. "Then we'll deal with Ghost and the hospital."

Six winked out of sight.

"That's a badass Legacy," Max remarked.

"She's got a couple of good ones," Sam told him.

"What've you got?" Max asked. His worry about Ghost was still evident in his eyes, but there was something else there now as well—curiosity.

"I talk to machines," said Sam. "What about you?"

Max shrugged. "Ghost is the most interesting of us, with her teleportation thing. That's why we call her Ghost, because she can pass through walls."

"And Nemo?"

"Can breathe underwater," Max said.

"I'm guessing your name isn't really Max, then," Sam said.

"Actually, it is," he said. "Haven't come up with a good nickname since my Legacy isn't that interesting."

"Oh?" said Sam. "What do you do?"

"Languages," Max told him. "I can understand what people are saying in any language. I figured it out one day when I was on the bus and these two guys were speaking to each other in Russian. I didn't know it was Russian. I just overheard them, and understood it. One guy was telling the other about a movie he'd seen, but he couldn't remember the name. I told him what it was, and he said, 'You speak Russian!' I said I didn't, and he got this weird look on his face."

"So, you can hear a language and speak it?"

Max shook his head. "I can't speak them, just understand them. Although some of the languages that I hear more often, like Spanish and Chinese, I'm starting to pick up."

"I bet you'd get really good at that if someone taught you how to use your Legacy," Sam suggested. "You could be an interpreter. Or a spy."

"You mean like if I went to the HGA," Max said.

"Or someplace like it," Sam offered.

Max was quiet for a moment. Then he said, "So, if you and Six weren't trying to take Edwige to the HGA thing, why did you come see her?"

"We were hoping to protect her from guys like the ones who showed up," Sam told him. "What were you guys doing there if you weren't trying to take her?"

"Like I said, we were just talking to her. Then when we saw you guys there, we maybe tried to get her to come with us."

"Come with you where?"

"We have a place," Max said vaguely.

Sam let it go. Max was just starting to open up to him, and he didn't want to press him too hard for details and have him stop now. "And who is 'we'?" he asked instead.

Max looked uncomfortable. "I probably shouldn't talk too much about it," he said uneasily.

Give him a little space, Sam told himself. "I'll be right back," he said. "I need to make a call."

He walked off a short distance, keeping an eye on the boy while he phoned James. He quickly told him about the incident and asked him to look into the kidnappers, then returned to Max. "Let's go sit down," he suggested. He pointed to a bench that sat in the shade of some trees.

Max nodded, then followed Sam to it.

"Were you checking in with your parents?" Max asked.

Sam laughed. "Something like that—someone who can hopefully help us figure out who took Edwige," Sam said. "She's not the first person with a healing Legacy to go missing."

"Really?" Max said. "Why would someone do that?"

"That's what we're trying to find out," Sam told him.

Max shook his head. "You sure it's not someone trying to take her off to that academy?"

"They don't kidnap people," Sam told him. "Or shoot them. Whoever those guys were, they weren't HGA."

"But they made it a law that we're supposed to go," Max countered. "And they want us for that Earth Garde thing. Have you seen the ads with the president's kid? They're trying to make it sound like summer camp."

Sam, thinking about Melanie, said nothing about that. Instead he said, "The HGA is training people how to use their Legacies. Believe me, I know from experience that you get better a lot faster if you have someone who knows what they're doing teaching you."

"If you think what they're doing is so great, how come you aren't working for them?" When Sam didn't answer right away, he added, "It's because of her, right? Six?"

"She's not exactly a joiner," Sam said. "So we compromised. We're helping out in other ways. But what made you so suspicious of the HGA?"

Max was quiet for a moment. Then he said, "My parents sent me to boarding school when I was fourteen. Military school, actually. It was horrible."

"Why'd they do that?"

Max looked off into the distance. "Let's just say I got into some trouble."

He didn't elaborate on that point, and Sam didn't push him. Max obviously had a story, but wasn't ready to share the whole thing. Not yet. But he kept talking. "Anyway, it wasn't a good time for me. But my parents wouldn't let me leave. Eventually I cheated on an exam just so I would get expelled. It was the only way out. My father didn't talk to me for two months after that. Not a word. At dinner he'd sit there talking to my mother and sister, but wouldn't even look at me. It was like I didn't exist anymore. Like I'd died. When he finally did talk to me, it was to tell me I was being sent to another military school. He'd found one that would take me even though I'd been kicked out of the last one. It was even worse than the first one. So I didn't wait to get kicked out. I left. I couldn't go home, so I hooked up with some other runaway kids and lived here and there. Then when my Legacy kicked in about six months ago, I started looking for other people like me."

Again he stopped talking, staring off at nothing. Sam could practically feel the wheels in the kid's head turning, and he wondered what he was thinking about. He'd clearly had a difficult life. Sam felt bad for him. But he also needed information.

"How did you and Nemo meet up?" he prodded.

Max smiled a little. "Where else?" he said. "Online. In a group for people developing Legacies. It's been shut down since then. You know, because the government was monitoring it and kids were getting dragged out of their houses in the middle of the night."

"I don't think that ever happened," Sam said.

Max shrugged. "Maybe. Maybe not. Anyway, it wasn't safe anymore. But by then, we had met up in real life. We decided to create a group for people who didn't want to go to the HGA. A sort of family."

"Are there really that many of you who don't trust the HGA?" Sam asked him.

"Enough," Max said.

Sam thought about McKenna and his son. "I don't suppose you know a guy named Seamus?" he said. "Communicates with insects?"

"No," Max said. "But we're not the only group. There are a bunch of them out there. Some of them we keep in touch with, some we don't."

"How did you hear about Edwige?"

"Probably the same way you did," Max said. "We pay attention. Search online for anyone who seems like they might be interesting. We read about this girl who could heal, so we decided to check her out. We try to get to them before you—before anyone else does."

Something still didn't make sense to Sam. "But you were trying to take her against her will," he said.

Max looked away, saying nothing.

"Wait a minute," said Sam. "You'd had contact with her before you showed up."

Max waited a long time. Then he nodded slightly. "We'd talked with her online," he admitted. "She'd started to suspect that she had a Legacy. But she was afraid what her grandmother would think if she told her."

"Evella?"

"Yeah," Max said. "She's super-religious. I guess she thinks what's happening with the Legacies is, I don't know, evil or something. Anyway, Edwige didn't want to tell her about herself. A couple of days ago, Edwige emailed Nemo saying she was thinking of contacting the HGA. We decided we should come here and try to talk her out of it in person."

"But that didn't go so well, did it?" said Sam.

"No," said Max. "When Edwige saw us, she freaked. Her grandmother thought we were trying to hurt her. Then you and Six showed up. You know the rest."

"Why didn't you just tell us what you were doing? We thought you were kidnapping her."

"We thought *you* were kidnapping her," Max countered.

"Meanwhile, somebody really was trying to," said Sam.

He hesitated a moment before going on. Max was opening up to him, but he felt that at any moment the boy might close up again. He remembered how it had felt struggling with his own developing Legacies. One minute, he'd wanted to talk all about it. The next, he'd wanted to talk about anything *but* what was happening. It wasn't easy being a teenager under normal circumstances; being one under extraordinary circumstances was even more difficult.

Then Max said, "There she is."

"Edwige?" Sam said hopefully.

"Geppettogirl," said Max, shaking his head.

Sam looked. The girl was setting up at the other end of the square.

"Come on," Sam said, starting to stand.

"Let me talk to her," Max suggested.

"You?" said Sam. "Why you?"

"People know who you are," Max reminded him. "You've been on *television*. If she has a Legacy and hasn't reported it yet, there's a reason. If she thinks you're after her for some reason, she might run."

"Okay," Sam said. He realized this was the opportunity he'd been looking for, a chance to help Max trust him.

Max walked toward the girl. Sam watched, on alert for any sign that Max might run or do anything else that would require interference. When he reached her, he said something and held out his hand. The girl shook it. Then Max talked for quite a while. The girl's expression changed, and she began to glance around. For a moment, Sam thought she might bolt. But she didn't. Then Max turned and pointed to Sam. The girl looked, frowning. Sam nodded.

She turned away, and talked some more with Max. Then

she started putting things back into the cardboard box that she'd unpacked not long before. Max beckoned Sam over with his hand.

When he got there, Max said, "Sam, this is Rena."

"Hi," Sam said. "It's nice to meet you. I like your work."

"You were here before, with that girl."

Sam nodded. "We saw your videos online."

"You came all the way to New Orleans to see me?" Rena asked.

"Well, not exactly," Sam admitted. "But we were really happy we found you."

"How come you ran off?"

"Long story," Sam said.

"I got time," Rena said.

"You know, I never got to have that po'boy. How about we get lunch?"

Rena picked up the box with her things in it. "Come with me," she said. "We can go to my uncle's place. No po'boys, but I think you'll like it. And we can talk."

They followed her down the street and around the corner, away from the touristy square. Crossing the street on which Edwige's shop stood a few blocks farther up, Sam noted that there was still a police cruiser parked there, the lights flashing. He saw Max glance in that direction as well, and resisted the urge to put his hand on the boy's shoulder.

Two blocks later, Rena stepped through the doorway of a small restaurant called the Crawfish Pot. Inside, it was easy to see why it had that name. The entire place was filled with the steam from pots that boiled on three stoves in the kitchen. A handful of picnic tables covered in red-and-white-checked plastic cloths were crowded with people talking loudly and picking crawfish, corn on the cob, and potatoes from mounds piled in the center of their tables.

Rena led Sam and Max through the kitchen, where a big man wearing an apron stood stirring the contents of several pots on a stove. Rena made some hand motions to him. He looked at Sam and Max, then made motions back at her. They were communicating in sign language, Sam realized. Rena signed something else, and the man nodded. Then Rena led them into a small room where there was another picnic table.

"This is where the staff eats," Rena said as she set her box down on a chair. She picked up some newspapers that were stacked on another chair, then spread them out on the table like a tablecloth and took a seat.

Max and Sam sat as well, Max next to her and Sam across from them. A moment later, the man they'd seen in the kitchen came in, carrying a steaming bowl of food. He dumped it on the newspapers, then set the bowl down.

"Thanks, Uncle Smalls," Rena said. She made a sign, placing the fingertips of her open palm against her lips and moving it down and away from her face.

"Yes, thank you," Sam echoed. "This looks fantastic." He mimicked the sign Rena had made. Her uncle nodded, then left them alone.

"He can read lips, but he doesn't talk," Rena told Sam and

Max as she handed them napkins from a pile on the table. "You all know how to eat crawfish the right way? You pinch the tails and suck the heads."

She proceeded to show them. Within minutes, Sam's and Max's fingers were sticky with crawfish juice and butter.

"This is fantastic," Max said, tossing an empty shell into the bowl.

"You never had crawfish?" Rena asked.

Max shook his head. "We don't have them where I'm from."

"Where's that?" said Rena.

Max darted a glance at Sam. "Somewhere else," he mumbled.

Rena gave him a quizzical look, but didn't press him for details. Instead, she asked, "Which group are you two with?"

"Different ones, actually," Max told her. "Sam and Six are kind of official. Me and Nemo are on our own."

Rena snorted. "Let me guess. You're fighters?"

"Fighters?" Max said. "What do you mean."

Rena looked from him to Sam. "You don't know about the fighters? I figured that's why you were here. Thought maybe Yo-Yo sent you. I told him I wasn't interested, but that's never stopped him before."

"Who's Yo-Yo?" Sam asked.

Rena picked up another crawfish, broke it in half, and put the open end of the head in her mouth. She sucked noisily. "That's a long story."

Sam grinned. "I got time."

"First, answer me a question," Rena said. "Why'd you all come looking for me?"

Sam wiped his fingers on a napkin. "Like I said before, we saw your videos."

Rena cocked her head and raised an eyebrow. "So you thought you'd offer me a TV show or something?" she said.

Sam laughed. He liked her cockiness. "We wanted to see if you're legit or if it's a really good act."

"And what did you decide?"

Sam looked into her eyes. "I think you're for real," he said.

"And what if I am?"

"You know you're supposed to report your Legacy," Sam said.

"Yeah, I know," said Rena, nodding. "Maybe I just haven't gotten around to it yet. Besides, what kind of use is what I do to this army they're putting together?"

"Earth Garde isn't an army," Sam said. "It's more like a, well, scouting group or something."

"Right," said Rena in a tone that suggested she didn't believe this for one second. "And I bet they all sit around a campfire and eat s'mores." She looked at Max. "And why are you here?"

"Um, trying to help a friend," he answered.

"She have a Legacy too?" Rena asked.

"She can heal," Sam said when Max didn't answer. "My girlfriend, Six, and I came to talk to her too."

"But not together," said Rena, indicating Max.

"No," Sam confirmed. "There were some other people

84

interested in her too, though."

Rena's uncle came into the room, interrupting the discussion. He signed quickly to Rena, a worried expression on his face. Rena signed back, then looked at Sam and Max.

"You talking about Edwige, right?" Rena said.

"How'd you know that?" Max asked her.

"Uncle Smalls says there was trouble over at their place. Evella got hurt."

"Evella?" Sam said. "No, it wasn't her. It was a girl."

"My friend Ghost," Max explained.

Rena signed some more with her uncle, who shook his head and repeated the signs he'd used before.

"It was Evella," Rena said. "One of the customers was there when the ambulance came. Said there was a lot of blood."

"What about Ghost?" Max said, his voice filled with worry.

"Wasn't no girl there," Rena insisted.

Max looked at Sam. "Where is she?"

Sam took out his phone to call Six. "I don't know," he answered. "But I think we'd better get to the hospital."

CHAPTER SEVEN

SIX
NEW ORLEANS, LOUISIANA

BEING INVISIBLE HAD ITS ADVANTAGES, BUT SIX wished that not being seen meant that she also couldn't be felt, so she wouldn't have to dodge the tourists walking down Bourbon Street. Nemo had chosen the most crowded thoroughfare in New Orleans to walk down. Six had bumped into half a dozen people, trying to keep up with the girl. Fortunately for Six, most of them had been too distracted to notice.

Ahead of Six, Nemo turned a corner. Six, having to wait for a group of bros to cross in front of her, fell behind. By the time she reached the corner and followed after Nemo, the girl was nowhere in sight. Six walked faster, looking into the various stores and restaurants she passed, but there was no sign of her. Then she spied a flash of blue.

Nemo was a block ahead, walking fast.

Six continued tailing her as the girl zigzagged through the Quarter. Finally, she stopped at a car, a beat-up green Chevy Tahoe, and opened the door. She got in, started it up, and pulled away. She was driving toward Six, going slowly. Six, tired of trailing the girl and not wanting to try to follow the car, stepped into the street and materialized. Nemo hit the brakes, bringing the SUV to a stop.

Six stayed in front of the Tahoe, blocking Nemo from driving away. She saw the girl look behind her, but they were on a one-way street, and a delivery truck was coming up behind the Chevy. Nemo glared at Six through the windshield. Six glared back.

The truck behind Nemo stopped, waited a minute, then honked for her to move. Nemo in turn honked and rolled down her window, gesturing at Six to let the driver behind her know she couldn't go anywhere. Six went invisible. She saw Nemo mouth a curse and smack her hand on the horn again. Now she looked like she was blocking the street for no reason.

The driver of the truck honked again, then leaned out his window and shouted, "Move it!"

Nemo scanned the area in front of the Tahoe. For a moment, Six thought she might hit the gas and try to run over her. Instead, the girl opened her own door and got out, leaving the Tahoe running while she started yelling at the truck driver.

Six used the distraction to slip into the Tahoe and shut

the door. Hearing the sound, Nemo whirled around. Six, materializing, leaned out the window and smiled. "Need a ride?" she said.

Nemo swore again, loudly.

"Suit yourself," said Six, and started to drive away.

Nemo ran after her, banging on the window. Six stopped. She cocked her head, indicating that Nemo should go around to the passenger side. Nemo, scowling, did so, opening the door and then slamming it hard when she was inside. Six continued driving.

"That wasn't a bad try at losing me," she said.

Nemo snorted. "I'm not stupid, you know. I picked that street on purpose, so you'd have a harder time following me."

"Did I say you were stupid?"

Nemo didn't respond at first. Six stared her down.

"Not in so many words."

"Not in *any* words. Now that that's out of the way, can we talk?"

Nemo snorted. She looked out the window, anxiously tapping her fingers on the seat. Six studied her, noticing things she hadn't before. Like Nemo's fingernails. They were chewed to almost nothing, and painted the same blue color as her hair. And beneath her faded red hoodie she was wearing a T-shirt that said *Ask Me About My Antisocial Tendencies.*

"Nice shirt," Six said.

"What can I say," Nemo replied. "I'm a people person."

Six looked in the rearview mirror. The back of the Tahoe

was crammed with stuff: duffle bags, clothes, bottles of water and energy drinks, discarded chip bags, camping equipment. It was obvious that Nemo, Ghost, and Max had been living out of the SUV for some time. "So, who did this thing used to belong to?" Six asked Nemo.

"We didn't steal it, if that's what you're getting at," Nemo snapped. "It's mine."

"Yours?" Six said dubiously. "You're barely old enough to have a license."

"Okay, so it's my parents'," Nemo admitted. "I borrowed it."

"Your family lives in Florida?" Six asked. "Or is it Virginia? I'm thinking Virginia."

Nemo looked at her.

"You've got Florida plates but a Virginia inspection sticker," Six said. "Plates are easier to switch out."

Nemo glanced at the windshield. "Crap," she said. "I might have switched the plates," she added after a moment.

"Hopefully with another green Tahoe."

Nemo snorted. "Like I said, I'm not stupid."

"How long have you three been living out of here?" asked Six.

"A while," said Nemo. "Couple of months. We stay at campgrounds, mostly. Sometimes crappy motels where we can pay in cash."

Six didn't ask her where they got the cash. Instead she said, "How have you managed to stay ahead of the police? Your parents must have reported you missing and the SUV stolen. Switching plates only works for so long."

Nemo didn't answer her immediately. She looked out the window. Six wondered if the girl had reached the limit of what she was willing to share. She'd already said more than Six had expected her to. Then again, there was something about her that suggested she actually *wanted* to talk. She seemed tired. Maybe tired of running.

"Not everybody's parents care where they are," Nemo said quietly. "And nobody ever drives this thing. They probably haven't even noticed it's gone."

"I moved around a lot when I was growing up," Six told her. "Ohio. California. Nova Scotia. New York. Mexico. Colorado. I'm probably forgetting some of the places. Always trying to stay one step ahead of people who wanted to kill me."

"Looks like it worked," Nemo said.

"My Cêpan was murdered when I was thirteen. Tortured in front of me, then stabbed through the heart."

Nemo turned her head and looked at Six. "Cêpan?"

"She was kind of like my guardian," said Six. "Basically, my mother. Her name was Katrina."

Nemo looked away again. "That sounds hard."

"It was," said Six. "I learned to be tough. Like you have." She paused, then added, "But I also learned that sometimes you have to trust other people."

"I'm not going to the HGA," Nemo declared.

"I already told you, we're not involved with them. I mean, I know people doing that, obviously. But it's not my thing either."

"What *is* your thing?" Nemo asked.

"Saving the world," Six said. "Haven't you noticed?"

Nemo gave her a withering look. "Seriously?"

"Seriously," Six said.

Nemo said nothing.

"How did you meet Max and Ghost?" Six asked her.

"We connected in a subreddit about people developing Legacies," Nemo said. "A lot of it was posers making stuff up, but there were some legit people in there. Eventually, we took it off-line and made our own family."

"Are they runaways too?"

"They have their own stories," Nemo said. "They can tell them if they want to. Assuming Ghost is alive to tell hers."

Six's phone dinged. She fished it out of her pocket and looked at it. "Shit," she exclaimed.

"Bad news?" Nemo asked.

Six hesitated. She didn't want to tell her what Sam's text said. If Nemo knew Ghost was missing, she'd probably freak out. On the other hand, they now had to get to the hospital, and Nemo would wonder why.

"It's Evella," she said, going with a partial truth. "Something's wrong." She handed her phone to Nemo. "Look up University Medical Center and tell me how to get there."

Nemo did as she was asked. Fifteen minutes later, Six pulled the Tahoe to a stop in the hospital's parking garage. She and Nemo got out, found their way inside, and stopped. **WE'RE HERE. WHERE ARE YOU?** Six texted Sam, then waited for a response. It came a few seconds later.

"Second floor," she told Nemo.

They rode the elevator up, then exited into a large waiting area. Sam and Max were there, and Six was surprised to see the girl from the park was with them. Sam walked over to Six, while Nemo went over to see Max.

"What the hell is going on?" Six asked Sam.

"I don't know yet," he said. "All I know is that Evella was hurt, and Ghost wasn't there when the police and paramedics arrived."

Six swore. "They must have come back and taken her too," she said. "We should have stayed."

"You know we couldn't," Sam reminded her. "Garde? Runaways with unregistered Legacies? We've got enough problems right now."

"How's Evella?" asked Six.

"She's in bad shape, but I think she'll be okay. She's in surgery now. And we've got another little problem. The police are here, and they have questions."

"You didn't talk to them, did you?" said Six.

"No," Sam answered. "They haven't even seen us. But I don't think we should hang around here for very long."

"What about Evella? I know she's not our primary concern"—Six glanced over at Rena, Max and Nemo—"or even our second or third concern, but she could cause problems if she tells the police anything she shouldn't."

"I called James," Sam said. "I let him know what's happening. McKenna is going to handle it. In the meantime, I do have some news about Edwige."

"You know where she is?" said Six.

Sam shook his head. "No, but Max told me something interesting. According to him, Edwige was in on what they were up to."

"What?" Six said. "She wasn't being kidnapped?"

"Not by the three of them, if he's telling the truth."

Six sighed. "That's a big *if*," she said.

"I believe him," Sam replied. "Between you and me, I think he's looking for help dealing with his Legacy, plus some other issues. Nemo is the real holdout here. Did you get anywhere with her?"

Six gave a short laugh. "Yeah," she said. "We're best buds now."

As if she'd overheard them, Nemo came storming over. "Where's Ghost?" she demanded. "Max says something happened to her."

"We should go somewhere else and talk," Sam said. "There's a cafeteria downstairs. Have you guys eaten?"

"I don't care about food!" Nemo said. "I want to know where Ghost is."

"Keep it up, and the police will have some questions for all of us," Six told her.

Nemo paled.

"Like Sam said, let's talk about this downstairs," Six said. "It's going to be okay," she added. "Remember what I said about trusting people?"

Nemo didn't reply, but she also didn't make another demand. Instead, she seemed to shrink into her hoodie. Sam waved Max and Rena over, and the five of them walked to the elevator.

In the cafeteria, they found a table. Six and Nemo went and got themselves some food, then came back and sat down. Six tore into her sandwich, but Nemo only picked at her salad.

"First, Ghost," Sam said. "We don't know for sure yet, but we think the people who took Edwige might have come back for her. That's what makes the most sense, anyway."

"She was hurt really badly," Nemo said, shoving her tray away angrily. "If they don't help her, she's probably dead."

"If they did take her, they want her for her Legacy," Six said. "They won't let her die. And they've got Edwige. She can heal her."

"Or maybe they didn't want her talking, and decided to make sure she couldn't," Nemo suggested.

"I think Six is right," Sam said quickly. "So, the sooner we find Edwige, the sooner we find Ghost. In the meantime, Rena has a story you guys need to hear."

"It's really Yo-Yo's story," Rena said.

"You know someone named Yo-Yo?" asked Max.

"His mama started calling him that when he was a baby," Rena said. "Because one minute he'd be crying, and the next laughing. He's my best friend since we were five and he moved next door to me and my uncle. He's got a Legacy too. Kind of unusual, I guess, best friends both getting them. Nice, though. We had someone built-in to talk to about it."

"What's his?" Max asked her.

"Fire," Rena said. She laughed. "Damn fool almost burned his own house down when it first showed itself. Set his bedspread on fire. He got it under control pretty quick, though. Got to where he can make a fireball on his palm and send it where he wants it to go."

"That can be useful," Six said, thinking about how many times that Legacy had helped John.

Rena nodded. "That's why the fighters wanted him."

"Fighters?" said Six.

"This is the part I wanted you to hear," said Sam.

"Yo-Yo wanted to take advantage of his fire thing. There's a ton of stuff online. A lot of it is fake, like everything else on the internet, but some of it isn't. Yo-Yo stumbled across this group that was for real, though. They take kids with powers and train them to fight."

"Like an army?" Max asked.

Rena shook her head. "Like each other. Or people without Legacies who think they can beat them. They organize fights and people bet on them."

"That's disgusting," Nemo said, breaking her silence. "Like something they'd do a thousand years ago."

Rena shrugged. "It's kinda like boxing," she said. "People like fighting. I'm not saying it's right or anything, but right doesn't always figure into it."

"Did Yo-Yo agree to fight?" Sam asked.

"They offered him money. A lot of it. Told him if he was interested, to meet them somewhere and they'd take him to the place where they train."

"What makes them think they know any more about training people with Legacies than the HGA does?" Sam said.

"I don't know," said Rena. "It's not like they sent a brochure or anything. I only know what Yo-Yo said. Anyway, he decided to do it. I told him not to, but he's stubborn."

"He went?" Six asked.

"About two months ago," said Rena. "At first, he sent me texts saying he was fine. Said the place was nice, and they were training him how to do his fire thing in ways he could never have imagined. Said there was a place for me there if I wanted it."

"Then what?" said Sam.

"Messages started coming less and less. Then he wrote me and said he was in a little bit of trouble. Needed some money. Didn't say why. But I said I would help."

Six remembered the articles Lexa had shown them about the antiques shop that had been robbed by dolls. "Like a couple of rare-coins level of help?" she asked.

"Maybe something like that," Rena answered.

"What did he need the money for?" asked Six.

"He never said. My guess is, he bet on himself and lost. That's something Yo-Yo would do. Anyway, he asked me to meet him in Texas, so I did. Took a bus there, met him at a truck stop diner."

"Texas," said Six. "Is that where these people are?"

"I think so," Rena said. "Yo-Yo never really got to that

part. He was more anxious about his money. I gave it to him. I asked him to come home with me, but he said he had one more fight he had to do, then he'd come home."

"Let me guess," Six said. "You haven't heard from him since."

"Not a word," said Rena. "His phone number still works, but he doesn't respond to my texts or calls."

"Why did you think we worked for those people?" Sam asked her.

"Yo-Yo told them about me. Said they were interested. Said they'd never heard of anyone who does what I do."

"Well, that's probably true," Six told her. "We haven't either."

"No?" Rena said. "I guess I'm special. You think the people Yo-Yo is mixed up with took Edwige and that other girl?"

"That's what we need to find out," said Six.

"A lot has happened today," Sam added. "We know a guy named Jagger Dennings was part of the group who came after Edwige. He got away."

"I know that name," Rena said. "Yo-Yo mentioned him. I remembered it because of the singer from that old group. The Rolling Stones. My mama loved that song of theirs, 'Gimme Shelter.'"

"Mick Jagger," Sam said.

"That's him," said Rena. "Yo-Yo said Dennings was one of the guys training him."

"And did Yo-Yo know Edwige?" Six asked.

"Sure," said Rena. "Like I said, everybody around here does."

Six thought for a moment. "If Yo-Yo mentioned Edwige to the people he's with, that might be how they found out about her," she said. "And if they're the ones taking healers, they'd definitely want her."

"To heal their fighters," Sam said, finishing the thought.

Six crumpled up her napkin. "This gets weirder and weirder. We've got to get back to the plane."

"You have a plane?" Rena asked, one eyebrow lifted.

"Want to see it?" said Six.

"Maybe," Rena answered. "What's the catch?"

Six tapped her water bottle on the table. "The catch is, it looks like we're taking it to Texas, and you'd be coming with us."

"To look for Yo-Yo?" said Rena.

"And the others," Six said.

"If Ghost might be there, we're coming too," Nemo said.

"Yeah," Max added, although he sounded less sure.

Six looked at them. There was no way she was going to put any of the teens into a dangerous situation unnecessarily. Especially not Nemo, whose temper could get her into trouble. She had a feeling Rena could handle herself under pressure, and she and Sam may not have a choice about involving her if they were going to track down these fighters. For now she would settle for having them all off the streets. They could figure the rest out later.

"Okay," she said. "Let's go." She stood up and took the

keys to the Tahoe out of her pocket. "We've got a ride," she told Sam.

Unexpectedly, the keys levitated out of her hand and flew to Nemo's. "Yeah," Nemo said, waggling them triumphantly. "But this time, I'm driving."

CHAPTER EIGHT

THE SOUTH TEXAS SCRUBLAND, DOTTED WITH CACTI and trees that seemed to have been withered by the unrelenting sun into twisted shapes, didn't provide many opportunities for remaining hidden, but dusk was coming on now. Sam felt Six let go of his hand, and they were suddenly visible again.

"You sweat a lot," she remarked as she wiped her hands on her pants.

"Hey," Sam said. "It's hot."

It was. Well into the nineties. And the drive hadn't been an easy one. They'd had to stay far back from the car carrying Rena to the compound, relying on directions radioed from James, who was tracking her via a small implant in her upper arm. He was also babysitting Nemo and Max, who, despite protesting, had been left on the plane.

Setting everything up had been easier than expected. They'd started by sending a text to Yo-Yo's phone, saying that Rena was ready to join him and see what the fighters had to offer. Given that she hadn't heard from her friend in a while, a response came back surprisingly quickly. Yo-Yo—or more likely someone pretending to be him—had given Rena instructions to meet them at the same truck stop where she'd met Yo-Yo before. From there, she would be escorted to the final destination.

Of course, Rena had been miked, and had a tiny camera built into the frames of the fake glasses she now wore, so they'd monitored everything. She also had a tiny in-ear receiver so they could communicate with her. She'd played her part perfectly, saying she'd been thinking about things. She'd asked about Yo-Yo, and was told he was fine. Neither of the two men who met her at the diner were identifiable through facial recognition software. Nor had they given Rena any names.

The important thing was that they'd bought her story. Now, four hours later, Rena had been escorted inside a compound surrounded by a fence made of barbed wire. The camera in her glasses was feeding to a small handheld monitor that Six and Sam were looking at.

"Why isn't the sound working?" Six asked.

Sam smacked the monitor.

"Couldn't you try talking to it instead," Six asked.

The monitor crackled, and suddenly they could hear

voices. Sam grinned triumphantly. "Sometimes you have to show them who's boss," he said.

Rena was being shown around by a girl her own age who was called Sprout. "Our dorms are down here," Sprout said, leading Rena along a hallway. "Guys are in another part. Bathroom is here. And this is our room. You'll be sharing with me and Freakshow."

"Freakshow?" Rena said.

They were inside a small room that contained a pair of bunk beds and not much else. A girl sat cross-legged on one of the lower beds, reading a Wonder Woman comic book. She was short and heavyset. Her blond hair was collected into two pigtails, and she had a silver ring in one nostril.

"We all go by nicknames based on our powers," the girl said.

"So, why are you Freakshow?" Rena asked. "You don't look very scary to me."

Freakshow set down her comic book and smiled sweetly. "Give me your hand," she told Rena.

Rena held hers out. Freakshow touched it lightly with her fingertips. A moment later, Rena felt something crawling on her arm. She looked down and saw that dozens of small black spiders were crawling their way up her body. She screamed and shook herself, but the arachnids kept coming. It was as if they were glued to her skin. She flailed around, trying to wipe them off. Then, just as quickly as they'd appeared, they were gone and she was brushing her fingers against bare skin.

"What did you see?" Freakshow asked.

"You didn't see them?" said Rena. She shivered, recalling the touch of hundreds of feet.

Freakshow shook her head. "Only the person I touch sees the fear," she explained. "Everyone else just sees the reaction. Based on how you flipped out, I'm guessing fire or bugs."

"Spiders," Rena said. "And that's freaky, all right."

"I can make you see happy things too," the girl said. "But the scary stuff is more fun."

"Maybe for you," Rena said. She turned to Sprout. "Why do they call you Sprout?"

Sprout reached for a small pot that was sitting on the desk. A tiny shoot stuck out of the dirt, a thin stalk with two leaves coming off it. Sprout cupped her hands around the pot and focused on the little plant. It started to grow, new leaves bursting forth from the expanding stalk. Then a bud formed at the tip, exploding into a profusion of orange petals. It was a marigold.

"Pretty," Rena said.

"Thanks," said Sprout, setting the pot down again.

"How big can you get them?" Rena asked her.

Sprout grinned. "Big," she said.

"That could come in handy," Six remarked to Sam.

"How come you call them 'powers' and not 'Legacies'?" Rena asked Sprout.

"We don't like that word," Sprout said. "It's too formal. We prefer 'powers.' That's what they are, right?"

"I guess," Rena said. "So, do we get capes and tights too?"

"No capes," Sprout said. "Too easy to get caught in stuff." She laughed.

"What's your name?" Freakshow asked.

Rena told her.

"We're going to have to call you something else," Sprout said. "What is it you do?"

Rena looked around the room. Her camera honed in on one of the bunks. She went and picked up a teddy bear that rested against the pillow.

"Hey!" Sprout said. "Don't be hurting Mr. Honeyfoot."

"I won't," Rena promised her. "Just watch."

She held the bear in her hands. A few moments later, it lifted its paws.

"You're doing that with your thumbs," Sprout said, clearly unimpressed.

Rena set the bear down on the floor. It stood on its own legs. It turned its head from side to side. Then it began to march in circles.

"Okay," Sprout said. "Now *that's* cool. How long does it last?"

"Until I tell it to stop," Rena answered. She picked Mr. Honeyfoot up and held him again. His head flopped to one side. When she handed him to Sprout, he was just a stuffed toy.

"I don't know how that's going to help you win fights, but it's pretty awesome," Freakshow said.

"We should call you Annie May," Sprout announced.

"Annie May?" Rena said. "That sounds like a hillbilly name."

"No, *Anime*," Sprout said. "As in 'animation.' Because you bring stuff to life."

"Ooh, that's good," Freakshow said. "I like it. I second Anime."

"That's two votes to one," said Sprout. "Anime it is."

Rena nodded. "I guess that's okay," she said. She paused, then said, "So, I have a friend who's here. He goes by Yo-Yo, but I'm guessing you call him something else. He makes fire."

"We've got a couple of those," Sprout said. "What's he look like?"

"Skinny guy. Tall. Likes to wear diamond studs in his ears," Rena said. "Has a tattoo of Baron Samedi on his left arm."

"Baron who?" Freakshow asked.

"Skull-headed guy with a top hat," said Rena.

"Oh," Sprout said. "She means Sparky." There was a peculiar tone to the way she said it. Then she glanced at Freakshow, who suddenly found her Wonder Woman comic deeply engrossing again.

"What?" Rena said. "Is something wrong?"

"No," Sprout said, a little too quickly. "It's just that he's, um, not around right now."

"Not around?" said Rena. "What does that mean? He's not here? He left?"

"He's here," said Sprout. "It's just he . . ." She paused, then sighed. "He got hurt. In a fight. He's in the infirmary."

"But he'll be okay, right?" Rena asked her.

"Sure," Sprout said, sounding way too certain of this. "Sure, he will."

"Speaking of the infirmary, did you hear about the girl they brought in today?" Freakshow said.

"No," said Sprout. "Who is she?"

"I don't know. I just heard she was hurt pretty bad. Got shot or something."

Listening to the conversation, Sam said, "They must mean Ghost."

"They're bringing all kinds of new people in," Sprout commented. Then she looked at her watch. "Oh, it's time for practice. We should go. Freak, you coming?"

Freakshow got up, and the three of them exited the room. Sam and Six got another tour of the compound as the girls made their way outside. They went to another building, one that looked like an aircraft hangar, with corrugated metal sides and roof. From where Rena and the others stood, they could actually see the back side of it.

"This is where we train," Sprout explained as she slid open a door and they walked inside.

The view from Rena's glasses cam showed a huge open space filled with twenty-five or thirty people standing around talking. On three sides of the hangar there were bleachers set up. The center was just a sandy floor. Then a man walked into view.

"Dennings," Sam said.

Jagger Dennings strode into the center of the floor and stopped. He took a whistle that was hanging around his neck and blew it. "Everybody quiet down," he shouted. They did, almost instantly.

"They're afraid of him," Six said. "But why? They have Legacies, and he doesn't."

"We've got some new recruits," Dennings announced. "As well as some special guests. So, we're going to show them how things work here and what some of you can do."

"Special guest?" Rena said. "What does that mean?"

"High rollers," Sprout whispered to her. "People who bet on the fights. They sit in another room and watch. We never see them. Although sometimes, if you win a fight, you get introduced. I haven't fought in a betting fight yet. I want to, though."

Dennings looked around the hangar. "So, who is it going to be tonight?" he said. He was grinning. "Who wants to show us what they've got?"

Voices filled the air, and hands went up everywhere as kids clamored to be chosen. Dennings put a hand to his ear and with the other one urged them to scream more loudly. He turned first one way and then the other, as if listening for the loudest volunteer and looking for the most enthusiastic wave. Then he motioned for everyone to quiet down.

"That's what I like to see," he said. "Fighting spirit! He clapped his hands together once. "I want to see Freakshow down here."

Freakshow, sitting beside Rena, stood up. "Who am I

fighting?" she called out in a firm voice.

Dennings put his finger to his chin and seemed to ponder the question. Then he grinned and pointed. For a moment, it looked as if he was pointing at Rena, and Six and Sam heard her give a little gasp. But then Dennings said, "Sprout."

Sprout stood. She and Freakshow didn't look at one another as they walked down to the floor and over to where Dennings waited for them. They stood on either side of him as he put his arms around their shoulders.

"The two of you know what each other can do," he said. "So you should be prepared for this. Ready?"

Freakshow nodded, while Sprout said, "Ready."

"Then go!" Dennings said, and walked quickly away. He stood off to one side, watching the girls.

They faced one another. Sprout reached into her pocket, taking something out.

"Seeds," said Sam. "She came prepared."

The girl crouched, pressing the seeds into the dirt floor of the arena. As she did, Freakshow darted forward, wrapping her hand around Sprout's wrist. Sprout tried to pull away, but failed. Somehow, she managed to keep her other hand against the floor. Beneath it, green shoots snaked out. They grew rapidly, twining around Freakshow's ankles and moving up her leg. Leaves popped out, followed by blossoms of purple and blue.

"What are those?" Six asked Sam.

"Morning glories, I think," Sam said. "Smart choice. They wrap around everything."

As the morning glories wrapped Freakshow in their vines, Sprout closed her eyes. "It's not real," she said in a shaky voice. "You're not going to fall. You're not going to fall. You're not going to fall." Her whole body started to shake.

"Heights," Sam said. "She sounds terrified."

Freakshow, meanwhile, was using her free hand to try to tear the plants from her body. But they kept growing, thickening by the second, until they were like ropes binding her. The large flowers covered her body. Then the vines began to wrap around her head.

"Come on!" Dennings shouted. "Which one of you is stronger? Fight!"

Behind him, the onlookers in the stands took up the chant. "Fight!" they shouted. "Fight! Fight! Fight!"

As the morning glories engulfed Freakshow's head, the vines tightened around her, and her power seemed to fade. Sprout opened her eyes. With what was obviously enormous difficulty, she lifted the hand that had been touching the ground and pointed them toward her friend. Freakshow was lifted off the ground by the force of Sprout's telekinesis. Then she was thrown backwards, landing hard on the floor with a cry of pain. Sprout staggered a few paces, exhausted by the effort.

"Get up!" Dennings shouted, and the chant changed. "Get up! Get up! Get up!"

Freakshow tried. But the vines had wrapped around her like a shroud. Dennings and the other kids continued chanting for another minute, then Dennings walked over to where

Sprout lay on the ground. "Are you getting up?" he shouted. "Or are you giving in?"

Freakshow answered with an unintelligible whimper, her words impossible to hear. Dennings shook his head in disgust. Then he called out, "Drac!"

A gasp went up from the assembled crowd as a man emerged from the sideline. He had close-cropped black hair and pale skin. As he walked to where Dennings was waiting, the room grew silent. Sprout, who had gotten back on her feet and seemed to be over the effects of her friend's attack, now looked on.

Drac knelt on the floor. He pulled the vines, which had started to wilt, away from Freakshow's face and neck. Seeing him, she started babbling.

"Please," she said. "I'll try harder next time. I promise."

Drac looked at Dennings.

"Do it," Dennings ordered.

Drac now placed his hands on Freakshow's head, much as a healer might. But instead of a warm yellow glow emanating from his hands, a sickly green one spread out. It enveloped her head as she began to sob.

"Is he killing her?" Sam said, shocked.

The light surrounding the girl's head suddenly turned inky black. Drac removed his hands. His face had a peculiar look of satisfaction. On the ground, Freakshow wept.

"Your Legacy has been removed," Dennings said. "Now you're nothing but a normal human again."

Sam looked as Six. "Dreynen?" he said.

Six shook her head. "I don't think so," she said. "This looks different."

"Can you really completely remove a Legacy?"

"Permanently?" said Six. "I don't know. They seem to believe it. That's probably how he controls them."

"All right," Dennings said cheerfully. "That's all for right now. Everybody head over to the cafeteria for dinner." He indicated two boys, pointed at Freakshow, and said, "Get this one out of here."

Rena stood up and started to leave the hangar. But Dennings called her name. She turned and looked at him. "Stay a minute," Dennings said. "I want to talk to you."

She went over to him. "I've heard a lot about you from Sparky," he said. "I'm glad you decided to give us a chance."

"I heard he got hurt," Rena said.

"Nothing that can't be fixed."

"Can I see him?"

"Later," said Dennings. "Come with me." He put his arm around her and led her to a door at the back of the hangar. He and Rena walked outside. Dennings led her to a much smaller building about a hundred yards away. He opened a door and they stepped inside. It was filled with television monitors, several of which showed the main hangar from different perspectives. There were also several that showed the other buildings in the compound, and even the area outside the fence. Several men sat at chairs in front of the monitors. None of them looked up when Dennings and Rena came in.

"That's a pretty fancy setup," Sam remarked. "Someone spent a lot on that equipment."

"What's all this?" Rena asked Dennings.

"This?" he said, looking around as if he was noticing all the equipment for the first time. "This is just surveillance stuff. We don't want anyone trying to get in here who shouldn't be."

"Or out," Six remarked.

Dennings turned back to Rena. "I've got a couple of questions for you."

"Shoot," said Rena.

"What finally made you decide to come to us? I understand Sparky—Yo-Yo—tried to get you to check our operation out a couple of times, and you said no."

Rena shrugged. "Guess I changed my mind," she said. "He made it sound pretty good. Figured if you can help me learn to use my power better, that's something."

"You could do that at the HGA," said Dennings.

"I don't really like being told what to do or when to do it," Rena shot back.

Dennings laughed. "In case you didn't notice what happened back there, I'll be telling you what to do and when to do it. You don't have a problem with that?"

Rena shook her head. "Not as long as you pay me what Yo-Yo says you pay."

"And how much is that?" Dennings asked.

"You tell me how much you're offering," said Rena. "I'll tell you if it's enough."

Dennings laughed again. "A girl after my own heart," he said. "Okay, fair enough. We can talk about that once we decide if you're going to stay."

"Why wouldn't I stay?" Rena asked him.

"I know you just got here," Dennings said. "And we haven't explained all the rules to you. So I can't be too upset that you've broken one of them."

"Broken a rule?" Rena said. "I don't understand."

Dennings nodded. "Take a look at monitor number five," he said, indicating one of the screens.

Rena looked. The man sitting in front of the monitor pressed a button on the console in front of him, and a video feed started to play. It showed the battle that had just taken place in the hangar, but from the perspective of someone sitting in the bleachers.

"That's the feed from her glasses," Sam said.

Rena swung around to look at Dennings. He was no longer smiling as his hands reached for her face. "I think you'd better give me those." Then the feed cut out.

CHAPTER NINE

TEXAS

"WHAT'S THE PLAN?" SAM ASKED SIX AS THEY RAN towards the fence that surrounded the compound.

"We get in, get Rena, and get out."

"I'm not sure that qualifies as a plan," Sam said.

"We've gone in with less of one," she reminded him.

"And what about Ghost and Edwige?"

"One thing at a time," said Six.

They reached the fence and quickly made their way over it, coming down on the other side just as a group of twenty armed men approached from around the side of the nearest building. Too many to take care of using just telekinesis.

Six looked around. Several old vehicles, including a school bus, were parked nearby. Rusted out, with holes in its sides, the bus looked like it hadn't been used to carry anyone to school and back in years. Many of the windows were smashed, and two of the tires were flat, making it list to one side.

"Sam!" Six called out. "The bus!"

Sam turned towards it. Six heard the sound of an engine trying to turn over. Metal rubbed against metal. The bus sputtered, choked, gave up. It tried again. This time, an irregular pulse chugged beneath the hood. And then the bus began to move, slowly, like an old dinosaur taking its final steps.

"Forget making it move on its own," Six said. "Push it!"

She concentrated, adding her power to Sam's. Together, they lifted the bus and pushed it at the approaching group of men, who panicked and shot at it. Bullets pelted against metal and glass. The bus slammed into the men, most of whom scattered, some of whom found themselves under-neath it.

Using the ensuing confusion as cover, Sam and Six ran away from the men, who were now shouting to one another and running every which way as they attempted to get a lock on their targets. Six knew it wouldn't be long before they went in the right direction, either accidentally or after rul-ing out all the other ones.

Rounding the corner of the hangar, they were surprised to see Rena standing in the center of the open space. Alone. Six scanned the area, looking for Dennings or anyone else. She'd expected to be met by an army.

"Where is he?" Six asked.

She saw then that tears were running down Rena's face. The girl's chest was shaking as she quietly sobbed.

"What's going on?" Six asked her.

"He's going to kill Yo-Yo," Rena said, her voice hitching with every word. She took a deep breath and steadied herself. "If you don't leave."

"She's right." Dennings's voice crackled out of loudspeakers attached to poles around the compound.

"Dennings!" Six shouted. "Why not come out and speak to us in person? Give me a chance to kick your ass. Again."

"Easy," Sam whispered. "He's still got Edwige and Ghost."

Dennings's laugh rippled through the air. "Don't think I wouldn't welcome a rematch."

"Then why send out your welcoming committee?" Six said. "Why not come alone?"

"To amuse myself," said Dennings. "And maybe buy some time to get my people out of harm's way."

Six laughed. "Looks to me like you're *putting* them in harm's way," she countered.

"I guess we'll have to agree to disagree on that."

A rustling of feet made Six turn around. The men who had escaped the encounter with the bus unharmed appeared behind her. There were fewer than a dozen of them. She and Sam could easily handle them. They raised their hands.

"I wouldn't do that," Dennings warned. "Not unless you want someone to get hurt. And I don't mean you."

Six turned away from the men.

"Smart girl," Dennings said, making Six bristle. "Now

back to the matter at hand. As your young friend has told you, I'm willing to let her—and you—walk out of here. Right now."

"No deal," Six snapped. "We want Edwige and Ghost, too." Under her breath she added, "And every other kid you've got in here."

"Sorry," Dennings replied. "This isn't a negotiation. You get this one and safe passage out of here, or you get nothing."

"Or we could rip this place apart until we find where you're hiding," Six suggested.

"I think you know what will happen if you attempt to do that," Dennings said. "And believe me, I can be gone before you even get started."

Sam put his hand on Six's shoulder. "We've got Rena," he whispered. "We can come back for the others."

"He'll move them," Six said, frustration making her voice sharper than normal. "He's not stupid enough to stay here. He'll find some other place."

"Then we'll find him," Sam said. He looked into her eyes. "We can't win this one. Even if we destroy this place, it will just end up hurting the kids who are here."

Six looked at Rena. "Please," the girl said.

Six shut her eyes. She counted to five, calming herself. "All right," she said, and opened her eyes. "We're walking out of here." She turned to the others. "Come on. Before I change my mind."

Although Dennings's men eyed them warily as they left, they met no resistance as they walked to the front gate of the compound, which was open. Six never even looked back as she, Sam, and Rena started down the dusty trail that led into the scrubland.

Rena came and walked beside her. "Thank you," she said.

Six nodded. "I know what it's like to lose a friend," she said. "And you did a good job in there."

"You saw what they did to Freakshow," Rena said. "I think they did the same thing to Yo-Yo." She paused. "You think his power is really gone?"

"I don't know," Six told her. What she thought, but didn't say, was that Dennings and whoever else was behind the fights wouldn't have much further use for a kid without a Legacy. So why would they keep them alive? *Unless they're lying about what they can do,* she thought.

"He's made those kids some big promises," Rena continued. "Money. Not having to go to the HGA and follow their rules. The kids I met mostly seemed like the types who didn't exactly fit even before they turned into superheroes, you know? I think he makes them feel like stars. That whole nickname thing. It's like being in a club, or a gang."

"But then he hurts them when they fail," said Six.

"You've never been in a gang, have you?" said Rena. "That's what they do. Build you up, tear you down. Tell you that you aren't worth anything unless they say so. Make it so you want to belong even harder. I know it doesn't make sense, but that's how they do it. I've seen a lot of people get sucked in like that back in my neighborhood."

Six's thoughts flashed to Five again, and how he had

betrayed the rest of them after falling under the influence of the Mogadorians. She understood. Wanting to belong made people do things you never thought they would do. They were going to have to find Dennings, shut his operation down, and get the kids he'd conned some real guidance.

In the meantime, she had other problems. Namely, what she and Sam were going to do with the little group of Garde they'd collected. She thought about it all the way back to the SUV they'd parked a few miles away. And all the way back to the airport where the jet was waiting for them. When they were on board and seated, she still hadn't come to any decisions.

It was Nemo who brought it up. "So, now what?" she said once they were in the air.

"What do you want to happen?" Six said, turning the question back on her. "You're the one who said you don't want anything to do with being part of an organized group. You could just go back to doing what you were doing before we found you."

"You didn't *find* us," Nemo countered. "You got in our way. . . . And there's actually no one to go back to. It's just the three of us."

"So, you're not part of a bigger group?" Sam asked her.

"Oh, there are more people *like* us. Lots of them. But most of us are on our own. That's kind of part of the whole not-liking-groups thing."

"But you could be convinced," Six said.

Nemo shrugged.

Six looked at Max, who looked at Nemo. He was obviously still anxious about what Nemo thought. But what did *he* want?

Six considered the options. She could try to convince them to go to the Human Garde Academy. But if she couldn't support it herself, how could she ask Nemo and the others to? Especially Nemo. She had come to really like the girl, and for obvious reasons. They were very much alike. It would be like telling her younger self to do something for her own good. She already knew what Nemo's response to such a thing would be. But what was the alternative?

"What about you?" she said to Rena.

"Can't really go back to business as usual now," the girl said. "I want to get Yo-Yo out of there."

Six nodded. "Sam, can I see you in the bedroom?" she said, standing up.

Sam followed her. "Normally, I'd be happy to hear you say that," he joked as he shut the door to the cabin. "But I have a feeling that I know what you're thinking, and I also think it's going to make life much more complicated."

Six turned on the monitor affixed to the wall across from the bed. "Tell this thing to call McKenna," she said.

A minute later, they were talking to McKenna, whose face filled up the screen. "So, how many should I expect for dinner?" he said.

"About that," Six said. "How many bedrooms are there at our fancy home base?"

"Enough for company," McKenna replied. "Are you thinking what I think you are?"

"Maybe," said Six. She told him her idea, such as it was. "Until we can figure out what to do with them."

"I'm not opposed to it," McKenna said when she was done. "But there are some complications. Despite what they might have told you, the three runaways have people looking for them. People who are worried about them."

"You haven't reported them, have you?" Six asked.

McKenna shook his head. "Not as yet," he said. "But I'm going to have to. And that raises an additional problem—once they're reported found and safe, they'll be expected to report to the HGA."

"They're not going to want to do that," said Six. "Most of them, anyway."

"As I said, that raises a problem," said McKenna.

"We'll talk to them," Sam said. "See what we can do."

"You don't have much time," said McKenna. "As I said, their families are concerned."

"Got it," Six said.

"All right," McKenna said. "Now, on to other matters. We've had another missing healer."

"Who now?" Six asked.

"Her name is Taylor Cook. An American."

"You want us to go looking for her?" said Six.

"No need," McKenna answered. "She's been returned. To the HGA. She's there now."

"So, then, there's no problem."

"There is," McKenna replied. "A big one. Taylor has information on who has been abducting healers. It's a much bigger problem than we thought. And it might require you to work more directly with the Human Garde Academy, and possibly Earth Garde. I'd like you to go and meet with Nine."

"Yay," Sam remarked. "A family reunion."

"I'll let them know you're coming," McKenna said. "Captain Kirk can land in California, and once you've met with Nine, you can proceed to headquarters."

"What do we do with our guests while we're there?" Six asked him. "I don't know if it's a good idea to bring them along."

"Actually, maybe it is" McKenna said. "Let them see the facilities. Maybe one or more of them will decide to stay there."

He signed off. Six sat down on the bed, then lay on her back. "This is getting complicated," she said.

Sam lay beside her. "You like complicated," he reminded her. "Actually, you're kind of the definition of complicated." He took her hand. "That's what I like about you. Don't worry. It will all be fine. And we'll get to spend some time with my dad, and Nine too."

They lay there for a while, not saying anything. Six closed her eyes. Maybe she could at least get some sleep before they landed.

There was a knock on the door.

"Are you two almost done in there?" Nemo's voice carried through the closed door.

"Why?" Six answered. "What's going on?"

"Oh, not much," Nemo said. "Only the pilot is missing—and no one is flying the plane!"

THE LEGACY CHRONICLES

CHRONICLES

INTO THE FIRE

CHAPTER ONE

SAM
SOMEWHERE OVER CALIFORNIA

"IT'S NOT RESPONDING."

Sam looked at Six, a worried expression on his face. Moments ago, they'd discovered that the pilot of the jet taking them to the Human Garde Academy in California had vanished into thin air. Now, the plane's controls were locked. And if Sam couldn't fix them, the flight was going to end much sooner than expected.

He closed his eyes and concentrated—hard—on connecting with the plane's flight navigation system. His mind reached out, searching. He sensed a vague buzzing, like voices coming from far away. He tried to reach them, but couldn't make sense of anything that was being said.

"It's like they're speaking a foreign language," he told Six, his voice tight with frustration. "Right when something starts to make sense, the language changes. The messages are all scrambled."

This had never happened to him. Ever. He could always connect with a machine's internal circuitry and talk to it, tell it what to do. Now, though, he found nothing. It was as if the plane's memory had been completely erased. Or he had been locked out. He attempted once more to reach the plane's electronic central nervous system.

"Well?" Six said.

Sam shook his head. "Nothing."

"Nothing?" said the girl with turquoise-colored hair standing behind Six. "Translation—we're going to crash."

"We're not going to crash, Nemo," Six said sharply. She looked at Sam and lifted her eyebrows, silently asking, *Are we?*

"Of course we aren't," Sam said, trying to sound confident even as the plane's nose suddenly dipped and an ominous popping sound came from the engine on the right-hand wing. The Gulfstream listed, then seemed to drop more quickly.

"Go strap yourself in," Six ordered Nemo. "Max and Rena too. Now."

Sam sat down in the pilot's seat. Six took the copilot's position.

"I think we're going to crash," Sam said quietly.

"All right," said Six. "Plan B."

She took out her phone and dialed Peter McKenna, the man for whom the pair had recently started working, investigating Garde-related incidents. When McKenna answered,

Six said, "We have a little problem." She explained as quickly as she could what was happening.

"You're going to need to switch to manual control," McKenna said calmly. "I'll walk you through it. Start by disabling the computers completely. They've been compromised."

Step-by-step, he took Six and Sam through the process of turning off the plane's electronic systems. "Sam, can you control the plane's mechanics now?" he asked.

Sam reached out, this time with his hands. He gripped the plane's yoke and pulled back. He sensed the plane adjusting, and then the nose lifted.

"It's working," he said. He looked over at Six and grinned. "Looks like all those hours I spent playing Birds of Steel will come in handy after all."

"Don't get too comfortable," McKenna said through Six's phone. "This is the easy part. You're still going to have to land her. We're going to set a heading for Petaluma Municipal Airport. It's a little less than an hour until you get there."

Another popping sound came from outside, and the plane shuddered.

"Something is happening with the engines," Sam said. "Something not good. We might not have an hour."

"Then let's get started," McKenna said.

After running through the procedure with them until both Sam and Six could recite the steps from memory, McKenna signed off to call the airport and make arrangements for their arrival. "I'll call back when I'm done," he promised.

"I assume this means we're not crashing?" Nemo said.

She and Max were standing in the open cockpit doorway. Behind them, Rena peered over their shoulders with a worried expression.

"Nope," said Sam. "Well, probably not."

"Too bad," Nemo said. "I was kinda hoping we'd get to use the inflatable slide."

"I don't think this plane has one of those," Max said seriously. "Are you sure everything is okay?" he asked Sam.

"Absolutely," Sam assured him.

"So, what happened to that Kirk guy?" Nemo asked.

"Good question," Sam said. "We haven't had a chance to think about that yet. You know, what with all the not-crashing and everything."

"Did you see what happened?" Six asked Nemo.

Nemo shook her head. "I went to ask him if I could have a soda," she said. "I couldn't find him anywhere. He was just . . . gone."

"People don't just disappear from planes while they're in the sky," Max said firmly.

"Maybe he jumped," Rena suggested. "He could do that, right?"

"Theoretically," Sam said. "But we'd know if a door had been opened."

"Maybe someone like Ghost came on board and took him," said Nemo.

"Could they really do that?" Rena asked.

"I don't know. Maybe," Six said. "Teleporting to and from someplace that's moving is difficult. Doing it from seven or eight miles up? While traveling six hundred miles an hour? It seems impossible. I've never seen anyone do that."

"What other explanation is there?" Sam said.

"How about we figure out what happened to James once we're safely on the ground," Six suggested. Looking over her shoulder at Nemo, Max, and Rena, she added, "You three go sit down."

"Okay, Mom," Nemo said sarcastically. "Come on, guys. Let's get out of here before she makes us clean our rooms."

"I think I like her," Sam said to Six as the three retreated to the main cabin.

"Don't tell her I said so, but I think I do too," said Six.

"Probably because she's a lot like you," Sam suggested.

Six shot him a glare. "Just fly the plane," she said.

Twenty minutes before they were scheduled to arrive in Petaluma, McKenna reconnected via Six's phone. "Everything is set," he told them. "Weather is calm. They've cleared the runway. Emergency services are standing by."

"Emergency services?" Sam said.

"Standard procedure in situations like this," McKenna said. "You'll be fine. I told air traffic control that I'll talk you through it. Now let's fire up the plane's EVS. It will help you land in the dark."

Fifteen minutes later, as the plane skidded to a stop on the tarmac, Sam breathed a sigh of relief. "You were right," he told McKenna. "That was nothing."

"Except for the part where the landing gear is on fire," Six remarked, looking out the window as a fire truck, its lights flashing, raced towards them.

Not long after, they were allowed to exit the plane. At the foot of the stairs were two familiar figures: Dr. Malcolm Goode and Nine. Sam embraced his father, who hugged his son tightly and said, "Not bad for a first landing."

"Don't I get a hug?" Nine asked Six.

"Don't you need two arms for that?" Six replied.

They both laughed as Six wrapped her arms around him. "It's good to see you," she said.

"Aww," Nine said, squeezing her tightly. "You missed me."

Nine let go of Six and turned to the three young teenagers standing together and watching the reunion. "You're not wearing uniforms, so I'm guessing you're not the cabin crew," he said. "That means you must be Nemo, Rena, and Max."

Nemo only grunted, but Max rushed forward and held out his hand. Sam, watching, thought that the young man acted as if he were meeting a favorite celebrity. He also couldn't help but notice Nemo reacting to Max's enthusiasm with distaste.

"Come on," Nine said after shaking Rena's hand as well. "We'll ride back to the HGA. You all must be exhausted. McKenna and I have arranged for some people to look over the plane and see what they can find out."

"HGA?" Nemo said. She glared at Sam and Six. "We were supposed to be going to New York. You said—"

"This wasn't the plan, Nemo," Sam interrupted. "Not at

first, anyway. But then we got some new information."

"And then Kirk disappeared and we were going to crash," Six added with less patience. "You think we planned *that*?"

Nemo shook her head and said nothing.

"Are we good?" Nine asked.

"Yeah," Sam said. "We're good."

They walked to the parking lot, Nemo silently bringing up the rear.

"A van?" Six said when she saw the vehicle Nine was leading them to. It had the Human Garde Academy logo painted on the side.

"What?" Nine said as he slid the door open. "It's perfect for taking the kids to soccer practice and picking up groceries."

The ride to the Human Garde Academy took almost ninety minutes. It was close to midnight when they arrived, and Max and Rena were already asleep, their heads tilted to the side. Nemo was hunched down, her head covered by her hoodie; but given how suspicious she seemed to be of everyone, Sam suspected she was wide awake, watching everything that happened.

"We'll put you up in the dorms," Nine said as he pulled the van into a parking spot. "Tomorrow, you can have the full tour. Oh, and we can talk about who it was who tried to kill you." When no one laughed, he added, "Seriously, you couldn't be any safer if you were locked inside a vault. Someone would have to be insane to try to mess with you while you're at the Academy."

"Unless it's someone *at* the Academy who's trying to mess with us," Nemo said under her breath.

"Sam, you can bunk in my place if you want to," Dr. Goode said.

"That would be nice," said Sam. "We can catch up." He turned to Six. "Do you mind keeping an eye on these three?" he whispered.

"No problem," Six said. "But next time, you get to babysit the kids while I go out with the girls for drinks and boy-watching." She squeezed his hand. "Go on. I'll see you in the morning."

Nine escorted Six and the three teenagers to the guest dorms, while Sam walked with his father to one of the town houses that acted as faculty housing.

"It's nothing fancy," Dr. Goode said as he opened a door and motioned for Sam to step inside. "But it's all I need."

Sam sank wearily onto a couch while his father took a seat in a chair. "So," Dr. Goode said. "Anything exciting happen lately?"

Sam sighed. "It's been a long couple of days," he said. "It's hard to believe that a week ago, Six and I were sleeping in a tent and not worrying about anything. Then again, I guess that's kind of par for the course when it comes to Garde life."

"Never a dull moment," his father agreed. "And things are good with you and Six?"

"Yeah," Sam answered. "They are."

"You sure?" his dad pressed.

"No, they're great," Sam said. "I'm just not positive we're

totally on the same page right now about what we're going to do. You know, with the rest of our lives."

"It may not seem like it, but you're still a teenager, Sam," his father said, laughing. "You have a lot of time to figure that out."

"I know. It will be fine."

"I was surprised when Nine told me you and Six were coming. He didn't say why, though. What's going on?"

Sam didn't know how much Nine actually knew about the situation either and found himself wondering what he should—or could—tell his dad. What he and Six were doing for McKenna was supposed to be a secret. Not even other Garde were supposed to know about it. That had changed now, but how much? Sam felt weird keeping information from his father, but he also didn't want to put him in the middle by having him know more than Nine might.

"We're following up on leads about kids with Legacies," he said, keeping it vague.

"Like the three you brought with you?"

Sam nodded. "What about you?" he asked, changing the subject. "Is everything going all right for you here?"

"It's great," Dr. Goode said. "I love working with the kids. We've got a diverse group. Lots of different Legacies."

Sam yawned. His father laughed. "I know it's not as exciting as jetting around the world," he joked.

"I'm sorry," said Sam. "I haven't gotten much sleep lately, and—"

"Let's get you to bed," his father said, standing up. "I've

got a guest room, although I mostly use it as a library. Sorry about the boxes of books."

He showed Sam into the room, which was indeed filled with cardboard cartons. His dad cleared three of them off of the bed. "Bathroom is down the hall," he said. "Get some sleep. Nine will probably try to have you up at dawn for a morning swim."

"He's on his own for that," Sam said. "I didn't bring my swimsuit."

"Good night," his father said. He paused in the doorway. "It's really great to see you, son."

"You too," Sam said.

Minutes later, he was asleep.

✧✧✧

Much too soon, Sam was awake again as the smell of coffee filled his nose. He opened his eyes. Six was standing in the doorway, a cup in her hand.

"Rise and shine," she said.

"I'll rise," Sam said, sitting up. "But I think shining will take a little longer. What's going on?"

"Rena, Nemo, and Max are getting a tour of the Academy," Six told him. "Nine is waiting to talk to us." She handed him the coffee. "Maybe this will help."

Minutes later, the caffeine coursing through his system, Sam walked into Nine's office with Six. "Wow," he said when he saw the large, light-filled room. Its windows looked out onto a grassy lawn, and beyond it the Pacific Ocean was visible in the distance.

"Not bad, right?" said Nine, grinning. "You sure you two don't want to rethink taking staff positions here?"

"We're good," Six said. "This is okay, but our new place has a penthouse view. Plus, you can get takeout in ten minutes. Here, we'd have to wait at least, what, two hours?"

Nine raised an eyebrow. "Sounds fancy," he said.

"Speaking of our new home," Sam said, addressing Six, "Have you spoken to McKenna this morning?"

"I did," she replied.

"Any sign of James?" Sam asked.

"No," said Six.

"I had Lexa and some of her people look over the plane," Nine said. "They found a device that was scrambling the signals to and from the onboard computer. That's why you couldn't interface with it. It's a sophisticated piece of equipment. We're reverse engineering it now."

"People?" Sam said. "We?" He looked at Six again.

"We're working together with Nine and his . . . people," she said, sounding unenthusiastic. "On this, anyway."

"McKenna thought it would be a, how did he put it? A mutually beneficial arrangement," Nine said. "He likes big words, doesn't he?" He leaned back in his chair. "So, could this Kirk guy be in on what happened?"

"I guess anything is possible," Sam said. "But I really doubt it."

"Why?" said Nine.

Sam shrugged. "I just don't think he would do something like this."

"Okay," Nine said, sounding dubious. "Then why would someone take him? He doesn't have a Legacy, does he?"

"No," Sam said.

"So why take him and leave five people who do? What reason could someone have for wanting to kill the rest of you?"

"Maybe they weren't trying to kill us," Six suggested. "Maybe they were just trying to scare us."

Nine considered the suggestion. "Again, why take him then?"

"Because he was the pilot," Sam said. "Isn't that reason enough?"

"They could have just killed him," Nine said. "Are any of the three kids healers?"

"No," Sam told him. "But there was a healer in New Orleans. They got her already."

"They," said Nine. "You're assuming the same people who took her sabotaged the plane."

"Who else would it be?" Six countered.

"The Foundation," Nine suggested.

"I think I'm missing something here," Sam said. "What's the Foundation?"

"The people who took our student Taylor Cook and the other healers you were investigating," Nine told him. "That's what they call themselves. You really need to get up earlier. Six and I already talked about this."

"From what you told me, the Foundation sounds way

more sophisticated than what Dennings is doing," Six said. "I mean, they might be connected somehow, but at the moment I think we should assume they're two different problems. The immediate question is what we're going to do with these kids."

"What do you want to do with them?" Nine asked. "Technically, they're supposed to come here."

Six snorted. "Since when have you been concerned with technicalities?"

"Are you suggesting that I lack respect for law and authority?" asked Nine. "I think I'm offended."

Six sighed. "You know how I feel about this," she said. "What am I supposed to do, tell them that I agree with them but have to play by the rules? None of them want to be here."

"Well, Nemo doesn't," Sam reminded her. "I don't think Rena feels that way. And I think Max could easily change his mind if—"

A commotion in the hall outside interrupted them. A moment later, the door burst open and Rena came in. She was followed by Max and Nemo, who were arguing. Rena looked at Sam and Six and shook her head. Lastly, a girl with blond hair came in. She had an exasperated expression on her face.

"Come on, Nemo," Max said. "This place is great."

"Whatever, Max," Nemo shot back. "Just because you have a crush on Legacy Barbie here."

"Hey," the blond girl said. "Leave me out of this. I just gave you the tour. That's all."

"Six, Sam, this is Ellie," Nine said, as if everything was fine.

"Hi," Ellie said edgily. She looked at Nine. "Can I go now? Please."

"Sure," Nine said, and Ellie left.

"So," Nine said to the trio of teenagers. "Did you enjoy the tour?"

Max and Nemo scowled at one another and said nothing. Rena said, "It's an impressive place."

"You're welcome any time you want to come," Nine told her.

"Considering there's a law that says we *have* to come here, that's really big of you," said Nemo, glaring at Nine.

Nine smiled at her. "Six and I were just talking about that."

"I bet you were," Nemo said.

"And I was saying to Six that a setting like this isn't necessarily right for everyone," Nine continued.

"Oh yeah?" said Nemo.

"Oh yeah?" echoed Six.

"It's great for students who want to learn to make the most of their Legacies," Nine said, ignoring them. He looked at Rena. "And someone like that would be welcome here anytime."

"Thanks," Rena said. "But before I can think about that, I want to help get Yo-Yo away from the people who have him."

140

"Yo-Yo?"

"Her friend," Sam explained. "It's a long story."

"I've been thinking about it," Rena said. "And I have an idea. I don't think you're going to like it, though."

"What is it?" Sam asked her.

Rena took a deep breath. "I want to go back," she said. "Back inside."

"No," Six said immediately.

"I said you weren't going to like it," said Rena. "But hear me out. I can pretend that I tried coming here for a little while, decided I didn't like it, and ran away. I can go back and say you all were horrible to me and tried to make me do things I didn't want to do."

"That's exactly what they *are* trying to do," Nemo muttered.

Rena ignored her. "You've got all kinds of spy gadget stuff," she said. "You can fix me up so you can keep an eye on me. I'll go in, get Yo-Yo, and see what I can do about Edwige and Ghost while I'm at it. You remember Edwige and Ghost, right?"

"Of course we remember them," said Six. "And we're working on it."

"Well, I'm suggesting a way to work on it a little bit faster," Rena told her.

"It's still a no," Six said. "We just tried using surveillance equipment, remember? Dennings figured it out."

"Maybe you need better equipment," said Nine. "We've been working on some things here that—"

"You stay out of this," Six said.

"Just saying that I think it's a good idea," said Nine, crossing his arms over his chest.

Six snorted. "Well, then it's a good thing she's not your responsibility," she snapped.

Nine looked at Rena, then back at Six with a smile on his face. "She would be if she enrolled at the Academy."

CHAPTER TWO

SIX
POINT REYES, CALIFORNIA

"JACKASS!" SIX SAID, SLAMMING THE DOOR.

Lexa looked up from her seat at her desk. "Nice to see you again too."

Six dropped into a chair and uttered a groan of frustration. "Not you," she said. "Him."

"Help me out here," said Lexa. "Are we talking about Nine or Sam? Or maybe somebody else?"

"Both of them, actually," Six answered. "Nine is the one I want to smack at the moment, but it's Sam's fault we're here at all."

"Got it," Lexa said, returning her attention to her computer screen for a moment to check something before turning back to Six and asking, "What did he do this time?"

"He's going to get them killed," said Six.

"I'm going to need you to be more specific again," Lexa said.

"Rena," said Six. "Probably Ghost and Edwige and Yo-Yo, too, once Dennings figures out what's happening. And he *will* figure it out. Sending Rena in there is ridiculous."

Lexa nodded. "Got it," she said.

"So, you agree with me then," said Six. "He's out of his mind, right?"

"Actually, I still don't have a clue what you're talking about. But I assume it has to do with the kids you picked up in New Orleans. As for Nine being out of his mind . . ." She shrugged. "Speaking of kids, did you ever find that girl from the videos?"

"Yeah, that's Rena," Six confirmed. "And I'm not real happy with her right now either."

Lexa picked up the cup of coffee resting beside her keyboard and took a sip. "Sounds like everybody's on your bad side today." She looked at her watch. "And it's not even ten o'clock yet. What's going on?"

Six told her everything. "It's not like I don't want Rena to stay here," she said, wrapping things up. "I'd like *all* of them to stay here, if that's what they want. And Max probably will. Nemo, who knows what will happen with her. But Nine is encouraging Rena to do this totally stupid thing, and he's only doing it to piss me off."

"Mm-hmm," Lexa murmured.

"What?" said Six.

Lexa held up her hands. "I didn't say anything."

"I know that sound," said Six. "That's the sound you make when you don't agree but don't feel like getting into it with someone."

Lexa grunted.

"Just like that," Six said, pointing a finger at her. "You think he's right."

"I didn't say anybody was *right*," Lexa argued. "But maybe it's not such a bad idea. This Rena, can she handle herself?"

"No," said Six. "I mean, yes, she's tough. But Denning isn't going to believe for one minute that she ran away from us. I mean, why would anyone do that?"

"I can't imagine," said Lexa.

"Fine," said Six. "Maybe it is believable. It's still a terrible idea. She could get hurt."

"Somebody can always get hurt," Lexa reminded her. "Let me ask you this. If Sam was being held by somebody you knew was hurting him, wouldn't you do anything you could to get him out?"

Six narrowed her eyes but said nothing. Then there was a knock on the door.

"Somebody around here who knocks?" Lexa said. "Must not be Nine. Come in!"

The door opened, and Sam's head appeared in the crack. "Hey," he said, sounding uncertain. "Can I come in?"

"No," said Six.

"Yes," said Lexa.

Sam walked inside and shut the door behind him. He eyed Six warily as he passed by her, went over to Lexa, and gave her a hug.

"That's more like it," Lexa said. "Now sit."

Sam sat. "So," he said.

"Lexa's on your and Nine's side," Six said.

"Oh," said Sam. "I didn't realize there were sides. I thought we were all working *together* now." He waved at Lexa. "Welcome to the team, I guess."

"Someone is a little bit mad that Nine is acting like Nine," Lexa told Sam.

"I am not mad!" Six objected.

"She's mad," said Lexa.

"Noted," said Sam. Then, to Six, he said, "Nemo says she wants to leave. Now."

"I think I'm with her," said Six.

Sam nodded. "I'm kind of getting that. But here's the thing. Rena wants to stay. Max does too. That leaves Nemo the odd one out. And you're the only one she trusts. Well, sort of trusts. So I was hoping you could maybe talk to her."

Six stood up. "Fine," she said.

"Great," said Sam. "She's stomping around the grounds somewhere. Max is tailing her to make sure she doesn't take off, so she shouldn't be too hard to find."

"There are cameras all around this place," Lexa said. "I'll find her." She turned to one of the handful of monitors set up around her desk. It displayed video feeds from around the campus. "There she is," she said, pointing to the screen.

"Heading for the beach. But once she leaves the lawn, alarms will sound."

"Do me a favor." said Six. "Turn them off. Let me follow her as far as she'll go."

Lexa hesitated, then nodded. "I can disable the security temporarily," she said.

"Thanks," said Six.

She exited the office, leaving Sam and Lexa to catch up. She went outside. It was gray and cold, and the air smelled like the ocean. A light rain was falling as she walked around the grounds of the Academy and across the expansive lawn, and headed towards the coast. After a few minutes, she saw Max ahead of her. She increased her pace, catching up to him.

"How is she?" Six asked him.

He pointed ahead. "She's not stupid. She knows I'm following her. But I can tell she doesn't want to talk to me."

"She probably doesn't want to talk to me either, right?"

Max shrugged. "Probably not."

"You head back to the Academy," Six told him. "No point in everyone getting wet."

She walked on. After a minute, she saw Nemo. She was walking down a path that led to the beach. Unless she started swimming, there was nowhere for her to go, so Six took her time following her. She considered turning invisible, but Max was right—the girl wasn't stupid. Nemo would know they wouldn't let her get too far out of their sight. Now wasn't the time to try to fool her.

Nemo paused, bent down, and removed her sneakers and socks. She carried them in her hand as she walked to the edge of the surf zone and stood there. A wave came in and broke, rolling up the sand. Water covered Nemo's feet for a moment before retreating. She stood there, staring out at the gray-green ocean as rain dimpled the surface. Six walked up and stood beside her. She left her shoes on.

"Thinking about swimming to Hawaii?" she said to Nemo.

Nemo didn't say anything for a minute. Another wave came in. Six stepped just out of its reach. Nemo didn't move.

"This is prime great white territory," Nemo said. "From here down to Monterey Bay. They come to breed, and because there are a lot of seals to eat. They call it the Red Triangle because a huge percentage of shark attacks on people occur here. But they only bite humans because we look like seals when we're in wet suits."

"You like sharks?" Six asked.

Nemo nodded. "They're cool." She looked over at Six. "Doesn't mean I want to swim with them, though. I can breathe underwater, but I still look like a seal to a hungry great white. Maybe if I had animal telepathy. Does that work on fish?"

"You'll have to ask Nine," Six answered. "He's the animal whisperer."

"What's the deal with the two of you?" Nemo asked.

"He's like the bossy big brother who's always trying to one-up you."

Nemo snorted. "So that's why you're so pissed off that he agrees with Rena."

"I'm pissed off about that because I don't want her to get hurt," Six retorted.

"And because he's trying to be the boss," Nemo suggested.

Six started to deny it but then said, "He does that. It's annoying."

Out of the corner of her eye, she saw Nemo smile a little. But the girl didn't say anything in response. Instead, she turned and walked a little farther down the beach, to where a large rock jutted out of the sand. She climbed it and sat down. Six followed her and sat beside her.

"The Farallon Islands are out there," Nemo said, pointing. "There's nothing else, really, except more great whites. A couple of scientists live at a research station there, studying them."

"How do you know so much about sharks?" Six asked.

Nemo shrugged. "I've read a little," she said, obviously trying to sound casual about it.

Six suspected there was more to her interest. "Maybe you should consider being a marine biologist. That breathing-underwater thing would come in handy."

"Actually, that's kind of how I figured out I had a Legacy," Nemo said after a moment. "My family was vacationing at a lake. I was swimming and wanted to see if I could dive to the bottom. I held my breath and swam down. It wasn't that deep—maybe ten feet or so. I was lying there, and I started watching some little fish swim around and wondering what they were. Then I realized I'd been there way longer than I should have been able to stay and still wasn't running out of air. At first, I thought I was just really good at holding my breath. Then I figured it out." She looked at the ocean. "I haven't gone swimming in the ocean yet, though."

"How come?" Six asked.

Nemo shrugged. "It's just so . . . big," she said.

She's afraid, Six thought. *Good. I can work with this.*

"Sam made me try scuba diving when we were in Thailand," she said. "No sharks, but we saw eels. They were cool."

Nemo rewarded her with a genuine smile. "That sounds like fun," she said. Then the smile faded, and she looked sad again.

"Max wanting to stay here doesn't mean he doesn't want to be your friend, you know," Six said, guessing what she was thinking.

Nemo nodded. "Yeah, I know."

Before Six could continue, her phone buzzed. She took it out and looked at the screen. There was a text from Sam: **THEY'VE LOCATED KIRK**.

Six texted back: **ON MY WAY**.

"I've got to get back," she told Nemo. "And you really shouldn't be sitting here in the rain. So how about this—you come back with me. You don't have to stay here permanently. That's a promise. We'll figure something out. For now, though, be nice to Max. He needs you to be his friend."

She felt Nemo tense up.

"And maybe I'll talk to Nine about going with you underwater, so you won't have to worry about anything," Six added.

"Deal," Nemo said.

Relieved, Six stood up. Together, they walked back to the Academy.

✧✧✧

Rena and Max were hanging out talking to some students, and Six left Nemo with them, then went back to Lexa's office. Sam was still there, and on one of Lexa's monitors, McKenna was talking to them.

"What's going on?" Six asked.

"We've received a signal from Kirk's implant," McKenna said.

"Implant?" said Six. "What implant?"

"He was—is—part of a program testing implants in military personnel," McKenna explained. "Among other things, the implant acts as a locating device. Somehow, the signal was either inoperative or blocked. But now it's working."

"So, where is he?" asked Six.

"Montana," McKenna replied.

"Great," said Six. "When do we go get him?"

When nobody answered her, she looked at Sam and lifted her eyebrows.

"That's what we were talking about when you came in," Sam said. "We think it might be a good idea to move forward with Rena's suggestion."

Six grunted. "Of course you do," she said. She turned to

look at McKenna. "You too?"

"We still don't know who took James," McKenna said. "But as we've discussed, the logical conclusion is that it's someone connected to the operation Dennings is running. Since you discovered their previous location, they had to move to another one. If that's where Kirk is, this is our chance to find them."

"Right," said Six. "But we can do that without sending Rena in. Sam and I can go."

"Yes, you could," McKenna agreed. "However, there are other considerations."

"Like what?" Six asked.

"The possible connection to the Foundation," McKenna said. "From what we know, they're operating a kind of black market in those with Legacies."

"Right," said Six. "But I thought we figured that they weren't the same people Dennings is working for."

"I don't think they are," McKenna confirmed. "Despite its methods, the Foundation presents itself as an altruistic organization whose intention is to do good."

"By kidnapping healers?" Six said.

"Indeed," said McKenna. "Nevertheless, that's how they apparently see themselves. Whoever is behind what Dennings is involved in, it's more like organized crime. Purely for profit. At least, that's my theory. However, that's not to say that they're not connected. Which is why I think sending in someone who can get a more thorough look at what's going on there could be helpful. If you and Sam go in, you could probably retrieve Kirk and the kids who are there. But if Rena goes in and convinces Dennings that she's there of her own free will, she'll be able to feed information back to us that might help on a larger scale."

"Or get herself killed," Six suggested. "He had no problem shooting Ghost or Evella. And is there an update on Evella, by the way?"

"She's going to be all right," McKenna said. "I've had her moved to a private hospital, in case Dennings or the people he works for try anything more. And your point is taken. However, I think he knew Ghost would be healed."

"I'm sure that made being shot a lot better," Six snarked.

"You saw how he seemed to remove that girl's Legacy when she lost the fight," McKenna continued. "If he in fact did so, that has enormous implications."

"That's putting it mildly," said Six. "It would change everything. Someone with that kind of technology, power, whatever could do a lot of damage, especially if they got their hands on untrained kids."

"Exactly my point," said McKenna. "So if Rena can get inside and find out more about that, it would prove very, very useful."

"Or we could get in, get Dennings, and make him talk," said Six.

"As I've said before, I don't think he is the real power behind his organization," McKenna said. "And I don't think whoever is would let Dennings live long enough to tell us anything. We already know they have people with Legacies working for them, and we know they're more than willing to kill if they think they're in danger of being found. They would have no problem eliminating someone like Dennings."

"Or someone like Rena," Six pointed out again. She was out of arguments, and she still didn't like what they were suggesting. She settled into a sullen silence, while Sam and Lexa looked at her uneasily.

"I've spoken to Nine about equipping Rena with—"

"Nine?" Six interrupted. "Now you're talking to him without involving me and Sam?"

"Nine is familiar with the Foundation, due to Taylor Cook's experiences," McKenna said. "We've agreed that—"

"So now we're working for Nine," Six said flatly. "I get it."

"You're not working *for* me, Six" Nine said from behind her. "You're working *with* me. You know, like you told Sam earlier today."

She glared at him as he took a seat.

"Sorry I'm late," Nine said. "I had to meet some of my students about an extracurricular project they're working on. Where are we?"

Six listened as McKenna explained what was going to happen. She didn't say anything. Obviously, the choice had been made. She didn't like it and thought they were making a mistake sending Rena back inside. But now she had to focus on keeping the girl as safe as she could. Still, the whole thing bothered her.

She had already said no to working at the HGA, and now

here she was doing exactly that. Well, not exactly working for them. As Nine had so characteristically pointed out, she was now working *with* them. And *them* was Nine and Lexa, two people she cared about very much, even when they made her crazy. So why was it irritating her so much?

She wasn't sure. She'd told Sam she was okay with it. But was she really, or had she just been trying to convince herself she was? Right now, she didn't have time to work it out in her head. She had to focus on the mission ahead of them. She glanced over at Sam. He was watching her. He smiled. It made her feel better. Not great, but better. She pushed the worrisome thoughts away and turned her attention to McKenna. Everything else could wait.

CHAPTER THREE

NEMO
POINT REYES, CALIFORNIA

NEMO CLUNG TO THE STALK OF KELP, KEEPING herself from floating to the surface fifteen feet above. It swayed gently, moving her back and forth, and she wasn't sure if the nausea she felt was from that or from a combination of excitement and nervousness.

"You're doing great."

Nine's deep, soothing voice crackled through the tiny waterproof earpiece tucked inside her ear canal. The thick neoprene hood she wore encased everything but her face, keeping her mostly dry, if not terribly warm. The water was a chilly fifty-five degrees, and her wet suit was exactly that— wet. The ocean seeped in through the wrists and ankles. Nine had warned her that it would be cold, but the first plunge underwater had nevertheless been a shock. She was still getting used to it.

She was also getting used to all the gear. In addition to the wet suit, she wore gloves, fins, and a weight belt that helped her stay underwater. It had been a lot easier swimming in the lakes she had swum in before, where all she had on was a swimsuit.

Beside her, Nine floated effortlessly in the water without holding on to any kelp. His body was perfectly horizontal, and his arms were crossed over his chest. He wore the same getup that Nemo did, but with the addition of a buoyancy vest, air tank, and regulator. He also had on a mask outfitted with a transmitter that allowed him to talk to her. Nemo, in contrast, wore only a pair of swim goggles that allowed her to see underwater. Her mouth and nose were uncovered.

"Relax," Nine reminded her.

That's easy for you to say, Nemo thought. She couldn't talk underwater and had to respond to Nine using the hand signals he'd taught her earlier in the day. Now she gave him the OK sign to let him know she understood.

"When you're ready, you can release your death grip on that poor kelp, and we'll try swimming."

Very funny. Now I know why you make Six crazy. She looked at Nine and flipped him a signal she was sure he would understand, even though it wasn't one they'd practiced. His laugh flooded her ear.

Nemo steadied her breath. This required fighting against

her natural instincts, but she did it. Now she concentrated on keeping her body horizontal. When she was more or less there, she let go of the kelp. For a moment, she feared she would either sink or fly to the surface, but she stayed where she was.

"Excellent," said Nine. "Now, let's try swimming. Remember, slow, easy strokes. This isn't a race."

Nemo moved her feet and shot forward. She panicked and clutched at more kelp, then calmed herself and tried again. This time she moved slowly and steadily.

"Nice correction," said Nine, coming up to swim beside her. "Let's take a little tour."

The rain that had darkened the sky earlier in the day had given way to sunshine, and it filtered down through the water, illuminating the kelp forest as it passed through the golden-brown leaves.

"Beautiful, isn't it?" Nine asked.

Nemo nodded. It was more than beautiful. It was like nothing she had ever seen. She'd practiced her Legacy in lakes, but that had been nothing like this. This was the ocean, and it was huge and wild and dangerous. The thought of sharks was never far from her mind, although Nine had assured her that not only did they not swim within the kelp forest that grew in the shallower water, they could be controlled by his Legacy.

"Come look at this," Nine said, angling towards the bottom. All Nemo saw was some rocks and shells scattered around on the sand, but she followed as Nine went to a rock that looked just like all the others and hovered in front of it. Nemo joined him. Nine pointed to something no more than three inches long. It was covered in brownish spikes tipped in yellow, and at one end was what looked like two spiral horns. Nemo had no idea what it could possibly be, if it was some kind of anemone, or plant, or what. Then, ever so slightly, it moved, and she realized it was crawling across the surface of the rock.

"It's called a nudibranch," Nine told her. "A sea slug."

Nemo had never thought of a slug as something beautiful before, but the nudibranch was gorgeous in a strange, alien way. She watched as it moved what she assumed was its head back and forth.

"More than seventy percent of Earth is covered by water," Nine said. "And this is just one of the millions of things that live here. Most people will never see one up close like this. It's like you're an astronaut visiting another planet."

Says the guy who's from another planet, Nemo thought.

"Looks like we have company," said Nine.

Nemo looked up just in time to see something the size of a dog dart past. Then another one came by, and she realized that they had been joined by sea lions. The playful creatures swam around them, blowing bubbles. One of them dove down, picked up an orange starfish in its mouth, and came up to Nemo. It hovered in front of her.

"He wants you to take it," Nine said. "It's a game they like to play."

Nemo reached out and took the starfish in her hand. The

sea lion swam away, while another continued to circle them. Nemo held out the starfish, and the second sea lion took it in its mouth, spiraling away in a rush of bubbles.

"Looks like you've made some new friends," Nine said. "You ready to go back up? You don't want to stay under too long or you'll get hypothermia, even in that wet suit."

Nemo was not ready to go up, but she nodded. There would be other times. Now that she'd experienced the ocean, she knew she would be back again and again.

Which is exactly what Nine knew would happen, she thought as she followed him up towards the sun. Part of her hated him for introducing her to the magic of the kelp forest. Not that she had to stay at the Academy to go swimming. She could do that on her own. Still, it might be nice to have someone who knew what they were doing to show her what else she could do.

Her head broke the surface. Nine already had his mask off. "Pretty awesome, isn't it?" he said.

"Did you make them do that?" she asked.

Nine shook his head. "That was all them. If you want, next time we can go into more open water and I'll see about getting one of your shark buddies to do a swim-by. Sound good?"

"We'll see," Nemo said. "Maybe."

"Maybe," Nine echoed, rolling his eyes. "Come on. Let's swim in and get something warm to drink."

They swam to shallow water, then stood up and walked the rest of the way. Nemo couldn't believe how heavy she felt now that she was back on land. Compared to floating in the water, walking felt like trying to move through mud. When she reached dry sand, she took off her weight belt and dropped it with a sigh of relief.

"It's easier in warm water, of course," Nine said, shucking off his air tank and lowering it to the ground. He pulled his hood off and shook the water from his long, dark hair. "Not a lot of people can handle diving in this type of water. Cold. Low visibility. Sharks."

"I get it," Nemo said. "We're badasses. You can knock off the hard sell."

"No hard sell," said Nine. "What would I need to sell?"

Nemo barked a laugh. "This place?" she suggested. "The whole Human Garde thing?"

"Maybe I was just testing you," Nine retorted. "To see if you've got what it takes."

"Like I said," Nemo replied. "Hard sell."

"You're a lot like Six," Nine remarked. "No wonder I like you."

"And no wonder you annoy me," Nemo shot back, but not meanly. Despite all her reservations, she was starting to like Nine too.

"Let's go tell everyone what we saw," Nine suggested. "And see how Rena's coming along with her mission prep."

Mission prep, Nemo thought. *He makes everything sound so dramatic.* Then again, wasn't what Rena was doing a big deal? Going back into a dangerous place to help her friend. She was brave, that was for sure. Would Nemo do the same if it was Max who was being held? She was still really mad at him, but she thought she would. No, she knew she would. That's what friends did for each other. *So then why are you planning on running away and leaving him here?* she asked herself.

"Oh, shut up," she snapped.

Nine looked at her.

"Not you," said Nemo. "I meant, um, somebody else."

Nine cocked his head. "I'd say it was nitrogen narcosis, but you weren't breathing air from a tank."

"Like I said, not everything is about you," said Nemo, picking up her gear and trudging across the beach.

Half an hour later, showered and dressed in warm clothes, she walked into a classroom where Rena, Six, Sam, Lexa, Nine, and Sam's father were gathered. Max wasn't there, and she wondered if he was off with Ellie again. She felt a sharp pang of jealousy at the thought, but this disappeared as she watched what Rena was doing.

Rena was standing behind a table on which were arranged half a dozen dolls, action figures, and stuffed animals. She was holding a clown doll in her hand and staring at it with a look of concentration on her face. A moment later, the clown shuddered, as if waking up. Rena set it on the table, and it stood on its own feet, swaying slightly. It turned its head from side to side, the permanent grin painted there seeming to laugh at them all. The sight of it made Nemo shiver. She hated clowns.

"Tell it to juggle those balls," Nine said.

Rena nodded. She stared hard at the clown, which leaned over and picked up three small plastic balls that were lying on the table. It hefted them in its hands, then tossed them in the air, and started juggling.

"Great," Nine said. "Now try to make it do something unclown-like."

"Like what?" Rena asked.

"Tell it to strangle the Superman action figure," Six suggested.

"Like a clown wouldn't totally commit murder," said Sam. "No, see if you can get it to do something like ride the horse there."

"A clown could ride a horse," Six objected.

"Yeah, it *could*," Sam conceded. "But it's not generally part of the standard clown repertoire. Let's just try."

Rena looked at the clown. It dropped the balls it had been juggling and walked over to a plastic horse that stood a few feet away. The horse's usual rider, a cowboy figure, lay on its side next to it. The clown stepped over it and approached the horse.

"Tell it to get on," Sam instructed Rena.

The clown hesitated, as if it was unsure what to do. It reached out and touched the horse's neck. Then it pulled its hand back and just stood there.

"It won't," Rena said. "I can feel it resisting."

"Push it," said Nine.

Rena's forehead wrinkled as she concentrated. The clown didn't move. "It's not going to do it," Rena said.

"That's fascinating," Dr. Goode remarked. "It's like it won't do anything a typical clown wouldn't know how to do."

"I told you that's how it works," said Rena. She sounded tired, as if trying to get the clown to do what they asked had worn her out. "I can only make them do what they're supposed to. Paper butterflies fly. Ballerina dolls dance. Soldier dolls fight. Teddy bears . . . teddy."

"That doesn't make sense," said Six. "They're just plastic dolls, or paper animals, or stuffed toys. They don't have brains. They shouldn't be able to think about doing or not doing something. They should do what you tell them to with your thoughts."

"Maybe it's *how* you're telling them what to do," Nine suggested. "Maybe you can teach them to do other things. It would just take time."

Rena shook her head, and the clown doll collapsed. "You don't understand," she said. "I don't *make* them do anything. I give them the energy, power, whatever to do what they're already designed to do. I can direct them a little, tell them where to go and such, but they only do what they do."

Nobody said anything. Rena sighed. "It's like voodoo dolls," she said.

"Voodoo?" said Nine, laughing. "As in magic?"

Rena nodded. "Yeah," she said. "As in magic." When Nine smiled, she continued. "What? You think what we all can do isn't magic? Suddenly getting superpowers? Breathing underwater? Walking through walls? *Flying?*"

"It might *seem* like magic," Nine said.

"Can you explain it?" Rena asked. "With science?" She looked at Dr. Goode. "Can you?"

"We don't know exactly how the Loric energy works yet," he answered. "But I wouldn't call it magic."

"Mm-hmm," said Rena. "Well, let's get back to voodoo dolls. The way they work—and they *do* work—is that when you make them, you think about the person they represent. If you can, you put something of that person into them. Hair. Fingernails. A piece of fabric from their clothes. But you don't need to. It helps, but they work even if you don't. And they only work on the person they're supposed to represent."

"I'm not following," said Sam.

Nemo spoke up. "What she means is, the doll is made to do one thing. It's about the person who makes it as much as it is about the doll." She looked at Rena. "Right?"

Rena smiled. "Exactly right. They call it sympathetic magic. A voodoo doll is made to do one thing—affect a particular person in the way you tell it to. If I make one of Sam, I can't use it on Six. It won't work, no matter how many pins I put in it or workings I do with it."

"And you think it's the same with the action figures, or stuffed animals, or origami things?" asked Nemo.

"That's what I think," Rena said.

Six picked up the clown doll. "Okay. I get what you're saying. But do you think the people who work on assembly lines painting these things or filling them with stuffing really think about them all that much, enough to give them some kind of identity or purpose? Or what if they're made by machine? Machines don't think about it at all."

Rena shrugged. "Maybe it doesn't matter. Maybe it just is what it is. You paint a doll like a clown, and it's a clown. You make a dragon out of papier-mâché and sticks, and it's a dragon. What I do know is that when I make a certain kind of doll with a particular purpose in mind, it works a lot better. That's why I started making my own."

"Have you ever seen a Legacy like this?" Dr. Goode asked the others.

Nine shook his head. "No," he said. "But we'd never seen technopathy before Sam manifested it either. When you think about it, what Rena can do is a little bit like that. I still wonder if her skill can't be refined." He looked at Rena. "We'll work on that when you come back from your mission."

"About that," Nemo said.

"Don't you try to talk me out of it too," Rena said. "You know if this was one of your friends—"

"One of my friends *is* in there," Nemo said, cutting her off. "Ghost. And I'm not going to try to talk you out of it." She took a deep breath. "I'm going to come with you."

CHAPTER FOUR

SIX
POINT REYES, CALIFORNIA

"DON'T BLINK."

Lexa reached out, balanced a single contact lens on the end of her finger, and gently pressed it to Rena's eyeball.

"Good. Now let's see if it's working."

She walked back to her desk and typed rapidly on a keyboard. A second later, the screen filled with an image of the room.

"Look at Six," Lexa said.

Rena turned her head. On the monitor, Six's face came into view.

"That's amazing," Six said, the on-screen image of herself speaking in unison with the real thing. "How is there a camera in there?"

"Science," Lexa said. "But yeah, it's pretty cool. There's

an image pickup sensor and a built-in transmitter that sends the signal out so we can see what the wearer is seeing. A feed comes directly here, and you can also get it on a handheld monitor. The only thing is, they don't work well in low light, so if the wearer is in the dark, so are we."

"Does it feel weird?" Six asked Rena.

The girl shook her head. "Like a normal contact lens," she said.

"I want one!" said Nemo, who was standing next to Rena.

"Don't worry," Lexa said. "I've got one for you, too."

Rena swiveled her head around, causing the image on the monitor to change. She looked at Nine, who waved, and then at Sam, who gave a thumbs-up sign. Then she turned back to Lexa. "What else have you got?"

"These," Lexa said. She held up a small medallion and what looked like a single stud-style earring. She walked over to where Rena and Nemo stood. She handed the medallion to Rena. "I noticed your St. Therese medal," she said. "This one is just like it, only it has a listening device built into it. It will pick up voices from up to twenty feet away."

Rena pulled a necklace out from beneath her shirt and took it off, replacing it with the one Lexa had given her. "It's exactly like it," she said, looking at the nickel-size medal.

"I figure if Dennings noticed you wearing it before, he might not think anything of it," Lexa said. She turned to Nemo and held up the small silver stud. "And this is to replace the one in your nose."

Nemo took the jewelry and started working on switching

it out with her current piercing.

"We have to assume that Dennings will search you for devices," Lexa said to the girls. "Hopefully, he won't look too carefully at these."

"What if he does?" Nemo asked, securing the back to her piercing and turning it in her nostril.

"Then you tell him we made you wear them," said Nine.

"But our story is going to be that we ran away from here," Rena said. "So why would we be wearing anything you gave us?"

"An excellent point," said Nine. "*If* it comes to that, you tell Dennings that you *do* want to run away but that we kept such a tight leash on you that there was no way you could. So you agreed to *pretend* to run away and spy on him in order to *actually* run away."

"In that case, why wouldn't we just take out the contact lenses and throw the jewelry away once we were away from here?" said Nemo. "That's what I would do."

"Yes, you would," Nine agreed. "Unless you were afraid that not going along with us would result in some terrible consequences."

"Like what?" Nemo pressed.

"Look," said Nine. "No matter what you tell Dennings, he's going to be suspicious. He's already been found once. But from what you've told me, he's someone who thinks he's smarter than everyone else. That's what we're counting on. He doesn't really care whether you've run away or not. He only cares that he's got you."

"That's a terrible plan," Nemo said.

"Thank you," said Six. "Like I've been saying all along."

"Unless—" Nemo said thoughtfully.

"Unless what?" said Sam.

"Unless we tell him right up front that we have these," said Nemo. "Or one of us does, anyway. Or maybe not tell him outright but somehow let him know, like we're afraid to say it out loud. That way, we look like we were forced into it and are asking for his help."

Nine looked thoughtful. "That's not a terrible idea," he said.

"Can I see you outside?" Six said to him. "You and Sam."

She walked out of the room and into the hallway. When Sam and Nine joined her, she turned on Nine.

"Are you insane?" she said. "That's a *terrible* idea. All of this is a terrible idea."

"I know you're not exactly thrilled about it," Nine said. "But—"

"But nothing," Six said. "These are kids, Nine. And we're throwing them into the fire."

"Rena is the one who suggested it," Nine reminded her.

"That doesn't mean it's a good idea!" said Six. "Rena wants to save her friend. She isn't thinking about what could happen."

"I don't know," Sam said cautiously. "She saw what he could do in Texas, remember? She's already been in the fire once, and she came out of it in one piece."

"Because we went in and pulled her out!" said Six.

"Which we'll do again if we have to," Nine said. "They're both going to be implanted with microchips that will allow us to track them. If they get into any trouble—"

"*When* they get into trouble," said Six. "Let's not even pretend that they'll be able to get in there, find Yo-Yo and Edwige and Ghost, and get out again without anything happening. Something is going to happen."

"And *when* something happens, we'll be there to help them," Nine said.

Six looked at Sam. "Are you going to back me up here?"

Sam took a breath. "I know what you're saying," he replied. "And I agree with you that there's a very likely chance that something will happen that will require us to go in." He hesitated.

"But?" said Six.

"But I think it's our best chance of getting inside the operation before even more kids are hurt."

Six started to reply, but Sam continued.

"We don't know what condition Kirk is in," he said. "So even if Dennings has him, we don't know if he can do anything. And we don't know exactly how many kids he has with him already. But we know there are a lot of them."

"And you think it's worth risking two more kids to *maybe* find them and *maybe* get inside?"

"I know what I would do if it was you in there," Sam said.

"That's not the same, and you know it," said Six. "You know how to use your Legacy. You've got experience."

"I didn't when all this started," said Sam. "Not when I

saved John from the Mogs. Not when I promised to help you all fight. Then I was just ordinary."

"You were never ordinary," Six said. "And you had me and John and Nine and everyone else to help you when you needed it."

"And Rena and Nemo have you and me and Nine to help them when *they* need it," Sam said.

"And Lexa," Nine added.

Six let out a groan of frustration. "All right," she said. "I'm going to be outvoted anyway. But when this all goes to hell—"

"Then we'll let you say you told us so," said Nine.

"Like she wouldn't anyway," Sam said.

Nine looked at Six. "Those girls need to think you believe in them," he said. "Okay?"

Six nodded. She did believe in Nemo and Rena. She believed that they wanted to help their friends. She also remembered that wanting to help hadn't stopped Sam from ending up in a Mog prison and that she and the other Garde hadn't been able to keep him out of there. True, Dennings wasn't a Mog, but he was potentially just as dangerous. She kept these thoughts to herself, though. All she could do was prepare and protect Nemo and Rena to the best of her abilities.

"Let's go back in, then," Nine said, heading for the door to Lexa's office. "Smiles, everyone. Remember, we're one big, happy family."

"I'd forgotten how annoying he is," Six said to Sam as they followed him.

Sam put his arm around her. "Funny. I think I heard him saying something like that to Lexa about you earlier."

Back in the office, Rena and Nemo were practicing picking up conversations with their jewelry microphones. When Six and the others came in, Nemo said, "Are you done arguing?"

"We weren't arguing," Nine and Six said in unison.

Nemo looked at Rena. "They were arguing," they said in unison.

"Is everything working the way it's supposed to?" Six asked Lexa, changing the subject.

"Yep," said Lexa. "And until it doesn't, we'll be able to see what they see and hear what they hear."

"All right then," Six said. "Now what?"

"Now Rena texts the number she used before to reach Dennings's people," Sam said. "And then we wait."

Six turned to Rena. "Might as well do it now."

Rena took out her phone and pressed some buttons, calling up the number. "What do I say?"

"Here," Nemo said, taking it from her and starting to type. Her thumb and fingers flew over the keys. Before Six could tell her to wait a minute, she hit send. "There," she said. "Done."

"What did you say?" Six asked her.

"I asked if he wanted to Netflix and chill," Nemo said,

handing the phone back to Rena. "What do you think I said? I said I wanted to talk to him about something important. Well, I guess it's Rena who wants to talk to him."

Nine looked at Six. "She's like a mini you," he said. "It's like you have a kid, only she's almost the same age as you are."

"So more of a twin, then," Nemo suggested. "Anyway, that's what I said. Was that wrong?"

"No," Six answered after a moment. "It's fine. But next time, maybe run it by us first."

There was a dinging sound. Rena checked her phone. "Looks like next time is now," she said. "He responded. Well, somebody responded."

"What did they say?" Sam asked her.

"It says, 'I'm listening.' What do I write back?"

Nemo reached for the phone, but Rena held it out of her reach. Nemo rolled her eyes.

"Tell him you need to talk," said Nine. "In person."

Rena typed. She wasn't nearly as quick as Nemo had been, but a minute later she hit send.

Again, the response came quickly. "He wants to meet," Rena said.

"Where?" Six asked.

"Reno, Nevada."

"How far is that?" Six asked Nine.

"If you drive, probably around four hours," Nine said.

Six looked at her watch. It was 1:27. "Tell him you'll meet him at seven," she said.

"Wait a minute," said Nine. "You can't just drop them off

like you're dropping them off at the movies or something. They're supposed to be runaways, remember? How would two kids who were running away travel?"

"I'd steal a car," Nemo said immediately.

"Bus," Rena countered. "It's the cheapest, and you're not going to get pulled over by some cop who runs your license plate."

Lexa, typing away on her keyboard, said, "Bus from San Francisco takes about the same amount of time. If we drive them, they can be on the three thirty-five and be there around eight o'clock."

"Perfect," said Nine. "Text him back," he told Rena.

As Rena typed, Nine said to Sam and Six, "You two can follow in one of our cars. Once they make contact and find out what's next, we'll go from there."

"And what will you be doing?" Six asked him.

"I have things to attend to here," Nine reminded her. "Lexa and I will be backup support."

Sam looked at Six and nodded. "Sounds like a plan," he said.

"What about clothes?" Nemo said. "We don't have anything but what we've got on."

"Probably best to keep it that way," said Nine. "If you're running away, you're only going to have what you're wearing. Unless you want to take an HGA sweatshirt."

"I'll pass," said Nemo.

"Let's get going then," said Six. She looked at Nine. "Can I borrow the car, Dad?"

Fifteen minutes later, the four of them were in a Ford Explorer, headed for San Francisco. As Sam drove, Six lectured Nemo and Rena on what to say and what to do. Finally, Rena said, "I think we've got it."

Six sighed and settled into her seat for the rest of the ride.

When they got to the bus station, she and Sam bought tickets for the girls, then walked them to the waiting bus.

"We'll be following you to Reno," Six said. "Nothing bad is going to happen. And if you need to end this at any point, you just say so and we'll move in."

Rena hugged her. "We'll be fine," she whispered into Six's ear.

"I'm not really a hugger," Nemo said.

"Shocking," Sam said. "How about a fist bump?"

"That I can do," said Nemo, raising her fist and tapping it to his outstretched one. Then she looked at Six. "Seriously," she said. "We'll be okay. But thanks for worrying."

"Get on the bus before I change my mind," said Six.

With the girls on board, she and Sam returned to the Explorer and waited for the bus to leave.

"This is a whole new side of you," Sam said.

"What are you talking about?" said Six. "I don't have sides."

Sam snorted. "You're practically a dodecahedron," he said. "And I mean this mother-hen side. You're worried about them. It's sweet."

"Take that back!" Six said.

Sam reached out and took her hand. "It's *sweet*," he repeated. "I like it."

"I don't," Six said. "This is exactly why I didn't want to get involved with the Human Garde. Too much can go wrong."

Ahead of them, the bus's lights went on. The door shut, and the bus pulled away.

Sam squeezed Six's hand. "We'll just have to make sure it doesn't," he said as he started to follow.

CHAPTER FIVE

SAM
LIBBY, MONTANA

SAM PUSHED OPEN THE DOOR OF ROOM 11 OF THE Mountain Do Motor Inn and darted inside. He shut the door behind him and set a bag of food from the Golden Dragon Chinese restaurant on the small table that stood beneath the room's single window, which, if the curtains were open, would offer a spectacular view of the parking lot.

"Dinner's here, Mrs. Hubble," he said, using the name under which he and Six were registered.

"Great," Six said, coming over to inspect the bag. "I'm starving."

"I can't believe how cold it is out there," Sam said. "My hands are freezing."

Six pulled out a plastic container and handed it to him. "Here," she said. "Hold the egg drop soup for a few minutes. That will warm you up."

"Ahh," Sam sighed. "Better. The girl at the restaurant said we're in for more snow. I guess this is unusual for this time of year."

"Thank you, climate change," Six said, tearing open a packet of soy sauce with her teeth.

"What did I miss?" Sam asked as he sank onto the room's only bed. The mattress groaned in protest.

"Not much," Six said, pouring the soy sauce over a carton of pork with black bean sauce and poking into it with a fork. "The guy they sent to meet Rena and Nemo is grilling them, trying to trip them up. But they're sticking to the script."

She indicated the television. On the screen was an image, fed from the laptop on the bed, of a coffee shop. Rena and Nemo were seated at a table, across from a bearded man wearing a red-and-black-checked lumberjack coat and a red knit hat. Because the image was being fed through the contact lens cameras each girl wore, they only saw what Nemo and Rena were looking at.

"Whose camera is that?" Sam asked.

"Nemo's" Six answered. "You can switch between them, but they're showing the same thing right now, so there's not much point."

"Those things are amazing," said Sam. "Lexa really hooked us up." He turned up the volume and listened as the trio talked. The microphones implanted in the jewelry each girl wore was also working perfectly.

"You expect me to believe they just let you walk out of

that place?" the man said. "After what went down in Texas?"

"They didn't let us do anything," Nemo said, her voice dripping with hostility. "That's the point."

"They wanted everything their way," Rena added, perfectly playing her role as the more levelheaded one. "I don't like that. Besides, I want to see my friend Yo-Yo. Make sure he's okay. That's all I've ever wanted, even back in Texas. And Nemo wants to see her friend Ghost."

The man nodded at Nemo. "What is it you do again?"

"Breathe underwater," Nemo said.

The man snorted. "That'll come in real handy around here," he said. "And you make toys come alive?" he said to Rena.

"Something like that," Rena confirmed.

The man shook his head. "I don't know why the hell Dennings is taking a chance on you two," he said. "Personally, I think you're more trouble than you're worth."

"I guess it's a good thing you're not in charge, then, isn't it?" Nemo said.

The man pointed a finger at her. "Watch your mouth. You ain't there yet. I'd be more than happy to leave your asses right here."

"Whatever," Nemo said.

"She's pushing it," Sam remarked.

"You sound surprised," said Six.

"You still think we shouldn't have let her go, don't you?" said Sam.

"It doesn't matter now," Six answered. "She's there. Now

we just have to hope this guy buys their story."

A day had passed since Rena had boarded the bus in San Francisco. In Reno, they had met with a woman who grilled them just as the man in the coffee shop was, asking the same kinds of questions he was asking. Then they had been driven to a rest area and put into a van.

And then they had disappeared.

Sam and Six, watching the camera feeds and following the van at a discreet distance, had seen the feeds turn to static. Not knowing if the tech had failed or if Rena and Nemo had been physically injured or even killed, they'd panicked. But a minute or so later, the feeds were restored, and Nemo and Rena were staring at a stocky, pug-nosed teenage boy with buzzed blond hair who was holding on to them. They had been teleported to a new location, presumably to prevent anyone following them from knowing where they were going.

Fortunately, their microchips pinpointed their position in Montana. Six and Sam, who had trailed them the whole way, quickly detoured to an airport, where McKenna arranged for a private jet to take them to Montana. There, they had holed up at the motel nearby to monitor the situation. Given that James Kirk's tracking device was putting him in the same general vicinity, they hoped this would be the final stop.

The man in the coffee shop stood up. "Come on," he said.

"Here we go," said Sam.

The man walked out of the restaurant. Nemo and Rena followed. Nemo turned to look at Rena, and for a moment

Rena's face was looking out at Six and Sam. She looked exhausted.

The man walked to a pickup truck. "Get in," he ordered.

Nemo went in first, with Rena following. The man got in on the other side and started the truck.

"Where are we going this time?" Rena asked.

"Find out soon enough," the man said as he pulled out of the parking lot.

"Should we follow them?" Sam asked Six.

Six shook her head. "I think this is it," she said. "Besides, these roads are so deserted, it would be hard to stay out of sight. Let's wait and see where they end up. Then we can go in."

The truck wound its way up into the mountains, turning off the highway onto less-traveled roads until finally it was on what wasn't much more than a dirt lane twisting through the forest. Eventually, after almost two hours of driving, even this ended, and the man pulled the truck over.

"Get out," he said.

The two girls got out. Because of the darkness in the woods, it was difficult to make out much more than shadows. Nemo and Rena stood together. "Now what?" Rena asked.

"Now, we walk," the man told her.

"Into the woods?" Nemo objected.

"Into the woods," said the man.

"I've seen this movie," Nemo said. "We'll get ten yards in there, and you'll shoot us or something."

The man laughed gruffly. "You think we'd waste all this time just to kill you?" he said. He reached into his coat pocket and pulled out a pistol, waving it at them. "But don't try anything stupid."

He disappeared into the trees. Rena and Nemo followed. The snowfall wasn't deep this far into the forest, but it was thick enough to make walking difficult, especially as they were going uphill. For the next ninety minutes, they hiked farther and farther into the wilderness. The sound of their labored breathing filled the motel room.

"I feel guilty sitting here in a warm room while they're out there," Sam said, turning the sound down. "It's like watching a horror movie."

Six, who was testing the small receiver on which the girls' transmitters could be followed, set the device down. "There are all kinds of hunting cabins in those mountains," she said. "It's easy to disappear in there. My guess is that Dennings has found something like that. What we don't know—yet—is whether he's moved the whole operation here or just part of it."

"I don't think even he is stupid enough to risk having us catch him with all those kids again," said Sam.

"Agreed," Six said. "And that's what worries me. Why is he so willing to take these two in after what happened? And if Kirk is really here, what's he doing with him? I don't feel good about any of this."

On the television, the hikers stepped out of the trees. They were standing at the bottom of yet another mountain.

Snow fell lightly but steadily. Halfway up the mountain, lights burned in the darkness.

Nemo groaned. "More walking?"

"Relax, princess," their guide said. "Your chariot is here."

He pointed to an ATV parked at the edge of the trees. "Get on," he said.

"You're only supposed to put one person on the back of those," Nemo objected as the man straddled the front seat and started up the four-wheeler.

"Then you'd better not fall off," the man said. "I ain't a taxi service, so if you don't come now, you walk the rest of the way."

"Come on," Rena said to Nemo. "We'll be all right."

The two girls climbed onto the ATV. Reluctantly, Rena put her arms around the man in front, while Nemo squeezed in behind her and slipped her arms around Rena.

"Hang on tight," the man said, laughing, as he gunned the engine.

Viewed through Nemo's camera, the landscape bounced and shook as the ATV moved up the mountain. Its tires threw snow and dirt up in the air, and the girls grunted every time the vehicle leaped over a bump or slid sideways.

"I think I'm getting motion sickness," Sam said, watching their progress.

Nemo closed her eyes, and for a few minutes the screen was black, and all they heard was the sound of the ATV's engine. Then that came to an end. Nemo opened her eyes. They were parked next to a lodge. The three riders got off the four-wheeler, and the man led Nemo and Rena to a set of wooden stairs.

At the top, they entered through a doorway and went into a large, open room. The building was a cabin, and the walls were bare logs. Timbers crossed overhead, supporting the ceiling. Everywhere Nemo looked, her camera sent back images of animal heads mounted on the walls: bears, elk, deer, and mountain lions stared back with glassy eyes. There were birds, too, and fish, along with hunting rifles and traps. At one end of the room, a huge stone fireplace blazed with a crackling fire. The room was also lit by a huge chandelier made from deer antlers. Large windows provided a view of the woods below, which now were silvered with moonlight.

"Somebody likes shooting things," Six remarked.

As Rena and Nemo looked around, Jagger Dennings came walking into the room. He strode over to the girls and stopped.

"Didn't think I'd be seeing you again so soon," he said to Rena.

Rena shrugged. "Me either," she said. "But you know how it is. Things change."

"Yeah," Dennings said. "They do." He gestured around the room. "Although I guess I should thank you and your Garde friends. Because of them, I got to move into this place. A little nicer than the other one, don't you think?"

Rena shrugged. "It's pretty sweet. Smaller, though. Doesn't look like there's room enough for everybody."

"Ah," Dennings said. "Smart girl. You're right about that.

Not everybody made the move with me."

"Why's that?" Rena asked.

"Let's just say we've refocused our business model," Dennings replied. "Nothing to worry about, though. We can still use someone like you." He turned his attention to Nemo. "And I see you've brought along a friend. You didn't like what the HGA was offering either?"

"Not much," Nemo said.

Dennings continued to look at her without saying anything. Nemo stared back. Finally, Dennings said, "Well, I'm sure we'll find something to do with you." Turning his attention to Rena, he said, "That reminds me. I've got somebody who's been waiting to see you." He turned and called over his shoulder, "Sparky! Come on out. Your friend is here."

A young man appeared in the doorway. Tall and thin, with dark skin and close-cropped hair, he seemed nervous. He hesitated before running into the room and heading for Rena.

"Yo-Yo!" Rena shouted, and opened her arms. She hugged her friend for a long time. As she did, Six and Sam saw his mouth moving.

"Switch over to Rena's feed," Six said.

Sam did. By then, Rena and Yo-Yo had parted.

"I'll back it up a little," Sam said.

They watched Yo-Yo's mouth moving again. This time they heard him speak.

"You shouldn't have come back," he whispered. "I'm so sorry."

Sam switched back to the live feed. Now Yo-Yo was standing silently, looking at the floor.

"I love a reunion," Dennings said, clapping Yo-Yo on the back. "You and your friend have a lot of catching up to do, eh, Sparky?" To Rena he said, "Sparky here has some big news. Really exciting news."

"Yeah?" Rena said. "What's that?"

Dennings beamed. "He got his Legacy back. Well, Drac gave it back to him, after he showed us he deserved it."

Rena looked at her friend. Yo-Yo was still looking down at the floor.

"Come on, Sparky," Dennings said. "Show her."

Yo-Yo lifted his hands and cupped them in front of his body. He stared at the space between them. A few seconds later, a spark appeared, and a small flame burst to life. Yo-Yo held it in his hands as it burned.

"Look at that!" Dennings said. "Good as new!"

"What's this about?" Sam said to Six. "Why does Yo-Yo look so scared?"

"I don't know," Six said. "But I don't like it."

Back in the lodge, Yo-Yo pulled his hands apart, and the flame disappeared. He put his hands at his sides and hung his head again, as if using his power was somehow embarrassing or shameful. Dennings put an arm around the boy's shoulders, making Yo-Yo flinch.

"Pretty great, huh?" he said to Rena and Nemo.

"How'd you do it?" Rena asked.

Dennings held up a finger and wagged it. "That's a secret,"

he said. "The important thing is that Sparky here is back in business. And just in time."

"In time for what?" Nemo asked.

Dennings took his arm from around Yo-Yo's shoulders. "To play a game," he answered. "You two like games, right?"

Nemo looked over at Rena. "Depends on the game," Rena said.

Dennings nodded. "Sure," he said. "I get it. I promise you, this game is a good one. It's kind of like hide-and-seek. You've played that one, right, when you were kids? It's easy. Somebody hides, and somebody else tries to find them. You don't get found, then you win. In this case, if you don't get caught, I let you back in."

"And if we do get found?" Rena said.

Dennings frowned. "Well, then, I'm afraid you're out of the game."

"What's he setting them up for?" Sam said. "I don't like this. At all."

"Why does Yo-Yo need his Legacy back to play?" asked Rena.

"Let's just say it could come in handy," said Dennings. He looked at his watch. "The seekers should be here in a couple of hours. Then we can start."

"Who are these seekers?" Rena asked. "Other kids with Legacies?"

"No," Dennings answered. "No Legacies to worry about." He smiled, but there was nothing friendly about it. "But you'll want to make sure they don't catch you. Now, let's go over the rules. You'll get a fifteen-minute head start. Then the seekers will come after you. They'll have twelve hours to find you."

"Twelve hours?" said Nemo. "You expect us to hide out there in the cold woods all night?"

Dennings nodded. "You can always use Sparky's Legacy to start a fire to keep warm," he said. "Of course, that would probably give your location away. It's up to you. The game ends at ten o'clock tomorrow morning. Like I said, if you haven't been caught, you're in."

"How many seekers are there?" Rena asked.

"Good question," said Dennings. "Two. And to make things a little fairer for you, I'm adding one more person to your team. Cutter, bring their other teammate out."

The man standing behind the girls left the room. He returned pushing someone in front of him. The man's hands were tied behind his back, and he stumbled as Dennings's henchman shoved him to his knees.

When he looked up, Sam and Six were looking at the face of James Kirk.

CHAPTER SIX

RENA
THE MOUNTAINS OF NORTHWEST MONTANA

"I'VE GOT TO GET THESE CUFFS OFF," JAMES Kirk said.

They were running through the snow, or trying to, but Kirk kept tripping and falling. Already, five of their fifteen minutes had been used up. Soon, the seekers would be after them.

"Let's keep moving," Nemo said. "If we just keep going, we can get out of here and back to the highway."

"It's too far," Kirk said. "We're in the middle of nowhere. That's the whole point. This isn't about hiding. This is about fighting back. But I need my hands free." He nodded at Yo-Yo. "See if you can melt them."

He turned around so that the plastic zip tie securing his wrists together was facing Yo-Yo. The boy reached out and placed his fingertips on it. "This might be a little warm," he warned.

A spark appeared, turning into a small flame. Kirk gritted his teeth as the plastic heated up. As soon as it was soft, he pulled his wrists apart. He scooped up some snow and rubbed it on the burns. "Thanks," he said.

"Now what?" Rena asked.

Kirk looked around. "We go farther up," he said. "It's harder for us, but it's also harder for someone chasing us to have to climb."

They started to move. Dennings had sent them out without anything but what they had on them, which wasn't much. Rena and Nemo hadn't been planning to hike around in the woods and were trying to sell their runaway story, so they had dressed regularly and didn't really bring anything with them. Rena's sneakers were already soaked through.

"Do you two have any way of communicating with Six and Sam?" Kirk asked as they made their way through the forest.

"Yeah," Rena said. "We've got mikes and cameras."

"And tracking devices," Nemo added.

"Can they talk to us?" asked Kirk.

"No," Rena said. "But they can hear everything we say."

"Okay," said Kirk. "Sam and Six, I don't know our exact location, but I'm guessing you can follow our tracking devices. I'll try to keep us away from whoever is following us long enough for you to get here. Dennings kept me in solitary, so I don't know how many people are up here.

Sorry I can't be more helpful."

"Why'd he take you, anyway?" Nemo asked. "And how?"

"Same way he got Ghost and disappeared back in New Orleans," Kirk answered. "Someone with a teleportation Legacy. One second I was sitting in the cockpit, and the next I felt a hand on my shoulder. By the time I turned around, I was in the back of a van and someone was sticking a needle in my arm. I woke up in a cell in the basement of that lodge. The only reason I know where we are is Dennings talked about it. Almost like he wanted to be sure I knew."

"Was Ghost in there with you?" Nemo asked him.

"I don't know," said Kirk. "Like I said, I was kept away from everybody. I don't think so, though. I get the feeling there aren't that many people here. Yo-Yo, do you know?"

"They just brought me here yesterday," Yo-Yo said. "Told me I was getting a second chance to prove I belonged with them. They've been doing that—bringing kids here a few at a time."

Rena, already having a difficult time breathing while moving, asked, "Who are these seekers, anyway? People who work for Dennings?"

"I don't know," Kirk said. "This is the first I've heard of them."

"They don't work for Dennings," said Yo-Yo. His voice was tight. "They *pay* him."

"You mean they're his bosses?" said Kirk.

"No, his customers."

Kirk stopped. He looked at Yo-Yo. "What are you saying?"

Yo-Yo checked behind him. "We've got to go," he said. "We've got to hide. Quick."

"I need to know what we're up against here," Kirk pressed.

Yo-Yo licked his lips. "I don't know, exactly," he said. "But I heard some things. There are people paying to play this game—people who want to see if they've got what it takes to catch kids with Legacies." He hesitated. "And I heard something else. Heard it's not exactly hide-and-seek. Heard it's more like hunting."

"Hunting?" Rena said.

He nodded. "You see all those trophies hanging on the walls in that place? This here's a place where people come to hunt game. And right now, I think they're hunting us."

"And what happens if they catch us?" asked Nemo.

Yo-Yo didn't say anything.

"Yo-Yo?" said Rena. "What happens?"

"I don't know," he said. "I heard different things."

"Like what?" said Nemo.

"Like some of the kids who got sent here didn't come back," Yo-Yo told her.

"All right," Kirk said. "I think we should keep moving. Who these people are doesn't really matter at this point. What does is that they don't catch us, right?"

"And how do we make sure of that?" Nemo asked. "None of us can turn invisible, or teleport, or fly. The only one with a useful Legacy is Yo-Yo, and like Dennings said, we can't use it without giving our location away."

"We'll worry about that when we have to," said Kirk.

"Right now, let's get some more distance between us and them. Do any of you have a watch?"

"I do," Rena said. She looked at it. "It's been ten minutes."

"We won't get far in five more minutes," Kirk said. "So let's make them count."

"Maybe we should split up," Nemo suggested.

"No," said Kirk. "I take it none of you has wilderness training. But I do. Follow me."

They pushed on. The ground was getting steeper as they rose up the mountain. Making things worse, the snow had stopped and the clouds had dispersed. The moon, full and silver overhead, illuminated the woods where its light slipped in through the branches of the fir and pine trees. It was beautiful, but it also did very little to hide the four of them as they sought out a place to hide.

They were still climbing when a sound rent the air, a blast from an air horn.

"They're coming," Yo-Yo said. "The hunters." His voice shook with fear.

"What if we climb up in the trees?" Nemo suggested.

"Then there's nowhere to go if they find us," Kirk pointed out. "We need to stay on the ground." He looked around, surveying the forest. "All right. Here's the plan. We hide. We wait for whoever is coming to move past us up the mountain. Then we head down and figure out what's next."

"Maybe we could get back to the lodge and take the ATV," Rena suggested.

"We don't have the key," Nemo countered.

"I can start it without a key if we can get to it," said Kirk. "But that's later. Right now, we need to get under cover. We also need to make them think we're still going up."

"How do we do that?" asked Rena.

"You three hide," Kirk said. "Get behind or under anything you can find. Use pine branches to sweep away your footprints. I'm going to keep going so that there are tracks for them to follow. Once they've gone past me, I'll come back this way and we'll regroup and plan our next move."

He looked around at the three teenagers' faces. "It's going to be fine," he said. "Just keep calm."

"What if they find us?" Yo-Yo said.

Kirk pointed at Yo-Yo's hands. "Then you send a fireball at them and run," he said. "Now, go."

He turned and left them. Rena pointed towards a part of the forest where the trees grew more densely. "Let's go that way," she said. "There's more cover. I'll go last and wipe away the tracks. Try to step in each other's footprints so there aren't as many of them."

"How are we going to erase our prints?" Nemo asked.

"I've got an idea," said Rena.

Yo-Yo went first, taking big steps as he moved deeper into the darkness of the trees. Nemo followed. "Hey, longlegs," she said. "Can you shorten up the steps? Some of us don't walk on stilts."

Rena, going last, paused and concentrated on the snow. She focused her telekinesis and pushed, urging the snow to fill in their footprints and smooth them over. It mostly worked, and she hoped it was enough to fool their pursu-ers. At least the moonlight was shining on the prints Kirk had made leading up to and away from the hiding spot. That might save them.

The three of them found a place where two trees had fallen over. Although their branches had long since lost the needles that once covered them, the trunks were thick and provided something for them to hide behind. Nemo, Yo-Yo, and Rena crouched there in the snow, waiting. Afraid of making any noise, they didn't talk, and for a while the only sound was that of the wind moving through the branches of the trees.

Then they heard the soft crunching of footsteps on snow.

Rena, who was in the middle, reached out and took Yo-Yo's hand in one of hers and Nemo's in the other. She squeezed them gently, her heart racing. When a bird somewhere in the forest hooted, startling her, she bit her lip to keep from crying out.

Two shadows detached themselves from the darkness and moved into the moonlight.

"What did he say they could do?" said a man's voice.

"Fire," answered a woman. "That's the boy. One of the girls breathes underwater. The last one I didn't quite get. Something about bringing dolls to life."

The man snorted. "Not much of a challenge," he said. "Except maybe the fire kid. We should have asked for a dis-count."

"I think that's why he threw in the military guy," the

woman said. "At least he's got survival training."

"Looks like they all stayed together," the man remarked. "That'll make it easy."

"And boring," said the woman. "What's the fun of catching them all at once? I told you we should have gone on a big-game safari hunt instead."

"Anyone can do that," said the man. "Come on. The tracks go this way. Might as well get it over with. Didn't Dennings say if we catch them within two hours we get half our money back? We could still take that safari after all."

The two figures disappeared into the trees. Rena felt her heart slow a little, and she was able to breathe more easily again.

"Now what?" Nemo whispered.

"We wait for Kirk," said Rena. "That's the plan."

They waited. The cold had soaked right into their skin, and crouching behind the trees was uncomfortable. After what felt like an hour, Rena looked at her watch. Only ten minutes had passed.

"Where is he?" Yo-Yo said.

His voice was too loud, and Rena shushed him. A moment later, a light flickered over their heads. Someone had turned on a flashlight and was now shining it around the trees.

"I hear you," said the voice of the man they'd heard before. "Nice trick, trying to make us think you'd gone on ahead."

The three teens froze, saying nothing.

"Come on out," the man said. "Game's over. Let's all go back to the lodge and get warmed up. No sense freezing to death, kids." He laughed, and the sound sent shivers down Rena's spine.

Yo-Yo squeezed Rena's hand, and she realized they were all still linked together. She looked at her friend. He shook his head no. His eyes were wide, filled with terror.

"All right," the man said. "If you want to keep playing, we can play." A second later, a dull thud sounded, and snow tumbled down from a branch above where Rena, Nemo, and Yo-Yo were hiding. Rena looked up and saw an arrow sticking out of the tree trunk a few feet above their heads.

"I'll count to three," the man said. "If you're not out by then, we'll do this the hard way. One."

None of them moved. It was as if time had stopped. Rena felt her friends' hands in her own, but her body wouldn't move.

"Two."

Rena felt Yo-Yo's hand slip from hers. She turned her head and saw him starting to stand up. He had brought his palms together, and a ball of light was forming between his fingers. The glow was already spreading as the ball of fire grew stronger.

"Yo-Yo," Rena said.

It was too late. Yo-Yo stood up, revealing himself.

"Three," the man said, just as Yo-Yo flung his hands out. A fireball shot forward. The sound blasted through the night. A tree somewhere in the vicinity of the man burst into flame. Then Rena heard herself scream as an arrow whizzed past her head.

Another fireball was forming in Yo-Yo's hands, and he flung it at their attacker as Nemo and Rena stood up and looked around, trying to see what was going on.

"That's more like it!" the man shouted.

"Run!" Yo-Yo told the girls. "I'll take care of him."

"No," Rena objected. "We stay together."

The boy raised his arm to lob another fireball. Then he gave a shout of pain, and the ball flickered and went out. Yo-Yo hunched over, clutching his hand to his chest. "Get down!" he shouted at the girls.

"Are you okay?" Rena asked, kneeling behind the trees again.

"It grazed me," Yo-Yo said. "Hurts like a son of a bitch."

He showed her his hand. Blood was dripping from a slice on the side of his palm. Rena knew they had to bind it up, but before she could do anything, another arrow thwacked into a tree beside them.

"We're sitting ducks here," Nemo said. "We've got to move."

"What's going on?" The voice of the woman they'd heard before rang out. She sounded excited.

"They're pinned down in there," the man said triumphantly. "I think the fire starter is wounded. What did you find?"

"Nothing," the woman said.

Rena's hopes rose. She hadn't caught Kirk. But where was he?

She got her answer a moment later when he emerged from

the shadows behind them. "We need to make a run for it," he said. "Yo-Yo, can you do your thing?"

"I think so," Yo-Yo said.

"Then now's the time," said Kirk. "Biggest ball you can make. Throw it right at them, then we'll run back the way we came."

Yo-Yo nodded. He held his hands together. The wounded one was still bleeding, and it shook as he focused hard on the empty space his fingers made. There was a spark, then another. Then a ball the size of a grapefruit bloomed, swirling with orange and red flames.

"Don't miss," Kirk said.

Yo-Yo stood up and threw the ball of fire. It struck something and burst into flames. There was a scream. He had hit the man.

"Run!" Kirk shouted.

The four of them darted away from the tree. The man, who was on fire, was staggering around as the woman yelled for him to drop to the ground. Nemo, Yo-Yo, and Rena dashed into the trees. Kirk, bringing up the rear, shouted at them to hurry.

Rena heard a grunt. She turned and saw Kirk stumbling towards her. The front of his jacket was open, and on his chest a stain was blooming around the shaft of an arrow that protruded from his body. Then there was another whistling sound, and another stain. Kirk jerked and his mouth opened, blood spraying out and covering the snow.

He lurched forward. Rena held out her hands. Kirk

clutched at her, his fingers grabbing at her necklace. He fell, and the necklace was pulled away with him. He didn't get up.

"Rena!" Yo-Yo shouted. "Come on!"

Rena looked down at the body in the snow. She bent to retrieve her necklace, and an arrow whizzed over her head, making her fall back without the piece of jewelry. She got to her feet, turned, and ran into the darkness.

CHAPTER SEVEN

SIX
THE MOUNTAINS OF NORTHWEST MONTANA

SIX STOPPED WALKING SO ABRUPTLY THAT SAM almost ran into her.

"What?" he said.

"Did you hear that?" Six asked.

The in-ear receiver she wore was tuned to Rena's transmitter, while Sam was receiving Nemo's feed. Although the wrist monitor Six wore was receiving the video feeds from both girls' contact lens cameras, the smallness of the screen and the darkness of the woods made it impossible to tell what was going on.

"The shouting?" said Sam. "Yeah. Why? Did you hear something else?"

Six nodded. "Rena must be closer to them than Nemo is," she said. "Something happened."

"Is he dead?" said a voice in her ear. It wasn't Rena's and didn't sound like Nemo or Yo-Yo either.

There was silence, then some scratchy sounds, as if something was being dragged through the snow. Then a woman's voice said, "He is."

"Good," said the first voice. There was an odd quality to it, as if the speaker was in pain. "He was the only one with any survival skills. Without him they won't know what to do."

"The boy can still shoot fire," said the woman.

"Yeah, I noticed that," the man replied.

"Relax," said the woman. "It only burned your jacket and part of your arm. You'll live."

"It's my shooting arm," the man complained. "And in case you haven't noticed, it's pretty goddamn cold out here."

"We can stop at the lodge and get you another coat," said the woman. "They won't get far."

The man grumbled something unintelligible, and Six heard the sound of feet on snow. They were walking away from the necklace, which Six guessed Rena had either dropped or lost. But that wasn't what worried her at the moment.

"Patch through to Lexa," she said to Sam.

A few moments later, Lexa's voice was in her ear. "Where are you?"

"We just got to where they parked the truck. Now we're heading up the mountain," Six said. She hesitated a moment, then asked, "Are you still getting a read from Kirk's tracking device?"

"I'll call it up," Lexa said. Then, in a more somber tone, she said, "It's still tracking, but it's on recovery mode. No signs of life."

"Shit," Six muttered.

"What the hell is going on up there?" Lexa growled, her usually calm voice bristling with anger.

"Someone is hunting the kids," said Six. "Literally. Kirk was helping them get away, and—"

"How close are you?" Lexa interrupted.

"Not close enough," said Six. "Can you help us out?"

"I'll work with Nine on getting someone up there," said Lexa. "But it might take a little time."

"A little time is all we have," Six said.

"Got it," Lexa said, and disconnected the call.

"They're really hunting them," Sam said. "They're as sick as the humans who sided with the Mogs."

Six said nothing. Inside, she was raging with anger and frustration. She wanted to find Nemo, Rena, and Yo-Yo and get them out of there. Then, she wanted to find Jagger Dennings and the two monsters hunting the teens and show them what it was like to be on the run from someone who knew how to use her Legacies to their full extent.

She doubled the pace. She and Sam moved swiftly up the mountain, following the path that Cutter had led Rena and Nemo up. Without Rena's transmitter sending them her feed, Six tuned to Nemo's, hoping for clues as to where the three teenagers were.

What she heard was three frightened kids who were running for their lives.

"Are you sure he was dead?" Nemo said.

"No," Rena said, her voice trembling. "But I think so. There was a lot of blood."

"Fuck!" Nemo said. "This is all so fucked-up!"

"Yo-Yo, we need to bandage your hand," Rena said in a calmer voice.

Good girl, Six thought. *Keep them thinking about other things.*

"What's the plan?" Sam asked from behind her.

"First, we find these three and get them out," Six said. "After that, I don't know."

"We find the two who are hunting them."

"I'll be more than happy to spend a few minutes with them," Six told him grimly.

They reached the point where Cutter had transferred the girls to the ATV. Now, even though they were in great shape, they found the going tough. Six pushed herself on by listening to the voices of Yo-Yo, Nemo, and Rena as they looked for someplace to hide from the people pursuing them. They had bandaged Yo-Yo's hand. Now they were debating whether to go to the lodge and try to steal an ATV or keep moving on foot.

"Dennings will be waiting for us to try that," Yo-Yo argued. "I say we stay away from the lodge and head down the mountain on foot."

"My feet are blocks of ice," Nemo said. "My jeans are wet too. Rena and I aren't dressed for this. If we don't change or get warm, we're going to freeze to death before we get out of here."

"Nemo's right," said Rena. "My teeth are already chattering, and I can't feel my toes or fingertips. We've got to dry out somehow."

"Okay," Yo-Yo said. "There's another building. Some kind of barn or storage shed or something. Down the mountain a ways from the lodge. I heard Dennings tell Cutter to go get something out of it. We can try to go there. Maybe find some weapons while we're at it."

"Won't they be watching that place too?" Nemo said.

"You got a better idea?" said Yo-Yo. "Unless you can build us a cabin somehow, that's all I've got."

"We'll go there," Rena said decisively. "It can't be any more dangerous than trying to get down the mountain in this weather. Besides, Sam and Six are probably on their way to help."

"We are," Six said aloud, forgetting that they couldn't hear her.

"We have our tracking devices, and if they're listening, they'll know exactly where we are," Rena told the others. Then the sounds of talking were replaced by sounds of walking.

Six looked down at her wrist. She was wearing a GPS that showed their position in relation to the lodge, the coordinates of which she'd put in once they'd used the data from

Rena's and Nemo's tracking devices. They were only about fifteen minutes away.

All of a sudden, there was a screeching sound in her ear. She pulled the receiver out, seeing that Sam was doing the same thing.

"What was that?" Sam asked.

"I don't know," said Six, rubbing her ear. There was a ringing in her head. "It's like something fried Nemo's transmitter."

She looked at Sam as a horrible thought filled her mind. If the transmitter had been destroyed, it might mean Nemo had been hurt, or that Dennings had discovered it was a transmitter and removed it. Sam, likely realizing the same thing, said, "We've got to get to them."

Finding the barn was not difficult, and it's setting—below and away from the lodge—meant that it was hidden from anyone spying from the main building. This didn't mean it was safe, though, and Six and Sam weren't about to just walk through the doors. Instead, they first peered through one of the windows on the side. The inside appeared empty. Then Six noticed movement towards the back, plus a flicker of light.

"They're in there," she said with a sigh of relief. "But if they're smart, they've barricaded the door from inside. We need to get their attention."

Sam looked around. The barn was filled with pieces of furniture, boxes, and tools of various kinds. But one thing stuck out at him. It was an old pinball machine, sitting not far from the window. Why it was there, he had no idea. "This might do it," he said.

Concentrating his attention on the machine, he brought it to life. The lights around it suddenly flashed, and the various bells dinged as a ball was launched up the shooter lane and the flippers went wild. It wasn't the subtlest way of announcing their presence, but it did the job. A moment later, a worried-looking Nemo peered out from the shadows. Sam waved at her, hoping she would be able to tell it was him and not think someone was attacking them.

She did. She ran to the window, then to the door, which opened a crack. Sam and Six slipped inside, then they barricaded it again. Six looked at Nemo, who was trembling with cold. "Are you okay?"

Nemo nodded even as her teeth clacked together. "Yeah" she said. "Just hiding out from some nutjobs who are trying to hunt us down like a bunch of deer. The usual."

"We heard," Six said.

Rena and Yo-Yo appeared. Relief flooded their faces when they saw Sam and Six. "You made it!" Rena said.

"Let's go in the back," Six suggested. "Away from the windows."

Rena led them to the rear of the barn. There, they found a fire burning inside a large metal cauldron that hung suspended on chains from a steel frame. "Hunters and farmers use these for cleaning animals they kill," Yo-Yo explained. "You fill them with water and heat it to help de-hair hogs and such when you're skinning them. I saw my cousins do it once. It's kind of gross."

"It makes a nice fire pit," Sam said, holding his hands over the dancing flames.

"I don't think I'll ever feel warm again," Nemo said, standing close to the cauldron.

Rena looked at Sam and Six. "I think they killed James," she said, her voice breaking. "I tried to . . ." Her words trailed off, and she started to cry.

Sam hugged her. "It's okay," he said. "We're going to get out of here now."

Six addressed Yo-Yo. "Are there any other kids up there?" she asked.

"A few," Yo-Yo said.

"Ghost or Edwige?" Six said.

Yo-Yo shook his head. "I don't know who all is there. I only got here yesterday, and they kept me to myself mostly. Except when I saw Drac, and he restored my Legacy."

"Drac is here?" said Six.

"Yeah," said Yo-Yo. "Like I said, he's the one who fixed me up."

"How did—"

"Six," said Sam. "We really should get out of here."

"What's the hurry?" Dennings's voice filled the room. Everyone spun around, looking for him. Yo-Yo lifted his hands, forming a fireball. Dennings laughed. "Everybody's so ready to fight. Settle down. I just want to talk. You think I'd bring you all this way just to kill you? Not that I couldn't if I wanted to," he added. "The barn is rigged with enough explosives to send you all back to Lorien."

"What do you mean you brought us here?" said Six.

Dennings laughed again, his voice crackling through speakers in the barn's roof. "You think I wanted Rena and Whatshername?" he said. "Hell, no. I wanted *you*, Six. One of the originals. Why do you think I took your flyboy pal? Why do you think I let those two run around with their implants and their transmitters? I *wanted* you to hear everything. I *wanted* you and your human boyfriend there to come running to save these two. I knew you wouldn't let them get picked off."

"What do you want with me?" said Six.

"Like I said, I want to talk," Dennings replied. "Why don't you come up here to the lodge?"

"We've got nothing to talk about," said Six.

Dennings clucked his tongue. "I'm sorry you feel that way. Well, if you'd rather all of you die right now, I guess we'll do it your way."

"You know he means it," Yo-Yo said. "He doesn't care what happens to any of us."

"All right," Six said. "I'll come talk. But everybody else leaves."

"Sure, sure," said Dennings. "I mean, I can't promise my clients won't try to stop them, but four against two is pretty decent odds." He laughed. "Not that it helped your pilot."

Six swore and started to say something, but Sam put his hand on her arm. "I can handle this," he whispered. "It's two bad guys. I'll get everybody out, take them to safety, and come back. I'm pretty sure you can handle yourself." He smiled and lifted an eyebrow. "Okay?"

"No," said Six. "But I guess that's the plan."

"Come to the lodge," Dennings said. "Alone. And no one else leaves that barn until you're inside. I'll tell them when they can go. Oh, and don't try the going-invisible trick or everyone else dies."

His voice seemed to evaporate, and the barn was once again still except for the crackling of the fire.

"He's probably still listening," Nemo said.

"It doesn't matter," said Six. "Here's the plan. I go up there. When he says you can leave, you get out of here."

"That's not much of a plan," said Nemo. "What's to stop him from blowing this place up once you're there?"

"Because if he does, I'll tear that lodge—and him—to pieces," Six said. She spoke loudly, assuming that Nemo was right about Dennings listening in. "Besides," she added in a whisper. "McKenna knows exactly where we are and is sending help."

"Dennings will just move again," said Yo-Yo.

"He's not the one I care about," Six said. "You guys are. All right. I'm going."

They walked to the barn door. Six removed the boards they'd used to hold it shut from the inside, opened the door, and looked outside. She didn't see anything suspicious, but that didn't mean there was nothing out there. She turned to Sam, leaned in, and kissed him. "Be smart," she said. "I'll see you soon."

She slipped into the dark. Sam pulled the door shut behind her.

Six walked up the slope towards the lodge. She knew Sam was capable of handling himself, but still she worried. He had three other people to take care of—three people who had been through a lot and were frightened, exhausted, and edgy. She didn't know who those people hunting them were, but they'd already proved that they were more than willing to kill.

She passed through a copse of trees, momentarily engulfed in darkness, then emerged into the moonlight again. Ahead of her, the lodge loomed against the backdrop of the full moon. A lone figure stood on the porch, looking down at her. He waved.

"Come on up," Dennings called out.

Six mounted the stairs. "Well," she said. "What do you want to talk about?"

A second later she felt a sharp sting at her neck. Her hand flew to the spot, and her fingers felt something fuzzy and sharp. She pulled the tiny dart away and looked at it. Already her vision was fading. She tried to attack Dennings, but her body went limp. As she fell, he caught her.

"Oh, there are so many things to talk about," he said as he dragged her through the door and into the house. His voice sounded very far away. "Right after you see the doc."

CHAPTER EIGHT

SAM

THE MOUNTAINS OF NORTHWEST MONTANA

SAM LOOKED AT THE THREE TEENAGERS WAITING for his instructions. "You guys ready to get out of here?"

"Is Six going to be okay?" Nemo asked.

"Sure she is," Sam said. "She's faced way worse than Dennings. I'd be more worried about him than her."

Nemo snorted. "I don't care what happens to him," she said. "I hope Six beats his ass from one end of Montana to the other."

"She just might," said Sam, stifling a laugh.

"Okay, kiddies." Dennings's voice crackled through the barn. "Time to go. Good luck." He laughed loudly, and then there was silence.

"Okay," Sam said. "Let's move. Remember the plan—we get down the mountain. That's it. If we run into trouble, you let me handle it. And if for some reason we get separated, just keep going *down*. Get somewhere warm and dry, if you can. I can find you using your implants."

"What if something happens to you?" Yo-Yo said. "Those hunters out there mean business."

"The dude took down a Mogadorian warship," Nemo said. "I think he's got this." She looked at Sam, who was surprised that she knew about that. "Nine told me."

"You said there was an ATV, right?" Sam asked.

Rena nodded. "Back at the lodge."

"That would make things a lot easier," Sam said. "You three could take it and get out of here. Let's try that first."

He opened the barn door again, ready to leave. Before he could, an arrow embedded itself in the wood beside his head. Sam slammed the door.

"They found us," Yo-Yo cried. "Now what?"

"Stay away from the windows," Sam ordered. "Get into the back."

Nemo, Yo-Yo, and Rena did as he said, crouching down and moving into the rear of the barn. Sam stayed where he was, surveying the contents of the barn. Mostly it was just junk. But there were some tools—hoes, rakes, an axe—that could be used as weapons. *Except that the people out there have a crossbow,* he thought.

He risked a peek out one of the windows. The moonlight revealed nothing. But of course the people hunting them would stay hidden. Were they just going to wait out Sam and the others? Or were they planning something else?

He got down and retreated to the back of the barn, where he found Rena, Yo-Yo, and Nemo busily assembling something that looked vaguely like a large human figure made of boards, tools, and other things.

"What are you doing?" he asked.

"Nemo had an idea," Rena said.

"You know how Rena makes things come alive?" said Nemo as she used rope to affix a rusty sickle to the end of a broom handle. "Well, I thought we could make a kind of doll, and she could animate it."

The figure had a scarecrow-like appearance, an assemblage of odds and ends. And Sam was doubtful that it would even stand up successfully, let alone move.

"I've never done it with something this big," Rena said. "But I can try."

A faint thwacking sound came from outside.

"Why are they shooting arrows into the side of the barn?" Nemo wondered.

"As a warning?" Rena suggested.

Yo-Yo pointed to the nearest window. "No," he said. "To set it on fire."

Flames reflected in the window glass crackled eerily, and smoke drifted across the panes. The fire caught quickly, licking around the window frames.

"This place is going to go up fast," Sam said. "Especially if there really are explosives rigged. We need to get out."

Nemo stood back, looking at the Frankenstein's monster they'd created. "It needs a head," she said.

Yo-Yo pointed to the mounted head of a black bear that sat atop a stack of wooden crates. "How about that?"

A window shattered as a flaming arrow pierced it and flew into a pile of cardboard boxes. The dry material burst into flame, which crawled hungrily up the sides.

"It'll have to do," said Rena, helping Yo-Yo drag the bear head down. They tied the head to the rake handle neck, where it hung heavily.

"All right," Yo-Yo said to Rena. "Do your thing. It's getting real smoky in here."

Rena took a deep breath. She closed her eyes and held her hands out over their creation. Nothing happened. She wiggled her finger like Sam had seen her do in her videos, pretending to sprinkle magical dust over the lifeless form. Still nothing.

"I think it's too big," Rena said, frustration edging her voice.

"You can do it, Rena," said Nemo. "Picture it getting up and breaking out of here."

Rena tried again. Sam could see the strain in her face as she attempted to raise the creature. The heat and smoke were building up in the barn, and he knew they had only another minute or two before they would have to make a run for it. He was about to tell Rena to give up.

Then there was the scraping of metal on metal. One of the scarecrow's arms moved, lifting off the ground and rubbing against its snow-shovel leg. Rena gasped, and the arm clattered back to the ground.

"It's working!" Yo-Yo said. "Keep going!"

"It's hard," Rena said. "I can feel it draining the power out of me." But again she concentrated, this time holding her hands out with the palms facing the creature.

It moved. Tried to sit up. With no knees, it was struggling. Nemo and Sam went to it and lifted it. The thing towered over them and wobbled as they tried to steady it. Then it suddenly seemed to find its feet. Sam and Nemo let go, and it stood on its own.

"Can you make it walk?" Sam asked Rena.

The girl nodded, clearly already worn-out. The bear-headed thing moved, its makeshift limbs animated by her Legacy. It ambled towards the barn doors, passing through the smoke without stopping. Sam and the others followed, with Nemo and Yo-Yo helping Rena walk while focusing her attention on the giant figure.

Sam unblocked the barn door. "Stand away," he told the others. "Once this opens, all hell will break loose out there."

The others did as he said. Only the cobbled-together beast remained next to Sam. "When I open the door, send it out," Sam told Rena. "And whatever you can make it do, do it."

He opened the door using his telekinesis. Then Rena worked her magic, and the thing went striding out of the barn. Sam motioned for the others to come with him.

Outside, the two hunters had emerged from hiding, thinking that they were going to pick off their quarry easily. Instead, they found themselves confronted by something out of a horror film. Confused, they just stood there, looking at the thing coming towards them.

A spark flew from the burning barn and lit on the handle of the scythe that formed one of the arms. It started to burn. As if feeling it, the creature lifted its arm in the air and began to swing it from side to side.

"Come on," Sam said to the others, using the distraction as cover to make an escape.

Yo-Yo and Nemo followed him as he ran for the cover of the woods. But Rena remained standing behind the monster. Sam stopped and turned to go back for her, then paused. Backlit by the burning barn, Rena looked like some kind of sorcerer commanding her creation to do her bidding. She raised her hands, and the scarecrow moved with her. It was burning now, too, and probably wouldn't last much longer.

Rena pushed her hands out, as if shoving the giant thing, and it took a step towards the hunters. Startled out of their initial shock, they began shooting wildly, the arrows cutting through string and wood. One of the creature's legs buckled, and for a moment it seemed about to come apart. But it held, and took another step.

"What the hell is this thing?" the man shouted to the woman beside him.

She didn't answer. But the bear-headed thing did. It swung its scythe arm again. This time it connected with the man's neck, slicing through it as if cutting down a stalk of corn. His body slumped to the ground while his head rolled away across the snow, leaving a bloody trail.

Rena sank to her knees. The creature listed. Sam ran to Rena and picked her up, dragging her away as the thing she had been commanding fell apart, its rope tendons shredding as the fire destroyed them. It toppled onto the woman, who screamed as she fell to the ground under the rain of farm implements and wood.

"Can you walk?" Sam asked Rena.

The girl nodded but didn't speak. She and Sam rejoined Nemo and Yo-Yo.

"That was amazing," Nemo told Rena as the four of them began to move towards the lodge and the waiting ATV.

"I could feel it," Rena said weakly. "It *wanted* to fight. It did exactly what we built it to do."

"Talk later," Sam said. "We need to find that four-wheeler."

When they got to the lodge, Sam looked for the ATV. He found it right where Nemo and Rena had told him it would be. Staying under cover of the trees, he connected with the machine and started it, directing it to drive over to where they were hiding.

"Who knows how to drive one of these?" Sam asked.

"I do," said Yo-Yo. "My cousin has one we drive around out in the country."

"Get on," Sam said.

Yo-Yo swung his leg over the seat of the four-wheeler. Sam instructed the engine to start, and it revved to life. "Rena and Nemo, you're riding shotgun," he said.

Rena was seated, and Nemo was about to get on when

Sam felt a stabbing pain in his leg and his knee buckled. Looking down, he saw the fletched end of an arrow protruding from his thigh.

"Go!" Sam yelled at Yo-Yo, who wasted no time taking off. Sam grabbed Nemo's wrist and hobbled away, pulling her with him into the darkness. Ignoring the burning sensation radiating through his leg, he limped on, but every step was torture.

"We need to stop," Nemo said.

"We can't," Sam said. "She'll know we didn't all get away, and she'll be coming for us."

"Well, we can't move fast enough with you hurt," Nemo said. "We're going to have to figure something out."

Sam thought. He tried to remember what he knew about the lodge and the surrounding area from the aerial photographs McKenna had sent them.

"There's a lake," he said. "On the other side of the lodge. They use it for fishing."

"How far?" Nemo asked.

"Not close," said Sam. "But I think I can make it."

"And what do we do when we get there?"

"There might be a small cabin," said Sam. "Someplace to hide."

Nemo nodded. She put her arm around Sam's waist, and he threw his arm around her shoulders. Moving as quickly as he could, they headed in the direction of the lake. It was slow going, and at any moment Sam expected the remaining hunter to show up, but for some reason, she didn't. This worried Sam almost more than if she had, but he pressed on, hoping their luck would hold out.

When they came to the lake, they were disappointed. There was no cabin. However, out on the frozen surface of the water was a fishing hut. It would have to do.

Carefully, Sam and Nemo stepped out onto the ice. Using a sliding technique, they edged farther out, shuffling across the snow-dusted surface.

"Is it going to hold?" Nemo asked.

"It should," Sam said. "Otherwise the fishing hut wouldn't be there."

They were about twenty yards from shore, and the fishing hut was still impossibly far off, when a voice called to them.

"Not the smartest place to go," the woman called out.

Sam and Nemo stopped. They turned and looked at the shadowy figure watching them from the shore.

"That was some trick you pulled back at the barn," the woman said. "Impressive. But I don't see any—whatever that was—to help you here."

Sam's heart sank. She was right. He had made a choice, and it was the wrong one.

"Let her go," he shouted. "She's just a girl."

"How noble of you," the woman said. "But I paid for her, and I'm going to take her. If nothing else, it's payback for what you did to William."

"I wish I had a different Legacy," Nemo muttered. "If I could make fireballs like Yo-Yo, I'd toast her ass."

Sam, looking down, had an idea. "You've got exactly

the Legacy we need," he said. He concentrated on the ice, focusing his telekinetic ability and envisioning tiny cracks forming underneath them. He couldn't break the ice itself—it was too thick—but he could manipulate it a little bit. He heard the ice creak and groan. It was working.

Next, he focused on the water, drawing it up into the tiny fissures he'd made. The ice cracked loudly.

"What are you doing?" Nemo whispered. "We're going to fall through!"

"Exactly," Sam said. "And when that happens, you do your thing and swim for the fishing hut. There should be a hole in the ice."

"What about you? You can't breathe underwater."

"Well, you'd better swim fast," Sam said. Then, shouting for the benefit of the woman on the shore, he said, "The ice is giving way!"

The ice splintered. A hole appeared, and Sam and Nemo fell through it into the frigid waters of the lake. Sam had taken a breath before plunging in, but the shock of the cold almost forced it out of his lungs. His fingers clung tightly to Nemo's sleeve as they sank deeper into the dark water.

He forced himself to kick his legs. The pain was excruciating, but the icy water dulled it somewhat. Together, they swam up until their heads bumped against the ice. The full moon penetrated the inches of frozen water, but just barely, and Nemo and Sam moved through a twilight world of hazy shapes and bubbles as he took them towards what he hoped was the fishing hut.

More quickly than he had expected, his air began to run out. His lungs ached, and he found himself instinctively trying to breathe. His mouth flooded with water. He choked and panicked, pushing a hand against the ice in desperation. Then Nemo pulled him to herself. Her mouth found his, and she blew air into his lungs. He gasped, choked again, pushed down the feeling of drowning. He had air.

Now that he was able to think, he reached out with his technopathy, searching the fishing hut. To his relief, he sensed a battery-operated light inside. He turned it on. Not far away, a small spot of light appeared in the water. He and Nemo swam for it. Then Sam's head pushed up and through a hole in the ice.

Sam pulled himself out, flopping onto the floor of the fishing hut. Nemo's head popped up a moment later. Sam knelt and helped pull her through.

"I can't believe that worked," Nemo said.

"It almost didn't," said Sam. "Thanks for the air. Now let's hope that woman believes we drowned."

"I guess we can always go back down and swim the other way if she does," Nemo said. She looked around. "Think there are any blankets in this thing?"

Sam indicated two thick wool sweaters and two pairs of overalls that were hanging on pegs beside the hut's door. "How about those?" he said.

Nemo took one of the sweaters down and started taking off her wet clothes.

Sam shut his eyes. When he opened them again a minute

later, Nemo was dressed in the sweater and overalls. She had also found a pair of boots to put on. All of it was too big for her, and she looked like a kid playing dress-up as a fisherman.

"Now you," Nemo said.

"I can't get my pants off with this thing there," Sam objected, pointing to the arrow that still protruded from his calf.

"That's what this is for," Nemo said, holding up a fishing knife she'd found.

She cut Sam's pants around the arrow. She removed his boot and sock and slid the severed portion of his pants off.

"Now for the fun part," she said. "I saw this in a movie once. It might hurt a little."

It hurt a lot. Sam ground his teeth together to keep from screaming as Nemo sawed with the knife on the arrow's shaft. Then she used her hands to break off the barbed tip. Finally, she yanked the arrow backwards through his leg. But it came out cleanly, and there was very little blood. Nemo took a piece of cloth she found in a bucket and inspected it. "Not too many fish guts on here," she said, wrapping it tightly around Sam's leg and knotting it.

She helped him take off the rest of his clothes, until he was down to his boxers. Then she discreetly turned around while he took those off, too, and wrestled himself into the overalls and sweater. He smelled like a pile of trout, but he was dry and warm.

"Now what?" Nemo asked.

Sam eased aside a curtain and carefully peered out the window. There was still no sign that the woman was coming after them. Next, he checked the pockets of his wet pants. His phone was gone, probably lost during the fall into the lake. But McKenna knew where they were. He would send help. What was important was that Yo-Yo and Rena had (he hoped) gotten away and that he and Nemo were safe for the moment.

He sat down on a wooden box. "Now, we wait," he said.

CHAPTER NINE

SIX
THE MOUNTAINS OF NORTHWEST MONTANA

SIX OPENED HER EYES.

"Welcome back," said a voice she didn't recognize.

She tried to rub her eyes, but her hands were held down by straps of some kind. So were her ankles. There were also restraints around her legs, waist, and chest. That's when she realized that she was lying on her back on a metal table. Over her head, harsh fluorescent lights buzzed like angry gnats.

Suddenly, a face hovered over hers. She recognized it as belonging to Drac, the man Dennings had used to remove a kid's Legacy in Texas.

"You're even uglier up close," she said, her tongue thick in her mouth.

Drac grinned. "At least I didn't remove your sense of

humor along with your gifts," he said.

"What are you talking about?" said Six.

"You won't remember, of course," Drac replied. "I find it's easier that way."

"You're full of it," said Six. "You didn't remove anything."

Drac laughed. "You'll find out for yourself soon enough," he said. "But I assure you, I did. Although I must admit, I had doubts that the procedure would work on one of the originals. Human Garde are much less developed, as you know. Weaker. It's easier to work with them."

Six still didn't believe him. Without saying anything, she turned her head to see what was in the room. A tray of medical instruments stood nearby. She fixed her attention on it and tried to levitate it. Nothing happened.

"Go on," Drac said. "Try your other abilities. Go invisible."

"I'm not doing tricks for you," Six growled, although she did try to use her Legacy. Again, nothing happened.

"Really, I'm surprised no one has done this before," Drac said. "Once I figured it out, it was really quite easy."

"How did you do it?" Six asked him. She remembered the strange colored lights that had surrounded the girl Drac had performed on in Texas.

He looked at her and seemed to think about the question. "I suppose there's no harm in telling you," he said. "Not everything, of course. But the general idea." He disappeared, returning a moment later and holding up a small metal device. "This is the key," he said.

Six stared at the harmless-looking thing. "What does it do?"

"Do you know what causes your Legacies?" Drac asked.

"The Entity," said Six. "Everybody knows that."

Drac nodded. "The Entity, yes," he said. "I should have asked, do you know *how* it does it?"

"It just does," said Six. She hated that she was talking about this subject with someone like the grinning, oily Drac.

"'It just does,'" Drac repeated. "Actually, the answer is much more scientific than that. I imagine there are others studying this as we speak, looking inside the brains of those of you who have been fortunate enough to be blessed with these gifts. Trying to find ways to duplicate them, make them available to anybody who wants them. Or to the highest bidder."

An image appeared in Six's mind: A teenager strapped to a table, as she was, a girl with her head shaved and a portion of her skull removed. Were there people really experimenting on kids with Legacies? She didn't want to believe it, but she remembered what the Mogs had done. There were humans in the world who were just as twisted. People who would do anything to try and get power for themselves. Thinking about it, she was filled with rage, and struggled against her restraints. Again, she was helpless to break out of them.

"In simplest terms, the Loric energy creates changes to the pituitary gland," Drac continued, sounding as if he was teaching a science class. "I don't yet know *exactly* how this results in a person developing Legacies, but I'll figure that out. What I do know is that this device will interrupt pituitary activity and render a person incapable of accessing the energy."

"You put one of those in me?"

"You'll probably have a headache for a while," Drac said in answer to the question.

Six did have a headache, but she wouldn't admit it. "Sounds like a lot of bullshit to me," she said.

"And yet, here you are without your Legacies," said Drac. He looked at the device he held in his fingers. "It's science, not magic."

"Dennings said you gave Yo-Yo back his Legacy," Six said.

Drac nodded. "You saw for yourself that I did," he said. "There's no point in lying about it."

"So, whatever you did is reversible," said Six.

Drac frowned. "Oh, did I get your hopes up?" he said. "I'm sorry. Yes, the process is reversible. In your case, though, I'm afraid it doesn't really matter."

"Why's that?"

"Mmm, that may be one secret too many to share," Drac said.

"What are you afraid of?" Six taunted him. "That your procedure didn't really work? If it did, you don't even need these restraints to keep you safe from me."

"True enough," Drac said. "All right, then. As I mentioned, you're the first of the original Garde I've had the chance to examine. This is a unique opportunity to perform tests on your pituitary gland and harvest samples of its secretions."

Six let his words register. "You're going to milk me like a cow?" she said.

"A crude way of describing it, but yes," Drac confirmed.

Six had a flashback. She was in a Mogadorian cell. Being tortured. Feeling helpless. Then, she still had her Legacies. Now, she had nothing. Her heart sank.

"How's the patient?"

Jagger Dennings leaned over her. "Hiya," he said.

"Go to hell," said Six.

"Didn't remove her attitude, I see," Dennings said. "What about everything else?"

"She's powerless," Drac replied.

"Good," said Dennings. "The boss will be happy to hear that. When do you think you'll have a working serum, or whatever you call it? Something to give people Legacies?"

He sounded excited and hopeful. Six wondered, was he thinking he'd be one of the first to benefit from Drac's promises? Did he think he could get an injection and have a Legacy just like that? Suddenly, things made a lot of sense.

"Oh, not for some time yet," Drac said. "There needs to be more testing. Refinement. We can't rush something like this."

He's stalling, Six thought. She could tell by the tone of his voice. But why? There was something he didn't want Dennings to know. *Like maybe this device of his isn't working as well as he says.*

"Well, I've got some more subjects for you," Dennings said. "Cutter's bringing them down now."

Six heard the sound of footsteps, and then voices as more people entered the room. When she turned to see Yo-Yo and Rena standing there, their hands cuffed with plastic zip ties, the feeling of hopelessness inside her deepened. Her eyes met Rena's, and the girl's reflected the same thing.

"They tried getting out on the ATV," Dennings told Drac. "Too bad they didn't know about the stop strips Cutter put out on the trail." He chuckled, as if the whole thing was a big practical joke.

"What about the other two, boss?" Cutter said. "They're still out there somewhere."

"Helena will take care of them," said Dennings.

"Or they'll take her out," Rena said defiantly. "Didn't you see what we did to her friend back at the barn?"

"I saw it," Dennings said. "But Helena's smarter than Bill. She's the dangerous one. She won't get caught like that again. Your friends are probably already dead."

Six wondered what had happened back at the barn and why Sam and Nemo had gotten separated from Yo-Yo and Rena. A momentary panic overtook her. Were they dead? She forced herself to calm down. Unlike Dennings, Sam was someone she couldn't imagine anyone taking out, at least not very easily. If he was alive, he was her—their—best hope. And if he wasn't . . . she couldn't even think about that possibility. He *was* alive.

"Anyway," Dennings continued. "If they get anywhere near this place, we'll know."

"What do you want me to do with these two?" Cutter asked.

"Stick 'em in separate cells," Dennings ordered. "Make sure there's nothing in the girl's. And I mean nothing but concrete floor and walls. I don't want her making any kind of doll or whatever. Keep those fireproof mitts on Sparky's hands so he can't light up."

"Why not just shut them off?" Cutter asked.

"Because the doc here wants to do some experiments on them," said Dennings. "Don't worry about it, all right? Just do what I tell you."

"What about that one?" Cutter asked, pointing at Six.

"She stays where she is," said Dennings. "For now."

Cutter hustled Yo-Yo and Rena out. Six bristled with renewed anger as she heard the teenagers being pushed around.

"Guess you know how Superman felt when he got around kryptonite," Dennings said to Six. He leaned against the table and looked down at her.

Six didn't answer him. She was too busy thinking about everything she would like to do to him if she wasn't strapped down. With or without her Legacies, she would teach him a lesson he wouldn't soon forget. If he was still alive when she was done with him.

The sound of a cell phone ringing came from Dennings's pocket. He reached in and pulled it out, looking at the screen. He ran his finger over the surface. "Hey," he said. "What's up?"

Someone on the other end spoke for a minute. Then Dennings said, "All right. We'll be ready."

He hung up. "Mr. Bray is coming," he said to Drac.

"Here?" Drac said. He sounded surprised.

"He'll be here in an hour," said Dennings, who also sounded a little tense. "And he wants to see a demonstration of the serum."

"But I told you it—it isn't ready yet," Drac sputtered.

"Well, you've got an hour to get it ready," said Dennings. He turned and walked out of the room, adding as he went, "Don't screw this up."

After Dennings left, the change in Drac's mood was palpable. He slumped into a chair and rubbed his forehead. The smirking attitude of before was gone, replaced by a nervousness that practically radiated off him.

"Who's Mr. Bray?" Six asked.

"Shut up," he barked. "I'm trying to think."

"Whoever he is, he must be important," Six continued.

Drac ignored her. He stood and started doing something at a counter that ran along one side of the room. He picked things up and put them down, talking to himself the whole time. "It's way too soon," he said. "I *told* them that. Can't be rushed."

Cutter, returning from wherever he had taken Yo-Yo and Rena, walked in. Noting Drac's behavior, he said, "What happened?"

"Nothing," Drac snapped.

"Mr. Bray is coming," Six informed Cutter, knowing it would upset Drac.

Drac whirled on her. "I told you to shut up!" he said. He picked up a syringe and stalked over to the table. Pressing it against the crook of her arm, he started to slide the point beneath her skin. Then he paused and pulled it out again. "No," he said, seeming to speak more to himself than to Six. "No. I don't have time to do that." He threw the syringe across the room. "I need more time!"

"Calm down, doc," Cutter said to him. "You can't let Mr. Bray see you like this. He won't like it."

"I know that!" said Drac. "I know that," he repeated in a less-hysterical voice. "I just need to think."

"Think fast," said Cutter. "I'm going to go upstairs and get ready for him."

Left alone with Six, Drac ignored her completely as he frantically prepared for the arrival of the mysterious Mr. Bray. Although Six attempted to get him to talk, he ignored her, busying himself with pulling out vials and needles and other things Six couldn't see. Eventually she stopped trying to engage him and shut her eyes, attempting to relax. She didn't have a plan, didn't know what was coming, but she wanted to be as prepared as she could be.

Not long after, Cutter returned to the room. "He's here," he said.

"He's early!" Drac said. "He's not due for another twenty minutes."

"Tell him that," said Cutter. "He just showed up with that kid who can teleport. He and Dennings are on their way down now."

Right on cue, Dennings's voice could be heard as he came downstairs. "I think you'll be really pleased," he said as he entered the room.

With him was a man who looked anything but pleased. Short and big-bellied, he had thick black hair and equally black eyes. *Like a shark,* Six thought when he turned and looked at her. Mr. Bray.

"Drac here has been—"

"That's the Loric girl," the man said, interrupting. He came closer to Six, eyeing her as if she was an animal in a zoo. His expression was impassive, unreadable. Six half expected him to touch her, but he kept his hands at his sides.

"Have you harvested from her yet?" the man asked.

"No," Drac answered uneasily.

"Why not?"

"She only arrived earlier tonight," said Drac.

"Prep her," said Mr. Bray.

"But—" Drac began.

"I said prep her," Mr. Bray repeated in the same even tone.

"We have a serum derived from some other subjects," said Drac. "Maybe—"

Mr. Bray's face tightened. "I want *her,*" he said. "Don't make me ask again."

"All right," Dennings said. "All right. We'll get it for you. Cutter, why don't you bring Mr. Bray upstairs and make him comfortable. This will take a little while."

"How long?" Mr. Bray asked.

"About two hours," Drac answered.

Mr. Bray turned away from Six and left the room, followed by Cutter.

"Can you really do this in two hours?" Dennings asked Drac in a low, worried voice.

"I don't know," Drac admitted. "I can try."

"Shit," Dennings said. "You're going to get us both killed."

"I said I'd try," said Drac. "But it might kill her."

Dennings glanced at Six. "If you don't do it, he'll kill us," he said. "Seems to me it's an easy decision."

Drac picked up a syringe. He came over to where Six lay on the table. This time, he didn't stop when he put it into her arm.

CHAPTER TEN

"HOW LONG HAS IT BEEN?"

Sam automatically looked for his watch, remembered it was gone, and said, "I'm not sure. I'm guessing about an hour."

"Should we try to leave?" Nemo asked.

Sam thought about it. In the fishing hut, they were more or less safe. But they were also useless. Six was still out there, and even if Yo-Yo and Rena had gotten safely away, they were still vulnerable to anyone who might be following them. Despite Rena's impressive work with the bear-thing and Yo-Yo's ability to make fire, they were still at a disadvantage.

Then there was the cold. The change of clothes had helped, but Sam could tell that Nemo was suffering from her time in the icy water. She had her arms wrapped around herself, trying to get warm. But she needed more than that. So did he.

At least his leg was feeling better. It still hurt—a lot—but he was able to stand and move around.

"Well?" Nemo said, and Sam realized he hadn't responded to her question.

"You never give up, do you?" he said.

Nemo shrugged. "Not usually," she said. "Not when my friends need me, anyway. You don't either. You or Six."

Sam nodded. "No," he said. "Especially not Six."

"Then what are we doing sitting around in here?" Nemo said.

"That's a good question," said a man's voice from outside the hut.

Nemo shrieked, and Sam sprang to hold the door closed.

"Relax," said the voice. "It's me."

"Nine?" said Sam. He motioned for Nemo to get behind him, then opened the door a crack.

Nine was standing outside. "I never took you for the fishing type," he joked.

He came into the hut, and Sam shut the door. Nine nodded at Nemo.

"Did you find Rena and Yo-Yo?" Sam asked.

Nine shook his head. "No. But Rena's tracking device shows that she's somewhere here."

"Damn it," Sam said.

"They didn't get away," said Nemo sadly.

"Did you run into anyone?" Sam asked Nine. "A woman? A hunter?"

"No one," Nine answered. "I saw a lot of smoke and what looks like it used to be a barn. What happened there?"

"Long story," said Sam. "Six is here somewhere. We need to find her. Is anyone with you?"

"What? I'm not enough?" said Nine, pouting and pretending to be offended. "Actually, there's some help at the bottom of the mountain. Earth Garde. But they don't move as fast."

"We don't have time to wait," Sam said. "Let's go to the lodge."

The three of them left the fishing hut, walking out onto the ice. Sam kept his eyes open for any sign of the woman who had been hunting them. Had she given up, thinking he and Nemo were dead? He hoped so, but he had a feeling she was still out there, waiting to make another kill.

"Dennings is letting people hunt us," he told Nine.

Nine's face hardened. "Lexa told me," he said. He let out a long breath. "Why did Six go to meet Dennings?"

"He had us trapped," Sam explained. "And it's Six."

Nine looked at the device strapped to his wrist, pressing some buttons. "According to this, she's still somewhere near the lodge."

"Then something went wrong," said Sam. "Otherwise she would have either been out of there already or torn the place apart."

"What could stop Six?" asked Nemo.

"Not much," Nine said. "That's what worries me."

They reached the edge of the lake and safely stepped onto the shore. Sam's leg ached where the arrow had penetrated it, but he limped only a little as they walked back towards the lodge. They were halfway there, moving up the mountain, when Nine shouted, "Get down!"

A moment later, a bright light came into view, a single Cyclopean eye that burst out of the darkness—accompanied by the roar of an engine. A snowmobile crested the rise above them and came roaring down the side of the mountain. Sitting astride it was a single driver. The machine hurtled towards them with no sign of stopping.

Sam concentrated on telling the snowmobile to turn. The snowmobile jerked sideways, hit a mound of snow, and flew up. It lurched, throwing the rider off, and crashed into a tree, where it sputtered and stalled. The driver kept going, arcing up in the air and then landing on the ground before sliding down the slope.

Sam stood up and ran to where the body came to rest. The person was wearing a helmet, rendering the face invisible. Sam bent and removed it, revealing the face of the woman who had been hunting them.

"I can't feel my legs," she said.

Nine and Nemo ran over. Nemo leaned down and picked something off the ground. It was a pistol. She pointed it at the woman. Her hands were shaking, and the barrel of the gun moved up and down as Nemo said, "How's it feel to be on the other end?"

"Nemo," Sam said gently.

"Maybe I should put you out of your misery," Nemo continued. Now her voice was shaking as much as the gun was. She had started to cry.

"Nemo," Sam said again. This time he laid his hand on her arm.

"Why not?" Nemo asked, sniffling. "She was going to do it to us. She *did* do it."

"She's injured," Sam said. "She's not going anywhere."

Nine looked at his wrist. "Backup will be here soon," he said. "We'll tie her up and leave her for them. We have to get to the lodge."

Nemo lowered the gun. Sam took it. He searched the woman for more weapons, removing a knife and another pistol from the pockets of her snowsuit. He was looking for something to tie the woman's hands with when she spoke.

"The girl has bigger balls than you do," the woman said. "I would have killed you. I still would, if I could move."

"Then it's a good thing you can't," said Sam, knocking the woman on the back of the neck with the pistol. She slumped over, unconscious. "Let's go," he said to Nine and Nemo.

They left the woman lying in the snow. After trudging the rest of the way up the hill, they came to the lodge. "This is where I wish I could go invisible, like Six," Nine said.

They looked for a way in that wasn't the front door. There was one door on the lower level, but it was locked.

"Can't you just rip it off the hinges?" Nemo asked.

"Probably—but that would make too much noise," said Nine, testing the knob.

Nemo pointed to a small window set high on the wall. "Lift me up," she said.

Sam held her around the waist and hoisted her up. Nemo hit the glass with her hand, breaking it. Then she slid inside. There was a thud as she landed on the other side. They waited for the door to open, but it didn't.

"It's an electronic lock," Nemo said through the door. "It needs a key code."

Sam placed his hands on the door. He connected with the lock's chip, running through every possible combination. There was a chirp, then the sound of gears moving. The door popped open.

Nine and Sam slipped inside, joining Nemo. They were in a hallway. Walking along it, they passed several locked doors. Nine paused, listening.

"There are people in there," he said.

Sam laid his hand on one of the locks, again telling it what to do. The door opened, revealing a small concrete cell. Rena sat on the floor, her hands tied behind her back. When she saw Sam, her face lit up. Sam put a finger to his lips, signaling her not to make a sound. He knelt and used the hunting knife he'd taken from the woman to undo the plastic tie around Rena's wrists.

"Yo-Yo is in here too," Rena whispered.

Sam unlocked the next door, but the room was empty. He found Yo-Yo in the one next to that. He untied him. Yo-Yo immediately yanked the mitts from his hands.

"You three stay back," Nine told Nemo, Yo-Yo and Rena. "You'll be safer here."

Leaving the three younger teens behind, he and Sam walked the length of the hallway. As they reached the end, they heard voices and paused. There was a door between them and the next room, but it was solid metal, and they couldn't see through it.

"What's going on?" Sam asked Nine.

"They're arguing," Nine said. "It sounds like there are at least three of them."

"Do you hear Six?"

Nine shook his head. He looked at his wrist device. "But according to this, she's right behind this door."

The sound of the voices suddenly increased.

"Kill me and there will be no one who can help you!" someone yelled.

There was a gunshot.

Nine kicked the door, and it exploded inward. He and Sam rushed in. The first thing Sam saw was Six, strapped to a metal operating table. Her eyes were closed.

The second thing he saw was the man called Drac. He was holding his arm, and blood dripped through his fingers. A man Sam had never seen before stood on the other side of the operating table, holding a gun and scowling.

Footsteps thundered on the stairs leading from the upper level. Dennings appeared. He looked at the bleeding Drac, then at Sam and Nine. His mouth hung open in surprise.

Sam started to move, but the man with the gun pointed it at Six's head. "Stay where you are," he ordered.

Sam froze. So did Nine.

"What the hell is going on?" Dennings said.

"The doc here gave me something, but it isn't what it's supposed to be," the man with gun said.

"I told you it wasn't ready," said Drac.

The man grimaced in pain. "What's it doing?"

"It's altering your pituitary gland," said Drac. "I don't know what it will do, exactly."

The man shuddered. Sam worried that he would accidentally shoot Six. They had to do something, and fast.

"I'm going to kill him."

Yo-Yo's voice shook with rage as he pushed between Sam and Nine. Already, a glowing ball was forming in his outstretched hand. He faced Drac. "This is for making me and the others your lab rats," he said, getting ready to launch the ball of flame.

The man with the gun swung the weapon towards Yo-Yo and fired. Yo-Yo's eyes widened in surprise. The fire in his hands went out, and he crumpled to the floor.

Nine used the distraction to move with superspeed across the room, leaping over the operating table and slamming into the armed man. Sam took on Dennings, throwing himself at the big man and aiming a punch at his face.

Dennings countered, blocking Sam with one meaty hand. At the same time, he shouted, "Scotty, get down here!"

Sam kept fighting. But it was obvious that he was no

match for Dennings physically, so he tried another attack, this time pushing Dennings away with his telekinesis. Dennings faltered, and for a moment Sam felt a surge of triumph. Then a teenage boy appeared on the stairs. He was the same pug-nosed boy Sam had seen before when Rena and Nemo were in the van.

"Get us out of here!" Dennings said.

The boy came down the stairs and reached out, touching Dennings's shoulder. Dennings tried to pull away from Sam, but Sam flung himself forward, just managing to grab hold of Dennings's hand.

Then he felt the familiar vertigo that meant he was being teleported. The room disappeared, swirling away. The last thing he saw was Nine bending over Six to make sure she was okay.

The feeling of disorientation lasted only a few seconds. Then he felt himself solidifying, as if all his atoms had been pulled apart and were now being forced back together. For a moment, he couldn't breathe. Then his lungs went back to work, and he gasped in air. He smelled something salty and felt cold air on his skin.

He was on the deck of a boat.

"Looks like we got ourselves a hitchhiker," said Dennings.

Sam prepared to resume their fight. Then he saw the three men standing with guns pointed at him.

"Take him below," Dennings ordered the men. "Lock him up. I'll figure out what to do with him later. I've got bigger problems right now."

Two of the men came and took Sam by the arms. The third quickly knocked him in the back of his head with the butt of his rifle. Sam crumpled and was dragged across the deck and down some stairs. He was taken along a narrow corridor, then thrown into a tiny cabin. The door slammed shut behind him and locked.

"If he tries to get out of there, shoot him," a man's voice said.

Sam faded in and out. There was little in the room besides a bed affixed to one wall. He pulled himself toward it. In just a few minutes, everything had gone wrong. He had no idea where he was. He didn't know if Six was all right. He had no way to contact anyone who could help him.

He was all alone.

THE LEGACY CHRONICLES

UP IN SMOKE

CHAPTER ONE

"SIX?"

Six heard someone calling from far away. The voice, faintly familiar though she couldn't identify it, floated through the fog that surrounded her.

"Six, wake up."

She struggled to open her eyes. Lights flashed, blinding her, and she shut them again. Then she tried once more, squinting until she adjusted to the brightness. After a few seconds, a room came into focus around her. She was in a bed. Someone was standing beside her.

"Did you have a nice nap?" Nine said.

Six groaned. Her head ached. "Where am I?"

"HGA," Nine said. "The infirmary."

Images came flooding into her mind: being strapped to a table, a syringe, a face looking down at her. She recalled the feeling of something sticky and burning flowing into her veins. Her brain felt as if it was still swimming in it. She strived to force her way out of it.

"Try to relax," Nine ordered.

Six ignored him, attempting to sit up. Nine helped her, putting a pillow behind her. Six leaned back, exhausted. Her body felt drained of energy. Then she remembered something else. Her hand flew to her head.

"He put something in me," she said. "A device of some kind. He showed it to me."

Her fingers found nothing, though. No shaved area. No incision.

"Where the hell is it?" she asked Nine.

"Nothing turned up on the scan we did," he said.

Six let her hand fall to her side. "That bastard was lying."

That bastard was Drac. And if he hadn't implanted something in her, what *had* he done? She knew he'd injected her. She had no idea what it was he'd put into her, though, or what it had done. But she felt different. And that worried her.

"We don't know exactly what he did," Nine answered. "Yet," he added. "He hasn't said much."

"He's here?" said Six.

Nine nodded. "We grabbed him and that woman who

was hunting the kids."

Now Six started to remember. Rena and Nemo. A lodge in the mountains of Montana. It was all coming back to her, and as it did, she found herself becoming enraged.

"Kirk," she said. "They killed him."

She looked at Nine, who nodded. A dark look clouded his face.

"Who else?" Six asked. Suddenly, fear gripped her heart. "Sam?"

"No," Nine said. "Yo-Yo."

Rena's friend. The one she had gone there to try and help escape. Six had been against the plan from the beginning, and this was exactly why.

"The girls are both okay," Nine continued. "Rena's taking Yo-Yo's death hard, of course, but she's a tough one."

Another thought came to Six. Another jolt of worry. "If Sam is all right, why isn't he here?"

"Dennings used a kid with a teleportation Legacy to escape," Nine said. "He took Sam with him."

"Then you don't really know that he's okay," said Six.

Nine started to answer, then grinned weakly. "It's Sam," he said. "He's okay."

"You can't even convince yourself of that," said Six. "You're sure not convincing me."

"He's alive," Nine said more confidently.

"He *was*," Six countered. "How long have I been out?"

Nine looked at his watch. "About twelve hours."

Twelve hours. Half a day. A lot could happen in that amount of time. Six tried not to think about the more terrible things on that list.

"You know I'm not Little Mr. Sunshine," Nine said.

Six looked at him.

"But I really do think Sam is all right," Nine continued. "And we're going to find him. Okay?"

Six thought of several responses to this but said nothing. Instead, she just nodded.

"Good," Nine said. "Now that that's settled, I want you to do something for me. Use your telekinesis to hold this in the air." He reached into his pocket and pulled out a quarter, which he held up between his thumb and forefinger.

Six focused on the quarter. She imagined it hovering in the air.

Nine let go of the coin. It fell to the floor with a dull clink.

"What the hell?" Six said.

Nine bent down and retrieved the quarter. He put it back into his pocket. "Your Legacies are being blocked," he said.

"How?" Six said. "By what?" She recalled again the injection that Drac had given her. What had he done to her? Apart from the headache thundering through her skull, everything seemed normal.

"The injection . . ." she said. "Did he—"

"Whatever he put in you, it's interfering with your abilities."

"Interfering?" said Six, thinking back to something she'd seen Drac do to a kid in Texas when he'd appeared to remove her Legacy from her.

"Like I said, we're not certain," Nine answered. "He hasn't explained very much about what he did."

Six threw back the blanket that covered her and swung her legs off the bed. "Then he'd better *start* talking," she said as she attempted to stand up. "Where is he?"

She got to her feet, then began to fall sideways. Nine caught her and made her sit back down. Six shook him off. "I'm fine," she insisted. "Just give me a minute."

"You need to rest," Nine said.

"I can rest when I'm dead," said Six, standing up again. "Take me to him."

Nine started to argue, but Six looked at him. "Take me to him," she repeated. "Now."

Nine laughed. "Okay," he said. "I know that tone. Come on. But if you start to faint, I'm not catching you."

Six staggered to the door of the room. She had to fight to stay steady, but she was determined, and angry, and she used that as fuel to keep going. Nine opened the door, then led her into a hallway.

"We don't have a jail here," he said as they walked. "Not officially, anyway."

"But?" said Six as they stopped at an elevator and Nine pushed a button.

"But I might have put in some, shall we say, secure

holding areas," he said. "You know, just in case any of the kids got too rowdy."

The elevator door opened, and they got in. Nine pressed a sequence of numbers on the keypad inside.

"Let me guess," said Six. "They're on a floor that doesn't technically exist."

"Something like that," Nine said as the elevator descended. "We can't have students accidentally stumbling into areas they shouldn't be in."

"Of course not," she said.

The elevator came to a stop and opened onto another hallway. This one was lit by overhead lights, and Six got the feeling that they were now underground. She followed Nine as he moved down the corridor, which was lined on each side with steel doors. Each one had a small window in it, as well as serious-looking locking mechanisms.

"How many cells do you need?" Six asked.

"Secure holding areas," Nine corrected her. "And they're not *all* used for that purpose."

"Oh?" she said. "What else is happening down here?"

Nine glanced at her. "Secret things," he said. "Midnight dance parties and whatnot. You're not on the guest list."

"Fine," said Six. "Don't tell me."

Nine stopped at a door. He peered through the little window, then tapped his fingers on the nearby keypad. There was a click, and the door swung inward. "After you," he said to Six.

She went in. There was already someone in there, a man, and he turned to look at her.

"What are you doing up?" Peter McKenna asked.

Six, startled to see her boss there, said the first thing that came to mind. "Why aren't you in New York?"

McKenna looked at Nine, who had shut the door and was standing next to Six. "It's difficult to interrogate someone over Skype," he said.

Now Six noticed the man sitting in a chair behind McKenna. It was Drac. And he wasn't just sitting in the chair; he was secured to it with restraints on his wrists and ankles. He looked tired, but other than that, it didn't seem as if he'd been roughed up at all. Yet.

"Have you tried knocking a few of his teeth out?" she asked McKenna.

She stormed over to Drac and punched him, hard. "What did you do to me?"

Blood dripped from Drac's nose. Unable to wipe it away, he sniffed. "Having some trouble working your magic?" he asked, then chuckled.

Six hit him again, harder. His head snapped back. He screamed. "You broke my nose!" he whined.

"You took away my Legacies," said Six. "Not my strength. And I'm just getting started."

She reached down and took his right index finger in her hand. "I hope you're a lefty," she said. "Because these aren't going to work for a while."

"Tell her to stop!" Drac wailed.

Nine laughed. "*Tell* her to stop?" he said. "Have you met her?"

Six applied pressure to Drac's finger. "Okay!" he squealed. "Just let go!"

"I can talk and hold hands at the same time," Six said, not releasing his hand.

Drac glanced over at McKenna and Nine again. They shrugged. "Better listen to the woman," McKenna said. "She's gone rogue."

"It's only temporary," he said. "That's what you wanted to hear, right?" he added when Six didn't respond.

"Is it the truth?" Six asked.

Drac nodded. Six let go of his finger. Drac curled his hand into a ball as if this would prevent her from coming after his helpless digits again.

"How long?" she asked.

"I don't know," Drac answered. "In the kids I've tested it on, up to a week. But I've never tried it on an original Garde, someone who's had Legacies for so many years. You're stronger. It might not last as long."

"Might," Six repeated.

"It's all experimental."

"What exactly is *it*?" said Six.

Drac didn't answer right away. He looked like a little kid who was being forced by bullies to hand over his lunch money. Six reached towards him.

"It's a substance taken from the Mogadorians," Drac spat out.

Six froze. "What?"

"Their black ooze," Drac said. "Black goo. Whatever you want to call it."

Nine had advanced to stand beside Six. "Where did you get it?" he asked. His voice was tight, and Six knew that, just as she was, he was thinking about their encounter with the pool of black ooze Setrákus Ra had used to strip Five of his Legacies. Despite her feelings for her fellow Loric, it was a horrible sight, and the thought that the ooze might be working its way through her body made her sick to her stomach.

"I met someone—a scientist—who worked with the Mogs," Drac said. "And before you ask, his name doesn't matter. The Mogs killed him when he stopped being useful to them."

"And this traitor gave you the black ooze?" she asked.

Drac shook his head. "I stole it," he admitted.

"And you've been experimenting on Human Garde using this shit?" Six said. She reached out and wrapped her fingers around Drac's throat, preparing to squeeze, but this time Nine stopped her. "We need him to be able to talk," he said. He nodded at Drac's hand. "Break a finger instead."

"I'm telling the truth!" Drac blurted as Six forced his clenched hand open.

"Which is why I'm only breaking one," she said as she snapped his pointer finger.

Drac screamed. Six held his wrist tightly, so that he couldn't pull his injured hand away, and said, "Or maybe I should make it two."

"It doesn't hurt them!" Drac shouted.

"How do you know that?" Six shouted back. "How do you know what the hell it does to them? To us?"

Drac hung his head, sobbing with pain. Six let go of his hand. "You're pathetic," she said.

"I told you, the Legacies come back," Drac whimpered.

"Great," said Six. "But who knows what else it does to them. You're experimenting. On kids."

"What's the endgame?" Nine interrupted. "Why do this at all?"

"Because he's sick, that's why," Six snapped.

Drac shook his head. "Mr. Bray wants a weapon," he said. "Something that neutralizes Legacies."

"Why?" said Nine.

"Why?" said Drac. "Why else? Money. Power. In case you haven't noticed, there are a lot of people out there who aren't too excited about a bunch of teenagers running around with superpowers. Those people would pay a lot for something that can eliminate that problem. Also, that weapon could be used to control anyone with Legacies. You saw how those kids were afraid of me back in Texas. If someone knows you can take away what makes them special, they'll pretty much do anything you ask them to keep you happy."

"You turn them into slaves," said Six.

"More like disciples," Drac said. "Those kids are stronger than Dennings and the guys above him. If they wanted to, they could take him out and start their own little gang. But they don't. Why? Because he's their daddy. The alpha wolf. They want to be part of his family. They want him to love them. He's not stupid, though. Well, not entirely. He knows someday one or two of them will figure out that they don't need him. So he keeps them afraid of him by making them think we can take their Legacies away forever."

"Rena said you gave Yo-Yo back his Legacy," said Nine.

"Yeah," said Drac. "But I didn't really give it back."

"You just let the effects of the ooze wear off," Nine said.

Drac nodded.

"What about that device you *said* you implanted in me?" Six asked.

Drac grinned. "Oh, that? Just a little something I've been working on to administer the black ooze at regular intervals—like an insulin pump. It would last longer than the regular injection. But it's . . . still in development. Mostly, I made it to impress Dennings and his boss, Bray."

"Let's talk about Bray for a minute," McKenna said. "Nine says you injected him with something. Was that black ooze too?"

Drac frowned. "No, that's his pet project. Basically, it's the opposite of the black ooze. It *gives* you Legacies. Or, it's supposed to."

"It doesn't work?" asked Nine.

"Not so far."

"What's in it?" McKenna asked.

"Pituitary secretions," Drac explained. "From people with Legacies."

"You're crazy," Six muttered. "Seriously wrecked."

"Bray is obsessed with developing a Legacy," Drac said, ignoring her. "He hates that he doesn't have one."

"He's too old," Nine said.

"Plus, he's a dick," added Six.

"I didn't realize being a nice guy was a requirement," Drac said. "But I know he's too old. That's why he has wanted me to come up with some sort of serum to make it happen."

"You don't think it will work," Six said. "Do you?" She could tell by the way Drac spoke that he had doubts.

"No," Drac said after a pause.

"But you need Bray to think you can make it work," Six continued. "That's why you were so freaked out when he demanded a demonstration."

"I might have let him and Dennings think I was further along than I am," Drac admitted.

"Well, if we don't have to worry about that for the moment, let's get back to the black ooze," said McKenna. "With the Mogs imprisoned, there must be a limited supply. How much of it do you have left?"

Drac sighed. "Not much," he said. "I've been trying to replicate it, but I haven't been able to."

"At least that's some good news," said Six.

"Yes and no," Drac said. "Bray is getting impatient, and he knows I don't have much of the original black ooze left."

"Sounds like your problem," she said.

"It might become yours, too," said Drac. "Word is that Bray has made contact with some fugitive Mogs who are interested in making a deal."

Six and Nine exchanged a look. Was Drac telling the truth? Humans working with Mogs were nothing new, of course. Since the invasion, though, what was left of their numbers had been rounded up. Not that a few couldn't have slipped through the cracks. But would they really have the knowledge to make more of the black ooze? As far as anyone knew, it seemed as if only Setrákus Ra could—and he was gone.

Six turned to McKenna. "Do you know anything about this?"

McKenna shook his head. "I know someone who might, though. I'll go make a call."

McKenna turned to leave, but before he opened the door Drac said, "He has your kid, you know."

McKenna turned around. "What did you say?"

"Seamus," said Drac. "That's your kid's name, right?"

McKenna nodded once.

"Dennings has him," said Drac. "Took a special interest in him once he learned his daddy works for the government."

McKenna was silent for a long moment. "Why are you telling me this now?"

"Just thought you would like to know," Drac said. "Since we're sharing and everything."

McKenna looked at Six. "Keep him talking," he said. "I'm going to make that call." He glanced at Drac, then turned to leave. "Break whatever you have to."

CHAPTER TWO

SAM

UNKNOWN LOCATION AT SEA

SAM TRIED ONCE AGAIN TO OPEN THE DOOR USING telekinesis. And once again, the locking mechanism failed to respond. He sighed. He'd hoped it had been a simple bolt, but it was apparently something more complicated. This wasn't really a surprise, given that Dennings was used to dealing with kids who had Legacies and would have anticipated an escape attempt.

Since the cabin he was locked in was barely big enough to hold the bed he was sitting on, it had taken Sam all of ten seconds to figure out that there was nothing inside that was going to be of any use to him. The only other thing in the room was a small sink affixed to the wall, with a grimy, cracked mirror above it. The sink's faucet leaked, and every so often a drop of water dripped into the basin. Sam was sitting on the edge of the bed, counting the seconds between drops.

Four, he thought, watching the small orb of water forming on the faucet's mouth as it had hundreds of times since he'd begun his observations. *Three. Two. One.*

Drip.

Twelve. Eleven. Ten. Nine.

The door opened.

A tray slid inside, and the door shut again. On the tray were a plate with a sandwich on it, a plastic cup of water, and a paper napkin that looked as if it had previously been used to wipe up a spill of some kind. Sam knelt and picked up the tray. Balancing it on his knees, he took a bite of the sandwich. Peanut butter and jelly.

As he chewed, he listened. Without a window, he had no reference for where he was. His brief glimpse of the ocean when he'd appeared on deck had not shown him enough to have any idea *what* ocean he was on. He could be anywhere. And as far as he could tell, the ship wasn't moving. He heard no engines, no churning propellers, nothing to indicate that the vessel was traveling. There was the occasional clang or thump, but nothing useful. When he reached out with his technopathy, he found nothing to connect with, no computers or machinery to talk to.

He picked up the cup, paused a moment to wonder if the water might be drugged, then decided he was thirsty enough that it was worth the risk. Besides, the sandwich could also have been drugged, and he'd already taken a bite. He sipped the water, then took a longer drink as his parched throat welcomed the moisture and demanded more. The warm water tasted flat, almost stale, but he drained half the cup before forcing himself to stop and conserve the rest.

He took another bite of the sandwich, and felt something strange between his teeth. Pulling the pieces of bread apart, he found a folded-up piece of paper inside. His first reaction was disgust that it had found its way in there. Then it occurred to him that someone might have put it there on purpose. It had been folded in fourths, and while the outside was smeared with jelly and peanut butter, the inside was clean. There were numbers scrawled on it: 29.03083333, -118.28000000.

Sam instantly realized they were coordinates, latitude and longitude. But knowing *what* they were didn't help him understand *where* they were. At least not exactly. The positive latitude meant the spot was north of the equator, and the negative longitude meant west of the prime meridian; but that was still a lot of ocean.

He closed his eyes and tried to picture a flattened view of the globe. It had been a long time since he'd learned about maps, but he could still kind of visualize it. The equator cut through the top of South America, so 29 degrees north of that was somewhere around the bottom of the United States. And 118 degrees west of the prime meridian put that spot . . .

"Off the coast of Mexico," he said aloud. "More or less."

Not that this information helped him very much. Or was necessarily accurate. Besides, who would bother to send him map coordinates inside a sandwich in the first place?

"A radio would have been more useful," he said to himself. "Or a gun."

Not knowing what to do with the paper, he licked the remaining peanut butter and jelly from it, trying not to think about who might have touched it, and folded it back up. He stuck it in his pocket, then resumed eating his lunch. Dinner. Snack. He wasn't sure what time it was. It had been early morning in Montana when he'd been taken. And it had been dark when he'd appeared on the deck of the ship. How long ago had that been? Two hours? Maybe three?

His best guess was that it was still morning, probably not yet noon. He also realized that he was very tired. More tired than he should be, even having been up all night running around in the cold. His eyes started to close. He blinked, forcing them open, but they fought back. As he slumped to the side, he glanced at the cup of water falling off the tray and onto the floor and thought, *I should have drunk out of the sink.*

When he woke again, he was no longer in the same room, and his head was swimming. Through the fog, he could tell that he was in a larger cabin, seated on a metal folding chair. Actually, he discovered when he tried to move his arms, he was tied to the chair with some kind of restraints. All he could manage to do was bang the chair legs on the floor a little by bouncing the chair.

"Settle down," a voice said. "It's not like you've got anywhere to go."

Sam looked up and saw the mysterious man from the Montana cabin sitting in a much more comfortable-looking chair, watching him. He didn't know his name, but he recognized the face. It was the man who had been threatening Drac with a gun and who had shot Yo-Yo.

"Who are you?" he asked, his words coming out slurred from whatever drug was still lingering in his system.

"What difference does it make?" the man said.

Sam shut his eyes, trying to calm his spinning head. The man was right. It didn't matter who he was. What mattered was figuring out what he wanted.

"To be honest, I'd prefer if we'd gotten the girl," the man said. "Six."

At the mention of Six's name, Sam looked up. His thoughts found something to focus on, and he pushed his way out of his stupor to fix the man with a glare.

The man laughed. "That got your attention," he said. "Sorry if it hurts your feelings. She's one of the originals, though, and you, well, you're just an Earth kid who got lucky, right? Like all these other kids Dennings has got following him around like puppies."

Dennings. Was he around, too? Probably. After all, he was the reason Sam was on the ship in the first place, because he'd insisted on hanging on to Dennings when that kid teleported him out of the cabin.

"Tell me something," the man said. "How come it picks who it picks?"

Sam didn't understand the question. He must have

looked confused, because the man tried again. "The magic sky fairy," he said. "The Lorien god, or whatever the hell it is. The thing that gives people these powers."

"The Entity," Sam said.

"Whatever. How's it decide?"

Sam tried to shrug, then remembered his hands were tied. "Nobody knows."

"Come on," said the man, sounding angry. "There's gotta be some kind of system."

"Pretty sure it's random. Sorry you didn't make the list, if that's what you mean, but you're a little too old anyway."

The man grunted. "Wiseass. You think I don't know it only picks kids? Why'd you think I had Dr. Frankenstein working on a way to give them to me?"

Sam looked at him, not sure he understood. "What?"

The man laughed. "That imbecile who goes by Drac has been working on, I don't know what you'd call it, a serum? Something to give people these powers you and your friends got accidentally."

Sam's mind began to race. He pictured Six strapped to the table in the room beneath the lodge. What had they done to her? What the man was saying didn't seem possible. "How?" he said.

"I don't know all the scientific stuff," the man said. "Something about harvesting from the pituitary gland."

Sam shook his head. "That's not possible," he said. "You'd need to actually remove it, and you can't do that without . . ."

He stopped speaking as the horror of what the man was

telling him began to sink in. "You'd kill the person," he said. Again he thought about Six. His heart began to pound, and he pulled against his restraints.

The man, oblivious to Sam's rising panic, shrugged. "I guess," he said casually. "Not a big deal if they're already dead, though, right?"

"The kids you let people hunt," said Sam. "You take the glands out of them."

The man waved a hand. "I leave all that up to Drac," he said. Then his face darkened. "Although maybe that was a mistake. Whatever he put in me hasn't done shit."

Sam remembered the argument he'd heard the man and Drac having before he and Nine broke into the room. It was starting to make sense. Whatever this serum was that Drac was working on, he'd injected the man with some version of it.

The man seemed to be agitated now. He stood up and started to pace. He snatched up a handheld transceiver and pressed a button. "Cutter!" he barked. "Get up here."

He continued to pace, now talking to himself. "I should have kept a tighter leash on him," he muttered. "Who knows what he was doing, what he put in me." He threw the transceiver against the cabin wall, where it shattered. Then he held his head in his hands. "This goddamn headache!" he bellowed. "It feels like my brain's on fire."

Something was obviously very wrong. The man's demeanor had changed rapidly. Sam watched him walk back and forth, clenching and unclenching his hands as he shook his head. He was like a wild animal in a cage trying to find a way out.

There was a knock on the cabin door. The man answered it, and another man entered. Sam recognized him, too. He was the man who had met Rena and Nemo at the diner and taken them to the lodge. Cutter. Seeing him there, Sam wondered again what had happened to everyone back in the lodge. Was Yo-Yo alive? And most important, was Six? Now that he knew what Drac had been up to, his fear for her safety was growing by the second.

"How are you doing, boss?" Cutter said.

"How does it look like I'm doing?" the man snarled.

Cutter glanced over at Sam. Sam met his eyes and glared, thinking about how he was responsible for so many of the terrible things that had happened in the past twenty-four hours. A flare of rage surged through him, and he found himself trying to use his telekinesis to push the man into the wall behind him. When Cutter grinned and laughed, Sam realized that he knew what Sam was trying to do, and also that it had failed.

"I thought you would have figured out by now that you can't do it anymore," Cutter said. "Didn't you wonder why you couldn't connect with any of the machinery?"

Sam didn't answer. He'd assumed there was nothing to connect with on this old ship. Now, though, he realized that there should have been all kinds of machinery that he could access. And yet, there was nothing when he reached out. And he hadn't been able to open the cabin door either. What had they done to him? His thoughts flashed back to the compound in Texas, where Drac seemed to drain that girl called Freakshow of her Legacies. Had they done something similar to him?

The rage in him turned to fear. Without his Legacies, Sam was helpless. Panic seized him. But then just as quickly, he shut it down. He had been in tougher situations than this without powers. If he could survive what had happened to him in the Mog prison, he could handle whatever these guys threw at him. At least, he hoped so.

Cutter seemed to be waiting for him to reply to his statement, but before he could, Cutter's boss fell to his knees, howling in pain. He beat at his head with his fists, screaming. "Make it stop!"

"Mr. Bray!" Cutter said, rushing to him. He put his hand on the man's shoulder, but he shrugged him off with another wail, then collapsed onto his side.

Cutter took a transceiver from his back pocket and spoke into it, saying something in Spanish. Then he rolled the man, who Sam now knew was named Mr. Bray, onto his back. Bray was breathing heavily, and his eyes were wild, darting back and forth as he panted, trying to catch his breath.

The cabin door opened, and two men bustled in. They went to Bray, and one took his feet while the other put his hands under the man's arms. They lifted him, and Cutter said, "Take him down below. I'll be there in a minute."

When the men were gone, Sam asked, "What did Drac shoot him up with?"

Cutter ignored the question. He looked worried.

"Doesn't seem like he'll make it, if you ask me," Sam said, goading him.

"Shut up."

"I hope you have the antidote to whatever Drac used on him," Sam continued.

Cutter looked at him. "Maybe I do," he said. "The problem for you is, it might be inside your head."

Sam felt the cold grip of fear again. Cutter's implication was clear.

Cutter grinned maliciously. "No smart comeback to that? I guess Mr. Bray must have told you what we've been working on, me and Drac. Well, mostly Drac. But I've hung around long enough to pick up a few things. Figure I could do it on my own by now." He held up one hand and made a scissoring motion with his fingers. "Course, I'd have to cut you open, but how hard can that be? I've butchered plenty of deer. Can't be any harder than that." He laughed.

Sam had no idea how much of what Cutter said was just to rile him and how much was serious. If Drac really was using people with Legacies to make some kind of superhero drug, there was no telling what they had done to get the materials they needed for it.

"Relax," Cutter said. "I can't use you while you've got that black goo in you, anyway. Have to wait for it to get out of your system."

Sam had no idea what he meant. But the mention of black goo immediately brought back memories. Terrible ones. Was it possible that Drac had gotten his hands on some of the Mogadorian ooze? And was that what they had injected him with to strip him of his Legacies?

Cutter went to the door. "You can try to get out," he said as he opened it. "Won't do you much good, though, unless you're a long-distance swimmer. Besides, the guys have permission to shoot you if they see you running around. Best to just sit tight until someone comes to get you."

He left, shutting the door behind him.

Sam looked around the room. It seemed to be some kind of office or storeroom, filled with boxes and bits and pieces of equipment. A desk with a computer on it was positioned against one wall.

Before he could look at anything, he needed to get free. Each wrist was bound with a plastic restraint to one of the sides of the chairback. He couldn't break through them. However, the chair itself didn't seem terribly sturdy. It was possible he could break it if he tried hard enough. But it would be noisy, and attract attention if anyone heard it.

Then again, he thought. *What do I have to lose?*

The answer was, nothing. If someone did hear him, what would they do? He doubted anyone would actually shoot him. It sounded as if he was too valuable alive. Probably, they would just tie him up again. And even if they did try to shoot him, that was preferable to sitting there doing nothing.

He bounced the chair against the floor. It was wobbly, but it held. Fortunately, he was on a rug, which muffled the sound a little. He tried again, lifting the chair up and bringing it down. The jolt sent pain radiating up his spine, and he winced. He rocked side to side, testing the chair's joints. They squeaked.

He lifted up with his legs as high as he could, then let himself fall back down. The chair hit the floor with a thud that shook his body. There was a grinding sound, and the left-hand side of the chairback fell away from the seat. Sam tilted to that side, almost tipping over, but righted himself. He then leaned in the opposite direction while sliding his left hand down the now-loose side of the seatback. His hand came free, and he stood. A moment later, he had wrenched the other side off.

He expected someone to come to the door, but no one did. Either Cutter was incredibly confident that Sam wouldn't attempt to escape, or there really was an order to fire should he leave the cabin. Sam didn't have time to worry about it, though, as he needed to find something—anything—that could help him out.

He went over to the desk and looked at the computer. It was on. He searched around the desktop, found an icon for an internet browser and clicked on it. When it opened, he said a silent thank-you for his luck, then went to his email account. As it opened, he fished out the paper in his pocket and unfolded it. Then he typed a quick email to Six and hit Send.

As he was logging off, he heard voices outside, speaking in Spanish. Returning to where the pieces of the chair lay on the rug, he threw himself down on the floor on his stomach.

As the cabin door opened, he groaned, as if he had just that moment smashed the chair and had hurt himself in the process.

Two men entered, the same ones who had carried Bray out a little while before. Seeing him on the floor, they spoke rapidly to each other and dashed over to him. Sam kept his eyes shut, groaning as they rolled him over. He mumbled some nonsense words.

The men talked to each other in anxious tones. Then they shook him. "Get up," one of them said.

Sam fluttered his eyes.

"Get up," the man said again. This time, he took hold of Sam's wrist, while the other man took his other arm. They pulled him to his feet.

"Downstairs," one of the men said. "Now."

Sam allowed them to think he was still weak as they dragged him towards the door. He wasn't sure what he was going to do next, but he wanted to maintain the element of surprise. As they left the cabin, he thought about the email he'd sent to Six. Was she even alive to receive it? He prayed that she was. He couldn't even think about the alternative. She had to be okay.

Whether *he* would be okay remained to be seen.

CHAPTER THREE

SIX
POINT REYES, CA

"HERE'S WHAT WE KNOW ABOUT BRAY," MCKENNA said.

He, Six and Nine were in Nine's office, where McKenna had spent the past half hour on the phone with his contact. Six, still feeling the effects of the Mog ooze, had a pounding headache, which she would have been happy to deal with by trying to get more info out of Drac, but McKenna had called her and Nine up to share his findings with them. Now, she sat in a chair, wishing the jackhammering in her brain would stop.

"His specialty is drugs," Bray said. "He's one of the leading suppliers to the West Coast market, with ties to the biggest cartels in Central and South America."

"What about the Mogs?" Six said impatiently. "Is it true

what Drac said, that he's made contact with them?"

"It's possible," McKenna said. "There are still some Moga-dorians out there. We know that."

Six sighed. "Great," she said.

Before she could continue, her phone dinged, alerting her to an email. She pulled it from her back pocket, and when she saw that the message was from Sam, she opened it immediately. She clicked on the stream of numbers, and her phone told her they were coordinates.

"Guadalupe Island," she said.

"What about it?" asked Nine.

"It might be where Sam is," Six told them. She held up the phone. "I just got an email from him. He says he's on a ship."

"That's . . . lucky," McKenna remarked. "How would he be able to send you an email?"

"He might have used his technopathy," Six suggested.

"Or it might be a trick," said Nine.

"Only a couple of people know this email address," said Six. "It's from him."

"Okay," Nine said. "So he's on a ship. What's that ship doing there?"

"Nothing good, I'm betting," said Six. "I say we ask our friend downstairs about it."

She, McKenna and Nine returned to the room where Drac was being kept, his injured hand now bandaged. When he saw the three of them, he paled.

"Tell us about the ship near Guadalupe Island," Six said, abandoning preliminaries.

"I don't—" Drac said.

Six reached for his uninjured hand.

"All right!" Drac said. "It's one of Bray's hidey-holes. He has dozens of them all over the world."

"That's a start," said Six. "Keep talking. What kind of ship?"

"I don't know what it's called," Drac said. "A freighter? Something old. Big. The kind they transport stuff in."

"Does he?" asked McKenna.

Drac didn't respond right away.

"We know Bray is trafficking drugs," McKenna said.

"Drugs," Drac said. "Stolen whatever." He paused. "People. If it's something someone will buy, he'll sell it."

"So what's on this particular ship?" asked Nine.

Drac sighed. "It's mostly a floating arena," he said. "He keeps some of the kids there. Uses them to fight, like in Texas. High rollers fly in on private helicopters or bring their yachts out there to bet."

"People like Helena and William Armbruster?" McKenna asked.

Drac didn't answer.

"Helena?" said Nine. "The woman we brought in?"

McKenna nodded. "I got some interesting information on them as well."

"Oh?" Nine said.

"Helena Armbruster is the heir to Klumber-Bach pharmaceuticals," McKenna said. "She's worth billions." He looked at Drac. "My guess is that she's very interested in the work our friend here is doing. Isn't that right, Milo?"

Drac looked up, an expression of shock on his face.

"Milo Cerszik," McKenna said. "Although you changed it to Andrew Alderman when your work on human growth hormone was discredited by the medical community and Helena Armbruster hired you as a private physician."

"Wow," said Six. "This gets better and better."

"The line between legal and illegal pharmaceuticals isn't all that wide," McKenna said. "It doesn't surprise me that Bray would look for someone like Helena Armbruster to team up with. She's probably paying a lot of the bills. And one of her perks for underwriting the program is getting to hunt kids with Legacies. Is that right?"

Drac was silent. Six felt herself becoming enraged again. The way Bray and Drac and everyone involved with them treated people like they had no value except for how much money they could bring in was disgusting.

"What are we going to do with her?" she asked McKenna, thinking about the woman. "Won't her husband dying be big news?"

"Officially, she and William are out of the country," McKenna said. "I suspect there will be some story about how he died suddenly."

"And her?" Six asked again.

"That remains to be seen," McKenna answered.

"Maybe she should have an accident, too," Six suggested.

"It's not as simple as that," said McKenna. "She has friends in high places."

Six looked at him. "Higher than what?"

McKenna didn't respond. Instead, he turned his attention back to Drac and said, "What's Bray going to do with Sam?"

Drac glanced at Six as though he was afraid his answer would cause her to come after him. "Sam's Legacy could be very useful to him," he said. "If he can't make Sam work for him—"

"Sam would never do that," Six interrupted.

"Then he'll try to take it out of him," Drac finished. "Put it into someone who will. Or into himself. Like I said, he's obsessed with getting a Legacy. One like that, that no one else we know of has, would be a big deal."

"We need to get him out of there," Six said to Nine and McKenna. "What are our options?"

"Bray will expect you to be coming," Drac said. "He'll be waiting."

"Let's talk upstairs," Nine suggested.

He, Six and McKenna went back to Nine's office. Nine made a call, and a minute later, Lexa joined them.

"We're going to Guadalupe Island," Nine said to Lexa. "How soon can we be there?"

Lexa opened the tablet she'd brought with her, and her fingers flew over the screen. "Little over an hour," she said. "Except that there's nowhere to land on the island. Lucky for you, I have another idea."

"Care to share it?" Nine asked when Lexa continued to tap on her screen without saying anything else.

"I know a guy," Lexa said after another moment. "Runs a

dive boat operation out that way. Great white cage diving."

"And this helps us how?" asked Six.

"It helps us because his ship just happens to have a helipad on it," Lexa continued. "He uses it to ferry clients back and forth from Ensenada." She typed some more. "Those rich folks apparently don't like the eighteen hours it takes to make the trip by boat, so Stubby started flying them in."

"Stubby?" said Nine.

"Like I said, his business is great whites. Got a little too close to one while tossing chum in the water. Lost a hand." Lexa looked at something on her tablet, then grinned. "And he says he'll have a copter waiting for you in Ensenada. How many of you are going?"

Six looked at Nine. "I'm going."

"Your Legacies still haven't come back," Nine reminded her.

"I don't need Legacies to kick some ass," Six said. "Remember? And Sam is in trouble. There's no way I'm not going. He'd do the same thing for me—for any of us."

"You're right," Nine said.

"About that," Lexa said.

"About what?" Six asked.

"I reached out to John and Marina. You know, since they're both healers and they've dealt with the Mog ooze before. I figured they could help."

With everything going on, Six hadn't thought to ask them for help. Even if they hadn't been in touch lately, she knew they'd be there for each other when it mattered. "Yeah?"

"Sorry, they weren't available," Lexa said. "They must be off doing something else, but I left word for them. Hopefully, they'll contact us as soon as they can."

Six nodded, hiding her disappointment. "Okay," she said. "Thanks."

"All right," Nine said, flashing Six a sympathetic look. "Six is in." He turned to McKenna. "What about you? If Drac's telling the truth, your son might be out there, too."

McKenna nodded. "Maybe," he said. "But I think I can be more useful here, frankly."

"So, two?" said Six.

"Three," said Nine.

Six glanced at Lexa, thinking he meant her, but Nine shook his head. "Nemo," he said.

"Nemo?" said Six. "After what she's been through? Are you insane?"

"I think she might be useful," Nine said.

"What could she possibly—"

"She breathes underwater," Nine interrupted. "And this is all happening in the middle of the ocean. That might come in handy."

"You can't make her go," McKenna said.

"Of course not," Nine agreed. "But we can ask her."

Six and McKenna looked at each other. Six was about to offer a rebuttal, but Nine spoke first. "Totally her choice," he said.

"All right," she conceded. "But Rena is in no condition to be involved, especially after what happened to Yo-Yo, and I think Max should stay here, too."

"Agreed," said Nine. "Let's get Nemo up here."

As Nine picked up the phone and made a call, McKenna cleared his throat. "Do you really think the three of you can handle whatever is on that ship?" he asked. "Six, you still don't have your Legacies back. I know you're formidable even without them, but we don't know how many kids are out there, how armed Dennings and his people are or even exactly *where* they are. What we do know is that Bray is capable of anything and is willing to kill anyone or everyone who is a threat to him. This isn't a simple in-and-out mission."

"You said you could be more useful here," Six replied. "You're right. Arrange for backup."

McKenna shook his head. "It's not that easy," he said. "Law enforcement in that part of the world is unreliable. Someone like Bray has probably bribed everyone he needs to ensure protection."

"Then don't rely on law enforcement," Six told him. "Call in Earth Garde."

McKenna hesitated.

"What?" said Six. "Is there a problem with that?"

"Not a problem, no," McKenna said.

Six waited for him to elaborate. He didn't. "You don't want them to think we can't handle this on our own," she said.

"There are things about the situation I would prefer to keep on a need-to-know basis," McKenna said. "For now, anyway. The fewer people we can involve, the better."

Six looked over at Lexa, who only raised an eyebrow. Then she turned back to McKenna. "It will take us a couple of hours to get out there," Six said. "That should give you enough time to figure something out." To Lexa she added, "We'll be ready to go in thirty."

As Lexa left to make arrangements, Nemo arrived.

"What's going on?" she asked.

"How are you feeling?" said Nine.

Nemo shrugged. "Okay. You know, for being out in the cold all night being hunted by sociopaths, swimming under ice and seeing a couple of people get killed."

"We think we know where Sam is," Six told her. "A ship off the coast of Mexico. There are probably kids with Legacies there as well."

"Ghost?" said Nemo.

"We don't know," said Six. "Nine and I are going out there. And he thinks you might be able to—"

"I'll go," Nemo said. "That's what you were going to ask, right?"

"Right," said Nine.

"But you don't have—"

"I said I'll go."

Six looked at the girl. She felt as if she was looking at herself. In only a short time, Nemo had transformed from a petulant, somewhat obnoxious girl into someone who was determined to fight for her friends. It was a terrible way to come into her own, but it had changed her in ways most people could never understand. Six could.

"Why are you staring at me?" Nemo asked, nervously pushing a lock of turquoise-colored hair behind her ear, then crossing her arms over her chest.

"We leave in half an hour," Six replied. "Lexa will get you outfitted. Meet us out front."

Nemo nodded, then left.

"I'm going to make some calls," McKenna said.

"Stay here," said Nine. "Use my office."

Six left with him. Twenty minutes later, they reconvened in front of the building. An SUV was waiting for them. So were Lexa and Nemo.

"What took you so long?" Nemo teased as Six and Nine put their bags in the back.

"A private plane will take you to Ensenada," Lexa told them. "Stubby has arranged for a helicopter to get you to his ship. Anything you need, you know how to reach me."

Three hours later, as late afternoon shifted into early evening, a helicopter landed on the helipad of the *Nautilus Fathom*. Six, Nine and Nemo got out and were greeted by a tall man with a bushy white beard, shaved head and toothy smile. He extended his left hand to Six. "Hey there. I'm Stubby."

After shaking Six's hand, he shook Nemo's, then nodded at Nine's missing arm. "Looks like we've got something in common," he said, laughing. "Come on. We can talk inside."

He led them down a short flight of stairs to a lower deck, then along the side of the ship and into a cabin. It wasn't large, and the desk that dominated the space was heaped with papers and books and charts, so the four of them stood there and talked.

"Lexa said you're looking for a ship," Stubby said. "I'm pretty sure I know the one. It's been in the area for a couple of months. People going in and out a lot."

"And nobody thought to ask what's going on?" Six asked him.

Stubby shrugged. "This part of the world is kinda like the Wild West," he said. "Took me ten years to get the locals to stop trying to run me out of town. I didn't get here by sticking my nose into anyone else's business."

"Then why are you getting involved now?" Six asked him.

"Lexa tell you I have a niece at HGA?" Stubby said. "Deirdre. But we've always called her Little D. My sister is Big D. Little D does something with light. Never seen it myself."

"The kids call her Aurora," Nine said. "She's a good girl."

Stubby smiled. "Yeah. Well, she's how me and Lexa came to be acquainted. But I would help anyway. I don't much like seeing anyone be used the way it sounds like these kids are being used. So, what is it you need from me?"

"Well," Nine said. "Basically, we need to find that ship and get onto it."

"I know where it is," Stubby said. "As for getting onto it, seems like you need to do that without attracting attention, right?"

"Right," Nine said.

"Then your best bet is going at night," said Stubby. "Use

scuba gear and swim right up to it. How you get on after that, I don't know."

"We can manage that," Nine told him. "But how do we see our way to the ship at night?"

Stubby snorted. "Pretty hard to miss something that big," he said. "We can get you close on an inflatable. You drop in, swim to the ship. Unless they've got guards and floodlights, they're probably not even going to notice. From what I hear, the guy who owns that thing has everyone who might be trying to bring him down in his back pocket."

"Lexa mentioned something about great whites," Six said.

"That's why I'm out here," said Stubby. He grinned. "You're not afraid of a few sharks, are you?"

"Shouldn't I be?" Six said, looking pointedly at his missing hand.

"Just swim fast," said Stubby.

Nine put his hand on Six's shoulder. "You leave the sharks to me," he said.

"All right," Stubby said. "Sounds like a plan. Sun won't be down for a little while yet. Let's go get you geared up."

CHAPTER FOUR

SAM

SOMEWHERE AROUND GUADALUPE ISLAND, MEXICO

SAM CONTINUED TO FEIGN BEING UNSTEADY ON HIS feet as the men marched him along the deck of the ship. He stumbled, forcing them to hold him up, and when they cursed at him in Spanish, he mumbled incoherently. In his head, however, he was trying to formulate a plan. He sensed that if he went below and was put into Dennings's and Bray's hands, it would all be over. Without his Legacies, he was at a disadvantage. Once they had him securely restrained again, he'd probably never get out.

But what would he do if he somehow managed to escape? He was still in the middle of the ocean. He thought about the email he'd sent to Six. Even if she'd received it, it would be some time before she could get there with help. What would he do until then? Hide? The ship did seem to be huge.

Maybe he could find somewhere to lie low while he figured out what to do. *If it's either that or have them experiment on your brain, the choice is pretty clear,* he told himself.

The men dragged him down a flight of metal stairs, and they were on the main deck. He could see that they were headed for a door. Beyond that, he imagined, was another flight of stairs. Those would take him below, and that was someplace he was absolutely sure he did not want to go. Time was running out for him to make a move.

"Hey!" a voice called out.

The men stopped. A boy ran up to them, thin, with red hair and freckles. He said something in Spanish. The men replied, shaking their heads. The boy repeated what he'd said, this time sounding much more emphatic. Again, the men seemed to argue with him.

Something about the boy seemed familiar. Before Sam could think too hard about what it was, though, he sensed movement around his feet. Looking down, he was horrified to see cockroaches running over his shoes. Dozens of cockroaches. No, hundreds. They were pouring out of every crack and crevice he could see, a moving carpet of shiny brown bodies.

The roaches swarmed up his legs and the two men holding him. When the guards realized what was happening, they let go of Sam and started swatting at the bugs. Sam, acting on instinct, did the same. But the boy grabbed his hand. "Come on," he said.

The cockroaches were now covering the torsos of the two

men and starting to crawl over their faces. The men saw the
boy pulling Sam away, but when they opened their mouths
to shout, the bugs scurried inside. The men choked, trying
to spit out the roaches, and Sam heard the insects' bodies
crunching between their teeth.

The boy yanked hard on Sam's arm, and they ran, roaches
slipping from Sam's clothes and skin. They headed for the far
end of the deck, where another door awaited them. The boy
pulled it open, practically pushing Sam through, and followed behind him. They were at the top of a flight of stairs.

"Hurry," the boy said. "I can only control the bugs for so
long when I'm out of visual contact."

"Seamus," Sam said, the name coming back to him.
"You're Seamus McKenna."

The boy didn't answer.

"I know your dad," Sam said as they descended into the
ship.

"We can talk about that later," Seamus said. "Right now,
we've got to get to the others."

"Others?" Sam said. "What others?"

Again, Seamus didn't answer. He just kept moving, taking Sam down corridors and more stairs, going deeper into
the ship. They passed through another doorway and were
in a room filled with machinery. The engine room. Sam
reached out, trying to connect with the throbbing, noisy
heart of the ship. Normally, it would have been easy. But he
still felt nothing.

"Through here," Seamus said, opening yet another door.

Sam followed behind. This time they were in a room. And they were not alone. A dozen other teenagers were there, all of them staring at Sam.

"Hi," he said, waving awkwardly.

Seamus turned to him. "Did they switch you off?" he asked. "I'm guessing they did, or you wouldn't have needed rescuing."

"Yeah," Sam said. "They did."

"Great," said a girl standing nearby. "Now they know about us, and what did we get out of it?"

"All they know is that I helped him escape," Seamus said. "They don't know anything else."

The girl snorted. "It won't take them long to figure it out," she said. "Not with half of us missing at roll call tonight."

"We could show up," another girl said. "It's not too late."

"Yeah, it is, Alice," the first girl said. "The war is on."

"War?" Sam said. "Does someone want to tell me what's going on?"

"We mutinied," Seamus said. "And like Svetlana said, that means war when Dennings figures out what's happening."

Sam was beginning to put the pieces together. The kids Dennings had taken in had turned against him. At least some of them. He looked around the room. "You're half of the total number?" he asked.

"More or less," Seamus said.

"And the others?" said Sam. "They're loyal to Dennings?"

"Or afraid of him," said Svetlana.

"Or both," said Seamus.

Sam nodded. "I get it," he said.

"When we heard you were here, we thought it might be our best chance," Seamus explained.

"Except you're broken," said Svetlana. "So we're on our own."

Sam ignored the insult. He could tell that underneath the brash exterior, the girl was probably terrified. There were a dozen of them against at least that many others. Sam could feel the nervous energy in the room. Svetlana was obviously one of the leaders. If she panicked, they would all start to panic. He had to get them pulled back together.

"My Legacies might not be working at the moment," he said. "But I have something just as good, and that's experience. I've walked out of a Mog prison after they tortured me. I've fought alongside the original Garde. It takes a lot more than someone like Dennings, or Cutter, or Bray to make me afraid. Besides, our side has captured Drac. Also, I was able to send a message to my friends telling them where we are." He hoped talking about them all as if they were on the same team would make them feel better.

"Do you know for sure that they got this message?" Svetlana asked him.

"No," Sam said, deciding that being truthful was better than giving them hope and then disappointing them if Six hadn't received his email. "But I think they did. And that means they'll be coming."

Murmurs passed through the room, and he saw several faces light up with relief. He was winning them over.

"Let's start by figuring out what we've got to work with," he said. "Svetlana, what do you do?"

Svetlana's mouth quirked in a cocky grin. "I make bombs out of things," she said.

"Useful," Sam said. "Great. And you?" he asked, pointing at a boy.

The boy disappeared, then came back. "Invisibility," he said.

Sam continued around the room, asking each person what their Legacy was and making mental notes about how each could be used in a battle. When he was done taking inventory, he turned to Seamus. "What about the other side?" he said. "What Legacies are we up against?"

Seamus thought for a moment. "Gawain manipulates electricity," he said, thinking.

"Parvati duplicates objects," said Svetlana.

"Scotty teleports," Alice said.

"Him I've met," said Sam.

Seamus and the others listed another nine or ten kids and their Legacies. By the time they were done, Sam had a pretty good picture of the fight they were in for.

"The real danger is the guys without Legacies, though," Seamus said. "They'll kill us without even thinking about it. To them, we're freaks. Not even human."

Sam thought about the pair who had hunted Nemo, Rena and the others. The ones who had killed James Kirk. They had acted as if the kids were animals, trophies that they could kill for sport. What kind of people did something like that? Were the men (he had seen no women on the boat other than the girls with Legacies) working for Dennings the same? Or did they just do what they were told as long as they were paid?

Either way, they were the enemy, and Sam had learned the hard way that you usually didn't have time to try to change someone's mind when their primary interest was bringing you down. He wondered if these kids understood that.

He motioned to Seamus and Svetlana. "Can I talk to you for a minute?"

The three of them stepped away from the group.

"Dennings has been making you guys fight each other, right?"

Svetlana's face hardened, and she nodded curtly.

"Are the people in this room the ones who usually won, or the ones who usually lost?" Sam asked.

"I always won," Svetlana said. She hesitated. "The others . . ." She shrugged.

"The others—the ones still siding with Dennings—aren't the nicest kids," Seamus said.

"Cowards," Svetlana said sharply. "Cheaters. They think he will make them rich. He promises them the world. But he lies."

"The kids here, they want to get out," Seamus said. "They'll fight."

Sam nodded. "I'm sure they will," he said. "But Dennings and his crew will fight dirty. We need to be ready for that. You two are the ones who got everyone together, right?"

Seamus shrugged, while Svetlana nodded. For a moment, Sam felt as if he was looking at younger versions of himself and Six, and he wondered again if Six was okay. But he had to push the thought away and concentrate on what lay ahead.

"I need you two to be the generals here," he said. "The rest are going to follow your leads. And I need you to follow *my* lead. Okay?"

Seamus and Svetlana exchanged a look, came to an unspoken agreement and nodded.

"Good," said Sam. "Now, let's talk about logistics. This is a big ship. We need to figure out what our endgame is and how we're going to achieve it. At the moment, we can't get off this ship. That means we either need to take out Dennings and his side or contain them."

"I thought you said help was coming," Svetlana reminded him.

"It is," Sam said. "They are. But until they get here, we have to act as if we're on our own. So, what's the situation?"

"This lower deck is a series of interconnected rooms," Seamus said. They all lead into and out of each other. There are six sets of stairs going up to the next deck—two in the engine room, then two more at each end of the ship. If we secure the doors at the top of those stairs, nobody can come down."

"Or go up," Svetlana said.

"We've already been through this," Seamus said. "It's the most effective way to—"

Svetlana cut him off. "To trap *us* inside." She turned to

Sam. "Please explain to bug boy here that sealing ourselves inside this giant tin can is not the best idea."

"She's right," Sam said.

Svetlana shot Seamus a smug look.

"But narrowing the potential field of battle *is* a good tactic when we're outnumbered," he continued. "What I suggest is sealing off one end of the ship. That forces them to come at us from one direction. It also allows us an escape route if we need one. We should also have some people on the upper decks. What's the name of the guy who goes invisible?"

"Walter," Seamus said.

"He's an obvious pick," said Sam. "And who is the best at offensive attacks?"

Seamus cocked his head at Svetlana. "She is," he said. "She can turn almost anything into a bomb."

"Okay," Sam said. "Then Svetlana, Walter and I go topside. The rest of you will stay down here. We need to seal those doors any way we can."

"Alice can manipulate fire," Seamus said. "She can weld them shut."

"Good thinking," said Sam. "You're in charge of making that happen. Svetlana, you get Walter and come with me."

Svetlana left, walking towards Walter. Seamus stayed by Sam. "What if something happens to you?" he asked.

"It won't," said Sam. "But if it does, you and Svetlana keep everyone safe until help gets here."

A worried look passed over Seamus's face but quickly disappeared. Then he said, "You mentioned my father before."

"He's who I'm working with," Sam said. "I recognized you from the picture on his desk."

"Is he coming?"

"I don't know," Sam answered. "He could be. I know he's been looking hard for you and can't wait to see you."

Seamus turned away, staring at the group of kids behind them. Sam sensed that there was something he wanted to say.

"It's going to be okay," he said, trying to reassure the boy.

Seamus looked back at him. "How well do you know my father?"

"Not very," Sam admitted. "We've only been working with him for a little while. But he seems like a great guy."

"There's something you need to know about him," Seamus said.

Before he could continue, the sound of shots being fired echoed from somewhere on the ship. A moment later, a girl appeared in the room as if she had walked right through the wall. She was holding a hand over her upper arm, and blood was on her fingers.

"Ghost!" Sam exclaimed.

Ghost looked at him. "They're coming," she said.

CHAPTER FIVE

SIX
SOMEWHERE AROUND GUADALUPE ISLAND, MEXICO

AS THE ZODIAC SKIMMED OVER THE OCEAN, SIX looked up at the sky. Clouds covered the moon and obscured the stars. She had no idea how Stubby knew which direction to go in, but he piloted the inflatable without hesitation. To the starboard side, the outline of the island of Guadalupe was a solid patch of black against the clouds, dotted with occasional twinkles of light. The air was warm, and inside her wet suit Six was sweating.

Beside her, Nemo sat quietly. Six looked over at her. "You okay?"

Nemo nodded. "My stomach is a little queasy," she said. "I'll be fine."

The Zodiac rounded the northernmost point of the island, and farther out to sea, Six saw more lights.

"There she is," Stubby shouted over the noise of the motor. He steered the inflatable in a direct line to intercept the ship.

As the lights grew closer, Six's desire to be on board grew stronger. Sam was on that boat. At least, she hoped he was. *And whoever else is there had better pray that he's all right,* she thought.

Not long after, Stubby cut the motor. The Zodiac floated on the ocean, rising and falling with the swells. The ship was now visible as a huge shadow against the sky. Lights filled some of the windows and highlighted parts of the decks, but the ship itself was eerily silent.

"I don't want to bring her any closer than this," Stubby told them. He was looking through binoculars. "I don't see any guards, but you never know. And the sound could give us away."

"Isn't it strange that there's nobody on deck?" Six asked.

"Yes," Stubby said. "Then again, maybe they're all below, watching one of those fights they put on."

Or maybe something is wrong, Six thought. Because she didn't want to worry Nemo, she kept that to herself, but she looked over at Nine and caught his eye. He nodded, indicating he understood her concern and shared it.

"All right," Nine said. "Here's the plan. Compass reading on the ship is seventy-four degrees, so set your wrist gauge for that. They're illuminated, but the light isn't enough for anyone to see through the water. Keep your directional arrow between the notched marks on the dial, and you'll be fine. Once we reach the ship, we'll use what I've got in my bag to scale the side." He pointed to Nemo. "If anything happens to me and Six, or if we tell you to, you get yourself over the side and back here. Got it?"

"Got it," Nemo said.

As Six and Nine slid into their scuba gear, Nemo donned a weight belt and put on her fins. When they were all suited up, they slipped over the side of the Zodiac and bobbed in the water.

"McKenna is on his way to Ensenada," Nine reminded Stubby. "He's arranged for backup there and will contact your ship as soon as he arrives. He knows we can't wait for him to get here, so he'll be the cleanup crew if necessary. We need to get Sam out of there before Bray decides to cut him open."

"I'll be waiting right here for you when you need a ride home," Stubby said. "Good luck."

Nine turned to Six and Nemo. "We'll descend to thirty feet," he said. "Go nice and slow."

"You just worry about keeping the sharks away," Six said, raising her inflator hose and letting the air out of her BC, the inflatable vest that was keeping her afloat.

She sank beneath the surface. With her only light the faint glow coming from her dive computer, it was almost totally dark. She looked for Nine's and Nemo's lights, found them, and concentrated on clearing her ears as they sank together into the ocean. When they were at thirty feet, she added some air to her BC so that she stopped sinking and hovered in the water, kicking her fins gently as she made her body horizontal.

She looked at her compass, oriented herself, and started swimming towards the ship. Nemo was between her and Nine. As they moved silently through the water, Six saw shadows—big ones—pass below them. Then they sank out of sight. Great whites. Had Nine called them, or had he sent them away? She felt oddly strengthened by their presence, as if the sharks were escorting them to the ship.

For a long time, there was nothing ahead of them but night. Then a dark spot appeared in the gloom, and Six realized that they had reached the ship. They swam some more, and the hull appeared in front of them, a solid wall of steel. When they were close enough to touch it, Nine gave them the signal to ascend to the surface. They went slowly, adjusting to the change in pressure, and a few minutes later were once again on the surface. This time, they floated next to the massive ship. They were at the aft end.

As they floated, they heard noises coming from inside the ship, muffled bangs and cracks.

"That doesn't sound normal," Six said.

"No, it doesn't," said Nine as he opened the sack he had brought with him. "We'd better hurry."

He handed Six and Nemo four objects each. Two of them looked like clogs that had been cut short, so that they covered just the toes of the foot. The other two were circular, with one flat side and a pocket on the reverse side that they could slip their hand into.

"Take off your fins and slip the ends of your feet into these," Nine said, showing them how to put the shoe-like devices over their dive boots. "The tips have heavy-duty magnets in them. Then put your hands inside the other two."

Six and Nemo followed his example, handing him their fins, which he put into the bag.

"Now, you basically climb up the side like a spider," Nine said.

"What about our tanks and BCs?" Six asked.

"And my weight belt?" Nemo added.

"We'll leave them here, tethered to another magnetic clip," Nine said. "Whether they'll be here when we come back, or if we can get to them, is another matter. But this is where they'll be. Oh, and one more thing." He reached out and placed his palm on Nemo's forehead.

"What the hell?" Nemo exclaimed. "Your hand is hot."

Nine pulled his hand away, and Nemo rubbed her forehead. "What did you do?"

"Transferred one of my Legacies to you," Nine said. "Now you can talk to animals."

"Why'd you do that?"

"In case you have to go into the water without me," said Nine. "But don't get too excited. It's not permanent."

"What if *I* have to go into the water without you?" Six asked.

"You're still out of order, remember?" Nine said. "So just swim fast. You guys ready?"

The girls slipped out of their gear. Then they began climbing.

"The trick is to not look down," Nine said as they slowly made their way up the side of the ship.

It took about ten minutes to reach the top. There, they pulled themselves over a railing and found themselves on an empty deck. They hid the climbing equipment behind a barrel, then looked around.

"Where is everybody?" Nemo said. "I thought this place would be crawling with people."

"Something isn't right," said Six. "What were the noises we heard on the way up here? They sounded like explosions."

In answer to her question, the lights that lined the wall beside them flickered on, grew incredibly bright, then shattered, showering the deck with glass while plunging it back into darkness. At the same time, another explosion was heard, and a door at the far end of the ship flew open. Several men ran out, scattering across the deck as smoke billowed out behind them. There was yelling, then the sound of gunfire from inside. Next, a glowing orb came flying out of the doorway. It hit the deck and rolled. The men shouted in Spanish and ran, coming towards Nine, Six and Nemo.

"Go," Nine said to Six. "I'll deal with this and catch up with you. See if you can figure out what's happening."

Six turned and darted away from the chaos, calling for Nemo to come with her. The two of them ran the length of the ship. The lights all along their way had broken, and it was difficult to see anything in the dark. When they came to a door, Six pulled on the handle, but it was stuck fast. She moved on. Behind them, more explosions shook the night.

They rounded a corner, and Six collided with a boy who was standing there. He went sprawling onto the deck with a shout. A girl standing nearby leaned down and helped him up. The boy faced Six and Nemo and held out his hands. Sparks flew between them.

"Who are you?" the boy said.

"You don't know who she is, Gawain?" said the girl.

The boy looked more closely at Six. A grin spread across his face. "Oh yeah," he said. "I do. This is great." He lifted his hands, and the sparks formed a ball of crackling electricity.

The girl beside him put her hand on his arm. "No, you idiot," she said. "They're here to *help*."

Gawain frowned and looked at the girl. "Help?" he said. "But they're with—"

"Sam," the girl said. "They're with Sam." She looked at Six. "Right? You're here to rescue Sam?"

"That's the plan," Six said. "Who are you?"

"I'm Parvati," the girl said. "This is Gawain. You need to come with us."

Shouts came from the other direction, and Six turned around. "What's going on here?" she said.

"Some of us decided to fight back," Parvati told her. "Parts of the ship are blocked off. We were hoping help would come. It looks like it did. But we really need to get out of here."

"We should wait for Nine," Nemo said to Six.

"There's no time," Parvati insisted. "If we don't go now, we might not be able to get back to the others."

"Nine will be all right," Six said to Nemo. "Come on."

Parvati and Gawain turned and ran for an open doorway. Six and Nemo followed. They went through and down a flight of stairs to the lower deck.

"Sam will be so happy to see you," Parvati said.

"Is he all right?" Six asked.

"He's fine," Gawain said. "Never better. He's right up here."

Reaching the next level, they walked quickly down a corridor to another door. Parvati pulled it open as Gawain stepped inside. Six and Nemo followed, and Parvati came in behind them, shutting the door.

They were in a room containing a table covered in what looked like schematics of the ship. Big red Xs appeared at various locations. Several men were standing around the table, talking loudly. Hearing the door shut, they looked up. One of them turned around.

"Well, well, well," said Jagger Dennings. "Look who's here."

Six whirled around, reaching for the door, but Gawain sent her flying with a blast of electricity from his hands. Six hit the wall, and the breath was knocked out of her. She sank to her knees.

"Don't try to be a hero," Gawain said to Nemo, who stood still and looked at Six.

"We found them on top," Parvati told Dennings. "I told

them we were bringing them to Sam."

Dennings laughed. "Good thinking."

"She says Nine is here, too," Gawain said.

Dennings looked at Nemo. "Did you bring anyone else along with you?"

"There are more coming," Nemo said. "A lot more."

"Thanks for the information," Dennings said. He turned his attention to Six, who had yet to stand up. "Since you haven't tried to kill me yet, I'm guessing your Legacies still haven't come back. Drac may be nuts, but it looks like that black-goo stuff does the trick. Good to know."

There was a second door in the room, and Dennings walked towards it. "Bring them along," he said to the men.

"What about the traitors?" Parvati asked.

"We're working on that," Dennings replied. "Right now, I have a bigger problem."

Two of the men hauled Six to her feet. Another took Nemo by the arm and pulled her roughly towards the door.

Six resisted the impulse to fight. Even without her Legacies, she knew she could do some damage to the men holding her. But there were too many of them, and eventually they'd subdue her. She was also worried about what they would do to Nemo. If the situation got worse, she would risk it. Besides, Nine was still out there, and he would come. Also, she hoped that maybe they really were taking her to Sam.

They were not.

Passing into the next room, she was herded down another flight of steps, this one leading to a large, windowless room that was clearly below water level. It was outfitted as a hospital room and laboratory, with a few operating tables and cabinets filled with instruments. Several long metal tables were covered with all kinds of equipment.

Storming around the room, yelling at the three other men standing there, was Bray. The men looked anxious. He looked furious.

"I don't care if they're kids!" he shouted. "Blow their goddamn heads off. Better yet, get Scotty down here. He can transport us out of here and then we'll sink the ship. Let them all drown."

"Mr. Bray," Dennings said.

"What?" the man bellowed, spinning around.

When he saw Six standing there, a smile cracked his face. His eyes got big, and he clapped his hands like a little kid seeing the bike he'd asked for under the tree on Christmas morning. He giggled—he actually giggled. Then he ran over and stopped right in front of Six.

"I knew she would come." He laughed again. "I knew it!"

"I didn't like the idea of you having fun without me," Six said coolly.

"Oh, we are having fun," Bray said. "We're having so much fun. Aren't we, Dennings?"

"Sure, boss. Tons of fun."

Six heard worry in his voice. Something was obviously wrong with Bray. Anyone could see that. And whatever it was, it had Dennings scared.

Bray continued to stare at Six. Suddenly, one eye began

to twitch. His face reddened, and his mouth contorted in a grimace. He let out a wail of pain and grabbed his head with his hands.

"Get him on the table!" Dennings shouted.

Two of the men rushed towards Bray, but he snarled at them and held out his hands, bent with the palms up. A look of concentration appeared on his face, and he groaned as he tried to push the men away.

"What's he doing?" Nemo asked Six.

"It's working," Bray said, looking at the men who cowered in fear a few feet away from him. "It's working."

"He thinks he's using a Legacy," Six said.

"Shut up," Dennings snapped.

"He's crazy," said Six, ignoring him. "Whatever Drac did to him, it's getting worse."

"I said, shut up!" Dennings yelled.

Bray looked at them. He pointed a finger at Six. "I need what's in her head," he said. "Get Cutter."

"Cutter's trying to round up—"

"Get him!" Bray screeched.

Dennings turned to the men holding Six and Nemo. "Get her strapped to a table," he said, pointing at Six. "And put that one somewhere she can't get out. We'll deal with her when this is over. Then go find Cutter and tell him to get down here now."

The men holding Nemo turned her around and headed back towards the door they had entered through. Nemo struggled. "Let me go!" she said, kicking at them and trying to yank her arms from their grasp. But they were too strong. She turned and looked anxiously at Six. Why wasn't she doing anything? Nemo didn't understand.

The men hauled her out of the room, then down another corridor. Nemo halfheartedly resisted, but she knew she couldn't overpower them. Still, she wasn't going to make it easy for them. She swore up a storm and made them drag her.

One of the men turned and said something to her in Spanish. A second later, his head jerked back and he fell to the floor. The other man glared at Nemo and shouted something.

"Don't look at me," she said. "I didn't do it."

She felt something brush against her. Then the second man fell. A moment later, a boy popped into view. He was holding a heavy wrench, which he now dropped on the floor.

"Come on," he said. "We're getting out of here."

"Uh-uh," Nemo said. "That didn't work out so well the last time someone said that."

"You got a better idea?" the boy asked her.

"I'm going to help Six," said Nemo.

"Not alone you're not," the boy said. "We need help. We need Nine."

"You know where Nine is?"

"Who do you think sent me to follow you?"

Nemo looked at the men knocked out cold on the passage-way floor. The boy *had* rescued her. Still, she was unsure.

"I'm Walter," he said. "I'm one of the good guys. Sam is with us. Now can we get out of here before Tweedledumb and Tweedledumber come to? We've got more bad-guy ass to kick, and time's running out."

Nemo nodded. "Take me to Nine and Sam."

Walter reached out and grabbed her hand. "It's easier this way," he said as they both turned invisible.

Together they returned to the top deck. When they got there, they found themselves in the middle of a war.

CHAPTER SIX

SAM
SOMEWHERE AROUND GUADALUPE ISLAND, MEXICO

SVETLANA WAS VERY GOOD AT MAKING BOMBS.

As Sam watched, she reached into the canvas bag slung over her shoulder and pulled out a can of beans. Holding it in her hand, she concentrated on it until it started to glow. Then she tossed it in the direction of the men on deck. It exploded, sending them scattering.

"Why beans?" Sam asked her.

"It's what was in the pantry," Svetlana said as she powered up another can. "Also, hot beans hurt."

The two of them advanced down the deck. Without his Legacies, Sam was most useful as a second pair of eyes. Also, he had taken a gun from one of the men Svetlana's bombs had put out of commission, and he was ready to use it. The explosions had started several fires, and smoke billowed across the deck. And one of the kids fighting against them had blown out all the lights, which made things more difficult.

He hoped Seamus and the others were successfully fending off anyone trying to take control below. He had seen no sign of Dennings, which worried him. The man should have been leading the charge against the dissenters. That Dennings wasn't suggested that he had more important things to do, and that could only be bad news. Whatever was happening with Bray had already thrown the ship's crew into a state of panic. Sam could only imagine what was going on, and what he imagined worried him.

And then there was Six. Nine's appearance on the ship had surprised him. Learning that Six was alive and was there too had given him hope. But she hadn't appeared yet. Nine had gone to look for her. Sam wished he was the one who had gone, but Nine still had his Legacies and was better equipped to deal with whatever might happen. And so all he could do was wait and hope.

Someone appeared beside him, startling him.

"Sorry," said Ghost. "There's no way to warn people when I show up."

"We should tie a bell on you or something," Sam suggested. "Like a cat." He pointed to her arm, which was now bandaged up. "Are you okay?"

Ghost nodded. "It was just a cut. I'm fine."

"What's happening down there?"

"The sealed doors are still holding," Ghost said. "For now.

But I don't know how much longer. They're trying to burn through them. We've got this guy who manipulates hot and cold, and he's been freezing them out. But he's getting tired."

"Anyone hurt?"

"Nothing serious."

Ghost's voice was quiet but filled with anger. Sam could tell that she was a changed girl from when he'd briefly met her in New Orleans. In the short time she'd been with Dennings, something had happened. Not only was her ability to control her Legacy improved, her entire demeanor was more aggressive, less hesitant. Even her look had changed. She was wearing jeans, a black T-shirt and black combat-type boots.

"I didn't get to ask you before," Sam said. "Is Edwige here?"

Ghost shook her head. "They have her somewhere else. I'm not sure where, exactly. They've got places all over. They move those with the most important Legacies around. Healers especially."

Sam's stomach sank. Bray's operation was like Hydra, the mythical beast that grew two heads for every one that was cut off. Who knew how many hideouts he had, how many cabins and training facilities. There could be dozens, each with kids being used for their powers.

It made him angry all over again, and more determined than ever to find and stop Dennings once and for all.

"Svetlana!" he called. "Let's go back downstairs. We can do more good there."

Svetlana nodded, and Sam was about to turn and head back to assist Seamus and the others when two people came running towards them through the smoke. Sam raised his weapon, preparing to fire, then recognized them and lowered his gun. "Walter! Nemo!"

"Sam!" Nemo ran to him and, to his surprise, threw her arms around him. Then she saw who was beside him. "Ghost! You're okay."

She grabbed her friend, who hugged her back but, Sam noticed, didn't respond as enthusiastically to seeing Nemo. But Nemo hadn't picked up on it. "They've got Six," she said. "We have to go get her. Do you have your Legacies back?"

Sam shook his head. "Not yet," he said.

"Where's Nine?" Nemo asked. "Isn't he with you?"

"He was," Sam said. "He went to look for you and Six. You didn't see him?"

"No," Nemo said. "We ran into Dennings. He still has her. That crazy guy from the cabin is there, too. The one who shot Yo-Yo."

"Bray," Sam said. He wondered what had happened to Nine but didn't say anything.

"They want to do something to Six," she continued. "An operation, I think."

"We have to get to her," Sam said. "Now. Take me to her."

"I don't think we can get back that way," Nemo said. "They'll have found the guys Walter knocked out. They're probably coming after us."

"I can get you in," Ghost said.

316

Sam looked at her.

"I've gotten better," Ghost said. "A lot better. I just need to know where they are."

"The operating room," Walter said. "You know where that is."

Ghost nodded grimly, as if she was remembering something she would rather not. She reached for Sam's hand.

"Wait a second," he said. "I don't have my Legacies. We need someone else."

"I can only take one," Ghost said. "I haven't done more than that without . . . problems."

Sam thought quickly. Should he send Svetlana? She would obviously be able to defend herself. But she was also hot tempered and might do something to make things worse. He wished Nine was there. But he wasn't. Despite not having his Legacies, he knew he was still the best choice. Besides, it was Six. If anyone was going to help her, it was him.

"Let's go," he said. "But once we're there, you get Six out. Don't worry about me. She's the priority. Got it?"

Ghost nodded. She reached out her hand again. Sam took it.

A moment later, he was standing in the small cabin he had been placed in when he first arrived on the ship. He looked at Ghost. "This isn't the operating room," he said as the cabin door swung open and Dennings walked in. Instinctively, Sam prepared to fight him, but Dennings spun him around and had his hands cuffed before he could even respond.

"Ghost!" Sam said. "Get out of here. Find Nine."

Dennings laughed. "Yes, Ghost," he said. "Find Nine. That would save me the trouble of having to track him down."

Sam looked at Ghost. Her eyes were hard.

"You left me," she said, her voice shaking. "You all left me."

"We didn't leave you," Sam said. "They took you. You and Edwige."

Ghost shook her head. "You could have helped. None of you did."

Dennings looked at Sam and grinned triumphantly. "You really did just leave her there," he said, shaking his head as if he was disappointed.

"You're the one who shot her!" exclaimed Sam.

"Accident," Dennings said. "Besides, I fixed her up good as new. Better, even. Right, Ghost?"

She nodded. "Better," Ghost said. She looked at Sam. "Much better."

"What did you do to her?" said Sam.

Dennings put his hand on Ghost's shoulder. "Taught her how to use her Legacy," he said. "When she came here, she could barely teleport herself from one side of a wall to the other. Now, thanks to Scotty and me, she can go from here to the other side of the world, and take you with her. You might even get there in one piece."

"I told you, that wasn't my fault," Ghost snapped.

"Relax," said Dennings. "I'm just teasing."

Sam looked at Ghost's face. Now the changes he'd felt in her made sense. Believing that her friends had left her to die had warped her thinking. And Dennings had obviously encouraged her to believe this was true. Combined with helping her to strengthen her Legacy, it had made Ghost believe she could trust him.

"Listen," Dennings said. "I'd love to stay and talk about this some more. It's fascinating stuff, really it is. But I've got a mutiny to get under control." He addressed Ghost. "You got our guys inside that engine room, right?"

Ghost nodded.

"Good girl," Dennings said. "Well, go see if you can help Gawain and Parvati find Nine. I've got some things to do here."

Ghost gave Sam a last, withering glance, then winked out of sight.

"She's tough, that one," Dennings said. "You really shouldn't have left her there."

"We didn't—"

"I'm kidding," Dennings said, taking him by the shoulder and pushing him out of the room. "Jeez. Can't you take a joke?"

As Dennings herded Sam down the corridor, he whistled happily.

"You're pretty pleased with yourself," Sam observed.

"Yeah, well, it's turning out to be a good day," said Dennings. "First Six. Now you. Once we find Nine that's, like, a third of the original gang. Well, you're not one of the Loric, but you get it. I have to say, it's hard to believe you guys defeated the entire Mog army."

"We had all our Legacies," Sam said. "And we've kicked your ass, what, three times so far? I wouldn't be so confident if I were you."

Dennings pushed him, making him stumble. "Keep it up," he said. "We'll see how cocky you are when you're on the table next to your girlfriend, having your heads drilled into."

"Tell me something," Sam said. "Have you let Drac inject you with his magic potion?"

"Me?" Dennings said. "Nah. I'm not one of his guinea pigs."

"Why not? Seems like getting superpowers would be right up your alley."

"I'm good," Dennings said.

"You know it messes up their brains," said Sam. "You've seen it. You know what it's doing to Bray. It changes people. Makes them a little bit crazy, maybe."

"Maybe they were crazy to start with," said Dennings. "Anyway, you talk too much. How about you shut up for a while."

Sam could tell he had touched a nerve. Dennings knew that Drac's serum wasn't everything they wanted it to be. From what he'd seen of Bray, the man was definitely being affected by it. Whatever it was doing to him, it was obviously dangerous.

Not that that would stop people from taking it. Sam was pretty sure they probably already had buyers lined up, people who wanted power and would pay any cost to get it.

Even if they were warned, it probably wouldn't keep them from trying to get the Legacies they craved. And once they were hooked, they would come back for more, making Bray wealthy beyond imagination.

He had more that he wanted to say to Dennings. At first he held back, not wanting to anger him. Then he decided he didn't care. If Dennings was marching him to his death, he might as well go out fighting, or at least getting in a few shots.

"Don't you get tired of being Bray's errand boy?" he said.

"I thought I told you to shut up."

"Really, I want to know," Sam continued. "I looked you up after our first run-in. You were a big deal."

"King of the Mountain at World Wrestling Summit three years running," Dennings said.

"Right," said Sam. "So, how do you go from having endorsements and fans and million-dollar paychecks to doing the dirty work for a scumbag like Bray?"

"Things happen," Dennings said. "And he pays good."

"But you could be the boss," Sam said. "Run the whole thing. Especially if you had a Legacy of your own."

Dennings brought him up short and spun him around. "I don't know what you're trying to do here," he said. "You're not buying your way out by promising to turn me into Batman."

"I was thinking more along the lines of Solomon Grundy," Sam said. "But whatever. And I'm not trying to bribe you. I'd just like to know how someone goes from being King of the

Mountain to Cleanup on Aisle Four."

Dennings shoved him against the wall. "What about you?" he said. "Who the hell were you before you won the lottery? I'm guessing a scrawny little nerd who got pushed around by the jocks. Bet you couldn't get a girl to look at you to save your life. You think that girl—Six—would look at you twice if you couldn't do what you do."

"Actually," Sam said, "she liked me before all that happened."

"Sure," Dennings snapped. "She saw what a great guy you are inside, right? How much you care. How you're different from all the other guys who want to get with her."

"Personally, I think it's more his boyish good looks and the fact that he isn't a sociopath."

Dennings whirled around, and Nine punched him in the face. He flew backwards, landing on his ass and continuing to slide. Before he could even think about getting up, Nine was on top of him, pummeling him repeatedly as Dennings tried to protect himself. Nine hit him once more, and the big man was out cold. Nine got up and walked back to Sam.

"And that's with one hand," he said. "Guess that makes *me* King of the Mountain now. Do I get a crown or anything? Maybe a throne?"

"It took you long enough to get here," Sam said. "I wasn't sure how much longer I could stall him. Where were you?"

"Beating up ten or twelve henchmen," Nine said. "Turn around."

Sam put his back towards Nine, who inserted a key he'd

swiped from Dennings's pocket into the lock. The cuffs opened, and Sam pulled them from his wrists. "Ghost has gone over to the dark side," he said.

"A minor inconvenience," Nine said. "Help me pull the former king into his cell."

Together, they lugged Dennings into the cabin Sam had been occupying. Once he was locked in, they walked back down the corridor.

"Now, let's go get Six and get the hell out of here," Nine said.

"What about the rest of Dennings's crew?" Sam said.

"They're McKenna's problem," Nine said shortly. "I knocked them out and locked them up. He can figure out what to do with them. Unless they freeze first."

"Freeze?"

"I put them in a meat locker," Nine said. "The thing's huge."

"And the other Garde? We're not just leaving them here."

Nine sighed. "No, I guess not." He snorted. "I'll have to order more HGA sweatshirts."

"I'm serious," Sam said. "What's the plan for them? Especially the ones like Ghost who Dennings has brainwashed or done worse to?"

"I haven't thought that far ahead," said Nine. "I'm sort of at the making-sure-they-don't-cut-off-Six's-head stage of the plan right now. Which, if we keep talking, might happen before we can get to her. So can we table the whole what-will-we-do-with-the-kids thing for now?"

"Yeah. No. You're right," Sam said. "Ghost said Six is in the operating room."

"Excellent," said Nine. "You know where it is?"

"Downstairs," said Sam. "I think."

"You think?"

"I haven't been here a whole lot longer than you have," said Sam. "I didn't get the full tour. But that's where they were taking me."

"Downstairs it is," said Nine. "I don't suppose the black-goo ooze stuff has worn off?"

Sam tried to use his telekinesis. "Not yet."

"Mmm," Nine said. "Well, here. It's primitive, but it's better than nothing." He handed Sam a pistol. "I got it from one of the meat-locker guys. They had a lot of them. I gave the rest to Seamus and his bunch."

"You gave guns to the kids?"

"Does that make me an irresponsible adult? Cuz I couldn't care less. Anyway, they're dangerous enough on their own. The guns are just in case."

"In case of what?"

"I think we're getting close," Nine said as they descended some stairs. "I hear shouting. Down there." He pointed to the floor.

Sam strained to hear. Through the steel beneath their feet there was the sound of someone yelling. They followed it, moving along another long corridor until they came to one more set of stairs, which ended in a closed door.

"Think it's unlocked?" Nine asked as he descended the

stairs. "Or should we knock? Oh, what fun would that be?"

He kicked the door open.

"Sorry we're late," he said as he walked into the room. "Sam had to stop to pee."

Sam, following Nine inside, pointed the gun in front of him. He expected to be met by immediate attack, but none came. The people in the room—Bray and Cutter—stared at them in confusion. On an operating table, Six lay with her wrists and ankles bound.

"This again?" asked Nine. "Sam, untie her. You two, get on the floor. That's where I'm putting you if you try anything, so we might as well save some time."

Cutter, holding a syringe, set it down on a table and got to his knees. Bray, however, began sputtering. He held out his hands, pointing his palms at Nine. His face contorted in concentration.

"What are you doing?" said Nine. He looked at Cutter. "What is he doing?"

"Why isn't it working?" Bray shouted. Once more he pushed his palms towards Nine.

"Are . . . are you trying to use telekinesis?" asked Nine.

Sam, who was untying Six, freed her wrists, then started on her ankles.

"He thinks he has a Legacy," Six said.

"Oh," Nine said. He pointed at Bray. "Maybe you should try harder."

Bray grunted. His face was beet red with exertion.

"Careful," Nine taunted. "You don't want to overdo it."

Six, who was now free, strode towards the man. "Playtime is over," she said. "It's time to—"

Before she could complete the thought, Ghost appeared. She took Bray's hand, gave Six the finger and disappeared.

"Was that?" said Six.

"It was," Sam said.

"But—"

"I'm getting tired of this shit," said Nine. "Not that the Entity asked my opinion, but there are too many damn people getting teleportation as a Legacy."

"Where do you think she took him?" Six asked.

"Don't look at me," Sam said as she was doing exactly that. "I don't know."

"I do," said Cutter.

"What?" said Six.

"I said I do," Cutter repeated. "I know where she took him."

"Where?" Nine said.

Cutter shook his head. "Not until we make a deal."

Six raised her hand back to strike him. Nine stopped her. "He can't tell us anything if he's dead."

"I'm not going to kill him," said Six.

Nine looked at Cutter. "Talk."

CHAPTER SEVEN

NEMO
SOMEWHERE AROUND GUADALUPE ISLAND, MEXICO

"NEMO, COME ON."

Nemo looked at Ghost. Her friend was beckoning to her, urging her to come up the stairs and join her on the deck. But something didn't feel right.

"Where are Sam and Nine and Six?" she asked.

Ghost looked behind her, then back at Nemo. "I *told* you, they said to leave. It's not safe here."

"But we've got all Dennings's guys," said Nemo. "And most of the kids, too. There are only a few still out there. I'm going to help Seamus and Svetlana find them."

"Stop arguing," Ghost said. "Just come with me." She held out her hand.

Nemo almost reached out and took it. In her head, warning bells started to go off.

"Enough of this," said a man's voice. Then Dennings appeared in the doorway. He jumped down the entire flight of stairs and caught Nemo by the collar. He hauled her back up on deck, kicking and screaming.

"Ghost!" Nemo shouted.

Dennings clamped his hand over her mouth. "Come on," he said to Ghost. "They're going to hear her."

Ghost reached out to grab onto Dennings's wrist. Nemo lifted her foot and stomped on the man's instep as hard as she could. At the same time, she elbowed him in the stomach. He grunted in surprise, and his grip loosened. Nemo darted away.

"Sam!" she shouted. "Nine! Six! Help!"

Dennings lunged at her. She sidestepped him and ran. He chased her.

"Shut your goddamn mouth!" he yelled.

Nemo continued to cry for help, but no one came. She ran faster, staying barely one step ahead of the pursuing man, who moved much more quickly than his size would suggest he could. Nemo was quickly out of breath, and her cries for help faded to gasps as she looked around for an escape route. She found nothing.

They reached the bow of the ship. There was nowhere else to go. Nemo leaped up onto the small platform there. Behind her, invisible in the dark, was the ocean. She heard it gently lapping at the ship's sides. She smelled its salty tang.

As she stood there, watching Dennings rush towards her,

she wondered why Ghost hadn't run, too. She hadn't even seemed to be afraid of Dennings at all. And now Nemo saw her coming out of the darkness, calmly walking across the deck. Dennings stopped, barely out of breath, and waited for Ghost to catch up. She stood beside him.

"Now we're going," Dennings said.

"You shouldn't have run, Nemo," Ghost said.

"What, you're on his side now?" Nemo asked her friend.

"I'm doing this for you," Ghost said. "You can come with us, or you can stay here and die."

"I'd rather die," said Nemo.

"The ship is going to explode, Nemo," Ghost said. "I'm not kidding. Bray rigged it in case something ever happened."

Nemo looked at her. "That will kill all the kids left here," she said.

Ghost shrugged. "They should have fought harder," she said.

Nemo couldn't believe what she was hearing. Was this really Ghost talking? The Ghost she knew wouldn't let anyone get hurt if she could help it. But this Ghost was different.

"I'm only saving you because I owe you for helping me when I had nowhere to go," Ghost said. "Now we're even."

"I don't want to be even," Nemo told her. "I want to be friends."

Dennings made a noise of disgust. "Put it in a card," he said. "We're getting out of here." He jumped onto the platform. Nemo backed up against the low railing that was the only thing standing between her and the ocean thirty feet below. Dennings reached for her. Nemo wrapped her fingers around his wrist.

She fell backwards, pulling at the same time. Dennings, caught off balance, came with her, stumbling over the railing with a shout. Together, they fell through the darkness. Nemo looked up at the sky, wondering if they would fall forever. Then she hit the water. She went under, the breath knocked out of her. The ocean closed over her head.

At first she panicked. Then she remembered—she didn't need to breathe. She tried to calm herself. She had lost her hold on Dennings, but she could feel him somewhere nearby. The water was moving around her as he kicked for the surface and air.

Nemo kicked, too. Her head broke through the water, and she looked around. Not far away, Dennings was splashing and swearing. "I'll find you!" he shouted. "And when I do, I'll slice you open!" She saw him wave something in the air. Something long, pointed. A knife.

Above them, the ship rose into the night. Without the climbing gear, there was no way she was getting back on it.

"There you are," Dennings said.

She heard splashing as he came for her. She dived, ducking under and swimming down. She could stay there for as long as she needed to, waiting for Dennings to give up. But if Ghost was right about the ship being rigged to explode, she might not have much time left to warn the people still on board. She had to do something. But she couldn't go back up.

Not with Dennings ready to gut her like a fish.

Something grabbed her ankle, stopping her downward movement. Twisting around, she saw Dennings looming over her. Instinctively, she kicked out with her free leg. Her foot connected with his face, and he jerked backwards. But still he hung on. His fingers dug into her painfully. At any moment, she expected to feel a knife plunge into her. She kicked again. And again. Hoping to knock the weapon out of Dennings's hand.

All the while, they were sinking deeper, as if Nemo's body was a lead weight pulling them down. Then Dennings had her with both hands. He was pulling himself along her body, grasping at her arms.

As she tried to fight him off, Nemo's thoughts flashed back to what Nine had done on the deck of the ship. He'd transferred one of his Legacies to her. Could she really use it? She closed her eyes. Struggling in the darkness, she imagined herself calling out to the creatures swimming in the sea around her. Her mind filled with the image of sharks. Were they really there? Would they listen? Did she dare ask them to do what she wanted? What she needed.

Take him, she thought.

She opened her eyes. At first, she saw nothing but endless darkness and Dennings's shadow. She kicked some more, wiggling her body, and for a moment she was free of him. But he grabbed her wrist, pulling her towards him. His face came close to hers, his mouth clamped shut, his cheeks puffed out. He was running out of air. He had to either kill her here or drag her to the surface with him. His free hand reached for her neck.

Then, out of the gloom, enormous shadows emerged. The great whites moved silently through the water, rising as they came closer. Nemo's heart pounded in her chest as the creatures answered her call. There were two, then three. They passed within yards of her, and she felt the powerful strokes of their tails as the water swirled around her body.

Dennings sensed them, too. He looked around. When he turned back, his eyes were wide with terror. Then something pulled him backwards with great force. He was still holding on to her wrist, and Nemo's body jerked as she was pulled with him. Then there was a second pull, and Dennings was gone. In the shadows, Nemo saw a thrashing of bodies, then a cloud of darkness formed, swirling in the water like ink. The sharks circled, twitched their tails, dived back down. They separated, swimming in different directions, each carrying something in its jaws.

Nemo hung in the water for another few minutes, not sure if what had happened was real or her imagination. The ocean surrounded her, cradling her, and she felt strangely safe in the enormous expanse of darkness. She extended her senses, felt life around her and knew that she was home.

Then everything came back: Ghost, a bomb, Dennings. Had she really told the sharks to kill him? Had that actually happened? Or had she imagined it all, and he was still up there, waiting for her? She pushed the thought away, at least for the moment. It was too horrible to think about. She focused on the more important thing: getting back to her friends and helping them.

She swam. When she reached the surface, she saw that she had drifted away from the ship, and was going farther away at a rapid pace. She was in a current. She kicked, trying to swim back towards the ship, but she was being pulled away more quickly than she could swim. The ship was growing smaller.

She started to panic, not only about being taken out to sea, but because every second she was away from the ship was potentially one second closer to the explosion Ghost had promised. And where was Ghost? Had she teleported out of there? Even if she was there, would she help?

Nemo kicked harder, knowing that it was useless. She gave up in frustration, floating, feeling the ocean tug her farther and farther away from Sam, Nine and Six. She waited to hear an explosion, to see the ship erupt in flames. Her heart ached, and she felt useless and helpless.

Call the sharks.

The thought came to her like a voice cutting through the dark.

Call the sharks.

The idea terrified and thrilled her. Would they come again? And what would they do? The idea of being so close to them was both exciting and chilling, especially after what she had witnessed them do. What she had *asked* them to do.

She closed her eyes and extended her thoughts. What should she say? Sharks were simple animals. They swam, fed and reproduced. Could they understand a call for help? She reduced her need to the most basic word she could think of.

Come.

Come.

Come.

She repeated the word silently, sending it out into the water.

As before, she felt the presence before she saw it. She was learning how to connect with the creatures she summoned, to join with them and communicate the way they did. The shark that came to her was a large one, a female. It was old, scarred. Nemo didn't know how she knew this, but she did. The shark had swum in several oceans, covered tens of thousands of miles in her lifetime, never sleeping, always moving. She thought about nothing but survival.

The shark came up beside her. Her snout went under Nemo's arm, and Nemo's hand slid up the rough skin, her body inches from the crushing jaws that gave the animal its fearsome reputation. She imagined rows and rows of teeth, machinery designed for the ripping of meat and bone. Was this shark one of the three that had taken Dennings? Nemo tried not to think about it.

The shark moved, and Nemo's body was lifted, becoming horizontal as the shark sank beneath her. Nemo took hold of the massive dorsal fin, the solid V of cartilage that cut through the water. There were notches on it, like scratches in the trunk of a tree. Nemo gripped it with both hands as the shark sped up. Her body lay atop the great white's, and she felt its muscles move like the pistons of a train, side to side, propelling them through the ocean. Water streamed around and over them as the shark stayed barely submerged, carrying Nemo back to the ship.

When they got there, Nemo let go and slid off. The shark immediately dived, and Nemo felt its thoughts turn again to finding food. She thanked it for its help, knowing that the shark didn't understand the concept. She knew, too, that should they encounter each other under other circumstances, the shark would not remember her as a friend. It would not remember her at all.

She had, without even thinking about it, directed the shark to take her to where Nine had attached their gear to a line. The line was still there, and Nemo hung on to it as she contemplated her next step. She had gotten back to the ship, but she was still not *on* it. And there was nothing in the gear that would help her.

She briefly wondered if there was any animal around that could somehow lift her onto the ship. But there wasn't. Finally, she did the only thing she could think of. She shouted.

"Help!" she screamed. "Man overboard!"

She had no idea who might be around to hear her. She hoped it was somebody friendly and not one of the few people loyal to Dennings who hadn't been captured. But she would take what she could get.

"Help!" she shouted again. "Anybody!"

To her immense relief, a light appeared above her. "Is someone down there?" a boy's voice called.

"Yes!" Nemo yelled back.

The light disappeared, and Nemo felt herself start to freak out. But not long after, it returned. Then something fell into the water. Nemo reached for it and saw that it was a rope ladder. She started to climb.

She reached the top, exhausted and barely able to hang on. Hands grabbed her and pulled her over the railing, and she rolled onto the deck.

"How did you fall overboard?" asked Seamus, looking down at her.

"I didn't fall," Nemo said. "I jumped. It's a long story. Right now, we need to get to Sam and the others. The ship is going to explode."

Seamus wasted no time in pulling her to her feet. The two of them ran to the operating room, where Sam, Six and Nine were discussing what to do with the information they'd gotten from Cutter.

"What happened to you?" Nine asked when he saw Nemo.

"There's a bomb," Nemo said. "There might be a bomb. Ghost said there is."

"A bomb?" said Sam.

Six looked at Cutter, who was sitting on the floor, his back against the wall. "Do you know about a bomb?"

"There's a self-destruct mechanism built into the ship," he said. "Bray is paranoid about someone getting their hands on anything he owns."

"Where is it?" asked Nine.

"Engine room three," said Cutter.

"Take us there. Now," Nine ordered.

A few minutes later, they were standing at a small control panel, looking at a digital clock readout that was counting down.

"Less than five minutes," Six said. "That's not good."

"There's no way to evacuate this ship in that amount of time," said Sam. "Even if we had somewhere to evacuate them to."

"What about jumping overboard?" Nemo asked.

"We couldn't get far enough away," said Six.

"So, that's it?" Nemo said. "We're all going to die?"

"Not if we can disarm it," Nine said. "Anyone have a screwdriver?"

Svetlana stepped forward and handed him one. "What?" she said when Nine looked at her quizzically. "I thought I might need to stab someone."

Nine removed the screws securing the cover of the control panel. Inside, three red wires ran from the display and out of the box.

"I don't suppose we can just cut them," Nine said.

"You could," Cutter said.

Six, who was peering at the wires, produced a knife and inserted the tip beneath the wires, lifting them up.

"Except that would set off the bombs," Cutter said quickly.

Six pulled the knife away. "Bombs?" she said. "As in more than one?"

"There are explosives attached to the hull in two hundred different places," Cutter explained. "Only one wire actually controls the detonation device. If you cut that one, it deactivates. If you cut either of the other two, the sequence begins immediately."

"Which one do I cut?"

"I don't know," Cutter said.

"Don't play games with me," said Six. "Which one?"

"I *don't* know," Cutter repeated. "Bray told me about the bomb, but not how to defuse it. It's his way of messing with people's heads, reminding us that he's in charge."

Six put down the knife. "Any other ideas?" she asked as the timer counted down to four minutes.

"I have one," Sam said.

Everyone looked at him.

"But you're—" Nine began.

"I know," said Sam abruptly. "I know. But sometimes Legacies emerge in stressful situations, right? Maybe something like that could happen to bring back mine."

"Go on, Sam," Six said. "Try."

Nemo watched as Sam put his hands on the countdown clock. His face screwed up as he concentrated.

"Anything?" Nine said.

Six shushed him.

Nemo watched the numbers on the clock spinning backwards. Three minutes.

Sam groaned. He pulled his hands away, balling them

into fists. "Damn it," he muttered.

"Try again," Six urged.

Sam took a deep breath and put his hands back on the clock. A look of surprise flashed over his face. "I got something!" he said.

Nobody said anything. Nemo looked at the others. They were all watching the clock. Two minutes and twenty seconds remained.

"It's coming in bits and pieces," Sam said. His voice was steady. "I'm getting a little more."

Two minutes. Nemo felt her heart racing.

Sam's eyes were closed, and his face was suddenly relaxed.

"Sam?" Six said.

Sam didn't respond. But his lips were moving. "Almost. What? No. No!"

The clock suddenly jumped to thirty seconds remaining.

"You told it to hurry up?" Nine said.

Sam grimaced as if his head hurt. The numbers whizzed by. Twenty. Fifteen. Ten.

Nemo shut her eyes and waited for the sound of her death. It didn't come.

She opened her eyes. The clock had stopped at three seconds. She waited for it to finish counting down, but it didn't change.

"You did it?" she said.

"No," Sam said, sounding disappointed. "She did."

Beside him, Svetlana was standing holding the knife that Six had set down. One of the wires in the box had been cut.

"We had a one-in-three chance. Someone had to try," she said. "It was going to *kaboom* either way. Now can we please get off this stupid ship?"

CHAPTER EIGHT

SIX
POINT REYES, CA

"WONDERLAND?" SIX SAID.

"It's the name of a mansion," McKenna replied. "It was built in nineteen twenty-two by Harlin Pearsall, a famous silent film actor."

It was twenty-four hours after the events on the ship. Six, Sam and McKenna were in Nine's office. Nine was seeing to the processing and settling-in of fourteen of the kids rescued from Bray's floating prison and brought back to California. Parents needed to be notified. Statements taken.

An additional twelve kids—the ones who had sided with Dennings—were in lockdown. They were a bigger problem. Most wouldn't reveal their real names. A few had been identified through the DNA registry set up for those with Legacies, but the majority were kids who had slipped through the cracks and had never reported to the authorities in the first place. Figuring out who they were would take some time. Deciding what to do with them would take even longer.

That was Nine and Lexa's problem. Bray was Six and Sam's. Cutter had given them the name: Wonderland. In return, they had agreed not to introduce him to the sharks that had taken care of Dennings. Instead, he was sitting in a cell three doors down from Drac's, worrying about what they *would* do to him. And that's how they wanted it for now.

"And it's in Argentina?" said Sam.

McKenna nodded.

"Why?" Six asked.

"Partly because of Prohibition," McKenna explained. "It was illegal to make or sell alcohol in the United States at that time. That didn't stop people from doing it, of course, especially in Hollywood. But Pearsall had a reputation as a clean-cut fellow. His nickname was America's Son, because he always played good guys. In reality, he liked to party hard. He also had ties to organized crime. He built Wonderland as a place where he and his friends could go and live it up away from the prying eyes of the gossip magazines and the government. You could do that back then, before the internet made a private life impossible."

"But why Argentina?" said Six. "Why not Mexico, or someplace closer?"

"The distance was part of the appeal," McKenna said. "Also, South America was considered exotic. And it was cheap. He built Wonderland for well under a million dollars."

"And Cutter says this is where Bray is hiding out?" said Sam. "It seems kind of, I don't know, ostentatious for someone trying to keep a low profile."

"Wonderland changed hands in nineteen thirty," McKenna continued. "Pearsall likely owed the wrong people a great deal of money and gave it to them to save his neck. Whatever the reason, it was subsequently owned by a man named Thiago Godoy, better known by the nickname the Butcher of Tucumán due to his habit of cutting up his enemies and feeding them to his dogs."

"Charming," said Six.

"Indeed," said McKenna. "He had a number of other bad habits, including being a big fan of Adolf Hitler. Following the war, Wonderland became a refuge for high-ranking Nazi officers escaping prosecution. There are also reports that a number of the scientists involved in the experiments conducted by the Nazis found their way there and continued their work."

"Kind of like Drac," Sam remarked, shaking his head. "Monsters."

McKenna looked serious. "Well, that's where it gets interesting," he said. "Or, more accurately, disturbing."

"You're not going to tell us that Nazi scientists are running around down there, are you?" Six said.

"Not precisely," McKenna answered. "If any of them are still alive, they would be in their nineties now." He paused.

"However, they had students, followers they trained to continue their work in creating what they considered the perfect humans. Advances in genetic research have only encouraged them further. And something like the development of Legacies would naturally be of enormous interest to them."

"Drac," Sam said. "You think Drac is continuing their work."

"I did some more digging on our doctor friend," McKenna said. "His birth name is Milo Cerszik, which we already knew. Turns out his great-grandfather was one Blago Grgić. Grgić was a member of the Ustaše, a Croatian ultranationalist organization patterned after and aligned with the Nazis. He was also a doctor, and very interested in the Nazis' studies of eugenics. Drac himself is a direct result of his great-grandfather's work, which attempted to breed a superior human. The man used his own daughter as a breeding subject."

"Looks like that experiment failed," said Six. "And how interesting that he didn't bother to mention any of this before. I should have broken more fingers."

"We think this goes much deeper than what Drac has told us," McKenna said.

"We?" said Sam.

"I think it goes deeper," said McKenna. "I think Drac is continuing his great-grandfather's work. And I don't believe his story about getting the Mog black ooze from another scientist. I think Bray has some kind of connection to the Mogs, has had it for a long time. Just like Drac is descended from Grgić, I think Bray has connections stretching back to

Godoy. They're just the most recent faces of an evil that's been around for decades. Only now they have more technology, more resources, more power than ever before."

"Let's question Drac again," Six suggested.

"He's being questioned," McKenna said.

Six and Sam exchanged a glance. "By who?" Six asked.

"He's been transferred to another facility," said McKenna. "They're handling it there."

"When did this happen?" Sam said. "Does Nine know?"

"Yesterday," McKenna replied. "And this is not an HGA matter, so Nine is not in charge of the situation."

"Then who is?" said Six. "You?"

"Yes," McKenna said.

"So, where is Drac, exactly?" Sam asked.

"At a secure facility. One where he can be properly interrogated." McKenna looked meaningfully at Six.

"Hey, it got us the information we needed," Six said. "And as I recall, you told me to break whatever I had to."

"I'm confused here," Sam said. "Earlier, you said *we*. Now you're talking about a different facility and someone interrogating Drac. I thought we were our own thing."

"We are," said McKenna. "In as much as we act independently. But given the potential scope of what Drac and Bray were doing—are perhaps still doing—there are larger concerns. I felt it best to call in additional resources."

"Which brings us back to *who* those resources are," Six pressed. "If it's not us, and it's not anyone connected with the HGA, then who is it? The government? Because if you recall, I'm really not down with working for the feds."

"I understand your concerns," McKenna said. "For now, I'm asking you to trust that I'm doing what's best for the situation."

"Trust isn't really something I'm great at," Six reminded him.

McKenna nodded. "You've made that clear on more than one occasion," he said. "But I'll ask you again to please accept that I'm doing what's best."

"Best for who?" said Sam.

"For all of us," McKenna said.

Six looked over at Sam. He seemed on the verge of saying something. She could sense that he had questions, just like she did. But there was something else, too, something more. She knew him well enough to recognize the expression on his face. He was worried. So when he didn't say anything, it made *her* more hesitant to believe McKenna.

"What's next?" was all he said.

McKenna seemed to let out a breath he had been holding. "I think our best course of action is for you to go to Argentina," he said.

"Just us?" said Six. "What about Nine? Or Lexa? Or, well, any backup at all?"

"This particular mission has only one objective," McKenna said. "Terminate Bray. And I think you two can handle that with or without all your Legacies."

"Kill him?" said Sam. "You want us to kill him?"

"We—I—believe that Bray is currently the single most dangerous threat to the Garde," McKenna said.

"What about everyone working for him?" said Six. "If he's doing what you think he is, there are going to be lots of people involved. Drac, Dennings and Cutter are probably just the tip of the iceberg."

McKenna nodded. "Agreed," he said. "But Bray is also a despot, a control freak. I'd be surprised if he's trusted anyone else with all his secrets. If he's taken out of the equation, the rest will scatter like rats leaving a sinking ship, and we can pick them off one by one. But as long as he's alive, they think they're invincible."

"What if there are kids there?" said Six. "According to some of the ones we rescued, there are more at camps and hideouts and whatever all over the place. What happens to them if we take out Bray?"

"I understand your concern," McKenna said. "And I share it. But the fact is, we're running out of options. Bray is obviously unstable. And now he's desperate. We don't have time to try to infiltrate his organization again or do any of the large-scale things we would normally want to do in a situation like this."

"Yeah, but this is superrisky," Sam objected. "What if they decide to just kill all the Human Garde they have?"

"Bray is going to kill them one way or another," McKenna countered. "Either through his attempts to manufacture the serum, through the battles he forces them to engage in or by letting other people pay for the experience of hunting them. As I said, we've run out of time. Bray will expect us to come after him, so he's likely sped up his activities."

Sam sighed. "When do you want us to go?"

"One hour from now," said McKenna. "That gives you time to pack whatever weapons and gear you need and for me to finalize backup for you there."

Six wanted to protest, but Sam stood up. "Okay," he said. "We'll see you in an hour."

He left the office. Six followed. "Hey," she said, catching up to him as he made his way down the hallway. "What's going on? You didn't even put up a fight back there, and I could tell that you wanted to."

Sam stopped. "Something's not right," he said. He looked back in the direction of Nine's office. "He's not telling us everything."

"Obviously," Six said.

Sam started walking again.

"The armory is the other way," Six said.

"We're not going to the armory," said Sam, continuing to move. "We're going to the dorms."

Six followed him. "Why?"

"To talk to Seamus," Sam said. "When we were on the ship, he told me there was something I should know about his father."

"He didn't say what?"

"We were kind of in the middle of a situation," Sam said.

"How come you didn't tell me this before?"

"We had a lot going on," said Sam. "Remember? And honestly, I sort of forgot about it until things got weird in there just now."

"Do you think he'll talk to us?" Six asked.

"Maybe," said Sam. "Maybe not. Don't you think it's weird that McKenna hasn't been spending more time with him since we got back? Now that I think about it, I don't even remember seeing them reunite when McKenna came to pick us up."

Six thought back to the night before. "I don't either," she said. "But like you said, there was a lot going on. A lot of kids to keep track of. I wasn't really paying much attention to Seamus."

They reached the elevators, and Sam pressed a button. "Let's see if he's in a talking mood."

They took the elevator to the third floor. Getting off, they walked into the common area. There, several students were sitting and talking, including Nemo, Rena and Max. Seeing Six and Sam, they jumped up and came over.

"Nemo just told us about Ghost," Max said. "Is it true she's one of the bad guys now?"

"I didn't say she was a bad guy," Nemo objected.

"I think Ghost is upset and confused," Sam said. "Hopefully, we'll be able to help her."

"What about Edwige?" said Rena. "Have you found out where she is?"

"Not yet," said Six. "But we're looking."

"Do you guys know where we can find Seamus?" Sam asked them.

"He's in the room at the end of the hall," Nemo said. "I tried to talk to him, but he hasn't said much. Why? What's going on?"

"Nothing," said Six. "We're just checking on the new recruits and want to make sure he's settling in."

Nemo cocked her head and narrowed her eyes, but she didn't say anything. Instead, she just pointed. "Room three three nine," she said. "Good luck."

Sam and Six walked down the hall. When they reached the room where Seamus was staying, they knocked. There was no answer, so Six rapped on the door again. "Seamus? It's Six and Sam."

A few seconds later, the door opened. "What do you want?"

"To talk," Sam said. "See how you're doing."

Seamus looked past them. "Is my father with you?"

"No," Sam said. "It's just us."

Seamus turned and walked back into the room, leaving the door open. Taking it as an invitation to go in, Six and Sam entered. Sam shut the door behind them. Seamus went to the window and leaned against the ledge. He folded his arms over his chest. "Did my dad send you?"

"Actually, no," said Six.

"We don't have a lot of time," Sam said, echoing McKenna. "So I'll get right to the point. On the ship, you said there was something I needed to know about your father. What did you mean?"

Seamus looked away. "Nothing," he said. "I didn't mean anything."

"Are you afraid of him?" Six asked.

Seamus didn't answer. He turned and looked out the window at the nighttime sky.

"Seamus, when your dad first told us about you, he said that you ran away because you didn't want to come to the HGA," Sam said. "Is that true?"

"No," Seamus said softly. "I *wanted* to come here."

"Then why didn't you?" Six asked.

"That's a long story," said Seamus.

"You don't seem very excited to be here now," Six observed. "Or to be reunited with him."

Seamus turned around. "Did he tell you about my sister?"

"Only that you liked to use your Legacy to scare her," Six answered.

Seamus smiled, but sadly. "Yeah," he said. "I did do that. Cat was terrified of bugs."

"Why do you keep talking about her in the past tense?" Sam asked.

"Because she's dead," said Seamus. "He didn't tell you that either?"

"I'm getting the feeling there's a lot we don't know about your family," Sam answered.

"Well, if there's one thing my father is good at, it's keeping secrets," Seamus remarked. He moved from the window to the bed and sat down. "Cat—Catriona—and I were twins. When I developed a Legacy, my father thought Cat might, too. When she didn't, he decided to see if he could make one happen."

"You mean like—" Sam began.

"Like what Drac was trying to do?" Seamus said. "Basically. Only he had a whole team of government scientists working on it for him. And it was supposed to be safe. As we found out, though, it wasn't. At least, not for Cat."

"What did they do to her?" Sam asked.

"I don't even really know," said Seamus. "Some of it involved using my blood for transfusions. Bone marrow. Spinal fluid. They thought maybe whatever had been activated in me would activate in her."

"And she went along with it?" said Six.

Seamus nodded. "She wanted us to be the same," he said. "She always did. I mean, we both did. If one of us had something, we wanted the other one to have it, too."

"But you didn't want her to have a Legacy?" said Sam.

"No, I did," Seamus said. "At first. But when I saw what all the experiments were doing to her, I told my dad I wanted to stop. Cat, though, she wanted to make our father happy. Especially after what happened to our mother."

"So the part about her dying in the Mog attack was true?" Six said.

"Yeah," said Seamus. "After that, my dad became obsessed with Legacies and the Garde." He looked from Sam to Six. "With you. That's when he started campaigning to start a special task force. He didn't tell you any of this?"

"Not exactly," Sam said. "And none of that about you and your sister."

Seamus shook his head. "I think he went a little crazy," he said. He took a deep breath. "Anyway, then Cal got really sick. I don't even know what was wrong with her, exactly. But I know it had something to do with what they were doing to her. What *I* was helping them do to her. When she died, that's when I ran."

Six didn't know what to say. She knew what she *wanted* to say, which is that she knew they should never have trusted McKenna. But she wasn't about to say it in front of Seamus. If he was telling them the truth, could they believe anything McKenna had told them? And who was he really working for? She suddenly had a lot of questions.

Sam looked at his watch. "I hate to say this, but we need to go. Seamus, I want you to tell Nine everything, okay? He'll believe you. And he'll make sure nothing happens to you. When we get back, we'll sort this out. Okay?"

Seamus hesitated, then nodded. "Okay."

Back in the hallway, Six found her voice. "Do you believe him?"

"We have no reason not to," said Sam as they walked.

"So, what do we do? If what Seamus says is true, we don't even know who we're really working for. For all we know, they're using us to find this serum for themselves."

"I think we need to hear McKenna's side of the story," Sam said.

Six groaned. "Why do you always have to be so . . ."

"Objective?" Sam suggested.

"I was going to say irritating," said Six.

They passed through the lounge, which was now empty. Six was relieved, as she wasn't in the mood for pretending everything was all right in front of Nemo, Max and Rena. She waited impatiently for the elevator, and once they were in it, she tapped on the wall with her nails until the doors opened again and she and Sam were heading back to Nine's office.

She didn't knock. She threw open the door and went inside. McKenna was there, holding a cell phone to his ear. When he saw the look on her face, he said, "I think I need to call you back," then slipped the phone into his pocket.

"Is something wrong?" he asked.

"I don't know," Six said as Sam shut the door. "That's what we're about to find out."

CHAPTER NINE

SAM

POINT REYES, CA

"WHO WERE YOU TALKING TO JUST NOW?"

Sam faced McKenna, waiting for an answer.

The man started to answer, stopped, then said, "Karen Walker."

"FBI agent Walker?" Sam said.

McKenna nodded. "Although she's no longer with the Bureau. She now oversees a group called Operation Watchtower."

"And you're working with her?" Six asked.

"Yes," said McKenna. "So are you."

"Whoa, you'd better back up," Sam said. He knew Karen Walker, of course. Although she had initially worked with the Mogadorians in a misguided attempt to gain access to their technology, she had realized her error and sided with the Garde to fight against them. Her aid was instrumental in preventing the Mogs from conquering Earth, and Sam and the others were grateful for that. But he had never fully trusted her. She was ruthless, driven, and calculating. Hearing that she was somehow connected to what he and Six were doing with McKenna did not make him happy.

It made Six furious.

"You lied to us," she said. Sam recognized the tone in her voice. If McKenna didn't respond in a way that defused the situation, she was going to explode. Or walk out.

"No," McKenna said. "I didn't lie."

Those were not the right words. Six turned to Sam. "I told you—"

"I didn't know myself," McKenna said.

"What do you mean?" Sam said. "How could you not know?"

"I knew about Watchtower," McKenna answered. "But there are several aspects to the program, each with distinct responsibilities. Mine—ours—is to address issues related to Human Garde activity. Karen Walker's directive is different. Only when our assignments started to overlap was I put in contact with her. Until then, I didn't know she was involved."

"What do you mean 'overlap'?" Sam asked. Six was still standing there, and he took the fact that she hadn't stormed out of the room as a positive. But she wasn't saying anything.

"When we discovered that Bray is potentially trying to

weaponize Legacies, that crossed over into Walker's territory," McKenna said.

Now it was starting to make sense.

"Walker is trying to develop military uses for kids with Legacies?" Six said, breaking her silence. "Tell me that's not what you're saying right now."

"No," McKenna said. "At least, I don't believe so. As I said, I don't know everything about Watchtower. What I do know is that she's been a very useful resource."

"Oh, okay," Six said, her voice dripping with sarcasm. "That makes everything all right, then. I guess we should also ignore that you apparently caused your daughter's death by trying to do to her what we're trying to stop Bray from doing."

Sam cringed. He was obviously wondering the same thing after what Seamus had told them, but this was not how he would have brought up the topic. He looked at McKenna to see his reaction. He expected anger, at them or at Seamus for telling them what they knew. Instead, he saw sadness on the man's face. Deep sadness. McKenna looked as if he'd been gut-punched.

"What happened to Catriona was terrible," he said.

"Terrible?" said Six. "How about criminal? You're her father."

McKenna didn't respond immediately. When he did, his voice was soft. "I think about her every day," he said. "I'm doing what I'm doing because of her. For her and others like her."

"What you did killed her," Six said coldly.

"Catriona was already dying," McKenna said. "She had acute myeloid leukemia. She wasn't responding to treatments. I thought—I hoped—that perhaps we could somehow stop or slow the progression of her disease using blood or gene therapy from someone who had developed a Legacy."

"Seamus," Sam said.

"Being her twin, he already was the best option," McKenna continued. "Because he has a Legacy, we thought that maybe the regenerative capabilities could somehow be passed to Catriona. It was all extremely experimental." He paused. "And it didn't work."

"That's not quite the version we got from Seamus," Sam told him.

McKenna took a deep breath. "Seamus took Cat's death very hard. Particularly after already losing his mother. In his mind, a lot of the responsibility for both things was due to the Garde, the Entity, the Legacies. It all became jumbled together. It gave him something to be angry at, which helped him deal with what he was going through at the time, but ultimately became a much larger problem. And he was angry with me, too, of course. I understand why. He was afraid, and also I suspect felt a little guilty that he was alive when his sister wasn't. It was a lot for anyone to deal with. I did what I could to hold what was left of our family together, but I was grieving, too. I made mistakes."

Sam looked again at Six. The expression on her face had softened. She glanced at Sam, then at McKenna. "It must have been very hard for both of you," she said. Sam knew this was as much of an apology as McKenna was going to get.

"It was," McKenna said. "It still is."

"But we still have questions," said Six.

"I'm sure you do," McKenna said. "Unfortunately, it will have to wait. If you two are still going to Argentina, you need to leave. And if you're not going, I need to know so that I can make other arrangements."

Sam looked over at Six. He raised an eyebrow.

"We're going," Six said. She turned to McKenna. "I don't know what will happen when we get back, but I want to see this through."

Although McKenna only nodded in response, Sam could feel the relief coming from him. Their relationship had changed, there was no way around that, but for now they could focus on a shared goal.

"Argentina is an unpredictable place," McKenna said. "Walker doesn't want to involve their law enforcement or military, and I agree with her on that. Instead, she's arranged for some of her people to act as backup should you need it. They'll meet you at the airfield."

"No," Six said.

"No?" said Sam.

"I don't want her *people* involved," Six said. "I don't trust her."

"But—" McKenna said.

"We go alone," Six insisted. "Or we don't go."

McKenna looked at Sam, hoping for a counterargument,

but Sam only shrugged. He knew arguing with Six was pointless.

"All right," McKenna conceded. "No backup. I've got the most recent satellite photographs of Wonderland and the surrounding area loaded onto tablets you'll find on the plane. Have you picked up your weapons from Lexa?"

"We'll head there now," Sam said, preparing to go. Then he remembered something. "Who's our pilot?"

McKenna looked pained. "You're not going to like that," he said. "His name is Ignacio Soto. He's one of the guys Walker lined up." He held up a hand. "Before you say no, let me remind you that you're going to need someone who knows the area. He's from there. In fact, he's intimately familiar with Wonderland."

"He's one of Bray's?" said Six.

"No," McKenna said. "His mother was a maid there. He tagged along. Practically grew up there. He can help you get in and out."

Six groaned. "Whatever," she said.

"I think that's a yes," Sam told McKenna as he went over and started herding Six towards the door. "We'll be going now. Before she changes her mind."

They left the office and headed for the armory.

"This sucks," Six said as they went inside. "This whole thing. It sucks. Just so you know."

"What sucks?" Lexa asked, setting a knife down on a table that was spread with a variety of weapons.

"Very long story," Sam said. "No time. What have you got?"

"What do you know about Watchtower?" Six asked Lexa.

"No time," Sam reminded her.

"What do *you* know about Watchtower?" said Lexa.

"Great," said Six. "Apparently everybody knows about it except us."

"Well, we know now," Sam reminded her. "What's this do?" He picked up a black metal orb the size of a tennis ball.

"Incendiary device," Lexa said. "You depress the buttons on the top and bottom, toss it at what you want to set on fire and duck. Or you can activate it with this." She held up a tiny device. "Plant them, leave and blow them up from close to a mile away."

"Nice," Sam said. "I'll take three."

Lexa held up a black backpack. "You have six," she said, handing him the pack. "Each," she added as she gave Six an identical one. "Along with the usual assortment of things you can use to hurt someone or create a situation. Also, wrist communicators, in-ear receivers so you can talk to each other when you're not in the same place and snacks."

"Snacks?" Sam said. "What do they do?"

"Keep your blood sugar up," said Lexa. "They're snacks. Cookies, to be exact."

"Oh," said Sam. "I thought that was code for something else."

"So, about Watchtower," Six said.

"No. Time," said Sam, taking her by the hand and dragging her away.

"Good luck," Lexa called, waving. "Call me if you need anything. And kick some ass."

Six and Sam left the building, where they found an SUV and a driver waiting for them. As they rode to the airfield, Six looked out the window, not saying anything.

"So," Sam said after a few minutes of silence.

"I'm still mad," she said.

"I kind of figured that," he said.

Six turned to him. "What are we supposed to believe? The whole reason I didn't want to get involved with any of this is because you never know who to trust, or what they really want or who is actually pulling the strings."

"Life is messy, Six," Sam said, taking her hand. "It's kind of always like that."

"No," Six said. "Not always. Not with you."

Sam squeezed her hand. "Thanks," he said. "The thing is, it can't always be just us. Not if we want to help these kids."

"How much help have we really been? Edwige is still missing. Ghost has gone over to the dark side. Yo-Yo is dead."

"All of which would have happened with or without us," said Sam. "But you know what *wouldn't* have happened without us—without *you*? Nemo."

Six gave him a half smile. "She's turned out to be pretty badass, hasn't she?"

"Yes," said Sam. "And mostly because of you."

"I think Nine's little shark-talking trick helped," said Six.

"But you're the one who took a chance on her first," Sam reminded her. "You're the one who made her believe she was worth something. I get that you're pissed about McKenna, and Walker, and whatever this Watchtower thing turns out to be. And if you decide you don't want to be involved anymore when this is over, I'm behind you one hundred percent."

"Even if I decide that all I want to do is wander around the world sleeping on beaches again?" Six asked.

"Sure," Sam said. "If that's what you want."

When the car arrived at the airfield, they got out and boarded the waiting plane. As they entered the cabin, a man came out of the cockpit. Thirtyish, short, with dark skin and buzzed black hair. He held out his hand. "Ignacio," he said as he shook hands first with Six and then with Sam. "Nice to meet you."

"You too," Sam said. He looked around the plane, which was the same Gulfstream they had almost crashed in.

"Everything is fine," Ignacio said, noticing his attention. "I heard you had a little trouble with her. I've checked everything out. All you have to do this time is enjoy the ride."

"That's what I heard last time," Sam said, setting down his bag.

"I have some questions," Six announced.

"About the plane?" Ignacio asked.

"About Watchtower. And Wonderland. And Walker."

Ignacio grinned. "Let me get the plane in the air," he said. "Then we'll have ten hours to talk."

Six and Sam took their seats. Half an hour later, with the

G650 airborne, Ignacio emerged from the cockpit and joined them in the main cabin. Six and Sam, who had been looking at the information on Wonderland that was downloaded to their tablets, set the devices down.

"All right," Ignacio said. "What do you want to know?"

"How did you get involved with Walker?" Six asked.

"Do you know about my mother?" said Ignacio.

"We know she worked at Wonderland," Sam answered.

Ignacio nodded. "Right. Well, when she'd saved enough money, she brought me and my brother to the United States. She wanted to get us as far from the corruption she saw at Wonderland as she could. She took a job here cleaning motels. My brother and I would hang out with her after school, doing our homework or watching TV in one of the rooms. One day we watched this movie *The Silence of the Lambs*, about an FBI agent who hunts down serial killers. I thought that sounded like the coolest job ever, and I decided I wanted to join the FBI. Everybody thought I was crazy, except my brother and my mother. They told me I could do it. And I did. I got accepted into the Academy, made it through and went to work with the Bureau. That's how I met Agent Walker. When she was asked to work for Watchtower, she contacted me and asked if I would join her."

"Do you trust her?" Six asked.

"Wow," said Ignacio, laughing. "You get right to the point, don't you?"

"Well?" said Six when he hesitated. "Do you?"

Ignacio looked thoughtful. "One of the things I learned

hanging around Wonderland was that to understand why people do what they do, you have to figure out what motivates them. With some people, it's easy. They want money, or power. Bray is like that. You know that he's always going to make the choice that gets him more of those things, which means you can't trust him not to turn on you. With other people, it's trickier. It might seem like they want power, but what they really want is to not be afraid. Or it might seem like they're motivated by greed when really they're trying to protect someone they love. It's not always easy to figure out."

"That doesn't answer my question about Walker," Six said.

"I'm getting there," Ignacio said. "Agent Walker wants to make the world a safer place."

"Which still doesn't answer the question about whether you trust her or not," said Six.

"People who want to make the world a safer place can go either way," Ignacio continued. "Sometimes, they go after anything they see as a threat. Like people who think every shark should be dragged out of the water and killed. Because a handful of people get bit every year, they think we should remove the possibility of it happening. They don't think about the good that sharks do maintaining a balance in the ocean ecosystem."

Sam, thinking about their own recent experience with sharks, nodded. "Every shark is a bad shark," he said.

"Exactly," Ignacio said. "On the other hand, people who

want to protect other people can seek out ways to make others safer. Instead of killing the sharks, they try to find ways to make people who interact with sharks able to do it more safely. They invent shark repellent, or devices that keep sharks from coming near swimmers, or whatever. Instead of looking for ways to remove the thing they're afraid of, they look for ways to deal with it more effectively."

"And which type is Walker?" asked Six.

"You tell me," said Ignacio. "From what I understand, you've had experiences with her."

"Well, she started out trying to hunt us," Six said.

"Why?" Ignacio asked.

"Because the Mogs convinced her we were the bad guys," Six said.

"And then?" Ignacio prodded.

"The she realized she'd made a mistake, and she started helping us," said Six.

"So, she realized the sharks weren't the problem," said Ignacio.

"More like she realized the sharks weren't the sharks," Six suggested.

Ignacio smiled. "Good point," he said. "You sure you didn't go through the Academy?"

"Just because she realized she was wrong and helped us out a couple of times, that doesn't mean I trust her," Six argued.

"Your choice," Ignacio said. "But maybe you don't have

to trust her right now. Maybe you have to trust me. Can you do that?"

Sam watched Six's face, waiting for her answer. When she said "We'll see," he had to stop himself from laughing.

"Fair enough," Ignacio said. "Well, how about we get started going over the plan? The plane will fly itself for a little while. That gives me time to tell you everything I know and for you to get a little sleep before we land."

For the next few hours, they went over the diagrams of Wonderland. Ignacio proved to be an invaluable resource, telling Sam and Six about the mansion, the grounds and what they might expect to encounter there. When he went to resume control of the plane, leaving Six and Sam alone, Sam leaned back on the couch.

"I like him," he said.

"You like everybody," said Six.

"Not *everybody*," Sam objected. "I disliked Dennings from the second I saw him."

"Okay, everybody who isn't trying to kill you," Six said. "Hey, I figured out your motivation. You want to find the good in everyone."

"Does that mean you can trust me?"

"I don't know if it means I *should*," Six answered. "But I do."

"Aww," Sam said. "You're giving me feels."

"Ugh," Six said. "Your turn. What's my motivation?"

"You?" said Sam. "That's easy. You want justice. You

want good people to be rewarded, and you want bad people to be punished."

"Isn't that what everyone wants?" Six said. "I thought that was normal."

"It is for you and Batman," Sam said, kissing her. "Come on. Let's get some rest. I have a feeling it's going to be a long day."

Four hours later, the plane rumbled down a private airstrip in the rain forest of northern Argentina. When it came to a stop, Ignacio walked into the cabin. "All right," he said. "It's time for you to meet our secret weapon."

"Secret weapon?" Sam said as Ignacio opened the door. "What secret weapon?"

Ignacio exited the plane. Sam and Six followed. At the bottom of the steps, Ignacio was hugging a woman. She was even shorter than he was, with the same dark skin and hair. The two of them kissed each other on the cheek, then Ignacio turned around.

"Sam. Six," he said. "I'd like you to meet my mother."

CHAPTER TEN

SIX
THE RAIN FOREST OF ARGENTINA

VALENTINA SOTO NAVIGATED THE RUSTED-OUT FIAT up a narrow dirt road that led them to the gates of Wonderland. She was dressed in a pink maid's uniform. In the backseat, Six and Sam sat watching the trees of the rain forest pass by just beyond the windows.

"We're almost there," Valentina said. "When we arrive, the guards will ask me how I like the weather. I will answer that it is a lovely day for drying sheets on the line. This is code to let them know that everything is okay and that no one has placed any explosive devices in the car, or anything like that."

"What would you say if they had?" Six asked, curious.

"I would tell them that it was a good day for mopping the floors," Valentina said.

"But what if you were the one who planted the explosives?" Six continued.

"Then it really wouldn't matter," said Valentina. "As we would all be dead when the bomb exploded."

"I guess that's one way to look at it," Six remarked.

"What if the guards decide to look for themselves?" Sam said.

Valentina lifted her hand. She was holding a Browning Hi Power MK1 pistol. "Then we go to Plan B. But they won't. I am considered family here. They trust me. Once we are inside, I will park the car and let you out. When we are inside, you know what to do."

"Find Bray and take him out," said Six. "Then leave."

"Good," said Valentina as if she was the one leading the mission.

"If you don't mind me asking," Sam said. "Why did you come back? You could have just stayed in the United States."

"I could have," Valentina agreed, putting the car into a lower gear as it started up a long hill. "But Argentina is my home. I missed it."

"But why come back *here*?" Sam pressed.

Valentina looked at him in the rearview mirror. "Because the FBI asked me to. They gave my son a chance. I wanted to help."

"It just seems . . . dangerous," Sam said. "And you didn't have to."

"No, I did not," Valentina agreed. "All right. We are almost there. It is time for you to get in back."

She stopped the car, and they all got out. Valentina opened the car's trunk, and Six and Sam got inside. It was a very tight fit. "It'll only be for a few minutes," Valentina said as she shut the trunk.

"This would be a lot easier if I could make us invisible," Six said as the car started up again.

"And miss spending this quality time together?" Sam joked.

The car rattled along, making for an uncomfortable ride. But Valentina was true to her promise, and not long after, they felt the car come to a stop.

"Good morning, Emile," Valentina said cheerfully, her voice muffled but still understandable. "Lautaro."

"Good morning, Valentina," said a man's voice. "How do you like the weather today?"

"Wonderful," Valentina said. "An excellent day for hanging the sheets on the line. They will dry in no time."

There was silence. Then a thump sounded twice on the trunk. Six held her breath, preparing herself in case she had to leap into action. But they started to move again. There was another short drive. Then the car stopped, they heard a door shutting and a moment later the trunk lifted.

"Here we are," Valentina said, looking down at them.

They got out. Six and Sam had seen pictures, but Wonderland was even more beautiful in person. It sat at the very top of a hill, rising above the forest below it. Columns lined the porch, and vines twined around them, covered in white and yellow flowers. The grounds around the mansion were well maintained, the rain forest kept at bay so that the house seemed to float on an island of green in the middle of the lush fauna.

"As we discussed, there will be a small staff inside," Valentina said. "The night maid. The cook. Bray's bodyguard. Maybe some others."

"But no kids," Six said. "You're sure about that?"

Valentina nodded. "No. Not at this location."

Six was relieved about this. It was one less thing to worry about. At least for the moment.

Valentina got out of the car. She opened the back door and took out a cardboard carton holding cleaning supplies. Then the three of them continued on into the house.

They walked through a back door and into a hallway. "The kitchen is through there," Valentina said, speaking softly as she pointed to an open doorway. "Wait in the hall until I see what the situation is."

Six and Sam did as she suggested, although Six couldn't resist looking into the room. There, a harried-looking young woman was stirring something in a pot on the stove.

"Magda, why are you cooking?" Valentina asked, setting the carton on a table. "Where's Yanel?"

"She quit," the girl said. She seemed to be practically in tears. "And now I've burned the soup!"

Valentina walked over and took the wooden spoon the girl was holding out of her hand. Valentina looked into the pot on the stove. Then she took the pot, dumped it into the sink and ran water in it.

"He's going to kill me!" Magda said, beginning to sob.

"Calm down," Valentina said. "What's happening?"

"He's gone crazy," said Magda. "Crazier. I don't know. Last night he threw a knife at Yanel, and she ran out. I didn't dare. I was afraid he would hurt the girl."

"Girl?" Valentina said. "What girl?"

"I don't know her name," Magda answered. "She's just a girl. He had her brought here. They say she's a *curandera*."

"A healer?" said Valentina, opening a can of soup and pouring it into the pot.

Magda nodded. "He's sick," she said. "Sick in his head."

Six looked at Sam. Had Bray brought someone with a healing Legacy to Wonderland?

"Where is he now?" Valentina asked.

"In his bedroom," said Magda. "I can't go back there. Please don't make me go back there."

Valentina put her hand on the girl's arm. "You don't have to," she said. "In fact, I want you to leave. Don't worry. I'll cover for you." She paused a moment, then asked, "Who else is in the house?"

"No one," said Magda. "Everyone else is too frightened. He even ordered the guard out."

"It will be all right," Valentina assured her as she put the soup on the stove to heat. "Just go."

A moment later, Valentina came into the hallway. She was carrying a tray on which were placed a bowl of soup, a napkin and a spoon. "Did you hear?" she asked.

"It sounds like everyone is gone," said Sam.

"Magda is the maid," Valentina said, nodding. "Follow me to the bedroom."

Valentina walked down the hallway, through an empty dining room and down another hallway. As they approached a door at the end of it, they heard the sound of someone yelling. Valentina paused, listening. Then, she pushed the door open. Again, Six and Sam waited outside, pressed against the wall, sneaking glances inside.

The room was a disaster. Furniture was upended. Sheets and draperies, torn to ribbons, were scattered across the floor. The glass from a broken mirror glittered in the sunlight coming through the bare windows. On the walls, smears of food created the impression of hastily scrawled graffiti.

In the center of it all stood Bray. He was barefoot, wearing only a dirty white undershirt and a pair of pajama bottoms. His hair was greasy and stood out in haphazard tufts, and his face was shadowed, with stubble. In one hand was a hypodermic needle, which he had plunged into the crook of his arm. On the floor around his feet lay half a dozen more.

Then Six's eye went to one corner of the room. There, huddled against the wall, her knees drawn up to her chest, was Edwige. Her eyes were closed, and she was silently mouthing something as if she was praying. Six wanted to run to her, but she stayed where she was.

Bray looked up. He pulled the needle from his arm and grinned. "Valentina," he said. "Are you the only one who hasn't abandoned me?"

"I brought you some soup," Valentina said, keeping her

voice calm. "I thought you might be hungry."

"I am," Bray said. "So hungry. You can't even imagine. I feel like I haven't eaten in days. Weeks." He held up the syringe. "It's this," he said. Then he laughed, a weirdly high giggle that filled the room. "It makes me so hungry. Maybe you should run, Valentina. Maybe I'm going to eat you up."

Valentina ignored him, setting the tray down on the bed, then picking up an overturned table and righting it. She transferred the tray to the table, then stood aside, her hands folded in front of her. Six, watching Edwige, waited for the girl to open her eyes and see them. But she didn't. She remained where she was, seemingly frozen in place.

"Come," Valentina said to Bray. "Eat something. You'll feel better."

Bray lumbered over to the table. Picking up the bowl of soup, he lifted it to his mouth and upended it, pouring in the soup. Most of it ran down his undershirt, staining it red. He slurped and gobbled at what was left, using his fingers to scoop the soup into his mouth.

Valentina quietly moved toward Edwige. When she was close enough to touch her, she knelt and put a hand on the girl's knee. Edwige gave a startled shriek and opened her eyes. The noise attracted Bray's attention.

"Don't touch her!" he shouted. He threw the bowl to the floor, where it shattered.

"I thought perhaps she could help me in the kitchen," Valentina said.

"Her?" Bray said, laughing. "Help? She can't help. She's

useless." He stomped through the pieces of broken bowl. "Useless! She can't even fix what's wrong in here." He smacked his hand against the side of his head, then hit himself half a dozen more times.

Edwige turned her head away, burying her face against her shoulder. Bray charged at her, stopping right in front of the girl. He bent down and laughed loudly. "Useless!" he screamed again. He lifted his hand to strike her.

Six had had enough. She stepped into the room. She didn't want to kill him in front of Edwige, but she wasn't going to let him hurt her either.

"Bray!" she shouted.

Bray turned his head. For a moment, he just stared at her. Then he grinned. "You," he said. He pointed at her with a thick, stubby finger. "You're what I need to feel better."

He charged.

Six prepared to meet him. Without her Legacies, she had only her strength, and although that was considerable, Bray seemed to be fueled by something other than normal human anger. When he plowed into her, he knocked her back and off balance. She regained her footing and hit him hard in the chest. He grunted, stumbled and swung at her. She ducked, and his hand went over her head, spinning him off balance. Six dealt him a kick to the side, and he flew backwards, landing on the floor.

As he struggled to get to his feet, two figures appeared out of thin air. Ghost and Scotty materialized on either side of Bray. Seeing them, he grinned.

"Take the healer," he ordered.

Scotty went towards Edwige, reaching out to grab her. Before he could, Valentina's hand came up. In it was her gun. She fired. A red stain appeared on Scotty's shirt, and his mouth opened in surprise as he crumpled to the floor.

"No!" Ghost shouted. She pointed her hands at Valentina, and the gun flew out of Valentina's hand and clattered onto the floor as she herself was slammed into the wall and knocked out. Then Ghost whirled and glared at Six, her eyes filled with hatred. At the same time, she took something from her pocket and handed it to Bray. It was a syringe.

"Good girl," Bray said. "Now get out of here. Take Scotty. I'll handle this."

"I have one more thing to take care of first," Ghost said.

Six felt a surge of power. Sam, who had come into the room, shouted as he was swept back through the door, which slammed shut. Six heard him pounding on it, but Ghost was using telekinesis to keep it bolted shut, and whatever the door was made of, it was withstanding Sam's assault. Dennings had been telling the truth. The girl's Legacies were very strong.

Now, Ghost turned her attention to Six. Six braced herself, instinctively calling up her own Legacies. Then she remembered she was without them, and the next moment she was lifted up in the air. Her head drew close to the ceiling. Below her, Ghost looked up with an expression of satisfaction.

"Aren't you going to fight back?" she said.

Six tried. She willed her Legacies to return. She attempted

to muster even an ounce of power. Nothing happened. And with the others unable to help her, she was on her own. It was not a good feeling.

As Six waited to see what Ghost would do, Bray uncapped the syringe the teleporter had brought for him and plunged it into his arm. Then he yanked out the needle and tossed it aside.

"Leave," he said to Ghost. "I'll finish this."

Ghost frowned. She obviously wanted to argue. Instead, she continued to hold Six up as she went over to Scotty's prone body and placed her hand on it. She gave Six one last look, then vanished. Six, no longer held up by telekinesis, fell to the floor. Snarling, Bray started towards her. She leaped to her feet and once again prepared to meet him.

But after a few feet, Bray stopped. His face contorted, and he clapped his hands over his ears. One eye began to twitch, opening and closing rapidly. Bray's mouth twisted into a rictus of pain. His tongue lolled, dripping drool down his chest.

Slowly, he began to spin in a wobbly circle, his feet stomping on the trash that littered the floor. A moan escaped his lips, growing into a howl as he thrashed his head from side to side. The veins in his neck swelled, pulsating. When he turned back to face Six again, his skin was mottled, flowers of black and blue blooming across it. Six had never seen anything like this.

Bray staggered forward a step, reaching for her. His fingers twisted, turning in on themselves until the nails cut into his palms. Blood began to flow, dripping down his wrists. And still he howled, an unearthly sound of pain that had no words.

Behind Six, Sam finally got the door open and ran inside. Valentina too was stirring.

Edwige whimpered.

"Get her out of here," Six said.

Sam and Valentina pulled the frightened girl to her feet. Six stood between them and Bray as they hustled her out of the room. Then Sam came back to stand beside Six.

Bray began to claw at his face, his nails tearing at the skin. It was terrible to watch, and Six wondered if they should let him rip himself apart or put an end to it. Before she had to make the decision, Bray gasped. He made a choking sound, and his head flew back. Black bile erupted from him, splashing the ceiling and the wall behind him as it arced through the air. Then he collapsed onto the floor. He didn't move.

Sam and Six waited a minute before checking for a pulse. There was none. Satisfied that the man was dead, they went out into the hall, where Valentina waited with Edwige. "Take her to the car," Six told Valentina. "Sam and I will finish up here."

Valentina nodded. Holding Edwige's hands, she led the girl away. Six shucked off the backpack she was wearing and opened it, taking out one of the bombs Lexa had packed for her. She tossed it into the bedroom, where it rolled to a stop beside Bray's lifeless body. Then she and Sam went through the other rooms of the mansion, leaving a device in each one.

Then they went through the secret passageway that Ignacio had told them about and descended into Wonderland's lower depths.

There they found the laboratory and operating room. They were empty now, but evidence of what had taken place there remained: medical instruments scattered around, bloodstains on the concrete floors, vials of various-colored substances spilled on the countertops.

"Looks like Bray turned this place upside down, too," Sam remarked. "Should we take any of this back to analyze?"

"No," Six said, tossing the last of the incendiary devices into the room. "It all goes. Come on. Time to get out of here."

Back upstairs, they walked through the kitchen and out of the house. Valentina and Edwige were waiting in the Fiat. Edwige was sitting silently in the passenger seat, staring dully out the window at nothing. She barely reacted when Sam and Six got into the car.

"He did something to her," Valentina said. "Something bad."

Six leaned forward and looked closely at Edwige's neck. There was a scar at the base of her skull. The wound was only recently healed. She looked over at Sam and saw that he was staring at it, too. "Let's get out of here," she said to Valentina.

As they approached the guardhouse once more, Six was relieved to see that the guards had abandoned their posts and the gates were open. Once they were through the gate and driving down the road, Six turned to Sam. "Blow it up," she said.

Sam took out the controller Lexa had given him. He pressed the button. A moment later, the forest behind them erupted with a roar. Looking through the rear window of the Fiat, Six saw Wonderland turn into a cloud of fire and ash. She saw the two guards throw themselves to the ground. Smoke billowed into the sky, thick and black, as the bombs consumed the mansion and all its secrets.

Valentina kept driving. Six turned back around and once more placed her hand on Edwige's neck. "It's over now," she told the girl. "It's all over."

Edwige slept the entire flight back to California. Once there, she was taken to the HGA infirmary. Six and Sam went directly to Nine's office, where they found Nine with McKenna.

"Cutter was able to provide us with the locations of the other camps where Bray and Dennings were holding kids with Legacies," McKenna informed them. "We've shut them all down and taken the kids into our custody."

"How many?" Sam asked.

"Seventy-two kids."

"And by *we*, I assume you mean you and Walker," said Six.

McKenna nodded. "Walker's division has also taken responsibility for everything we retrieved from the ship and from the other camps."

"You mean the black ooze and the serum Drac was working on?" Six said. "Why aren't we taking the lead on this?"

"I've been given other directives," McKenna said. "Walker's team is better equipped to deal with that technology."

Six looked at Nine. "And you're okay with this?"

Nine shrugged. "I've got enough to worry about running this place," he said. "Especially with a bunch of new kids coming in."

"Am I the only one who isn't okay with it?" Six said. "Sam?"

Sam looked uncomfortable. "I'd like to know more about what exactly Walker is doing and what's she's planning to do with everything we've recovered," he admitted.

"I'm not entirely sure," said McKenna. "As I told you before, we work independently until—"

"Can we have a meeting with her?" Six interrupted.

"I don't see what that would—" McKenna began.

"You said if I didn't want to be involved anymore, you would be behind me," Six said, speaking to Sam. "One hundred percent. Remember?"

Sam nodded. "I remember."

"Well, I don't," said Six. "Want to be involved anymore."

"What?" said McKenna. "Why? This mission was a success."

Everyone looked at Six, waiting for an answer.

"Was it?" she said. "A dead kid and a dead agent, another kid still missing and dangerously pissed off at us, our Legacies gone, and now we find out we're actually working for some group no one wants to give us any real information about and who has taken the technology *our* mission brought back. Doesn't sound so successful. Not to me, anyway."

"Your Legacies will come back," Nine said. "And—"

"Save the speeches for your new students," Six said. "I'm out."

She walked to the office door, opened it and left. As she strode down the hallway, Sam ran and caught up with her. "You're bluffing, right?" he said. "To get McKenna to give us more information."

Six shook her head. "I don't trust him," Six said. "And I really don't trust Walker. How can we work with them?"

Sam didn't argue. He walked beside her as they left the building. The SUV they'd come from the airport in was still sitting there. Six was contemplating the pros and cons of borrowing it and driving away when she heard a voice say, "Going somewhere?"

She turned around. Nemo was standing on the steps, hands on her hips. "Ghost is still missing, right? You going to go look for her?"

Six sighed. "It's complicated," she said.

Nemo walked down the steps and came to stand in front of Six. "Know what it looks like?" she said. "Looks like you're running away."

"Like I said, it's complicated."

Nemo cocked her head and folded her arms over her chest. "Physics is complicated," she said. "Helping your friends, that's not. We're friends, right?"

"Of course," Six said.

"Well, I need your help finding my other friend," Nemo said.

"You mean your friend who tried to kill me?" said Six.

Nemo shrugged. "We all have bad days," she said. "Besides, she's been brainwashed or whatever. I know the real Ghost is still in there. So, are you going to help or not?"

Six looked at Sam, who was standing a little way off, watching the exchange. "I think the student has become the teacher," he said.

Six groaned. "All right," she said. "But we do this my way. Got it?"

"Is there any other way?" Nemo said.

"Get in," Six said. She opened the door of the SUV and climbed into the driver's seat. Sam got in on the passenger side, while Nemo settled into the back. Six started the engine.

"I don't suppose you have any idea where we're going," Sam said.

"You heard the girl," Six said as she drove towards the front gate. "To find Ghost."

"I got that part," Sam said. "I'm just wondering about, you know, the *next* part. Like, where she might be. How we'll find her. What we'll do if we do find her."

"*When* we find her," Nemo said.

"When we find her," Six agreed. "You worry too much," she added to Sam.

"Someone has to," Sam said under his breath.

Six looked in the rearview mirror. Nemo was looking back at her. Six winked. Nemo grinned.

"I still think you're bluffing," Sam said as the HGA building disappeared behind them.

Six didn't say anything. *We'll see*, she thought as they approached the gates and they started to swing open. *We'll see.*

A NEW ENEMY HAS BEEN UNCOVERED. FOR THE NEXT
GENERATION, THE BATTLE HAS JUST BEGUN. . . .
DON'T MISS THE SECOND BOOK IN THE
LORIEN LEGACIES LEBORN SERIES!

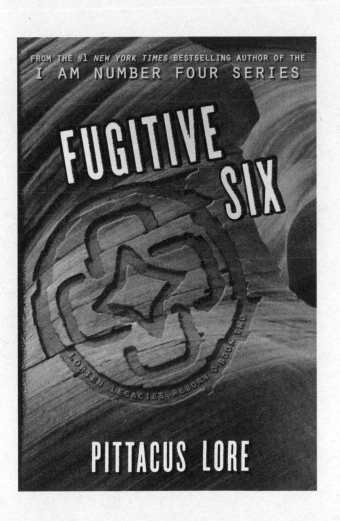

CHAPTER ONE

DUANPHEN
BANGKOK, THAILAND

DUANPHEN WATCHED THE BEGGAR AS HE SCURRIED through traffic with his bucket and rag. The boy couldn't have been more than twelve, small, with a mop of greasy black hair. He picked his cars smartly—shiny ones with tinted windows and drunk passengers. He splashed dirty water on windshields and stretched across hoods to ineffectively clean up, mostly smearing around more grime. Drivers rolled down their windows to curse at him but usually relented, shoved a note into his hand to make him go away and turned on their wipers.

It was after midnight and Royal City Avenue still pulsed with life. Motorcycles weaved through the traffic. Drunk clubbers stumbled into the street. Neon lights flashed in unison with their bars' competing bass lines.

Duanphen rubbed the handcuff around her wrist which attached her to the executive's briefcase. The metal irritated her. Just like this place.

Three months since she was last here. She hadn't missed it.

The beggar spotted Duanphen and her limo. Well, not *her* limo, precisely—it belonged to the executive; she was only watching over it. The black stretch was double-parked obnoxiously in front of a club where go-go dancers gyrated in the windows. The executive had been so excited when he saw the place that he was practically drooling; they just *had* to pull over. The rest of the executive's security had gone in with him, but not Duanphen. She was too young.

"Sweet ride," the beggar said in Thai as he stopped in front of her. He held out his rag threateningly. "Dirty, though. For a few bucks I'll wash it for you."

Duanphen regarded him coldly. "Go away."

The kid stared up at her, as if trying to decide if he should press his luck. At seventeen, Duanphen wasn't that much older than him, although her steely gaze made her seem it. She stood a shade over six feet tall, her long-limbed body like a switchblade. She kept her hair buzzed and wore no makeup except for some extra-dark eyeliner. Her petite nose was a crooked zigzag; it looked like it'd been erased and redrawn.

"I know you," he said.

"No."

"You're a hooker," he said with a laugh. "No! That's not right. Where have I seen you?"

"Doesn't matter," Duanphen said. "Get lost."

The beggar hopped in the air as the realization hit him. "You're a fighter!" he said, shaking his rag at her. "I know you! You're the one who cheats. The one—"

As if by magic, the boy's bucket tipped towards him and spilled water down the front of his pants. He gasped and shut up, staring at Duanphen.

Not magic. Telekinesis.

"If you do know me," Duanphen said, "then you know what I will do when I run out of patience."

The beggar looked at her wide-eyed, then took off into the crowd with a yelp. Duanphen pursed her lips. Calling her a cheater. What did that little idiot know about anything?

Duanphen had been doing Muay Thai fights since she was fourteen, a necessity to supplement the pittance she got working sixty hours a week at the garment factory, all to pay her rent at a roach-infested boardinghouse. Before her Legacies kicked in, Duanphen had lost more fights than she won, often getting her face smashed to a bloody pulp by girls twice her age.

Telekinesis, she discovered after the invasion, made the fights easier. An assisted leg-trip here. A deflected punch there. She went on a winning streak. She began to bet on herself. The competition got tougher, but her telekinesis got stronger, too.

It wasn't until an opponent managed to get her in a choke hold and Duanphen's electrified skin unexpectedly triggered that the fight promoters got wise. They called what she'd been doing "stealing" and gave her a choice: work off the debt or die. She considered fighting her way out, but they had a lot of guns, and blocking punches wasn't the same as stopping bullets.

Word soon got out that the local mob had a Garde for hire. That was how the executive found her. He knew a lot of people. He was a talker. An excellent negotiator.

That's what made him so valuable to the Foundation.

The Foundation paid off her debt and gave Duanphen a fresh start. They gave her more money than she could hope to earn in a thousand fights, plus clothes and a splashy apartment in Hong Kong. All she needed to do in exchange was watch over this smarmy executive and carry around his briefcase.

Not a bad deal at all, she'd thought. At least until she got to know the executive better. Men liked him, of course, because he was always making gross jokes and buying drinks. But, to Duanphen, he was a middle-aged creep, the kind of tourist she'd encountered a million times in Bangkok. He was always complaining about his cold wife and his kids who didn't talk to him.

The executive sauntered out of the club surrounded by a phalanx of brutish bodyguards. He had a lot of security—more added in the last few weeks, for reasons no one explained to Duanphen. The muscle cleared a path on the sidewalk, shoving aside gaudily dressed revelers as they escorted the executive to his armored limo. People craned their necks to catch a glimpse of what kind of man commanded such an entourage. The executive didn't look like much—a thatch of thinning blond hair, short, a potbelly, his designer suit wrinkled from the humidity, his salmon-colored shirt damp with sweat. Not famous, the onlookers probably thought, disappointed. Just some rich jerk. Bangkok was full of them.

Duanphen opened the car door for her rich jerk. He pinched her cheek affectionately and she died a little inside.

"Missed a banging good time, Dawn," he said, his words slurred from too much champagne.

"Mm," Duanphen offered noncommittally. She despised his butchered *farang* version of her name.

The executive interpreted Duanphen's murmur as encouragement. "One of these days you'll be old enough to make a proper piece of arm candy," he told her.

Duanphen smiled mirthlessly and clenched her fist. She slid into the backseat beside the executive, one of the other bodyguards taking the wheel.

"Meant to ask you," the executive said. "Happy to be back home?"

"No," she replied. "I hate this place."

"Really? I've always loved Bangkok." He waved his hand airily out the window. "Although it's more fun when you aren't bloody surrounded."

Duanphen knew the executive chafed at the extra security. His bodyguards weren't just the average bruisers anyone could hire around Bangkok; they were highly trained mercenaries. The Blackstone Group detachment had been his wife's idea—or, rather, his wife's command. She was in the

Foundation too and seemed to wield more power than her husband. That, at least, cheered Duanphen.

The rest of the executive's security piled into two cars, one behind and one in front. The executive sighed as his ungainly security force began the journey through the crowded streets back to his hotel.

The executive checked his watch. "Ah, running a bit late." He wiggled his fingers at Duanphen. "Let's get to business, shall we?"

Ostensibly, the executive was in Bangkok to sign some paperwork on a hotel he'd invested in. But while that work had made the executive rich, it was no longer his true occupation.

Duanphen offered him the briefcase. The executive unlocked it with his thumbprint, then lifted out its contents—a sleek tablet computer. This, too, the executive unlocked with his fingerprint, followed by a nine-digit code that he kept hidden from Duanphen. The tablet connected to a secure server via satellite uplink. The executive settled back, waiting to connect.

"A good turnout," the executive said approvingly. He liked showing off, so he didn't mind if Duanphen peeked at the tablet.

There were twenty people waiting for the executive in the e-conference. They were represented by icons—an infinity symbol, a snarling fox, a silver-and-blue star that Duanphen thought was the logo for an American football team. The mundane avatars of the very rich people in the executive's club.

A slithering blob of shadows appeared among the icons. That represented the executive himself. That was always how the auctioneer looked during one of these Foundation events.

"Good evening, all," the executive said, after unmuting his side of the conference and activating his voice modulator. "On the block tonight, we have the services of Salma G., for the weekend of January third through the fifth."

The executive called up Salma's picture and sent it out to the bidders. The girl had wavy brown hair that was long and unruly, plus a thick unibrow that made her look like she was deep in thought. In the image, Salma wore a tangle of scarves that were nearly indistinguishable from her billowy dress, patterns upon patterns. She sat cross-legged, fingers pinched together like she was meditating, her eyes gazing into the middle distance.

He muted the conference so he could smirk at Duanphen. "Nice costume on her, eh? The lads in marketing thought it'd be clever to give her a sort of gypsy fortune-teller vibe."

"I see," Duanphen replied.

"Don't need any of that when you're on the block, eh? Your face conveys exactly what you're for."

Duanphen touched her crooked nose but didn't reply. The executive had already unmuted the video conference and was again speaking to his international audience.

"The following specs were included in your dossier, but I'll summarize. Salma is sixteen years old. Moroccan. Speaks fluent Arabic, passable French and passable English.

No health concerns. Buyer must provide a halal diet. Salma's telekinetic control remains middling at best, so, if that's what you're interested in, we've got better assets available. Her real allure is her precognitive ability. She's perfect for a visit to the track or the casino, although we don't recommend attempting to use her Legacies to choose stocks or other long-term investments. Salma is geo-restricted; you've already been provided with lists of approved locations. Bidders are also reminded that you are purchasing *only* the use of Salma's Legacies and that any behavior viewed by the Foundation as untoward or detrimental to the asset will result in swift expulsion from the organization."

Duanphen knew that expulsion, in this case, meant death. It didn't matter how wealthy and powerful the Foundation's members were; if they broke the rules, they'd be punished.

"Righto." The executive cleared his throat. "As there's a great amount of interest in dear Salma, I believe we shall start the bidding at five million euros. Do I hear five million?"

Immediately, a handful of the icons logged out of the conference. The price was too high for some, but not all. The bidding went back and forth. Each time one of the icons pulsed, a little beep sounded and the bid increased by 250,000 euros.

Five minutes later, the auction was over. A weekend with Salma had gone for 10.6 million euros. The executive checked his account. The payment had already come through.

"Bastard'll probably make that back in a night." The

executive sniffed. He handed his tablet back to Duanphen and she returned it to the briefcase. "We ought to take a percentage of what the girl makes them at the tables, eh?"

"It is a lot of money," Duanphen said, in awe of the price the Moroccan Garde commanded.

"Eh." The executive shrugged. "Not so much."

They arrived at the executive's hotel. It was a lavish place, where the staff wore silk vests and bow ties and were always underfoot with warm towels and glasses of rose water. The executive loved it. He had the penthouse suite all to himself. Well, not quite all to himself. Duanphen slept in an adjoining room and a handful of the other bodyguards were always camped out in the hallway.

Some of the guards stayed in the lobby to keep an eye on things; the rest piled into the elevator with them. When they reached the top floor, they met two more bodyguards who were stationed outside the executive's suite.

"Keeping watch on an empty hallway," the executive groused. "What a great use of our resources."

But, as he neared his suite, the executive suddenly began to whistle a jaunty little tune. Duanphen raised an eyebrow. The little man was practically swaggering, swinging his arms back and forth like he was in a wonderful mood. Maybe he was drunker than she thought.

"Aw, you lads are just doing your jobs," he said. "I don't mean to be such a bastard. I just made a tidy pile of quid tonight, y'know? Ought to spread the wealth, as the poors love to say." He stopped abruptly in the middle of the hallway. "Come on, ya blokes," he said. "Gather round, eh?"

The guards did as they were told. Normally, they were a stoic bunch, but now they looked as upbeat as the executive. Some of them grinned as they formed an impromptu huddle. Duanphen arched an eyebrow. The Blackstone mercenaries were usually much more professional.

"It isn't easy work, what you do. I want to show my appreciation." The executive pulled out his overstuffed money clip and started slapping high-denomination Thai baht into the outstretched hands of his security guards. "Bangkok's a damn fine place for strapping bucks like you lot. Take the night off. Go out and enjoy yourselves. On me, of course."

As if the money wasn't enough, the executive handed over his Black Card to one of the guards, then tossed his entire wallet to another. He winked and waved them off, watching like a generous father as the hardened mercenaries jostled their way back to the elevator, arm in arm, laughing and cracking jokes.

Duanphen watched it all happen with her mouth half-open in disbelief.

"What . . . ?" She sounded bewildered. "What the hell are you doing?"

The executive grinned at her. "What's the matter, Dawn? You sure you don't want to join them? Go on, then. Have fun." He slapped his pockets. "Afraid I'm out of money, though . . ."

Duanphen stared into his eyes, which had a wide and spacey quality. "You're—" She gave up on the stupidly

grinning executive. "Hey, wait!" she called after the mercenaries, but the elevator was gone. Had they all gone crazy?

"Sir," Duanphen said, balling her fists. "You're acting
strange."

"Nonsense," the executive replied. He swiped his key
card and pushed open the door to his suite.

Immediately, Duanphen could sense something wrong.
The air was warm and sticky, not meticulously tempera-
ture-controlled like the executive preferred. And where was
that breeze coming from?

The executive stopped suddenly and pinched the bridge
of his nose. He shook his head as if he were coming out of a
dream.

"Dawn, what— Did our boys just rob me? Or—what came
over me?"

The answer stood right in the middle of his suite.

The young man was slender, his brown hair combed
from the side into a meticulously gelled swoop. He wore
expensive clothes—gray slacks, a black vest, a white dress
shirt. Duanphen thought he looked almost like a magician;
appropriate, as he'd somehow slipped in past the executive's
security. The broken glass from the balcony window probably explained that . . . although how had he managed to
climb all the way up here?

The executive was frozen. "You."

"Not easy, putting you in a generous mood while making
those Blackstone morons go all frat boy," Einar said. There
were dark circles around his eyes and he was out of breath,

like he'd just greatly exerted himself. He held up a finger. "Give me a minute, will you?"

Duanphen didn't hesitate. Clearly, this Einar boy was a threat. Maybe even the reason for the executive's added security. She charged towards him, the executive's metal briefcase held over her head as a weapon.

Wumpf! She didn't see it coming. A second intruder slammed into Duanphen's side, trucked her clean off her feet and sent her crashing through a coffee table. A burly and hunched figure in a dingy gray sweat suit, the hood pulled up.

Einar sat down in a plush armchair and stretched out his legs. He smiled at the executive. "You aren't the only one with a bodyguard. Shall we see how this plays out?"

Duanphen snapped back to her feet, facing down the looming figure in the sweat suit. He was big, but she'd fought bigger. She triggered her Legacy. A field of electricity crackled across Duanphen's body. One Taser-like blow from her packed enough voltage to put down an ox.

She had longer reach than the brute in the sweat suit and threw a series of quick strikes at his face—a jab followed by a vicious swing of the briefcase. He bobbed backwards on his heels, keeping his distance as Duanphen's lightning-charged punches crackled right in front of his nose. Duanphen was merely testing him though, gauging her range.

"Ha!" She unleashed a vicious arcing roundhouse kick. The sweat suit barely managed to get his forearm raised in a haphazard block.

Duanphen screamed and flopped to the ground, her shin bent at an impossible angle. She'd broken her leg on her attacker's forearm. It was like hitting a brick wall.

The pain caused her to lose control of her Legacy. The sweat suit was on her fast. He grabbed Duanphen around the neck and lifted her off the ground with ease, his fist cocked back.

"Stop!" Einar yelled. "Don't kill her! You weren't even supposed to *break* her!"

As ordered, the sweat suit dropped Duanphen. She writhed on the floor, whimpering, body curled around her broken leg.

Einar looked at the executive. "Him, on the other hand . . ."

Duanphen saw it happen. The executive managed, at last, to turn and run. But it was too late. Sweat suit grabbed him by the back of his neck, lifted him up and then—*crack*—down, slamming the executive spine-first over his knee like a dead branch.

There was a moment that Duanphen knew from her many losing fights, that sensation right before a knockout, when all the pain was erased by welcoming blackness. The pain in her leg was shrieking and intense. Too much to bear. She let herself slip . . .

And then she was being not so gently slapped awake. How long was she out? Seconds? Minutes? She was still in the hotel room, the breeze from the broken window somehow chilling her despite the humidity. With every slight shift of her body, new shards of pain broke free in her shattered leg.

Duanphen wanted to retreat from the agony, but she sensed that if she passed out again she might never wake up.

Einar crouched over her. He stopped slapping her once her eyes focused.

"Hello again," he said. He held up the executive's tablet. "How do I access this?"

Shakily, she pointed at the executive's body. "Finger-print."

Duanphen felt a sticky heat beneath her, warm and spreading. Was that . . . ?

"Yes, I know fingerprint. We already took care of that." Einar held up the executive's severed hand.

Duanphen gagged. She was lying in a puddle of blood swiftly spreading from the executive's body. In a moment of panic, she checked her own wrists, was relieved to find them intact. They'd simply ripped open the briefcase with telekinesis.

Behind Einar, the sweat suit wiped his gore-stained hands on a bedsheet. There was something wrong with his skin. Duanphen squinted, but Einar snapped his fingers in her face.

"Do you know the code?" he asked.

She shook her head. "Only he did."

Einar frowned. "Well. Got a bit overzealous, didn't we?" He stood up. "So here is the situation, Duanphen. Did I say that right?"

She nodded. "Yes."

"We're like you. Garde. I'm sure you noticed how your

coworkers suddenly started behaving strangely out in the hallway. That was me. I can control emotions." Duanphen flinched as Einar reached out, but all he did was touch her gently on the nose. "But I'm not doing that to you, dear."

"Wh-why?"

"My new policy is that I don't use my Legacy against our own kind unless absolutely necessary. I don't kill them either. Good news for you, yes? But you still have a choice to make. Option one: you deliver a message for me. Tell the Foundation I know who they are and that I'm coming for them. We leave you here, the guards will likely be back soon, they take you to a hospital, fix your leg, and then you find out what the Foundation does to assets who fail at their jobs."

Duanphen glanced at the executive's mangled body. This failure was not something the Foundation would forgive. "Option two?"

"Option two," Einar continued, "is you come with me. Help me out with what I'm doing."

Duanphen already knew which option she would choose, but she still had to ask.

"What . . . what *are* you doing?"

"Simple. I'm remaking the world."

THE WAR MAY BE OVER—BUT FOR THE NEXT GENERATION, THE BATTLE HAS JUST BEGUN!

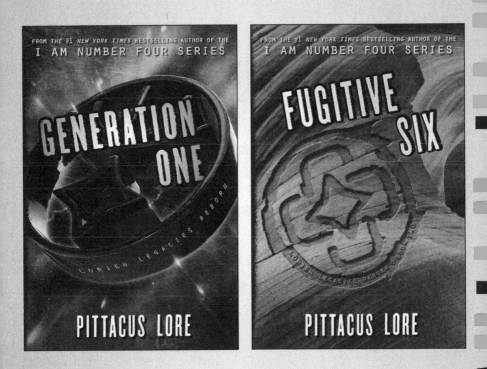

THE ADVENTURE CONTINUES IN THE LORIEN LEGACIES REBORN SERIES!

HARPER

An Imprint of HarperCollinsPublishers

JOIN FAN FAVORITES SIX AND SAM ON A NEW JOURNEY!

HARPER
An Imprint of HarperCollinsPublishers

DON'T MISS A SINGLE PAGE
OF THE ACTION-PACKED,
#1 *NEW YORK TIMES*
BESTSELLING
I AM NUMBER FOUR SERIES

HARPER
An Imprint of HarperCollinsPublishers

DELVE DEEPER INTO THE LORIEN LEGACIES WITH THESE COMPANION NOVELLAS!

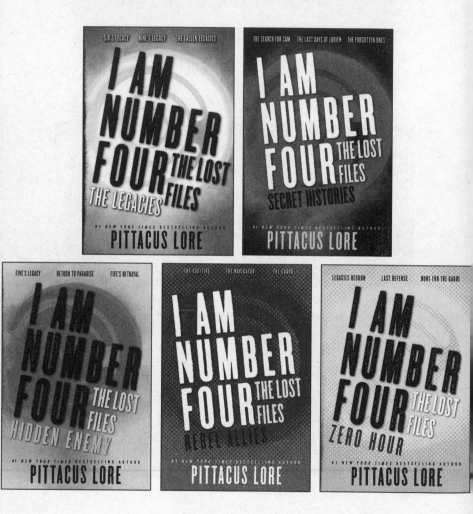

HARPER

An Imprint of HarperCollinsPublishers